FAR FROM
THERMOPYLAE

Belinda Harrison

Published by Gee Be Publications

Cover design: NEM Creative

ISBN-13: 978-0-6485604-1-8 (US/EUR Paperback)

Available titles in the Thermopylae Bound Series
(In reading order)

DEDICATION

For my own Ava, who is becoming an amazing, strong young woman in her own right. We all know if you hadn't come into our lives that this series would (probably) never have come into being ... NOW will you stop hassling me to tell everyone that?!

1

Pass of Coela, Southern Thessaly
5th rising, Moon of Anthesterion, 489BC

"Sander, you are no good to us here in your current state. You have to go back to Trachis. In a moon your body will be healed and you can return," I told him.

"No, please, I can stay, I ca—"

"This discussion is over. We cannot worry about you as well as any approaching enemies. Kleitos will take you back," I insisted, softening when I saw the flash of anger and pain dart across his features. "Look, I understand your frustration, I am sure you remember when I suffered from broken bones and had to stay in my room at the palace."

"I remember," he said, unable to keep the grin breaking out. "You were obnoxious and demanding and Skylar had to find endless patience, and new stories to keep you occupied."

I returned the smile. "I am sure you will not be quite as annoying for your wife and daughters."

He blew out a breath and nodded. "I suppose I should be grateful to see them again so soon."

"An excellent way to look at it," I agreed, squeezing his shoulder.

Sander and Kleitos had been out scouting for enemies when Sander's horse had slipped on the slick ground and he had fallen off, crashing onto a sharp rock and injuring his leg. The rest of us had been at the Pass, the constant rain and immobility grating on everyone's nerves, and it was almost a relief when Kleitos brought Sander back and we had to spring into action to attend his injury and get him ready to transport back to Trachis.

"I am ready," Kleitos announced, leading his and Sander's horses to where we stood, a cart attached to the back of his, and filled with material and straw. Sander would be travelling the day's ride south to Trachis in the cart in what we hoped was relative comfort but Lysistratos had also prepared a mixture of herbs to dull his pain.

Moeris and one of the younger ephebes helped Sander into the cart and I lay a blanket over him, placing his sword within easy reach. "Safe travels to you both," I said, taking Kleitos and Sander's arms and squeezing.

"I shall return as soon as I can," Kleitos nodded, Sander echoing his words.

I stepped aside to let the other soldiers offer their own wishes or exchange a last joke with their friend and headed back into the tent, welcoming the warmth and dryness the heavy leather overhead afforded. Torches had been wedged in the ground at regular intervals so it was not only warm, but bright as well – a stark contrast to the darkness outside.

I stood in the doorway and watched the cart pull away, recalling when Thaddeus and Hesper had visited me on one of those boring days when I had been confined to my room. I had been frightened to face them the first time I woke, sure they would be angry with me for Tritonos' death. But they did not blame me at all, wanting only for me to get well again. Hesper left to tend to their other children but Thaddeus remained, sharing his own tale of a similar injury a winter or so before I was born, and the perils of animals frightening other animals.

He told me he had been travelling with my mothers when a hare jumped across in front of his horse, Darko. The hare was trying to escape a snake, and when Darko caught sight of the slithering beast, he reared up onto his hind legs. Thaddeus had been walking beside his steed at the time, and he overbalanced, slipping down an embankment, breaking his leg and getting knocked out. He told me then, that no matter how careful we are, sometimes accidents happen – especially when serpents and horses are involved. He had hugged me and placed a kiss on my forehead, telling me to get some rest and that he would stay with me until I fell asleep. I closed my eyes, not quite asleep some time later when he whispered that even though he mourned deeply for Tritonos, he was glad Nikomachos and me were safe. I had not thought to ask Thaddeus at the time where he and my mothers had been going, but I wondered it now and I frowned; it was just another question about them I had no answer for.

The soldiers returned to their posts outside or jostled past me and into the tent. I wished for nothing more than to be alone and try to remember the other stories Mumma had shared with me while my body healed, but I joined them around the four torches clustered together in the middle of the sleeping area. Moeris and Lysistratos were the last to arrive, the former closing the flap of the tent behind them and gathering four amphorae. Moeris settled himself beside me, pouring the wine into cups Lysistratos brought over and handed out.

"We have neither heard, nor seen enemies for days. No doubt they have been kept at home by the rain and sodden trails we find ourselves amidst on this gods-forsaken night," our commander said, draining his cup and pouring another.

He had already had consumed at least two or three amphorae before Sander and Kleitos arrived back, not that I could not blame him, having taken one myself to sit alone with Philo for most of the afternoon. Both of us were only too aware of what today was. I had carefully avoided a number of the older soldiers, not wanting to be drawn into their memories and stories. But sitting beside them all now, and hearing the tone of Moeris' voice, I knew I would not be able to avoid it any longer.

"My friends, it is with heavy heart that we come together this night," he paused, draping his arm across my shoulders. I allowed him the gesture, knowing it was more for his sake than mine that he held me so close. "For those of you old enough to remember, it was ten winters ago this night that our beloved Princess Alexis, and her wife, Skylar, were taken from us by the Persian scum who would seek to take our lands. Our king's favored guard, Thaddeus, also lost his life as he attempted to save his friends. We mourn for them now, as we did then, never forgetting what they did for our city, nor the way they touched us so deeply.

"When our princess needed rescuing, Skylar was there for her. Skylar saved her from betrothal to a man who would have treated her with none of the respect or love Skylar did. Skylar ensured our people were safe when that man's family returned seeking Alexis again. And she did not allow an army to stand between her and her lover – vanquishing the entirety of them alone, fire her only companion."

I blew out a deep breath. Moeris only ever told *that* story after he had drunk too much. I did not know if it was true, but none of the other soldiers who were there ever corrected him. I had never asked for details. Had never wanted them; angry with Mumma that if it *were* true, why she had not been able to save herself or Mother Alexis when a mere five Persians came to the palace winters later.

"I ask you all now to raise your cups and join me in a toast." Moeris paused and took his arm from me so I could lift mine, waiting for everyone else to do the same. "To Thaddeus, who stood beside our king before he was known as such. Best friend, favored confidante when they were boys in Macedonia. He chose to join Agrias in the south, to stand beside him as protector and friend as he faced my people – the Malians – and spoke of his plans to create a thriving town and prosperous trade route at Trachis. Together they built what they had promised and I too came to call them both friend; pledging my sword to Agrias and leading his soldiers when he asked it of me.

"Thaddeus, who stood bravely by Alexis and Skylar's side the night they were taken, his own sword not enough to fend off the attackers and save himself. Thaddeus, whom Lysistratos' wife called Father until he was too early taken by the scourge of those from across the waters. We remember you and mourn you, this night more so than any other."

"To Thaddeus," I repeated, the soldiers around me doing the same, each of us taking long gulps of our wine. I caught Lysistratos' eye and we nodded to one another in respect. I lowered my cup again, preparing for Moeris' next words, having heard them every winter since that night, but feeling the sting of them just the same.

"To Princess Alexis, the beautiful daughter of our king and queen. A friend to all who met her, her gentle nature capturing many hearts. She left for Epirus as a child, her betrothal meant to keep our town safe. It was not to be though and when she returned to us, that danger followed her. Were it not for Skylar, and the love she found with Alexis, our princess would have been lost to us far earlier than she was. We called you friend, as well as Princess and we remember you and mourn you, this night more so than any other."

"To Alexis," I managed, my throat closing up as I recalled the quiet songs she used to sing me before bed. Moeris drained his cup, his eyes on me as the man beside him refilled it. He reached out to lay his hand on my forearm. I swallowed and nodded to him, dropping my gaze.

"And to Skylar, who was not seeking love when she arrived in Trachis, yet embraced it when it found her. She fought without fear for herself, her only thought to keep her princess, and then her daughter, Ava, safe from those who would attempt them harm," he paused again and reluctantly I raised my eyes to his and took up the words.

"She commanded the army jointly with Moeris until her last day, never faltering in her duty to the people of Trachis. She joined the army in their campaigns to make sure threats did not come to the palace."

"Until that last day," Moeris murmured. "It was only the trickery of the Persians which saw Skylar caught unawares. So we say now: to Skylar; the vanquisher of armies … and Alexis, the princess who loved her. We mourn you this night more than any other."

"To Skylar," the men shouted, my voice lost among theirs. I finished the last drops in my cup and pushed myself to my feet, a number of the newest recruits descending on Moeris. I heard their requests for the details of the fire Mumma used to destroy the army, but pushed through the flap of the tent before I heard his reply.

The cold outside hit me as it had on the beach as I stood by their pyres so many winters ago. I let the tears come, their heat stinging my eyes as they escaped and slid down my cheeks. A gentle arm around my shoulders announced Lysistratos' arrival.

"I wish we were with Eumelia – she must mourn for her father alone tonight," he said quietly.

I swiped at my face, knowing Lysistratos would never tease me about my tears, but still not wanting him to see me cry. "She will be reminded of her mother also, for with Thaddeus' death, so came Hesper's," I nodded, pleased my voice was even.

"Indeed," he agreed.

"It is good she has Phaidros with her; a helpless child who will keep her strong until you return to her side."

"Until we both return," he corrected me.

I inclined my head again, the hint of a smile on my lips. "I am not the one she wishes for most."

"Perhaps not, but she wants you safely back in Trachis just the same."

"I know," I murmured.

The tent flap opened again and Moeris stumbled out. He nodded to us both before gripping me tightly in an embrace. "I miss her, miss them both so much," he slurred.

I held him fiercely as I replied. "Me too."

With effort he released me, adjusting his cuirass and placing his hand atop the pommel of his sword. He cleared his throat, his voice gruff, but not unkind, when he spoke again. "Go get some sleep, both of you. I shall take first watch."

"It shall clear your head," Lysistratos grinned.

"Go," Moeris warned, swiping at the younger man. Lysistratos laughed and held the leather open for me. I made my way beneath the sagging roof of the tent to the small area I had made for myself among the other soldiers.

Ten winters had already passed since the night my mothers were killed. I could not imagine what the next ten would hold for me and those I loved, just as I had not known what it would then. I lay down on the hard ground and closed my eyes, hoping sleep would find me quickly and that the light of morning would bring with it clearer weather and a lighter heart, though I did not hold out much hope for either.

2

"Take this and go now," Spyros urged, thrusting the sword at Demetri. Demetri hesitated, leaving it where it was. "Take it as a reminder, as protection. Be safe. Go to Athens. Go to Epidaurus. They've got more accomplished healers than here in Larissa. Seek them out if you want to be ... who you are again. Be whoever you want. Use your skills as a metalworker to get coin, or do something else entirely. You have the skills."

Demetri nodded, taking the weapon and belting it to his waist. "Thank you," he murmured.

"You'll still need herbs for half a moon or so. Take what I've got left, you should be able to find more along the way." Demetri nodded again, accepting the pouch and adding it to the others inside his chiton.

"I won't forget you, or what you did for me, for what you've always done for me," he said.

"Nor I you," Spyros agreed. "But don't ever come back. It's not safe for you or me."

"I give you my word."

Spyros reached out, pulling Demetri into a quick hug. "Go," he said again, pushing Demetri towards the door.

Demetri crept out of the house, the street dark around him. He closed the door with barely a sound, looking both ways before deciding which way to go. He chose left, following the dirt road before turning into the first side street. Directly into the path of Phaeops, Eton and Megistias.

"Where do you think you're going, Beast?" Demetri didn't reply, gripping his waterskin tighter and taking a step back. "Get him," Phaeops sneered.

Demetri turned, drawing in a deep breath and making a run for it. He jumped over a hound who'd come to see what the noise was and turned the corner again. He ran past Spyros' house, the house *he'd* called home for the last twelve winters, and headed for the edge of town.

"Eton, tell my father we're going hunting and then catch us up. The beast won't get far," Phaeops panted, his voice reaching Demetri along the quiet street. Demetri extended his strides, putting a good distance between himself and his pursuers.

He had no idea where he was going to go, Athens was somewhere he'd always dreamed of visiting, maybe even living, but if he was going to make himself known to the metalworkers there, he'd need something impressive to set him apart and ensure he was given a job. Perhaps it was time he sought the Tymphaioi for the armor design he'd learnt about.

3

I crouched behind the large statue of Artemis. The marble chilled my hands and thighs. I shivered and gripped the goddess tighter. I could see in through the doorway of the Throne Room. Mumma Skylar was bound and guarded by four soldiers. She struggled to get free. Mother Alexis huddled against the wall. The soldiers were Persians – Nasrin had told me Persian soldiers wore yellow cloth on their heads and legs. A fifth soldier pulled Mother to her feet. He stood behind her, and held a knife to her throat as he looked at Mumma.

"The child is old enough to know the truth," he said. "Things shall soon begin to happen to her, just as they did you. Would you have her go through it without explanation? Would you wait unt–?"

"She is not of the line," Mumma shouted. "How many times must we speak of this? She has no mark. There is *no* connection with her."

"She *is* the one I have waited for and it is time for you to decide; shall you teach her or must I force your hand?" The Persian took his knife from my mother's throat. My stomach clenched as he sliced into her cheek. Mother whimpered but did not cry out as blood dropped to the ground.

"Stop!" Mumma commanded. With one hand free, she slammed it into the nearest Persian. His head whipped back and a bow fell to the ground.

"Sky, no, please," Mother Alexis pleaded as Mumma picked up the weapon.

"After the last time he was here, I swore I would never allow him to hurt you or Ava. No matter what," Mumma replied. Another Persian approached and she lashed out again. He ducked and her fist swung in the air above him.

The man with the knife has been here before? I frowned.

The Persian rammed into Mumma, knocking her to the ground as two others ran to his aid. She kicked and fought, but they overpowered her, pulling her up by her hair and re-binding her hands.

I wanted to help, but I was afraid. The men were big. They had weapons. I had nothing. I was just a child, shivering in the draughty courtyard in my tunic, my hair still wet from my bath.

The Persian with the knife pushed Mother Alexis into the hands of another soldier and grabbed Mumma Skylar by the throat. "You shall do what I tell you to do, when I tell you to do it." His tone was menacing but Mumma did not flinch.

"Go to Tartarus," she choked. She drew her legs up and kicked, catching him in the stomach. He doubled over, gasping. She fought to free herself but the men kept a tight grasp.

"You shall regret that," the Persian panted. "This night shall mark the beginning of all I have dreamed of. I knew before I came that you would never agree to teach Ava about her past," he said, straightening again. "Oh, I hoped you would change your mind of course, though given our history, I did not hold much hope. So, I have come up with another option." He picked up his knife.

"Which is?" Mumma asked.

He laughed. "If I told you that, it would not be a surprise, would it?" He put one hand on Mother Alexis' shoulder, and drew his knife back.

My vision went dark. A hand covered my eyes, another my mouth. My feet were separated from the cold ground. I attempted to scream, but could not take a breath deep enough to force any sound out. Whoever held me turned and ran. I struggled, kicking and squirming as Mumma Skylar had. The arms around me tightened immediately and the scent of beeswax and leather filled my nostrils. I stopped fighting. Papou Leandros had me, I would recognize that smell anywhere.

"No!" Mumma Skylar screamed. Her cry echoed around us. I knew the Persian with the knife had stabbed Mother Alexis. Papou paused. Tears welled in my eyes, but his rough palm prevented any from spilling down my cheeks. Papou began to run again, faster, his footsteps quieter now.

"The Throne Room, Thaddeus. Go," he said a moment later. He passed me into another familiar set of arms. "Take her to your father's house in town, you should be safe there. Do not return until I come to you," Papou ordered as I buried into Grandmother Melina's embrace, my tears finally escaping to wet my cheeks.

~

I was back in the courtyard of the palace, the statue of Artemis behind me, shielding me from Nasrin's gaze as she searched for me. Papou Leandros had insisted I remain with Nasrin in the andron, but I could not. I would not. My grandparents had hardly spoken in the days since my mothers had died, and when they did, they argued. I had never been close enough to hear what they fought about. But I would not be denied of it tonight. Papou Agrias may not have wanted me there, but I did not allow that to stop me.

Nasrin headed for the stables and I took my chance, sneaking between the columns and peeking around the doorway of the Throne Room. Papou Leandros was in his leather cuirass and his sword was tied in place at his thigh. The king and queen were in their official purple garments – all three of them having worn nothing but their current outfits the past few days. I retreated before any of them saw me, pressing myself against the cold stonework to listen.

"It is gone Melina, it disappeared when Skylar was ... when she ... It is just gone," Papou said, his voice low and halting.

"Could Ava have taken it?" Grandmother Melina asked.

"No, she was nowhere near them ... afterwards. You know that."

"But if she did?"

"She does not carry Skylar's mark, it is of no consequence," Papou replied angrily.

"How can we be certain? We have been beset by problem after problem since you and your daughter arrived. If you had not come here, then our daughter would still be alive."

"How quickly you appear to forget it was *you* who pushed our children together more than anyone else. You did not wish for Alexis to return to Epirus."

I did not know Mother Alexis had been in Epirus – only that Illyrian and Epirote soldiers had joined forces to take Trachis for themselves. My thoughts were interrupted by Papou Agrias' voice.

"Melina, please, if Leandros and Skylar had not come, we would have been enslaved to the Illyrians or the Persians many winters ago."

"The Persians were only here because of them," Melina cried. I shivered, a sudden chill running the length of my spine. "He cannot stay any longer," Melina continued after a pause. "Leandros, I hereby banish you from the city of Trachis in the region of Malis, land of the Malians, and the greater region of Thermopylae. You are not to return. Ever."

There was a short silence before Papou replied. "I understand."

No! He could not leave me too. My chest burned at his words and I burst from my hiding place and into the room, rushing to him. "No Papou! Do not leave. You cannot leave." I clung desperately to his thigh. I drank in the smell of the beeswax he used on his leather and sobbed.

He knelt down and took me into his arms. "My darling, I must," he whispered into my ear. "When it is time, I shall come find you and tell you everything. I give you my word,"

Arms tore us apart. Tears saturated my cheeks as I grabbed for him. "Swear you shall find me?" I screamed.

"I shall find you. I love you my darling and we shall see each other again." He smiled as the soldiers, his own men, took him from the room. He did not struggle or fight, just allowed them to take him away, his deep blue eyes never leaving mine.

~

The Throne Room disappeared, the hot springs south of Trachis taking its place. I was no longer nine winters old or in a time when nothing made sense and all I felt was betrayal and anger. The trickling water bubbled, soft as gentle rain as it passed over the submerged rocks and away through the thick undergrowth. Papou's retreating eyes hung in the air, his features changing into Mumma Skylar's as a shiver gripped me.

I knew I was dreaming – that she was not really there – but my heart soared at the sight of her, alive once more, as I had begged and wished and prayed for her to be.

"Mumma," I breathed. She smiled and held out her hand. I took it.

"My dear Ava." Her touch was cool, but not unpleasantly so. A heartbeat later her smile vanished and she became serious. "Time is passing and still you do nothing to avenge your Mother and me."

"I am a soldier, Mumma. I kill all the Persians I can."

"It is not enough. It is time you did more. Do you remember the necklace I always wore when you were a little girl?"

"The one with the black middle?"

"Yes. It is an extremely powerful amulet and it is time you had it."

"But how? It disappeared the nig–" She raised a hand to silence me.

"Listen now," she said. "You are already nineteen winters old. If you do not use the amulet within a moon, its power shall be lost to you. An advance party of Persians have landed on the east shores. They make their way through the Thessalian Plain towards you. Go now and destroy them. For us. With the amulet, you shall do great things. Kill every Persian in Greece and you shall be well rewarded."

"But whe–" She disappeared and I was left calling after her.

4

I woke gradually, the familiar ache of loss burning inside my chest, suffocating me with its presence. Ten winters may have passed since my mothers were taken from me but I still dreamed of that night with such vividness that it could have been days ago, not winters. The smell of Mother Alexis' sweet perfume and Mumma Skylar's leather armor consumed me where I lay and I squeezed my eyes tight against the onslaught of memories.

As a child I had wished every night for my mothers to return from the Underworld, for their embrace and soft words when nightmares pulled me from my sleep. For the soft melodies Mother would hum as she went about her day and for the respect Mumma commanded when she entered any room. The warrior I had become wanted more. I wanted revenge for the wrong that had been done to that innocent child. I wanted to launch attack after fierce attack on the dogs who had dared enter Greece's lands, stealing what was not theirs to take.

I inhaled deeply and blew the breath out slowly, trying to calm my rage and expel my hurt. I had often dreamt of my mothers, but their appearance in my dreams had become more frequent and their behavior far different in the week since I celebrated my nineteenth birthing day. They had started encouraging me, taunting me to act on the thoughts of revenge and destruction I held. I had always gladly done what they were now asking of me. As a hoplite in the Army of Thermopylae I killed every Persian I came across with nothing short of pleasure. But tonight was the first time

Mumma Skylar had mentioned her necklace.

The thought of having something more powerful than just the other soldiers to help me destroy the Persians and drive them from our lands once and for all was appealing. But if the Persians were already here, how long did I have to find it? And *where* was I to find it, this powerful amulet she wished for me to possess?

Papou Leandros' face drifted through my mind. *When it is time, I shall come find you and tell you everything,* he had said. What had he meant by that? What was he waiting for? His departure had hit me with the same ferociousness and sense of injustice as my mothers' deaths and I had still not forgiven Agrias and Melina for their decision. Papou had lost just as much as they had and it was not fair to send him away when I was the only family he had left. Part of my decision to join the hoplites had been to punish Melina for Papou's banishment. I was determined to become a respected and valuable soldier just as he and Mumma had been. I also wanted to use the soldiers and their nomadic lifestyle to escape Trachis, to distance myself from the memories of the familiar people and smells and the place I had been so happy in, until those nights. When I was accepted into the army in my twelfth winter, my relationship with Agrias and Melina became almost non-existent, and that suited us all; they no longer had a constant reminder of all they had lost, and neither did I.

The ache of the old wounds deep inside my chest lessened and I knew I would not get back to sleep. I opened my eyes, the flickering light from the torches threw long, dark shadows outwards from the poles which held the heavy leather overhead. Only an occasional 'drop' hit the skin above and I wondered if the constant rain that had kept our camp sodden for almost half a moon had finally slowed. There was less sagging around the poles above so maybe the gods had finally taken pity on us.

Papou's presence in my dream could not be coincidence. It had to be a sign that it was time we were reunited. I had not seen him since the night he was banished from Trachis, but somehow I was sure we had to find the necklace together. If there was a way to completely destroy our enemy he would want to be with me. He would want to make them pay for what they had taken from us. It was time I stopped waiting for him to come to me. I would go to him instead. I would leave the Pass and the other soldiers. Tonight.

I exhaled another long breath as the snores of the men surrounded me. When I had first moved into the barracks, their constant guttural noises had been unfamiliar and I had spent many sleepless nights and weary days. Now their sounds comforted me and it would be strange to sleep without them, but with what Mumma had said about the necklace and the approaching Persians, I would have to get used to the silence again.

I had heard whispers Papou was with the sheep herders deep in the

Pindos Mountain Ranges near the West Macedonian border. From where the soldiers and I were currently stationed, the Pindos Mountains were to our north-west. The terrain would be rocky and arduous in places, but if I started my journey tonight, I figured I could be there within three, or maybe four days. Papou would know where to start in our search for the necklace and if the Persians had only just arrived to the east, we should have more than enough time to retrieve it and get back to the Thessalian Plain to face them together.

I nodded to myself as a strange heaviness registered in my hand. I frowned and looked down. Mumma's necklace lay warm and solid in my palm. I pulled myself into a sitting position and stared at it in disbelief. *How did you get here?* I wondered. *Was Mumma responsible for giving it to me ... through my dream? How was that even possible? Maybe ... maybe even in the Underworld Mumma held command. Maybe she had met Hades, convinced him to let her gift me with her amulet. He would certainly appreciate the Persian souls I sent to him when I killed them. Maybe that was how she convinced him.* I did not know if any of that was plausible, but there was no denying that Mumma wanted me to have the amulet – to use it – so she found a way to get it to me.

It was just like I remembered; the black gem as long as my first finger but not quite as wide. Two thin pieces of silvery-red iron wound their way from top to bottom in a downwards swirl, effectively holding the gem safe inside. A second piece of looped iron was fastened to the top and the soft length of leather that had always kept it around Mumma's neck was laced through it.

I closed my hand around the amulet and brought it to my lips, sending up a silent prayer of thanks to Mumma. Now that I had her necklace, all I needed was Papou. We would destroy the approaching Persians, then ... who knew? Maybe we would set sail for Persia and destroy the rest of them. I would ask Papou to tell me what he had meant that night. What was the 'everything' he had to tell me, and why had he not returned to me as he said he would?

I dragged my bag closer and wrapped the necklace in the hem of my spare tunic. Until I was away from the camp I would not be able to wear it; Lysistratos would want to know where it came from and Moeris might recognize it.

"Lysistratos, it is time for you to take watch," Moeris' gruff voice announced, breaking into my thoughts. I put my bag back and looked up as the named man woke suddenly, encouraged by the nudge of Moeris' boot on his behind.

"I am awake, I am awake," Lysistratos muttered. He gathered his sword, helmet and cuirass, and pushed through the flap of the tent within moments of being roused.

Moeris laid a hand on my shoulder before taking his sword from his belt and sitting beside me. "Nightmare again?" he asked.

I nodded, knowing what he would think I had seen. "Yes, I have not dreamt of that night for some time, Morpheus has been kind to me."

"It must be because of the anniversary. Ten winters is a long time."

"It is," I agreed.

"When you first came to me and wanted to join the hoplites, you were nothing more than a child, ten winters old and so determined. But now look at you, a grown woman, as brave and loyal as any of the men here, and twice as lethal. Skylar would be proud," Moeris grinned, nudging me with his shoulder.

I smiled in reply. When I had first approached Moeris he would not let me join the soldiers; telling me I was too young. But he knew I would never give up and encouraged me to train hard and build up my strength, letting me stay with him in his room at the barracks instead of at the palace. He said he would invite me to apply with the rest of the epheboi in two winters' time, if I still wanted to, but he would not guarantee my acceptance. There was never any doubt I would fight fiercely for a position over the men and boys that spring.

"I hope so," I murmured. I had not told Moeris or Lysistratos about the new dreams that involved my mothers and I was going to have to lie to them about why I was leaving. That did not sit well with me but the journey was mine to make, and I needed to make it on my own.

I tightened my sandals and stood, sliding my scabbard along my leather belt and fastening it around the waist of my tunic. My sword – a two foot long xiphos – had once belonged to Mumma Skylar and when I was accepted into the army, Moeris had given it to me. I adjusted it so it lay comfortably against my left leg.

"I seek permission to leave this place for a time Moeris, will you grant my request?" I asked, reaching for my cuirass.

"Where is it you wish to go?"

"It is time I went … back … to Trachis," I replied.

He got to his feet. "Why?"

"To see the king and queen. As you said, it has been ten winters. There are words that need to be spoken between us."

I pulled the cuirass over my head, tying the leather lengths at my shoulders and adjusting the fit of the bonded leather and linen over my chest and stomach. I draped a coarse woolen travelling chlamys over my left shoulder, pinning it at my right, and pulled my bronze greaves up over my shins.

"Then I shall join you. King Agrias should not mind getting my report early," Moeris said, placing his sword back on his belt.

"No," I immediately replied. I softened my words by laying a hand on his arm. "This is something I need to do alone."

"At least wait until Helios provides light to guide you by."

I shook my head. "No, I must leave now."

"Ava ..."

"Please, Moeris, I have armor and weapons, and Philo. I will be safe." His brow furrowed as he considered my words. I knew Moeris thought of me as the daughter he never had, and I thought fondly of him in return, but the issue of my travelling alone had always been between us. I knew that when he learned the truth that I had gone north instead of south, he would be both angry and disappointed. That fact did not sit well with me either, but until I had Papou back and knew exactly how the amulet was going to help us in the war against the Persians, I would not speak of it to either he or Lysistratos.

Finally he blew out a breath. "Ensure you enjoy a fine meal from the palace kitchen tomorrow evening," he said, drawing me into his arms. "And take care crossing the rivers in the dark, the stone bridge over the Melas is in need of repair."

"I will," I said, my voice muffled against his shoulder.

"Be safe," he added as he released me.

"And you," I replied, picking up my bag. I pulled on my helmet, the familiar weight of the bronze was a comfort. My fellow soldiers preferred the more open Thracian type, whereas I favored the Corinthian, with its wide cheek protectors and long nose piece. It covered my features almost completely and it was impossible to tell my sex. I thrived on the anonymity of my gender and was afforded no special treatment or notice by the enemies we battled, attacking them with the same ferocity they fought me with. For all they knew, my helmet had been passed down from generation to generation of soldier until it reached me. I tipped it upward and followed Moeris.

5

My shield and spear hung from racks by the door of the tent and I took the spear first, tying it across my back with a piece of leather and knotting it at the middle of my chest. Moeris took my shield, running his hand down the slightly domed bronze-covered wood as he looked it over.

"This has seen better days. You should take my aspis instead," he suggested.

I followed his gaze, noting the small lines that ran upwards from the middle. "It has always served me well, this time will be no different." I added bread, cheese and a waterskin to my bag.

I wanted to be comfortable with the weapons I was used to if the need arose and at two-and-a-half feet wide, my aspis was smaller and lighter than the one Moeris and the other soldiers used – but it still adequately covered me from collarbone to knee. I was capable of using a larger one if I had to, but found it easier to wield mine for longer periods.

"Your journey is short. Ensure you have it repaired while you are at Trachis." I nodded my response and took it from him, sliding my forearm into the two leather straps on the underside. "I also urge you once again to purchase a bronze cuirass. You must protect yourself better," he added.

"I did not need one when we fought at Marathon last summer. I bought the bronze helmet and greaves you insisted on, but I will not get a cuirass." Bronze armor was a sign of wealth and status among hoplites and I did not want any *obvious* lineage between the king and queen and I. Besides, Mumma had never had heavier armor and when I faced Persian opponents, they were drawn to my lighter clad body which was similar to their own. I relished the fierce fight with them, relying on my winters of training and superior weaponry to disarm them of theirs and rob them of their lives.

Moeris shook his head. "Stubborn as always," he murmured, opening the material of the tent and letting me pass through ahead of him. "I shall fetch you a torch while you ready Philo."

"Thank you," I replied. As I made my way to the makeshift stables, I raised my eyes to the sky; the moon was round and bright, with few clouds concealing it. I was grateful, for it meant I would be able to travel further north than I had hoped tonight, and I silently asked Hermes to grant me such luck, as well as safety.

Philo was in a pen halfway down the row. He stood at fifteen hands high, his sleek, bronze-colored body catching the slices of moonlight that fell between the sheets of material behind him. His legs, mane, tail and face were black, his ears a combination of his two colors – brown with black outlines. He looked up as I slid the lengths of wood from the posts of his enclosure. He walked forward slowly and waited beside me, the top of his flank level with my armpit, as I put the wood back in position.

"We have to make a special journey, my friend," I whispered, stroking his nose. He whinnied in response and nuzzled my hand.

I took some cloth and laid it across Philo's back before fastening a bridle and bit over his nose and ears, settling the reins at the base of his neck and tying their ends together. I added two handfuls of apples from a nearby tub to my bag and secured it to Philo's rump with rope then led him back to the sleeping tent.

Moeris stood by the fire, speaking quietly to Lysistratos. I took the two unlit torches and flint our commander held out and stowed them in my bag. "I will see you soon," I said, as Moeris offered his arm. I took it, gripping him as tightly as he gripped me.

He nodded. "The Pass shall be safe in our hands and we await your return and our joyous reunion." Moeris stepped back, letting Lysistratos approach.

"Are you sure you do not want company for your journey?"

"Not this time, but if I was to ask anyone, you know it would be you," I replied.

He pulled me into a crushing hug. "Then be safe, keep your eyes and ears open. You know the signs to look for."

"I do," I nodded.

"Good. Bring news of home with your return, and give Phaidros a kiss for me."

"And for Eumelia?" I grinned, squeezing him tightly in return.

"Just tell her I love her and miss her," he replied and I heard the smile in his voice.

"I will." I knew Lysistratos was anxious to return to his wife and son when the Persians were driven from our lands not just because of the anniversary tonight, but in general. Now that I had my mother's amulet, I hoped I could fulfil his wish sooner rather than later. "Till we meet again, my friend," I told him as he released me.

I rested my aspis on top of Philo's head and took the hair at the base of his neck, jumping up and swinging my leg over his back. The heat of his body seeped through the sheer cloth below and warmed mine as I settled against him. With a final nod to Moeris and Lysistratos, I pulled on the reins and turned Philo east, squeezing my thighs against his sides to propel him forward.

I knew the two men would keep watch until I was out of sight and I quickened Philo's pace. If my intention had really been to go to Trachis, I had to follow the Spercheios River east until I reached a narrow section I could cross before turning south. The crossing was only thirty-one itinerary – or a candlemark's ride – from camp and on such a clear night, and the bright moonlight, I did not know how long I would be visible across the flat plain for. The mountain ranges I actually intended to enter, were fifty-seven itinerary away and at the point of the Spercheios River crossing, I had to turn north rather than south.

*   *   *

When I reached the river crossing, I slowed Philo and looked back. I could not make out the tent, the stables or the fire I knew to be burning. Satisfied that I would be as hidden from Moeris and Lysistratos as they now were from me, I pressed my sandals into Philo again and turned him north-east towards the Othrys Mountains.

I followed a well-worn path over the small rise, which was more a hill than a mountain. The moon's glow lit our way for a while, but soon the forest closed in around us and it was lost above the canopy of dense foliage. I recognized some of the trees; a cluster of oaks, a lone beech and a large number of black pines. Their grouping along the mountain path was just as it had been on the warm Pyanepsion night five winters ago when I had last been there. I had heard Papou was near our camp and had slipped away on Philo, shoving handfuls of hard nuts from the oak and beech trees into my bag to keep us fed as I searched for him. The moon had been bright and full, making its way through the thick branches when a light breeze wound through the leaves.

Instead of finding Papou, Philo and I had come across an elderly couple being terrorized at the hands of thieves. I had pulled on my helmet and taken to them with spear and sword, wounding two of the three before the largest of the group sliced deep into my leg. I had crumpled to the ground beside the body of the old woman, her throat slashed and draining her of both blood and life. The thieves fled into the mountains and the elderly man wept as he tended to my wound. He ripped a section from his wife's dress and wrapped it tight around my leg as I told him about my fellow hoplites, and he left to get help.

The night was warm, but I had shivered uncontrollably, a combination of injury and shock ravaging my body. Philo had approached cautiously, avoiding the spilled blood of the old woman and my leg. He had wanted to help me, yet shied away from the pools of red. Finally he settled himself on the ground behind me, and it was only his warmth that kept me alive until Moeris and the soldiers arrived.

I shuddered with the memory and pulled my chlamys tighter, sliding from Philo's back so the fire I struck to light our way did not distress him. Philo had put his love for me ahead of his aversion to the spilled blood that lay on the ground that night and I knew if the situation was ever reversed, I would do everything and anything I could to save him.

My recovery from the wound had been slow and painful. Moeris had sent soldiers to search for Papou, but they did not find him. After that, he kept a much closer eye on me and urged me to confide in him if I had word that Papou was near so we could look for him together. But I never heard he was again.

I rubbed at the scar on my thigh as I shook the memory from my mind.

*   *   *

Philo and I travelled north through the Othrys Mountains for candlemarks and when Eos, Goddess of the Dawn, peeked over the tops of the trees, we arrived at Lake Xynias. The lake dominated the area, the jagged mountains so far on the opposite side that it was impossible to tell exactly where the lake ended and the mountains began. Tracks led off to the east, north-east and north-west sides. The east path was wide but overgrown with grass on its way to Mount Othrys. The north-east track was thin and stony, following the lake as far as the northern section of the Othrys Ranges and the Thessalian Plain beyond. But it was the north-west path I intended to use to get me to Papou and the Pindos Mountains beyond the Plain. The route was well-worn along the Apidanus River, used by all traders and travelers to the area, and it would take Philo and me between the mountains on the other side of the lake, rather than over them.

I directed Philo to the north-west path towards some large boulders a little further along, finding that two were submerged on the edge of the lake, a gap between creating an inlet where one could enter the water. Either side of those, were two larger slabs which effectively hid the path from sight, and the inlet from the path, when I stood between them. They looked as though they had all once belonged to the mountains of the area and I wondered if it was god or mortal that had seen them positioned where they were now.

A large shrub, a tree really, had taken root about halfway up the side of the outer rock on the south end of the path. Its multiple trunks intertwined to form a solid base for it to grow. I rested my aspis against the rock below it and reached out, the twisted bark rough beneath my hand. The texture reminded me of the way Mumma and Papou's calloused palms had dragged across my soft ones when I was a child. My own now resembled theirs.

Narrow green leaves and big flowers with bright red petals and yellow cores grew on the branches above my head. Large, round fruit peeked invitingly from the foliage and at first I thought they were apples. On closer inspection, I realized they were not and left the fruit where it hung.

I took my helmet off and placed it beside my shield, deftly loosening the knot at my chest and adding my spear to the collection. Untying my bag from Philo, I took my empty waterskin and approached the inlet. The water was clear and lapped gently against the bank as I submerged the waterskin, goose pimples immediately breaking out on my arms. Bathing or dipping my limbs into anything other than the warmth of the hot springs at Thermopylae was always a shock, and it was only through a sense of duty that I filled the skins for the soldiers when asked. Philo joined me at the water's edge, taking great mouthfuls of the cool liquid as I sucked in a long draft from my waterskin.

When we had drunk all we could, I led Philo back to the tree and placed my sword beside my other possessions. I sat with my back against the solid rock, my weapons within easy reach on one side, and Philo on my other, his head and most of his flank shaded from the sun, just as I was. From my bag I took Mumma's necklace, slipping the leather over my head and tucking the gem into the front of my tunic beneath my cuirass. The steel was cool and foreign against my skin, but not unpleasant. I had never worn any jewelry except the leather bracelet Papou had given Mother when she and Mumma were married. It was still supple and comfortable and the Heracles knot had never once loosened. Jewelry was just not something we soldiers adorned ourselves with. Lysistratos and a few of the men wore medallions – Lysistratos' father having passed it down to him when he was a small boy – but that was about it.

I leant my head back, my thoughts drifting to my friends back at the Pass of Coela and I sent up a silent prayer to the goddess Athena to aid and protect them while I was away. I hoped Moeris would not be too angry when he discovered I had not gone to Trachis, but more than that I hoped he would not come after me. I rested my hand on Philo's head and closed my eyes, Hypnos bringing me sleep short moments later.

6

Making sure the sword was belted tight to his waist, Demetri added his waterskin to it, took a deep breath and dived beneath the freezing water. Phaeops and the others weren't far behind but he couldn't run anymore. He was exhausted. He didn't know how far he'd be able to get in the water either, but at least he could use his arms instead of his legs.

His chest was on fire, not just because he'd been running for over a candlemark with barely a rest, but because of the wounds that weren't quite healed. The herbs Spyros had applied before he left Larissa, and the ones he'd used since, had helped, but he had lost a lot of strength in his upper body, strength he'd relied on over the winters in the metalwork shop to lift steaming vats of liquid silver for the coins he made or to shape iron for swords.

He broke the surface and drove himself through the water, gasping between strokes, hoping his eyes were deceiving him at how far away the opposite bank appeared.

7

I stood on the beach. Eos' dawn made the sky pink. The cold wind chilled me but I did not pull my himation tight as the others on the beach did when they huddled together. I remained alone. Cold and alone.

Waves crashed against the sand. It drowned out the voices around me. Wooden torches stood around the three funeral pyres. I stared at the pyres. They were made high by the branches of olive and laurel trees.

Papou Leandros took two torches and lit them from a third in the sand. Moeris and two other soldiers stepped forward and shielded the flames. Papou waved me over. I shuffled forward and with one arm he lifted me up.

This would not be the first time I had seen their faces since they died but I knew it would be the last. I drew in a breath and closed my eyes, wanting to always remember what they looked like in life rather than death.

"You have the coins?" Papou asked.

I opened my eyes again and nodded, holding them up for him to see. He nodded back and took me to Mother Alexis. She looked different, yet somehow the same. Her face was pale, no pink in her cheeks as there usually was, just a blue tinge. That blue was even darker around her lips. I desperately wished she would open her eyes so I could see the green that matched mine, for her smile to light up her face. But she did not. Mother Alexis was gone.

I forced open her mouth and placed a coin between her lips, doing the same with Mumma Skylar's before shutting my eyes again. I sent up a silent prayer to the ferryman, Charon, to take them both safely across the Acheron River and help them find peace together in the Underworld. I wriggled in Papou's grip and he put me down in front of Mother Alexis' pyre.

~

Cold fingers scampered down my back as my mother's lifeless features suddenly transformed into living animation. The coin fell from her lips as she swung her legs over the edge of the pyre and blocked Mumma's body from view.

"My sweet girl, we are so proud of you, you have taken the first step," she smiled. I tried to move towards her, but my feet and ankles were stuck firm. "Soon you shall face the Persians and I know you shall do what you must. Do not ever forget how much we love you, and how much we are counting on you to avenge us."

Then she was gone.

* * *

I woke, no longer leaning against the rock but sprawled on the ground; head in the sun and legs in the shade. I shielded my eyes from the glare and crawled back beneath the tree, finishing what was left of the water in my waterskin. Philo stood nearby, munching on the leaves above his head and I wondered if I had kicked out in my sleep and woken him. It would not be the first time.

Despite having dreamt of the day we burnt and buried my mothers, I would not sit and dwell on their deaths – on a past I could not change – I needed to keep moving. I stood and plunged my waterskin into the lake again. I considered stripping off and immersing the rest of my body in the freezing depths so I could numb more than just the hand that touched the water, but I knew that numbing memories was far more difficult than numbing body parts.

When the skin was full again I secured it, and my bag, to Philo's rump and belted my sword around my waist. One of the fruit from the tree was split open on the ground, the imprint of Philo's teeth deep in the half-eaten inner when I picked it up. It was almost as big as my hand, with a thick skin and hundreds of small red seeds inside the fleshy outer. I recognized it as a pomegranate; a sweet, sticky fruit I had last eaten the night my mothers were sent to the Underworld. I frowned and threw it aside. The apples I had in my bag would do for my breakfast – I did not need further reminders of that night today.

Water slapping loudly against the rocks of the small inlet drew my attention and I raised my eyes. The earlier ripples were now churning between the hard surfaces and splashing over the bank. I slipped my hand into the holds on my aspis and unsheathed my sword, approaching the small gap with caution.

I stepped into the water, the cold piercing my skin around my sandals like needles. I positioned my body against one of the rocks and peered around its edge. I immediately saw the cause of the change in the calm water; a fully clothed person splashing their way across the expanse. Voices travelled over the water and I narrowed my eyes. A group ran along the north-east bank. I could not tell whether they were pursuing or cheering on the figure in the water, but he or she was starting to tire.

I threw my shield and sword up onto the bank and waded out until I was standing thigh-deep in the icy water. I braced one hand on the rough stone and dragged a young man through the gap and onto dry ground by his short chiton.

He sucked in giant gulps of air. "Thank you," he panted.

The group on the north-east path neared. They had weapons. Spears by the look of it. They would be on us in a matter of minutes. "The ones on the bank – are they friends of yours?" I asked.

"No. Definitely not friends," the boy choked, shaking his head and rolling onto his side.

I gathered my weapons and re-sheathed my sword as I studied him. His eyes were a deep brown flecked with yellow, his nose, which was neither thick nor thin, sat between flushed cheeks and his lips were slightly blue above a strong chin. His hair was the same shade as his eyes and his arms and legs were deeply tanned. I wondered what he had done to be pursued by such a group.

He pushed himself to his feet, placing his hand on his waist as he leaned forward and tried to bring in enough air to speak. "You should take … your leave. They've been … chasing me for quite some time. When they catch me …"

"Did you wrong them?" I asked, ignoring his suggestion.

"No. But they've done … many wrongs to me." I stared hard at him. I had no reason to trust him, for all I knew he had been sent as bait. However, I had made no fire when I stopped. There was no reason to think they had known I was there. Besides, in this weather who would *willingly* swim in Lake Xynias?

"Stay here," I told him, gathering my spear and tying it to my back.

"You must go, this is my fight. Please," he implored.

Again I ignored his words and took Philo's reins, leading him out of the inlet. There were several trees nearby and I looped the reins over a branch as I murmured, "Wait for us here, boy." He whinnied in response and nuzzled at my shoulder. I gave him a quick pat on the nose and returned to the inlet.

The boy was where I had left him but was now upright and breathing almost normally. I picked up my helmet and pulled it over my face, pointing to the sword sheathed at his waist as I approached. "Can you use that?" I asked.

His face registered surprise at the change in my appearance but he nodded. "Yes."

"Good. I will not leave you here alone."

"But they …"

"Believe me, all they will see is the uniform, they do not need to know anything more."

He hesitated but nodded again and offered me his arm. "I … I'm Demetri."

I gripped his forearm and we shook. "Ava."

Demetri pulled his sword from his waist as I took mine. We stood with our backs to the water and waited, shoulder to shoulder, for the owners of the nearing voices to appear. One by one, they rounded the large rock and skidded to a stop, puffing hard, spears in hand. They spread out in a line, effectively blocking our exit unless we were prepared to take to the water. There were six of them altogether - a challenge, but not impossible to defeat. They had the advantage though; I would bet my entire winter's earnings that they had fought together before. Demetri and I were strangers, I knew nothing of his ability with a sword, or any of his weaknesses, and he knew none of mine.

"Enjoy your run, Phaeops?" Demetri asked, no humor in his voice.

The largest of the boys in the group took a step forward; I assumed he was Phaeops. "You swim well, Beast. We thought you'd drown before you got halfway across the lake and deprive us of our fun," he sneered. "I see you found a soldier to tell your sorry tale to."

"I said nothing," Demetri replied, his hands tightening on the grip of his sword.

"You may take your leave, Soldier. This boy is no concern of yours," Phaeops said.

"When you outnumber him six to one, he becomes my concern," I told him, using the technique Moeris had taught me to sound more masculine.

Phaeops stared at me, then back the way they had come. He was probably wondering if I was alone or if the rest of my men were somewhere nearby.

"Our business to settle has nothing to do with you. Take your leave now or we'll consider you an enemy too."

"If you want him, you will have to fight me as well," I countered, raising my sword and positioning my shield across the left side of my body as I did when in phalanx formation.

Phaeops addressed Demetri again. "What lies did you feed this soldier before we arrived?"

"I told you; I said nothing," Demetri insisted.

One of the boys placed a hand on Phaeops' shoulder. "It doesn't matter what he said, this soldier is no more inclined to believe him than anyone did back home."

"You speak true, my friend. The words of a defiant slave mean nothing to those with the power to punish," Phaeops laughed.

His words surprised me. I had not expected Demetri to be a slave – he looked strong and healthy and he had no brand that I could see. But if he was, it made me wonder what he had done, and why he was running.

Phaeops tucked his spear beneath his arm. "Prepare to meet your fate, Beast." He charged forward. I jumped in front of Demetri and met Phaeops with a wide swing of my shield. The satisfying clash of bronze against wood bounced off the rock walls around us as I disarmed him and he fell to the ground, dazed, his spear landing beside him.

"I've got this," Demetri yelled, placing a well-aimed kick in Phaeops' midsection.

I nodded as the other boy who had spoken charged ahead like Phaeops had. I ran towards him, flattening my aspis above my shoulder as he tried to spear me with his weapon. It stuck deep, the head protruding just above my arm on the underside. I swung my sword in a wide arc, barely missing his stomach as he released his grip on his spear. I spun, dropping low to the ground, taking his feet out from under him as I slashed my blade across the fatty flesh of his calf. He screamed as I sprung up again.

The four boys who had so far been watching on, raised their spears. I unknotted mine and threw it towards them, barely having time to cover the few steps back to Demetri, pull him against me, and put my shield above us, before their weapons rained down. The spears bounced off the bronze and littered the ground, taking the embedded spear with them.

I lowered my aspis in time to see Phaeops on his feet and charging again. He slammed his shoulder into my shield and I felt rather than heard the bronze come apart above me. I fell back, my breath knocked out of me as his body covered mine.

Demetri suddenly flew above us and Phaeops' weight disappeared from my chest, giving me the chance to draw my breath back in. I was aware of little else other than the wheezing of my chest and the occasional touch from the sparring boys on my left until Demetri rolled me over yelling, "move!" The sound of rushing footsteps finally registered and I threw aside my shield, which hung uselessly from my arm by the leather straps, its body broken in two. I rolled onto my stomach, crawling in the opposite direction to Demetri, hoping to draw the boys away from him to deal with myself.

I had only travelled a few feet before I found myself unable to move any further. I looked back. I was pinned to the dirt by a sword in the end of my chlamys. Demetri's sword.

8

I frowned and raised my eyes, but it was not Demetri's hand at the end of his weapon, but one of the four spear throwers. Phaeops lay motionless on the ground, blood spilling from a gash on his forehead. Demetri thrashed uselessly in the grip of two others and the one I had cut down earlier continued to screech in pain.

The holder of Demetri's sword turned with a frown. "Enough! Eton, take him back to where we camped last night and see what you can do for him. We'll finish things here and join you." Eton nodded and pulled his injured friend to his feet, half-carrying, half-dragging him from the inlet.

The boy returned his attention to me and lowered his face to mine. "*You're* not going anywhere," he growled. He planted his foot on the back of my hand, crushing my fingers between the hilt of the sword and his sandal until I cried out. "I'll take this," he added, sliding my weapon out of my open hand.

Blood pounded in my ears. I could count on one hand the number of times I had been disarmed in a fight and I refused to be beaten by these … bullies who thought odds of six to one were a fair fight. I considered using Mumma's amulet against them but for one – I did not know how, and two – something told me that using *that* particular weapon against mere boys would not be fighting fair, and if nothing else, I always fought fiercely, but fairly. I would find another way to get my sword back.

He crossed to Demetri. "You'd better pray to whichever god you think will listen that Phaeops isn't dead," he warned. Demetri spat in his general direction, but the boy evaded the saliva coming his way and planted his fist in Demetri's stomach. Demetri slumped forward, still held tightly by his captors.

The boy held up my sword, smiling as he sliced the air in front of him. He was stiff and uncoordinated, having obviously never used one before. My breathing finally returned to normal and, with Demetri's sword stuck in my chlamys, I realized I had a weapon to fight back with. I tried to dislodge the sword from the dirt without drawing attention to my movements, but it had been driven in too deep. I had to make a decision; the boy would soon get bored of playing with my sword and might consider running Demetri through with it. The amateur movements he made told me that Demetri's death would be slow and painful if he did so.

I gathered a deep breath and stood straight up. My chlamys ripped loudly and three heads whipped around to look at me. I tugged Demetri's sword free, but before I had time to lift it, the point of my own was pushed painfully against my throat and I stilled.

"Don't move," the boy demanded.

"Wait, Megistias!" Demetri cried. "We can make a deal."

"You don't have anything we want," Megistias laughed, glancing at Demetri.

"I do … please, I do. Soldier, I … I need you to trust me, can you do that?" Demetri asked, turning his urgent gaze on me. I frowned beneath my helmet, which of course he could not see. *What was he up to?* I wondered. Megistias looked between us and after a moment I nodded. Demetri obviously had a plan and, for now, I had to trust that he knew what he was doing. Maybe whatever he had was the reason they had chased him. Maybe it was another weapon.

"Release him," Megistias ordered.

They let Demetri go as he spoke again. "I'll flip a coin. If I win, the soldier and I leave and you don't pursue us. Ever."

"And if I win?" Megistias asked.

"Then you can take what I've got to offer, and be free to do with us as you wish. You can even return me to Larissa if that's what you want."

"Show me what you have that's so valuable first."

Demetri nodded and stepped cautiously in my direction. I frowned again, wishing I knew what he had in mind. "I need some space," he announced, addressing Megistias specifically.

Megistias hesitated then withdrew the weapon at my neck and stepped back a few paces. "Keep your hands where I can see them, both of you," he insisted.

Demetri nodded and held his arms out on either side of his body, his eyes never leaving mine as he approached. Maybe his sword was valuable and he intended to offer that to Megistias if he won. I tightened my grip on the hilt, instinct telling me to be prepared for anything. Demetri slowly raised his hands towards my helmet and suddenly I understood; he was going to use me as a bargaining chip.

"You do not want to do this," I whispered, taking a half-step back.

"Trust me," he murmured in reply, flashing me a dazzling smile. I was caught in a moment of indecision. It was impossible to ensure the coin would come down on the side he wanted it to, yet his unexpected grin implied he thought the odds were higher in his favor. I squeezed the hilt of his sword again, but did not retreat any further. He took the thick bronze at my chin and drew my helmet off, stepping aside so the boys could see what he had revealed.

"She's a girl," one of the boys cried.

"I can see that," Megistias snapped, his anger quickly turning to joy. He approached, dropping to his knees and unfastening my greaves so he could run his hands down my exposed calves.

"What are your terms again, Beast?" I kicked out but found only air as he stood with a laugh.

Demetri put his body between the two of us, facing Megistias. "If you win, you can do what you want with the two of us. We won't fight or run, or cause you any trouble, you have our word," he said.

I squeezed the sword in my hand, fury now coursing through my body rather than caution. *Demetri* may not be prepared to run or put up a fight, but there was no way in Tartarus I would sit by compliantly and let them to have their way with me. They would have to kill me first, or I would figure out how to use the amulet against them – fair fight be damned.

Demetri was close enough to me that I briefly considered grabbing him and fighting our way out of the inlet to get to Philo, but he held no weapon and it was possible I would get him killed if I tried it.

The two boys who had been holding Demetri slapped each other and grinned wickedly. Megistias looked me up and down, his ugly smile turning into a snarl as he nodded. "I'm satisfied with the terms."

"What are you calling?" Demetri asked, putting his hand into the folds of his chiton.

"Heads," Megistias replied without hesitation.

Demetri retrieved a coin and held it up. "Ready?" he asked.

"Hurry up," Megistias growled, scratching at the inside of his leg.

Demetri placed the coin on the top of his thumb. It was a ridiculous bet to make, he *had* to know that, and he *had* to know that I would not let them take me quietly. We may be strangers, but he should know that a warrior would never let themselves be taken without a fight.

Demetri threw the coin high up into the air. I drew a breath, closing my eyes and sending up a silent prayer to the gods. The coin slapped onto his palm and I waited, heart racing and adrenaline kicking in.

"It's tails," Demetri called. There was a collective groan from the other boys and I released the breath I had been holding and opened my eyes.

"Flip it again, best two out of three," Megistias suggested.

Demetri shook his head and put his coin back. "That wasn't our deal."

"I don't care about the deal. We're going to kill *you*, then have some fun with *her*." Megistias rushed at us, my sword raised above his head. I pushed Demetri aside, hoping he landed somewhere near my broken shield. It was no sword, but it would have to do as a weapon until I retrieved mine.

I clasped both hands around the hilt of Demetri's sword and blocked Megistias' wild swing mid-air. The impact travelled through me, but my feet were positioned accordingly to deliver a counter attack. I flicked my wrists to the right, pushing down and around in a circle to disengage my sword from the boy's hands. It clattered to the ground, sending up a puff of dirt. Megistias growled and came at me again, but before his outstretched fingers found me, I stepped aside, spinning on my toes and bringing down the pommel of the sword hard onto the back of his head. He landed with a thud in the dirt and did not get up again.

Demetri had managed to do some damage to the other two boys with either his fists or my aspis; they leaked blood from various parts of their faces. But now he knelt awkwardly on the ground, held upright by his hair by one as the other stood over him, his spear at the ready.

"Beg for mercy," the standing boy demanded.

"Never," Demetri replied.

The boy raised the spear higher and steadied his weight. My own spear lay nearby and I crossed to it without hesitation, drawing it level with my face before hurling it forward with everything I had. It found the desired target with deadly accuracy. The boy screamed, releasing his weapon and dropping to his knees as he clutched at his hand and the spear that was now stuck in it. Demetri threw his elbow back, his captor's nose cracking as it broke. He grabbed at his injury while Demetri scrambled out of reach.

I picked up my sword and re-sheathed it as Demetri went to fetch my spear from the wounded boy. "Leave it! Come on," I yelled. I scooped up my helmet and slammed it back on my head. Going against everything I had been taught as a hoplite, I left my greaves and broken aspis where they were, determined to get Demetri and me to safety before the boys started to give chase.

I grabbed Philo's reins from the branch, urging him forward by the leather straps. Demetri was right beside me and I threw his sword to him, grabbing Philo's mane and springing up onto his back. Demetri took my offered hand, jumping up as I pulled him into position behind me. He put his hands on my waist shouting, "go!"

I turned Philo north along path and kicked my heels into his flank. He took off with a sudden jerk and I was thrown back against Demetri. His hands tightened around my waist and kept me from slipping off the side of my steed. He seemed to know what my next move would be before I made it and he leaned forward with me, driving Philo on and away from danger.

9

When we reached the opposite side of the lake I straightened up, pulling hard on the reins and slowing Philo.

"Whoa now ... easy boy," I crooned. He panted and puffed, his heartbeat clattering beneath my thighs as his strides slowed. We took up a slower pace until I drew him to a complete stop. I stroked Philo's neck as Demetri slid from his back.

My own heart hammered just as fast as Philo's, although it was not entirely caused by the adrenaline of our quick retreat – Demetri's chest had been firm at my back and his arms tight around my waist as we rode, the bottom of my chlamys and tunic soaked through where his wet clothing had met mine. I had felt his body responding to our closeness as we rode, and was angry with mine for doing the same. I ignored the hand Demetri offered and dismounted smoothly to land beside him.

He lowered his hand without comment. "Thank you for helping me," he nodded. "I gather you're heading north and I won't keep you any longer."

"And where are *you* heading?" I asked.

"I seek the Tymphaioi who live in the south of the Pindos Ranges near Mount Tymphristos. After that, I plan on going to Athens."

I raised my eyebrows. "The Tymphaioi?"

"Yes. The fierce tribe of warriors from Aetolia. Do you know of them?"

His information about where the Tymphaioi lived and what tribe they belonged to was far from accurate, and with the difficulty he seemed to have had evading six boys from his hometown, I could only imagine how he would fare if he indeed found the warriors he spoke of.

"Would you like to share some breakfast with me before you continue on? I imagine your journey so far has not afforded you the luxury of regular meals," I offered, ignoring his question.

He considered my request, eventually nodding. "Thank you," he murmured.

I pushed my helmet up off my face as Demetri shed his chlamys and laid it on the ground, seating himself beside it. I untied my bag, giving Philo an apple before joining Demetri and handing him my waterskin. "Who told you the Tymphaioi lived in the southern Pindos Ranges?" I asked, breaking off some bread and cheese and handing them to him as he returned the water.

"People believe slaves are deaf, but we hear a lot," he replied.

"So you *are* a runaway slave. Where is your brand?"

"Spyros believed the practice of branding to be barbaric and preferred instead that we wear neck irons to mark our place in the eyes of others."

"And where is your iron now?"

"It doesn't matter."

"You removed it? Then maybe I should take you back so Spyros can return it to you."

"You can't do that, please," he breathed, his face panicked as his eyes met mine.

I took a bite of bread. I had no intention of returning him; the path to Larissa was not along my route, but his desperation to be free of the town did intrigue me. "You need not fear me taking you back, but you are misinformed about the Tymphaioi. You are travelling in the wrong direction to find them," I told him.

Demetri frowned. "It's not Tymphristos they inhabit? I was sure if I headed south to Lake Xynias and through the Othrys Mountains I would find them."

I shook my head. "No tribes like the Tymphaioi live farther south than the mountains here. They are to the west."

"Then I shall alter my course and enter the mountains at this place," he said, pointing to the hills behind me.

I frowned. "Then your journey would be foolish and fruitless. You could travel for moons without ever finding them. You would die from lack of food, or by their hand when they saw you before you did them."

"You don't think I can find food or shelter for myself in the mountains?" he asked, his face flushing as he spoke.

I shook my head. "I did not say that."

"But you don't think I can protect myself or get where I want."

I inhaled deeply. This boy was not my concern, if he wanted to go off chasing in the wrong direction who was I to stop him? I had even less intention of taking him to find the Tymphaioi than I had of taking him back to Larissa. I needed to make my way to the Macedonian border and beyond to find my grandfather. I exhaled loudly, relenting. If I let him enter the mountains here, certain harm would find him, and after making such an effort to escape whatever life he had had before, it did not seem like a fitting end.

"Look, the Tymphaioi tribe is in Epirus on the eastern slopes of the Pindos Ranges, near the northern border of Thessaly and southern Macedonia. They call the region of Tymphae home. You need to travel north, not south, or you will never find what you seek."

"You're sure of this?"

"Yes," I replied. We sat in silence and finished the food. My admission meant that, for the time being, we were headed in the same direction. "If the boys from the lake continue to pursue you, it will not be long before they reach us, we should continue north," I told him.

He shook his head. "They won't follow. They'll return to Larissa and tend their wounds, no doubt finding another slave to torture until their strength is regained and they can come looking for me again."

"You seem to know their ways well," I remarked as I stood to tie my bag to Philo's rump. Demetri only nodded. "What will happen to your family if that boy Phaeops dies?"

"It's not relevant," Demetri replied with a shrug.

I paused, his lack of compassion stirring my anger. "Not relevant? You would leave your family to suffer at the hands of those boys for *your* actions? Without thought of helping them or at the very least, warning them?"

"No! I leave no one behind," he cried, scooping up his chlamys from the ground and turning his back as he tied it hastily in place.

I crossed to him in two short steps and grabbed his arm, spinning him to face me. "Tell me why those boys chased you from your home. What are you accused of?" If I let him accompany me I needed to know I was not aiding a criminal.

"I worked for Spyros the Celator, chief coin maker in Larissa," Demetri replied, and I let him shake off my grip. "Phaeops and his friends are the sons of some of the richest men in town and for almost five winters they've forced me to make coin for them after dark. A moon ago, Spyros caught me with extra silver. I'd always been so careful, only taking small pieces when he had gone for the day, but I was careless and didn't make certain he'd left before I took what I would need for Phaeops' demands. I told Spyros what was happening and he flogged me in front of each boy I'd named until I was near death."

"Could you not find proof to substantiate your claims?" I asked.

"And who would believe the word of a slave against Larissa's favored sons?"

I only nodded for he spoke the truth; the word of a slave was worth very little to most people. "So Phaeops took revenge on your family?"

Demetri shook his head. "I have no family. I was found on the path outside Larissa, left to die of exposure by parents who had no use for me."

I fell silent, his words tugging at me – the loss of my parents had been devastating, but to *never* have anyone to love or care for you, for them to abandon you on purpose, was surely far worse.

"I ... my apologies," I murmured.

He shook his head. "It doesn't matter. It made the decision to flee easier when I found out the punishment Phaeops had planned for me." I was about to ask what that punishment entailed, but he continued before I could. "I left under a cover of darkness, but they saw me and chased me here, telling their fathers they were going hunting, which I suppose was not entirely untrue," he said, with a dark laugh.

"You have travelled quite a way without them catching you."

"Yes, but the waters of Lake Xynias would have claimed my body if you hadn't pulled me from its icy depth this morning."

"That may well be true," I agreed. "Is that why you are searching for the Tymphaioi? Do you want to take them back to Larissa with you so they can avenge the wrongs done to you?"

"No. I seek them for their knowledge. They wear a certain kind of armor and I'm hoping they'll teach me to make it."

I smiled and raised my eyebrows. "That is a bold wish. The Epirote tribes are not known for their willingness to share anything with we neighboring Greeks, whether that be land, food or the secrets of their armor. What do you plan to do with the knowledge if, by good fortune, you are able to get the Tymphaioi to part with it?"

"Take a sample to Aristides, the new Archon at Athens. I'll offer my services to craft it for him personally. His armor would be the talk of Greece and no weapon would be able to penetrate it."

I nodded to myself, I had met Aristides at Marathon and it was possible he would be interested in such armor. "Why Athens? Why not Sparta? With their inherent fighting spirit would *they* not want to own the toughest armor ever crafted?" I asked.

"I can't really explain, but I feel a ... pull towards Athens more so than Sparta. I feel that Athens is where I belong. Besides, I think Aristides would pay me far more to have the advantage over his Spartan rivals and if I decide I don't want to remain in Athens forever, I'll need coin to get wherever I want to go. Maybe somewhere near the sea ..." he trailed off.

I nodded again. His logic made sense and I had to admire his plans, even if I doubted he could get the information from the Tymphaioi in the first place. "Well, for now we are travelling in the same direction so if you want, we can go together," I said, surprised to find myself suggesting it. I did not need – or want – a travelling companion, but I could hardly take the offer back now. At least it would not be too far before our paths separated us.

"I owe you my thanks once again," Demetri nodded.

I took Philo's mane and mounted him, reaching out so Demetri could pull himself up behind me. When he had settled into place, I pressed my thighs against Philo's sides and he started to move.

*   *   *

"You've got a fine steed, where did you purchase him?" Demetri asked as we trotted along beside the Apidanus River.

"He was not a purchase," I replied. "His father belonged to my family and his mother came from the rich breeding grounds of Larissa, which I imagine you are well familiar with."

"You've been to Larissa?"

I shook my head. "No. I was only a child and stayed at home while my Mumma went to choose a suitable mare."

"Your mother? Why was your family's slave not in charge of that task, or your father if your house had no slaves?"

I took a deep breath, having had no need to speak of my parents' relationship for many winters. I kept my eyes on the path ahead as I answered him. "My grandfather went with Mumma. I have never known my father. It was only ever my mothers and I."

He put his hand on my arm and I turned my face to his. He was frowning. "Mothers? As in more than one?"

"Yes."

"I do not understand. Was one your father's second wife?"

"No. My mothers were lovers. Betrothed. We lived together as a family," I replied, pulling Philo to a stop again and swinging my leg over his neck to slide from his back.

"Betrothed?" Demetri repeated, joining me on the ground. "I heard women who took other women as lovers were banished to the island of Lesbos, told never to return unless they changed their ways … To seek one of their own for companionship or love brings only persecution and banishment. It's a shameful love."

I rounded on him, staring hard, the quick anger that was never far away filling me. It had been winters since I had heard that particular view, but the words hurt all the same. "You are mistaken. The women of Lesbos *choose* to live on the island so they do not fall victim to words like the ones spewing from your mouth." I poked at his chest.

"Hey!" he cried, slapping my hand away.

"Have you ever noticed how men are frequently expected and

37

encouraged to take a young boy as a lover – to teach him the ways of the sword, the arts, or a trade?" I prodded him again. "In the great Trojan War, Achilles and Patroclus often openly displayed their affection for one another, and when Patroclus was killed, Achilles took life after life as revenge for the death of his lover and no-one begrudged *his* motives." A third thrust at his chest. "Why could two women not share a bond like that? Why could one woman not fight whoever she had to, to defend ... to save another? To save her wife from an enemy? Why is that so hard to understand?" I shouted, my chest heaving.

"I said stop poking me," Demetri growled, pushing me square in the chest, the surprise of his action clearly written across his face.

The heat within boiled and I turned, placing a hand on the cloth atop Philo. I recognized the rage building in my blood, heating me from the inside. My hatred. My sorrow. I had not lost control for a while now but I needed to get to the Thessalian Plain and find the Persians – they were the ones who deserved the fury coursing through me, not Demetri. *They* had never spoken words of shame when it came to two women being together, but they had broken a bond of love I thought could never be broken and it was time they paid for it.

"Wait. Don't go," Demetri pleaded. "Look, I'm sorry. I'm just repeating what I've heard. That doesn't mean it's what I think. I didn't understand when you said you had two mothers. Now I do. I've only heard whispers about girls and women sent from their homes to spare their families the shame. I don't care if a man or woman takes another or the opposite as their lover. I judge people only as I find them – liking or disliking them for how they treat me, not for who they love."

His quick apology surprised me. "I have to go," I murmured, tightening my grip on Philo's mane.

"Please don't. I didn't mean any disrespect to you or your family." He reached out tentatively, placing his hand on my arm. It took all my restraint not to throw it off again and I wondered if Demetri could feel how little hold I had on myself. He took his hand away but stepped between me and Philo, his eyes finding mine, and it looked like he was choosing his next words carefully. "Your mothers no longer walk in this world with you, do they?"

"No," I replied.

"Were they killed because they loved one another, is that why you defend them so fiercely?"

"No," I repeated taking a step back and starting to pace. "They were killed by the Persian filth who continue to ravage our lands. They were held prisoner in the palace, refusing to do what the Persians wanted until they were killed for their disobedience. I was there. I saw the yellow caps. I heard my mother die." My voice cracked on the final word.

"Ava," he whispered, halting my steps when he took my hand. "I'm sorry." I swallowed loudly but said nothing. "How long have they been gone?"

"Ten winters."

"It seems we're both orphans then," he stated.

I had never thought of myself as an orphan – just alone. "Y-yes, I suppose we are," I stammered. The heat in my veins was starting to dissipate, replaced by another feeling I was less used to. I stared down at our entwined fingers. I felt vulnerable, exposed. I did not like it. I did not share my feelings of that night with anyone – mostly there was no need – everyone I spent time with had been there. They remembered what happened, they had their own grief, or regret or anger to deal with. I let Moeris tell me of his hurt and regret, but I never spoke of mine. And I never spoke of it with strangers when I met them. Ever. I drew away from Demetri. He did not try and stop me.

He held out Philo's reins. "May I continue on with you for now?" he asked quietly.

I hesitated, torn by the duty I felt to see him safely away from his pursuers now that I had intervened, and my want to be alone to close up the rifts he had opened inside me. To ensure words and feelings I had kept inside remained that way. He had drawn them out of me too easily. I did not know if I could trust myself with him, and that had never happened before.

I eventually nodded and took the reins from him. "Do not push me again," I told him.

"I won't … so long as you don't poke me," he replied with the hint of a smile.

"Agreed," I nodded.

10

Demetri's hands held my waist firmly and, just as it had earlier, my body reveled in the contact, even though I tried to stop it. I could have walked beside Philo – or had Demetri do it – but I did not want our journey to be that slow.

When the sun finally started its descent behind the mountains, I was relieved to see a sheltered area at the side of the path. I steered Philo in that direction, eager to get away from Demetri's close proximity and the warring emotions he stirred within me.

"We will camp here tonight and continue on in the morning," I announced, slipping from Philo's back and rounding his rump to collect my bag. The knot holding the bag in place was stuck – the end having slid back in on itself, tightening the cord and making what was usually a simple task, more difficult. I tugged on it without success, cursing under my breath until Demetri came to stand beside me.

"Can I help?" he asked.

I had dealt with the problem before but I was tired and my fingers were starting to numb in the evening chill so I stepped aside with only a nod. I watched the way Demetri's nimble fingers manipulated the rope. They were long and elegant, working quickly but efficiently to get the job done. I wondered what it would feel like to run my own down their graceful length and for a moment considered doing just that. I caught myself in time, closing my hands tightly to censor the thought.

"Thank you," I said as he handed the bag to me. "Would you see to

Philo while I prepare something for us?" He nodded and took the three apples I handed him. I found a place beneath a large oak tree to set about dividing up the bread and cheese.

Demetri spoke quietly to Philo as he fed him the fruit and I made out a couple of the hushed words; he was thanking Philo for bringing him north. "Should I find some wood?" he asked as he joined me.

I shook my head and handed him the food. "No. A fire would make us an easy target if Megistias and his friends *did* decide to follow us."

"Oh, of course."

I was still hungry when we finished the small meal so took two more apples from the bag, holding one up to Demetri in question. He nodded and I threw it to him. The day's events replayed in my mind as I ate and one memory in particular piqued my curiosity.

"Hey, Demetri? Before you flipped that coin back at the lake, it seemed like you *knew* it would come down on the side you wanted it to. How could you be so sure?"

He smiled. "Do you want to see the coin I used?" I nodded and he crossed to my side, taking a small pouch from beneath the folds of his chiton and opening it. "Larissa is well known for two things; one you know of already – the high quality of the horses bred and sold there. The other, is its coins." He passed over a small piece of silver and I studied the picture on the side facing me. "When I have silver in my hands, the two are intimately connected."

"It is beautiful," I murmured, tracing the raised outline of a horse. It stood, body facing right and head to the left, looking back over its flank. The individual strands of its mane and tail dipped and rose beneath my finger, the simple beauty impressive.

"Horses are beautiful creatures, my favorite if truth be known. They're loyal and strong, and very hard to put onto a coin. I've spent candlemarks watching the horse trainers on the plains outside Larissa rear foals or break wild stallions they found wandering on their lands. I take what I've seen and try to recreate that in the silver."

Demetri leaned over, a long finger tracing the horse's body as mine had. I could imagine him sitting beneath a tree on a bright spring day and using those fingers to sketch the designs for his coins, but the idea of him actually *making* them was harder to imagine. From what I remembered of my great-grandfather Ophelos' metal workshop in Trachis, the men who worked there were muscular and dirty, cramped into a darkened room, a hot fire burning in the corner providing the only light. They crafted our weapons as well as our coins and there was always silver and bronze smelting in pots above the flames as they pounded away with their hammers and the other tools they used. I could not match that image and Demetri in my mind, even though his arms were well muscled.

"You made this?" I asked.

"I did," he nodded.

"You are very skilled, are the other Celators in Larissa as talented as you?"

"We all had our different talents," he replied simply. "Turn it over."

I did, looking up at him in surprise. "It is the same on both sides. That is how you knew you would win when you flipped it – both sides are tails."

He nodded again. "I waited until Megistias called heads before choosing this one from my pouch."

"You have others you made, similar to this?"

Again he nodded and retrieved a second coin. "This holds the head of Athena on the obverse and Hephaestus on the reverse. If Megistias had called tails, I would have selected this one instead."

I studied both sides, easily recognizing the images of the great god and goddess. "Your detail is incredible, far better than coins that have passed through my own hands," I said, handing them back.

"Thank you." He dropped the coins into the pouch and hesitated. I watched him, wondering what he was considering. He drew his hand to his chin and rubbed at it. "Would you like to see the others I have?"

"Very much."

He hesitated again, but then drew his legs up, pulling his chiton tight across his knees and upending the contents onto the material. Returning the two coins he had already shown me to the pouch, he arranged the other five in a neat line, handing the smallest to me.

"That one isn't as round as the ones I just showed you and the picture of the horse isn't as clear. It's also supposed to be in the center of the coin."

I held it up to the fading light. It was significantly different to the first two – tiny and thin, with broken lines forming the outside of a horse standing and looking to the right. There were no lines indicating the individual strands of its tail and the reverse side showed traces of the picture above, like it was wearing through.

"How many winters old were you when you made that?" I asked, passing it back.

"Eight."

"And you are how many now?"

"Eighteen."

I nodded. That explained the fragile state it was in. "Why did you keep it all this time?"

Demetri shrugged. "It was my first and Spyros told me that every Celator should keep the first coin he made with his own two hands." I nodded again and he passed me three of the four remaining coins.

The obverse of each showed a horse; the first was standing and looking off to the side, the second prancing, and the third had a hoplite on its back clutching a spear as the horse reared up on its hind legs. I turned them over. I once again recognized the heads of Hephaestus and Athena on two of the coins, the last showing the face and body of a sea nymph. The detail Demetri had managed to put onto such small items was remarkable and I could see why Larissa was famed for its coins.

"Why the sea nymph?" I asked, giving them all back.

"I'm not sure," he shrugged. "I kept dreaming of her until finally I put her on a coin."

I nodded. "You should forget about the Tymphaioi and their armor design. *Those* are what you should show Aristides at Athens. The owls on their coins are serviceable, but you would add so much more … depth to them. Have you considered putting your designs onto shields or armor?"

Demetri smiled and drew his sword from its sheath. "I have made swords as well as coins over the winters, but this is the only one I have ever put pictures onto."

I took the sword when he offered it, holding it up so the blade caught the rays of light as I studied the weapon in its entirety. It was well-crafted, solid but not too heavy, not quite brand new, but not chipped away as though it was used frequently either. The blade was smooth iron, sharp and leaf-shaped. Lengths of dark leather laced the width of the wooden hilt and when I squeezed it in my hand as I had at the lake, I realized it was to help with the grip. The simple idea was effective and I considered doing the same to my own weapon. The guard was also iron, but both sides were covered with the tiny pictures Demetri had spoken of. I leaned closer, making out horses, gods, nymphs and triremes, all perfectly formed in the silver.

"This is amazing," I murmured. "I would be proud to stand side by side with my fellow soldiers displaying these details on our swords or shields."

He smiled and took his weapon back. "Thank you." He re-sheathed it and packed away the coins he had shown me, picking up the final one and staring intently at it. I waited for him to give it to me, but he drew a deep breath and closed his hand around it instead, raising it briefly to his lips before returning it to his pouch with the others.

"You are not going to share that one?" I asked, my brow furrowing at his sudden reluctance.

He shook his head and would not meet my eyes. "I … I shouldn't have shown them to you at all. They are just … for me. I can't use them for trade, therefore they shouldn't be seen by others."

I stood abruptly, frowning as I paced back and forth across the path. "You carry no coin to trade for food or other items at the agora? That is a foolish decision. Did you not consider what you would need before you fled? How did you expect to survive long enough to reach the Tymphaioi?"

Demetri's brow creased into deep lines and he drove his hand into his chiton again, producing another pouch. "Of course I considered what I'd need. I've traded *a lot* to obtain Athenian coins from traders, and collected many more from beside men sleeping off the effects of Dionysius' spoils. I made sure I had what I needed to find the Tymphaioi and continue south to Athens. Don't be concerned that you'll have to provide for me now that my journey has changed direction." He gathered both pouches and hid them beneath his chiton again before pulling his chlamys around his shoulders and getting to his feet.

"Well … good," I said, unable to think of a better response. It was not hard to imagine what he would have had to trade for the coins. I doubted he had ever had any material possessions, and that could only mean he had traded on his body.

"I'm going down to the river to wash. You should rest … sleep." Demetri announced, turning his back on me.

"I do not need you to tell me when I need to rest," I growled.

"Fine, but don't follow me," he insisted.

"Why would I?" I started to pace again, furious at his suggestion that *I* was the one who needed to rest. There had been many times when Lysistratos and I had travelled all day and through the night to reach our destination – when we snuck away from Marathon to go back to Trachis for one. Or as we travelled home with the rest of the soldiers from Athens weeks later. There was no reason to think that this journey would be any different.

*

Demetri cast another look behind him, glad that Ava hadn't followed him as he'd asked. He removed the pouch of herbs Spyros had given him, they were almost gone and he'd have to find more before long. He had a quick look around but couldn't see any plants he recognized. He placed the pouch on the ground and crouched at the water's edge.

With practiced efficiency, he loosened the chiton from the top half of his body, peeling it down to hang over his belt and unwinding the cloth covering his chest. He made the herbs into a paste like Spyros had shown him and rubbed them in. It didn't hurt when he did it anymore, but it still felt strange. Unnatural. A loss.

*

I blew out a breath and slowed my steps, reminding myself that being chased, forced to sleep beneath trees and swimming across a freezing lake before fighting six boys was not what Demetri was used to. He had left his home under duress, and even if he had found safety from Phaeops and his friends for a few candlemarks each night, I doubted he had spent the time sleeping. I also suspected he had never held his own in a fight, slaves were often beaten or punished, but they were never permitted to raise a hand against their attacker – which would explain why he had looked so surprised when he pushed me earlier. I was sure that until today Demetri had *never* fought back against Phaeops and his friends, or anyone else.

My eyes fell on his sheathed sword and I wondered how he had come to have it. Who had it belonged to? None of the boys at the lake seemed to recognize it and I was fairly sure that Spyros would not have let him to keep such an expensive item. I would give Demetri his space tonight, but tomorrow I would ask him about it.

I raised my eyes to the path we had come from. The light was almost completely hidden behind the mountains, the trees reduced to dark forms. No one seemed to be pursuing us, the only sound the gentle chatter of the nearby river. I crossed to one of the trees and pulled my chlamys around my arms as I lay down, staring up into the darkness between the black pine's branches and listening for Demetri's return. Mumma's necklace slid across my chest, reminding me of its presence and I took it from beneath my tunic, holding it against my lips. In only a couple of days I would see Papou again and together we would finish what the Persians started ten winters ago.

From the corner of my eye I caught a glimpse of Demetri and turned over so my back faced him, saying nothing as he silently settled himself.

*

Demetri returned to the clearing. Ava looked like she was asleep, or was at least pretending to be, and he was grateful she was turned away from him as he re-adjusted his chiton, the material sticking to his chest where he was still wet. He lay down beneath a nearby tree and it wasn't long before his soft snores broke the silence.

11

I rolled over, Eos' dawn bathing the path in front of me with its cool light.

"Good morning." I sat up quickly, reaching for my sword. "I'm sorry, I didn't mean to frighten you," Demetri smiled, offering his arm. "Did you sleep well?"

I ignored his outstretched palm, pushing myself to my feet to belt my sword at my waist. My sleep had been filled with dreams of Demetri and I in intimate embraces and even though I was now awake, the feel of him was burned into my brain, leaving me with a disconcerting warmth in my body.

"Er ... yes. You?"

"Better than I have in days," he replied. "I filled the water skin. I'll have to buy my own when we find a suitable town or trader, I lost mine in the lake yesterday."

"Good idea," I nodded. "We should continue on. By foot," I added hastily, making my way to Philo. I did not want him so close to me after what I had dreamed.

Demetri nodded and I took an apple for each of us from the bag, handing them out before tying it to Philo. I took my helmet and slipped it onto my head, keeping it back from my face as we followed the river north again along the path.

"I want to ask you about your sword."

"What do you want to know?" Demetri replied.

"Did you steal it from the metalwork hut before you left?"

Demetri shook his head. "No. It was a gift from Spyros."

I frowned again. "A gift? Why would he do that? You said he beat you until you were almost dead. Why would he then gift a sword to you … unless he expected you to take your own life with it for being disobedient?"

"It wasn't for that." His words were so quiet I almost missed them. He took a deep breath, releasing it all the way before he spoke again. "Spyros bought me when I was six winters old. He took me to his home where I worked for him and his family. At harvest time, I often received lashings for watching the horses in the nearby fields and drawing what I'd seen in the dirt, rather than gathering the wheat. The news travelled back to Spyros and when he sent for me one evening, I thought it would be to tell me he was selling me. Instead, he gave me some papyrus and asked me to draw what I saw. When I was finished, I showed him and he wondered aloud if my pictures could be put into silver. He knew if the coins could hold them, that I would be of more value to him in that manner than as a field slave."

"Something tells me you were of great value to him."

Demetri nodded. "I made him extremely wealthy and his Celator's workshop well known, but when he found me with the silver a moon ago he wasn't alone. Eton's father was with him and demanded I be punished for the lies I told about his son and his friends. Spyros had no choice; he couldn't be seen to favor me just because I was gifted. I was still only a slave."

"So the sword was recompense for his actions?"

Demetri shook his head. "It was for protection. Spyros also learned what Phaeops planned to do to me. So, as soon as I'd recovered enough from his beating, he told me to take the sword and leave. He told me I'd more than repaid the debt my purchase had cost him and he took my neck irons from me, telling me I was free. He wished me well but told me never to return to Larissa – Eton and Phaeops' fathers would make him kill me for running. I promised him I wouldn't, and left."

"Do you think he always intended to free you one day?" Demetri seemed confused by my question. "You said that Spyros thought the idea of branding was barbaric, but without one unless you *tell* someone you were a slave, they would never know," I explained. "You are free to go and seek work wherever you want without that immediate recognition. If Phaeops' friend had not said anything at the lake, maybe even *I* would not know."

Demetri grew quiet, his brow furrowed as he considered my words. Maybe even as a slave, there had been those who cared for him. I was glad he had not died in the lake or by Phaeops' hand. He deserved the chance to become something more than an unloved orphan or a slave to be beaten.

"I didn't think of it like that but perhaps Spyros *did* intend to free me one day," Demetri finally conceded.

I let the silence drag out as we walked, but watched his deep frown from the corner of my eye. Eventually I reached out, placing my hand on his arm. It was warm and the smattering of hairs were soft, fine where they brushed against my calloused palms. "I did not mean to upset you."

He looked at my hand and as I lifted it, he covered it with his own, keeping it in place as we walked. "You didn't upset me," he said, meeting my eyes. "I was just thinking of the difficult position I put Spyros in. I see now that the only way to keep both me and his family safe was for him to send me away. But now he'll have to find someone to replace me, and that won't be an easy task. I was there so long, I didn't need anyone to assist me when I worked, he'll make less coin this winter due to my carelessness."

"The blame does not lie with you. Phaeops and his friends carry that burden."

"I should have stood up to them earlier."

"And you would have found yourself in the Underworld."

He whipped his hand from mine. "I ca—"

I stopped walking, taking both his arms and turning him to face me. "You know I am right. Those boys would have tortured you one way or another until you were dead. Or maybe they would have attacked Spyros to bend you to their will. Either way, getting caught with that silver may have been for the best; it allowed Spyros to help you without suspicion falling on him ... and you have received your freedom."

I released the hold I had on him, gathering Philo's reins again. He was quiet a long time, finally nodding. "That's enough about me for now," He looked back to the path. "Riding will see us to our destinations faster, if you don't mind us doing so."

I nodded in reply – he had been more than forthcoming with his answers when I questioned him and my body was back under control. I jumped onto Philo's back. Demetri waited until I was settled before joining me, his hands resting only lightly on my waist. I clicked my tongue and Philo started to walk.

*   *   *

We travelled in silence until the sun was high overhead and just as Demetri's movements had matched mine when we galloped away from the lake, so they did as we trotted along the northern path. Each gentle lift and lower of our behinds was perfectly in tune with one another and I was surprised that Demetri held himself so assuredly. He would have never owned a horse, but I wondered if Spyros had let him ride them after that day with the papyrus.

We left the Apidanus River when it met the Thessalian Plain, turning north-west and continuing along the well-worn path, both of us silent and lost in our own thoughts. It was rare for me to share Philo like I was. Over the winters I had carried plenty of soldiers or farmers on my horse, but they had been injured and laid across Philo's back, not astride him as Demetri and I were. For a brief moment I wondered what Demetri's body would feel like under my hands. I managed to control the growl threatening to emerge from my throat. I did not want to think of Demetri like that, did not usually think of anyone like that. Curse that dream. I was not inexperienced with men, but the times I had been with them had been under different circumstances – it was expected of me.

"Can I ask you something?" Demetri asked, interrupting my musings. I nodded, grateful for the distraction. "Are you really a soldier? You fight as if you've had training, yet you're here, alone, with no other soldiers at your side. Did you learn to fight so you wouldn't get bothered when you travelled?" I drew in a breath. "I don't want to upset you or argue, I just … wondered," he added quickly.

I blew out the breath. "I *am* a soldier. A hoplite in the Army of Trachis, in the region of Thermopylae. My Mumma was head of the army before she died and I joined when I was twelve winters old. The rest of the men are guarding the Pass of Coela, south of here."

"Why aren't you with them?"

"I … I have something else I have to do."

He was quiet for a moment, his fingers tightening ever so slightly where they were splayed out against the sides of my thighs. "Women aren't normally allowed to join armies, unless it's for entertainment. Do the men of *your* army know or do you keep your helmet and armor on so they are unaware?"

"They know," I replied. I was about to add that Spartan girls were trained as soldiers just like their boys were, but Demetri slid his hands from my waist up onto my cuirass just below my breasts and the bold action rendered me speechless.

"Your cuirass fits you … well. To an enemy your true identity is well disguised and when you spoke to Phaeops, your voice was deep and different to how you really speak."

I nodded and swallowed loudly, his breath tickling my ear. "My commander taught me to do that. It is another way for my gender to remain hidden during a battle."

"An important skill to learn," he noted. "Why did you want to be a soldier? Was it because of your Mumma? Were both of them in the army?"

I shook my head. "Only Mumma Skylar was a warrior. Two of our soldiers joined other Greeks against the Persians and when they returned from Sardis the winter after my mothers' deaths, I knew I wanted to join them. They spoke with pride of their part in the destruction and victory and of how many Persians they had killed. I was determined to know that feeling for myself. I would have done anything to feel Persian blood on my hands, whether I became a soldier or not."

"I imagine you would have," Demetri murmured. "Can I ask you something of a more intimate nature?" he added, his hands covering mine on Philo's reins and pulling him to a stop.

I hesitated, wondering how much more intimate he wanted to get. He did not know it, but what I had just told him about Kleitos and Sander's return from Sardis was not something I had shared with anyone else. I nodded.

"As a soldier, I expect you've had many … experiences. I know that when an army is victorious there's often a feast with wine, women and men for the celebrations." Demetri paused, his chest rising and falling quickly behind me. I wondered if some of his thoughts, just as his movements, had been following mine, if he too was overly aware of the body travelling so close to his.

"There are often rewards for a victorious soldier," I agreed with a nod.

"And did you partake of those rewards? The men? The women?" he asked, his voice catching on the last word.

My heart hammered and I was sure the sound would reach him. "Yes. I would not have wanted to offend our hosts by refusing."

He slid from Philo's back and stepped towards the trees. I watched him, wondering if he was angry. He should not be – it was my duty to accept such gifts. "It was expected. I did what any soldier did when presented with the same gift; I honored it," I explained.

Demetri turned back, the color high in his cheeks. He offered me his hand, gripping my fingers tightly as I joined him on the ground. I noted the determination on his face and waited for him to speak again.

"So you have had experiences with both men and women," he confirmed, reaching out with shaking hands to lift my helmet off and drop it beside us.

"I have," I nodded.

"And which did you find to be most satisfying? Do you intend to follow in your mothers' footsteps with your preferred choice of lover?" he asked.

My breath constricted in my chest and I slowly shook my head. "I … I do not have a preferred choice. I enjoy both."

"I see," he murmured, taking a step closer and entwining his fingers with mine again. His body radiated warmth that started at our entwined fingers and quickly spread through the rest of me.

"And you? Do you prefer the company of men or women for pleasure?" I managed. He slid his palms to my waist and up beneath my cuirass, drawing me closer, and the heat between us grew. "I prefer the company of women," he whispered, leaning forward to kiss me. His lips were soft yet firm, and just as warm as the rest of him.

"I see," I replied when we parted.

"Perhaps I should show my thanks for your help at the lake in a way you're more accustomed to," he said, a shy grin lighting his lips. His hands went to my shoulder to untie my chlamys.

"Wait," I insisted, covering his hands.

"Wh–get down!" he shouted, eyes wide as they suddenly focused on something behind me.

"What?" I frowned.

"Get down," he repeated, pushing me roughly as an arrow flew past my right ear. A second followed barely a moment later, lodging itself in my left shoulder.

"Ah," I cried, landing heavily on my back as I clutched at my arm. Demetri was immediately beside me, his back to the oncoming danger. His face showed no pain and he was not bleeding from anywhere obvious; the arrows had missed their second target.

He stared intently at the barb sticking out of my flesh and moved my hand, bracing his own against my collarbone. "This is going to hurt," he warned.

I nodded and drew in a breath as he nodded back. He tightened his grip and tugged the shaft of the arrow, freeing the head from my skin and throwing it aside.

I groaned, grinding my teeth together, refusing to cry out again. "We have to get to Philo."

"It didn't go in far, we'll tend to it properly as soon as we can," Demetri said at the same time. He grabbed the long length of my chlamys and wound it tight against the flowing blood.

My gaze went to the direction the projectiles had come from. A line of men were spread out across the Plain. Dark yellow cloth covered their heads and they wore robes of red over white, non-metallic chest pieces with sleeved, colored tunics beneath.

"Persians," I growled. There were at least thirty of them. My blood instantly boiled, heartbeat doubling with renewed adrenaline, the pain in my shoulder all but disappearing at the sight. I pushed myself to my feet, pulling Demetri with me as I searched for Philo. He was about ten feet away to our left, eyes wide, hooves stamping and nostrils flared as he snorted.

"Come on," I said.

The Persians rearmed their bows and as they took aim, I realized they were not pointing them at me and Demetri, but at Philo. "No!" I cried, rushing towards him. The Persians released their arrows, each finding its mark deep in Philo's flesh. He fell heavily to the ground. "Philo, oh gods, no, Philo …" I whispered, covering the short distance between us.

I dropped to my knees beside my faithful steed, laying a hand on his flank. Tears wet my cheeks but I did not wipe them away. "Oh Philo, forgive me. Forgive me."

"We have to go," Demetri urged, his hand on my shoulder.

"I am not leaving Philo," I replied, his wounds swimming before my eyes. The arrows were deep and he whinnied as I touched him gently. His life was streaming from him at an alarming rate. I did not know what to do first. I wanted to take the arrows out, as Demetri had done for me, but there were so many. I would do him more harm than good.

Demetri tried to pull me to my feet. "Leave me alone," I yelled, wrenching my arm from his grip.

"Ava, they're coming for us."

"I will not leave Philo here to die. Go if you want."

"I'm not leaving without you, but we can't help him if *we're* dead."

Demetri was right but I would not leave my most faithful friend. The Persians would have to kill me first. Or I would kill them. I shivered as heat spread through my chest and the skin high up on my shoulder blades itched uncomfortably. The Persians should not even be here yet. I was supposed to have more time to find Papou. *He* was the one who should be here facing them with me, not Demetri.

12

Ares held the frail old woman in his arms, the two of them hidden from the mortals on the Thessalian Plain.

"She is ready. It is time to release her wings," he told her.

"I hope I have the strength to make it so. I have waited so long for you to command it of me."

"I know you have, Rizpah, but as I told you when you suppressed them, she was not ready. I had to craft her into the warrior I needed. We needed."

"And she has become a fearsome warrior. You have molded her well," Rizpah noted.

"We shall see," Ares murmured. "Release them and ask your kin to prepare a room for her at my palace. If she is akin to others of the line, she shall require half-a-moon's rest once she has harnessed the amulet's power. I want her with us when she wakes."

"As it pleases you, Master." Rizpah raised her gnarled hand, the slightest of tremors accompanying the movement. She swept her hand across Ava's back and the small nodes came to life, rising slightly beneath her tunic and cuirass. "It has begun."

"It has and I thank you for your loyal service all these winters. We have not always seen eye-to-eye but you have always done what I have asked."

"It has been my honor to serve you," Rizpah nodded.

"Our entire number shall gather to witness the emergence of our Chosen One. Can I convince you to remain at my palace until she arrives?"

"No. I do not have long left, I would rather go to Stymphalos to meet my kin once I make my final change."

"I understand, though I hope you shall stay with me this day. I want you to witness what your line has been created for."

"If you wish me to, then I shall remain, though I am certain I would know of her, wherever I was."

"When she has shown us what she can do, I shall take you to Lake Stymphalos myself," Ares nodded.

"Thank you, Master."

"We await your demonstration, Chosen One," Ares grinned.

13

I put a hand to my breast, finding my cuirass warm to the touch. Had the amulet sensed the Persians' presence? It was, after all, them who Mumma had told me to use it against. I took the leather cord from my neck and looked up at the approaching soldiers; their arrows were by their sides but they advanced in two short lines.

"What are you doing? What is that?" Demetri asked.

I ignored his question and held the necklace up. The gem was no longer a deep black; it glowed bright orange and warmed my hand. Mumma had said it was powerful and I did not doubt her – how else could it have changed color? *But how do I call forth your power?* I frowned.

The itch at my shoulder blades intensified and I squirmed beneath my clothing. *The amulet was causing the reaction of my skin. How? Why?* A blinding pain down my back stopped any further thoughts and I rocked forward, my hands springing open and releasing the amulet. It fell to the grass in front of me, the intensity of its light unwavering. I ripped the fibula from my chlamys and pulled it off, the wrapped length at my arm hanging limply. I tore at the ties of my cuirass and dragged the bonded material over my head. I threw the leather aside, the pain at my back subsiding somewhat now I was free of it.

"Ava, what is it?"

"I do no–argh!" Piercing agony seized me again. It was as if two swords were being driven deep into my flesh. I arched back, my throat exposed to the sky as the screech of a bird called overhead.

"Ava!" Demetri pleaded.

The sensation intensified to an almost unbearable level. I could not reply. I squeezed my eyes shut, wishing only for relief from the pain.

Demetri grabbed me under my armpits and pulled me to my feet. "We have to go." I shook myself free and rounded on him, shoving him hard in the chest with both hands. He fell awkwardly to the ground. "What are you doing?"

I screamed and fell to my knees again as the bird screeched a second time. I looked up, seeing nothing in the clear blue sky. I pulled my tunic out from my right shoulder blade. There was no sword piercing my skin, only the shameful bump I had kept hidden from everyone for almost ten winters. But it was different today. Longer than I remembered. Darker too.

I staggered to my feet. *Was the bump on the other side the same?* Before I could find out, the darkened flesh split and separated, a long black point pushing its way out of the skin. It broke through my tunic, continuing to grow. Finally I looked to my left side, finding a second point extending through the material there. I watched, horrified, as the protrusions grew and grew. They were soon longer than my arms and I strained my neck to watch both at once. As they lengthened, the pain diminished.

When the pointed rods reached three or four feet into the air, black tendrils dropped towards the ground. They were longest at the end furthest from me and almost reached the dirt. My heart pounded beneath my chest. I trembled as they swayed in the non-existent wind and became thicker. In the space of a few moments, the tendrils turned from thin wisps of black into large, full wings. I had to reposition my feet to accommodate the sudden weight behind me.

"What …?" Demetri gasped.

I could not look away from my new wings but I was no longer horrified at what I was seeing. I reached out a tentative hand, taking the softness between my fingers. They were as soft as the wings of birds. Firm. Beautiful. Functional. A shiver ran through me and Mumma Skylar appeared, her face lit in a magnificent smile.

"Ava, you look so beautiful," she murmured, circling me and extending her own hand to touch my wings.

They obeyed when I lifted them, stretching out either side of me, large and imposing. Fear and complete calm engulfed me in equal measure. They were part of me, they were natural. I knew I would be able to use them as effortlessly as I moved my arms or legs. I looked past Mumma to the Persians. They stood with their mouths open, staring first at me, then at each other.

Mumma followed my gaze, smiling when she faced me again. "You are ready to take your revenge. You can destroy them all. Pick up the amulet." I bent down, re-gathering the object. The warmth of it travelled through my hand and up my arm. It filled me with clarity and a further sense of deep calm.

"What are you doing?" Demetri asked.

"Stay out of my way," I warned as fire rushed through my veins. I was unstoppable, invincible. I would destroy the Persians before me. I would be impossible to wound, the amulet would protect me. I would use my wings to fly high above their swords and arrows. I could lead an army of my own, crush the Persian forces whether they numbered twenty or two hundred. I would be the most revered soldier anywhere in the world. I wanted it more than I had ever wanted anything in my life. I craved it. I would have it.

"Do you feel it?" Mumma whispered. I nodded. "Then do it. Make them pay for what they have done."

"What about Philo?" I asked, my breath shallow.

"Forget about him, destroy the army before you."

"Forget him? How can you say that?"

"Who are you talking to?" Demetri asked.

Mumma frowned. "Very well then. Heal him with the amulet, but do not miss your chance to take what you desire most."

My eyes settled again on the Persians. They had started to move forward, but slowly, their bows still at their sides. I crossed to Philo and knelt beside him.

"Ava, what are you doing?" Demetri asked again. "We have to go."

"Be quiet and let me concentrate," I snapped.

"Hold it over him," Mumma instructed. I did so, the orange in my hand intensifying in both color and heat.

Without further warning, shots of light as bright as Zeus' thunderbolts burst from the amulet and raced to each of the arrows in Philo's flank, completely destroying the wood until not one trace was left in his skin. The light returned to the amulet just as quickly as it had come. Philo snorted, tossing his head as his body jerked then went still; the only movement the shallow rise and fall of his stomach with each hiccupping breath. The orange inside the amulet swirled before turning light purple then to red.

Power and fearlessness coursed through me again as my hatred for the men in the red robes and yellow caps reasserted itself. I got to my feet and faced them, angry and ready, as they ran towards us. I held the amulet up. I wanted this. I would have my revenge. Nothing would stop me destroying every one of the oncoming soldiers.

The amulet grew steadily hotter, the blood beneath my skin mirroring its heat. I silently commanded my wings to enlarge behind me, and I flapped them slightly as I waited. When the amulet's heat rose to an almost intolerable level in my palm, I knew it was time. *Go!* I commanded.

A massive thunderbolt erupted from the amulet, racing through the air until it found my target. The Persian soldiers burst into flames. Their screams filled the air as they ran back and forth, crashing into one another and grabbing uselessly at their arms and heads.

I grinned when they dropped to the ground, their fires out, the thunderbolt burned out with them. No more did their screams of anguish fill the air on the Plain, the only sound my breath, loud in my ears.

I shivered as Mumma Skylar disappeared but I did not mind; she had seen me. I had done it. I had destroyed them all with just one thunderbolt, just like she wanted. I wished more Persians would come. I would set fire to them all. I would inflict more destruction and pain on my enemies than they had ever known. I would become known as the vanquisher of armies, just like Mumma Skylar. I knew now that Moeris' tale of Mumma and the army at Trachis was true. She had used the amulet against them, I was sure of it. It explained too why it was she, and not Mother Alexis, who had been with me just now.

I stared at the smoking mound of bodies. I would be even stronger than Mumma. I would use the amulet against every Persian man, woman or child I came across. I would kill them all until I took my last breath. I would travel east, sail to Persian soil and take my lethal assault directly to them. They had no idea what deadly destruction was about to find them.

The rank smell of burnt, mortal flesh reached me, and with it, the power inside vanished and my knees buckled. I swallowed the bile gathered in my throat. My head throbbed and tremors racked my body as my wings retreated. *Did I really just sprout wings and destroy thirty Persian soldiers with Mumma's amulet?*

I looked to Demetri. He scrambled away from me; his ashen face and wide eyes providing the answer.

I opened my fist and stared at the gem in my hand. The fiery red had returned to a black mass set inside the iron. It looked like just a harmless piece of jewelry. How had it been able to make me feel so ... powerful, so different? I had never felt such a desire to harm and kill. I had always welcomed battle, especially against the Persians, but to want to harm women and children? The thought sickened me and I retched.

I needed to find Papou. He would know about Mumma using the amulet to destroy the army. Had wings come out of her back too? If so, it must be the amulet that made them appear because I was not borne of her body, but of Mother Alexis'. But the knobs on my back had been there since ... since just after they died.

I squeezed my eyes shut. It was not the first time I had been faced with questions I had no answers to. Answers I wanted from *them*. The child I kept protected deep beneath my breast suddenly rose to the surface with such ferocity that it hurt. She wanted desperately for her mothers to return from the Underworld and provide the answers she so badly sought.

The sound of sandal on dirt pulled me from my grief and I swallowed hard as I opened my eyes. Demetri was on his feet, making a wide berth around me as he ran. I did not blame him for leaving, after what he had seen happen to me and what I had done to the Persian soldiers he *should* leave. What if he had tried to stop me or stood between them and me? Would I have turned on him? Would I have been able to stop myself from hurting him? I doubted it. What I had felt had been too strong to fight. I had not *wanted* to fight it. I had enjoyed it. I swallowed again, my stomach threatening to return the apple I had eaten earlier.

I frowned, realizing that Demetri was not taking the path to the north or the south. He ran towards the pile of Persians. He nudged one of them with his toe and a puff of dust rose into the air. He jerked back as though stung.

"What did you do?" he cried in disbelief. "What was that?"

I did not reply. I picked up my cuirass and crawled across to Philo, putting a hand on his flank. His breath was still shallow, his heartbeat faint beneath my hand. The amulet was still in my palm, but I did not dare use it on him again. The feelings of power it had given me had been seductive, but I did not want feelings that were not true to who I was. I looped the leather around my neck, my shoulder reminding me painfully of my own wound that I needed to attend sooner rather than later.

Demetri stood by the Persians, muttering and throwing glances in my direction. Finally he made his way back towards me, but when he spoke, he kept his eyes firmly on the path to the north. "Philo needs help. I think the town of Gomphoi is closest. I'll go and find someone for him."

"How long will it take you to get there?" I asked.

"I don't know," he replied, meeting my eyes.

I pushed myself to my feet, my knees still weak from the amulet's influence, not missing the flinch or the step back Demetri took. "Thank you," I said.

He only nodded in reply before turning his back and leaving. I sank to the ground, wondering if he would come back or if it was just an excuse to leave.

14

I watched until Demetri was out of sight before focusing once again on Philo. His stomach still rose and fell with uneven breaths. His wounds wept, turning the dirt beneath him red. I had to decide what to do not only about him, but my shoulder as well. I had no herbs with me. I looked around the Plain, seeing no plants that would aid me, just the smoking pile that had once been thirty Persian soldiers. I turned quickly from them. I needed to focus on one thing at a time.

I pulled my cuirass over my head, the throbbing intensifying as I lifted my arm. I drove my teeth into my lip to draw the pain to another area and worked quickly to secure the leather at my sides. Realistically, Demetri might not return. He might not even go to Gomphoi or tell anyone of our whereabouts. I did not want to leave Philo, but he needed more help than I could provide alone. My bag and waterskin were both trapped beneath him and there was no way I could lift him to free them, so I was without food and water. My mouth was already dry, but even if I could get to the skin, I doubt I could have stomached it.

I peeled the end of my chlamys away, sucking in a sharp breath when one section stuck to my skin. My fingers were soon coated in warm, sticky blood but I continued to remove the material as quickly as I could. I inspected the damage; the diamond-shaped hole was as deep as the first knuckle on my finger and twice as wide. I held the flesh on either side and peered in; there were no exposed bones, but I could barely raise my arm above my chest when I tried to. Blood streamed from the opening and I knew that simply re-wrapping my chlamys around it would not protect it enough if I had to travel for candlemarks to seek help.

My eyes fell on the Persians again. The ash. Maybe I could use that to stop the bleeding. The thought made my stomach turn but I pushed myself to my feet and strode over to them anyway. As I neared the bodies, the stench hit me again and I held my arm across my face to shield the acidity. My battle with them was not like any I had been in before – I was hardened to the sight of blood and gore and the grimaces of death plastered for eternity on sunken faces. But the Persians' deaths could not be measured against those. Their clothing lay on the ground, singed, but mostly intact. What had once been their skin and hair was gone, leaving no obvious sign that what lay beneath the material had ever been men.

I squatted down, reaching out a hand to the nearest soldier. My fingers pressed through the grey matter, no solidity to it; just light, airy pieces of smoke that flew around me when I disturbed them. I tried to touch him again, but again the dust disappeared into the air. It did not make sense. It should have been like charcoal from a burnt-out fire; dense and tinting my fingers black where I touched it. Over and over I drove my fingers towards the soldier's body, but the more I persisted, the more it blew away. Finally I stood, kicking at the remains of the clothing, and sending hundreds more black wisps into the air. I shuddered, the unmistakable feeling of another's presence finding me.

"Demetri?" I whispered, turning. Mumma stood beside my horse. She smiled. I ran to her, so many questions on my lips. She disappeared before I arrived. "Wait," I cried, spinning as I searched for her again. "Please, do not leave."

"You have begun, my dear Ava. Soon you shall have all the power you desire." Her voice was beside and all around me, but there was no sign of her. "Rest now. You must regain your strength. You shall face more Persians soon." I shivered again and knew she was gone. I was alone on the Plain.

My knees trembled and I sunk to the ground. Intense fatigue engulfed me. I had to resist it. I could not rest. I had to get help for Philo. I had to forget about Demetri and his journey north and focus on my own. I needed to find Papou before I came up against the Persians again. I ... slept.

*

Demetri had argued with himself the entire way to Gomphoi, and in the stretches of silence between him and the men since. He knew he had to tell Ava everything. She deserved to know. He would have if they hadn't been interrupted by the Persians ... by what she had done. He still wasn't sure what to make of that, how to understand what he'd seen, what she'd done.

But he was only too aware that sometimes people weren't exactly who you thought they were or who they appeared when you first met them. He wasn't revolted by her. He didn't want to leave her behind. He needed to see her again, find out what she was and what it meant. Maybe then he could tell her who he was.

*

I woke to find the sun low in the sky, my mouth desperate for water and my shoulder aching. The flow of blood from my wound had lessened while I slept and I rolled onto my back, pressing a tentative hand against Philo's flank. He was still breathing. I sent up a silent prayer of thanks.

My head was clear again but I had wasted precious time sleeping. Evidently Demetri was not coming back and, as much as I hated the thought, I knew I had to leave Philo and go find help for him in Gomphoi myself before I continued on to find Papou.

I may not have been surprised at Demetri's desertion after what I did, but it still hurt – and I did not want to look too closely at why that was. It had been a long time since I had let anyone draw me into talking about my past. Into talking about anything other than battle strategy or their own lives, and whatever Demetri had started to feel for me, or what he had wanted to do other than kiss me would now be the farthest thing from his mind. Maybe to him I had become like Phaeops and his friends – taking unfair advantage of a position of power to torture and harm those weaker than me. Maybe he was right. I got to my feet, pleased that my legs had returned to their stable selves, and gathered up the end of my chlamys.

I knelt close to Philo again and stroked his face. "I will return as soon as I can with help," I whispered. His eyes remained closed and his breathing did not change, but I chose to believe that he heard me and would not die before I returned.

I straightened, pinning my chlamys back in place around my shoulders and retrieved my helmet, tucking it under my arm and starting north towards Gomphoi.

*   *   *

The sun had almost disappeared when I saw the approaching mule and cart, along with three figures jogging beside it. I recognized one of the shadows and an unexpected flare of joy bloomed at the sight of him. Demetri had kept his word; he was bringing help for Philo. It seemed I had cast him aside and doubted him too easily, just expecting that he, like so many others, would leave me before I had the chance to know them very well. And I had not *wanted* to get to know anyone in ten winters. Lysistratos had broken through some of my walls, Eumelia too, but that was different – I had known them before – and in some ways we were closer than friends; we were almost family.

When the three of them arrived, the man holding the mule brought it to a halt. The other gave me a brief nod and made his way to the back of the cart.

"You returned," I murmured as Demetri's eyes met mine.

"I said I'd get help for Philo," he replied. "Agapios, this is Ava. Ava, Agapios," he added, pointing between the two of us. Agapios held out his arm, pausing a moment in the action.

"What?" I frowned, taking his arm anyway.

"N-Nothing. Just … for a moment you reminded me of someone Andronikos and I met long ago," he replied, indicating the second man with him but continuing before I could question him further. "Demetri tells me you found some trouble."

"Yes, Persians," I nodded.

"It is worrisome they have made their way this far west," Agapios said. "At least they fled when they had inflicted their cowardly damage and left the both of *you* unharmed. Take me to your horse and we shall get him back to Gomphoi, I can tend him properly there."

I nodded again, appreciating that Demetri had not told Agapios what really happened. In the dimness I doubted the small pile of bodies would be visible, and for that too, I was thankful.

Demetri handed me a waterskin. "You should drink this."

"Thank you," I replied, taking it from him and greedily drawing in the cool liquid as I led them back to Philo.

Agapios and Andronikos attended to my steed, prodding and inspecting the holes made by the arrows before applying some sort of medicine to each of them.

Demetri held out a pouch. "I got some herbs for your shoulder. You can apply them or … or I could help you."

"I can do it, but thank you," I nodded, taking them and the clean length of cloth he offered. I unwound the end of my chlamys and Demetri trickled water from the waterskin over the top. I sucked in a breath when the cold hit my skin.

"Apologies," Demetri murmured.

"It is not your fault, keep going," I told him, carefully cleaning the blood from around the wound. "Thank you for the herbs, and for coming back," I said as I applied the herbs and Demetri re-dressed the injury.

He only nodded in reply and tied it off, tucking the ends under the last coil before crossing to Agapios and Andronikos. He helped them wind more cloth around Philo's flank, covering his injuries and keeping the herbs where they needed to be. Demetri freed my bag and waterskin, setting them aside as he and Andronikos drew the straw laden cart closer, the three of them hefting Philo onto a smaller cart and pushing it up two lengths of wood into the main one.

Agapios addressed me as he turned the cart back towards Gomphoi and lit a torch to guide us. "His injuries are severe. I can only pray that the herbs we have applied are enough to see him through the night, but you should prepare yourself." I nodded, my heart sinking. Maybe I *should* have used the amulet on Philo again. I still could of course. Except I was afraid of what it would make me feel – that overwhelming desire to harm or kill innocents – I did not want to feel that again. I did not want to subject Demetri to another demonstration of its power either. I just had to pray that Philo was strong enough to recover from the wounds on his own. I retrieved my bag and burst waterskin from the ground and followed.

Andronikos pointed to the skin. "I can mend that for you," he offered.

"Thank you, I would appreciate that. How long until we reach Gomphoi?"

"Around three candlemarks, perhaps a little longer, we shall have to travel slowly for your horse's sake and the river crossing at the Pamissos can be dangerous in the dark."

"Does Agapios have room to care for him until he recovers? I have coin to pay for whatever he needs."

"We have room for all of you, you may stay as long as you need," Andronikos replied.

"I will be continuing my journey tonight, but I thank you for the offer," I said.

Demetri's head whipped up, meeting my eyes with a deep frown. "You said you wouldn't leave Philo."

"And in the middle of a plain with Persians attacking, I would never consider it. But they are gone now and he needs time to rest and recover. I have to … to keep going. You are free to make your own decision about what you will do." Demetri opened his mouth to speak, but I held up my hand. "Any debt you felt you needed to repay for what happened at the lake yesterday has been settled by you bringing Agapios and Andronikos. You do not owe me anything."

Demetri was quiet for a long moment. "I'll stay in Gomphoi with Philo until you return," he finally said.

I swallowed my surprise. Maybe he did not completely despise me for what I had done to the Persians. Maybe I had once again dismissed him too easily.

"Thank you," I nodded.

15

"Where is she?" Ares asked, his frown deepening as he took in the dark, empty expanse.

"Look, there are tracks leading north," Rizpah replied. "A cart, and it was carrying something heavy."

"The horse," Ares murmured. "Perhaps a merchant passing by?"

"There are no tracks to the south. Maybe our Chosen One woke and went for help for her steed."

"I cannot imagine she is already awake. Every Ker before her has needed at least half-a-moon to recover before they were ready for me to test again, with Skylar it was almost a moon."

"The Valkyrie told us she would be different. This could be just one variance she possesses."

"Perhaps. Come, we shall follow the tracks and see what we can find."

*

Agapios and Andronikos' stables were large and clean and Agapios and his slaves set about making Philo as warm and comfortable as possible. Andronikos mended my waterskin and refilled it, packing more bread, cheese and dried fruit for my journey. He again extended the invitation to stay, at least until morning, but I declined the offer. The sooner I reached the herders and Papou in the Pindos Mountains, the better. We stood now in the darkness outside the stables, a torch each as we made our goodbyes.

"Tell us before you leave; your mother, was she a warrior named Skylar with bright blue eyes and long, dark hair the color of yours?"

"It could not be, Agapios, you know it as well as I do," Andronikos chided, a frown etched across his forehead. He met my eyes and added, "Apologies Ava, we have met few women soldiers. Agapios believed he recognized a similarity between you and a woman we once met. But the woman we knew preferred … preferred the company of women, not men. She could not be your mother as he suggests."

"She was not just someone we once met, Andronikos. If it were not for Skylar, you and I would not have been reunited; we would have never had the chance to be together far from what was destined for us in Nafpaktos," Agapios insisted.

"Please, there is no need to argue. You are both right – Skylar was my mother and she still preferred women to men. I was born from another's body. When did you meet her?"

"It would be over twenty winters ago now," Andronikos replied.

"And h–"

"I am sorry, I am eager to be on my way," I cut over Agapios.

He hesitated before inclining his head and offering his arm. "Perhaps when you return for your horse and your friend, you shall favor us with explanation?"

"If the gods see fit to reunite us then I will do so," I replied, gripping him tightly as a slight shiver slid down my back.

Agapios moved aside, Andronikos holding his arm out to me. "Travel safely and return soon. We would love to learn where Skylar's travels took her once we parted." I only nodded and took his outstretched limb.

"If I do not see Demetri before I leave, would you give him a message?"

"Of course. What is it?"

"Tell him that if his journey calls him away from Gomphoi before I return, that I understand and he should go. Maybe one day we will meet again."

"I shall ensure he knows, though I do not imagine he shall allow you to leave without further words," Andronikos said.

"We will see."

"You are headed north?"

"I am."

"Then you shall need a thick himation. The snow has begun to fall on the mountains and you shall need more than just your chlamys to give you warmth. Here," he said, passing me the named item.

"Thank you," I smiled, taking it and placing two coins in his palm.

"There is no need for this, you have already paid us more than you should have for the food we gave you and the necessary herbs for Philo's recovery."

"Take it, please," I replied, closing his hand around the coins. "I owe you much for your assistance today."

Andronikos gave a curt nod and I re-entered the stables to say goodbye to Philo. I had already left my helmet beside his head. I wanted him to see it when he woke and know I was with him in spirit. I hoped it would encourage him to regain his strength for when I returned.

*

"She appears well," Rizpah noted. "No appearance of fatigue."

"And intending to continue north by the sounds."

"What is to the north? You told her only to head to the Thessalian Plain to find the Persians."

"The boy spoke of the Tymphaioi warriors. They could be useful if she can convince them to join her against the Persians. I shall allow her the journey for now."

"You are not going to take her to Olympos? I thought you wanted to test her again."

"I do, though with her awake and travelling on already, I am curious to see what she does. Perhaps she shall be eager to attempt to use the amulet on her own again, just as her mother was when it was her turn."

"And if not?"

"Then I shall encourage her to. I shall take you to Stymphalos and call on you again when the time comes. Perhaps you shall want to be with us after all."

"Perhaps. There are many who are impatient to see who she becomes."

"Many indeed," Ares muttered.

*

I followed the northern path from Gomphoi, stopping only when I reached the Peneus River sometime later. It would have been impossible for me to cross the flowing tributary without ample light, or help; and I had neither. The rain had been relentless as I travelled, my torch more often dark than bright and several times I had lost the path, crashing painfully into branches, tree trunks or rocks.

A large tree overhung the river and I pulled the himation around me as I crawled beneath it. The thick foliage kept the rain from my head as I pulled a second torch from my bag, struggling to get the wet end to light. When finally it caught, I found a space large enough between two of the roots at the base of the tree to prop it up and warm my hands by.

I ate a meal of cheese and bread as I dried out, the day's events I had managed to *not* think about so far surfacing: Meeting the Persians on the

Thessalian Plain. Their arrows lodging deep in Philo's stomach. Mumma appearing and telling me to use the amulet. The rush of power the amulet sent through me as I held it. The big, black wings that sprung unbelievably from my body and the utter destruction I had caused, reducing the Persian soldiers to nothing more than piles of dust. A tear slid down my cheek as I slipped my hand beneath my tunic, feeling for the lump on my shoulder blade. It was still there.

And Demetri; his skill with coins and iron. His revelations about being a slave and an orphan. The way he had looked at me – desired me – when he kissed me. How much I had wanted him in return. The way his lips had felt on mine, soft yet certain. How I would have let him kiss me again. Done more. I swallowed, surprised at that last thought. I could not deny it was true, but since when did I want for another's body when it was not simply expected? Since when did I let myself feel anything for anyone, let alone a stranger? But how much of a stranger was Demetri really? There was of course much I did not know about him, but the short time we had spent together had seen me easily share my past, which I had never done with the men or women I had been with over the winters.

I leant my head against the tree trunk, staring down at the flickering light from the torch. I wondered what he was doing.

"Ava," a quiet voice said.

I jumped, looking up to find Demetri soaking wet, his hair plastered to his head and a thick himation that mirrored mine hanging heavily from his body. He looked solemn and the jolt of happiness that flickered uninvited inside me at his sudden presence disappeared.

"Philo?" I asked, my voice catching on his name.

Demetri shook his head. "I'm sorry. He … his injuries were too severe. He wasn't strong enough."

A sob escaped my lips and I buried my face in the folds of my himation, pressing my eyes hard onto my knees. Philo was dead. The only living gift my mothers had ever given me, gone. Taken by the same enemy that took them. Why had the amulet not healed him? Why had I not tried again? I knew the answer – anger and bloodlust had taken me over and I had taken it out on the Persians, destroying them for hurting him. Maybe I should have tried again in Gomphoi, away from Demetri and Andronikos and Agapios. I should have done more for him, just as he did for me that night in the Othrys Mountains. I had failed him. My side warmed as Demetri sat down, rubbing my lower back as the tears came.

"How long have you had Philo?" he asked when my sobs subsided long moments later.

I wiped my face and took a deep breath before I replied. "Fifteen winters."

"Would you tell me about him?"

I drew another breath but nodded. "I was four when Mumma Skylar's horse, Skotos, sired him. I was not allowed ride him until my sixth winter. But after that, we spent candlemarks each day building a silent language of communication and trust until I only needed to alter my position on his back slightly and he understood what I wanted. We used wheat bales to represent rocks or fallen trees, and he never once failed to clear them when I asked it of him."

"He was a loyal friend to you," Demetri murmured. "I ... I hope you'll accept my apology for his death. If I hadn't tried to ... if I hadn't distracted you we might've seen the soldiers and had time to get away. Instead, you saved me and lost Philo."

I turned to look at him. He stared out beyond our circle of light and my heart went out to him, to the guilt and regret I saw written on his face. I reached out and lay my hand on his arm. "Demetri it was not your fault." His eyes met mine. "I do not blame you for what happened. I blame the Persians. I blame myself." I stood and started to pace beneath the tree, my anger re-ignited as more memories returned.

"They were laughing when their arrows hit Philo, Demetri. *Laughing.*"

"I heard them," he replied quietly.

"I knew they were ruthless and callous, but to laugh?"

Demetri pushed himself to his feet and reached out a trembling hand, halting my movements. "They were heartless and cowardly. I can only imagine what they would've done to us ... to you, if they'd had the chance. But you didn't let that happen."

"No, I grew a huge pair of wings and used an amulet to make sure they never harmed any human or animal again," I snapped.

He took a deep breath, blowing it all the way out again before he stepped closer. I swallowed as his cold fingers traced the leather at my neck and he gently freed the gem from my tunic. "This is a very powerful weapon," he whispered. "Are you ... was today the first time ... have you always been able to do what you did?" he stammered.

"Today was the first time," I replied.

He nodded in acknowledgement. "May I ... take it from your neck?"

It was my turn to nod. He drew the leather over my head, cradling the amulet reverently in his hand and tracing the iron with his long fingers. The pounding of my heart beat loudly in my ears as he stared at it with such intent.

"Where was it made? Do you know what it is made of?" Demetri asked.

"It belonged to Mumma Skylar. I do not know anything about it, or where she got it, but it went missing the night she and Mother Alexis died."

His eyes met mine. "Missing? Then how do you have it?"

I drew another long breath. "A few nights ago, Mumma appeared to me in a dream and told me I should have it. When I woke up, it was ... in my hand," I said, aware of how improbable the explanation sounded.

"Oh," Demetri murmured. He raised the necklace then took it to the torch at the base of the tree. He held it close to the light and I joined him, wondering what he saw. "This silvery-red wrapped around the stone here, it's a type of iron called hematite. The stone itself looks to be amber, but that's only found on the coast of the Baltic Sea far away to the North, and even then it's difficult to acquire."

As I took the amulet from him, our fingertips grazed, sending the barest of thrills through me. "I think I once heard Mother Alexis' parents say that Mumma's ancestors came from the North lands, but I am not sure if that is right, I was quite young. Of all the memories I have of my childhood that is not a clear one." I held the amulet up, watching the way it caught the light from the torch as it swung back and forth.

"If she was from the north, then it has to be jet."

"What does that mean?"

"Separately, jet and hematite are fairly harmless. But together … well I think we both know the answer to that." He paused and I waited for him to go on, breath held tight in my chest. "Hematite is said to be a protective element and jet; well you'll hear very few healers speak of it. It's said to be one of the most powerful stones known and most of them have never come across it personally. It's used by darker healers."

"Oh," I whispered, staring at the small gem.

"Maybe you shouldn't wear it against your skin as you have been. Use this." Demetri took his two coin pouches from his chiton, transferring the contents of one to the other before passing me the empty one. "This was all I had with me when I was found on the side of the road. It must've belonged to my parents."

"Maybe I should take the other one instead," I suggested, leaving it in his outstretched hand.

He shook his head and placed it in my palm. "I want you to have it."

I nodded and gripped it, pushing the amulet inside the fur-lined opening. "Thank you, it will keep it well protected."

Demetri took the leather cord that had held the pouch at his waist and slipped it over my head. I watched him, his eyes following the movement of his hands as he rested the encased amulet against my cuirass.

"The amulet frightens me," he admitted.

"But you still came to find me. To tell me about Philo."

"Yes," he nodded.

"Thank you … do I scare you?" I asked a moment later.

Demetri flattened his hand against my chest, the tips of his fingers tightening in the top of my cuirass as he raised his face to mine. "A little." The dark inners of his eyes grew, reducing the warm brown to mere outlines. I recognized the look, recognized the want to succumb to primal yearnings, to feel your heart beating fiercely in your chest and know you were alive. Part of me wanted it too, to feel something other than terror or anger or pain, to forget everything that had happened – even just for a little while. To be lost together.

I raised my hand, intending to put it on Demetri's chest. He flinched and took a step back. "W-we can't stay here tonight, it's too exposed. We should go to Tricca," he stammered, removing his hand.

He bent to retrieve the torch from the roots of the tree and I saw he had paled. "Are you alright?" I asked.

"Yes," he replied. I was not sure I believed him. "I left your helmet in Gomphoi, Andronikos wanted me to bring it, but I ... I left it so he could mark where he buries Philo. I hope you don't mind," he added.

My guilty thoughts at Philo's demise resurfaced, effectively extinguishing my stirring desires. "I do not mind. I am grateful for all you have done for me."

Demetri only nodded in reply and held the torch up. I pulled my himation closer around me as we left the dry canopy of the tree, stepping out into the teeming rain and onto the path that would lead us to Tricca.

16

We followed the Peneus River for a time, crossing it by taking a careful path across six large rocks in the water. The rain lessened the further we went but the temperature dropped, confirming we were still heading north towards the mountains. As the rain abated, so did the clouds, and the moon intermittently made its way down to light our path. We arrived in Tricca before dawn and Demetri secured a room for us with a local trader. We were shown to our lodgings and gratefully discarded our sodden himatia and bags.

My shoulder ached uncomfortably and the cloth Demetri had applied back at the Plain was soaked through with blood. He joined me beside the small table and looked it over.

"You need that re-dressed. I'll get some new herbs and cloth," he said simply.

I nodded and while I waited for him to return, I removed my sandals, chlamys and cuirass, hoping they would all be dry by the time we were ready to leave. I crossed to the bed and laid down, Hypnos claiming me before Demetri returned.

I shivered and opened my eyes to find Mumma Skylar standing at the foot of the small bed. "I had imagined this journey of yours to be an unaccompanied one, but this boy continues to appear," she said.

"He is no threat to what you ask of me. I shall use the amulet to kill every Persian I meet," I replied.

She rounded the bed, her hands clasped behind her in an unfamiliar gesture as she peered out the window. "He may be of some use, for now. The armor he seeks from the Tymphaioi shows he has a warrior's instinct. I admire that. Continue to the north towards them and I shall decide what to do with him once you have the armor."

"Do not harm him, he is good and kind …" I pleaded.

"The decision shall not be yours," she replied, disappearing as I shivered once more.

*   *   *

I woke in the dimly lit room. My shoulder still ached, but not as badly as before and I found the bloodied cloth had been swapped for a clean one. I pushed myself up, swinging my legs over the side of the bed – my body better for the rest.

"You're awake," Demetri's voice greeted me. He sat at a small table, a smile on his lips as he picked fruit from a plate beside him.

"How long did I sleep?" I asked.

"All the candlemarks of the day," he replied. "I helped Korpos' … people …" *Slaves* I realized he meant. "Prepare some food for when you woke."

"Thank you," I said, joining him by the table and taking a fig. "Thank you for changing the dressing on my shoulder also."

"I hope I didn't overstep by doing it while you slept, but I didn't want you to fall ill from it."

"No, I am grateful for the gesture."

"When you've eaten, Korpos has offered us the use of his baths if you want to join me." I hesitated. If there was a bath instead of just a clay basin, I would have to completely undress before entering. It had been so long. Demetri already knew what the nodes on my back were, but I did not want a slave to see them. "I've asked that no one accompany us," Demetri added, as if following my thoughts.

"A-alright," I replied with a nod. Demetri had said baths, as in more than one, so maybe that meant we would not have to share, or wait for the other to be finished.

He gave me a tight smile and got to his feet. "Follow the hallway to the end; it's the door to the left."

When the door closed behind him, I took the pouched amulet from my neck and pushed it to the bottom of my bag. My spare tunic was still damp inside and I lay it over the chair to dry and started on the food. Before I was finished, the door to the room burst open again, Demetri and a smaller man rushing in.

"Please, young lady, come quickly," the man – our host Korpos – cried.

73

"What is wrong?" I asked, a familiar adrenaline rushing through my body at the pinched look on his face.

"My wife. She is with child and I do not know what to do," he replied.

"Take me to her," I nodded. Korpos led the way, pausing only when we reached the first door at the top of the stairs. He opened it and stepped aside for me to enter. Demetri was right behind me but I turned to him and shook my head.

"The birth of a child is only attended by women. You will have to stay out here with Korpos."

"But I have experience ... I ..." Demetri trailed off, his forehead pulled together momentarily in a frown before he nodded and asked, "What can I do?"

"Send someone to find a midwife or healer," I replied. He nodded again and I entered the room, closing the door behind me. I approached the bed where Korpos' wife lay, taking her hand when I reached her. "My name is Ava. I am here to help."

"Please, this is my first child. I am so frightened." She was young, probably only fourteen winters, but her color was good and she looked healthy.

"Do not be afraid, I know what to do," I told her, turning to the two slaves in the room. "I need towels, a blanket, a jug of hot water and a clay bath." They nodded and hurried out. "What is your name?" I asked the girl.

"Alecia," she replied.

"Well Alecia, you need not be concerned. Soon enough you shall meet your child."

She nodded as the slaves returned, struggling under the weight of the heavy clay bath. I crossed the room, taking the hot water, blanket and towels from Demetri, who trailed the women. "Thank you," I nodded, closing the door again.

I helped the women set the bath on the floor in the middle of the room, passing the jug to one of them as the other spread the towels out on the ground and placed a chair beside them. I helped Alecia from the bed, sitting her on the chair as an unpleasant memory surfaced; three moons ago I had been on a scouting mission and had come across a woman birthing her child by the side of the road. I had done all I could to help her, but she had a severe wound and there had been complications with the child. I had not been able to save either of them.

I blew out a breath. I would not let that happen tonight, besides, the circumstances were favorable – I had supplies and help – and Alecia was not already bleeding to death when I arrived.

"Have either of you assisted a woman with child before?" I asked the slaves. Both shook their heads. "As soon as the child is born I will pass it to you. It should be crying, if not, support its head and clean its mouth, you have to do it immediately, do you understand?" They both nodded this time.

"When it cries, clean the rest of its body with the water and then wrap it in the blanket to keep it warm."

They nodded again and I addressed Alecia. "When did your pains start?"

"When I woke this morning, but it worsened a candlemark later."

I sent up a silent prayer to the goddess Artemis, asking her to assist me with the birth. "When you feel the next sharp pain, I need you to push down as hard as you can for as long as you can, do you understand?"

"Yes," she replied.

*　　*　　*

For near on three candlemarks, I talked Alecia through her pains, at times encouraging, at others demanding that she do as I asked. When Alecia's arms could no longer hold her up, I sat one of the slaves in front of her so she could lean on her. The other woman mopped Alecia's forehead and waited for the baby to arrive so she could clean it.

The midwife arrived and a short time later, in a final outpouring of blood and exhaustion, he arrived; a healthy baby boy. He cried as he entered the world, cradled in my hands, hardly any mess on him at all. The midwife took him, checked him over then handed him to the nearest slave, who cleaned his face and wrapped him in a blanket, awaiting further instructions. She inspected Alecia as the rest of us breathed a sigh of relief.

"Your help is most appreciated," the midwife said, turning to me. I nodded in reply and left her to see to the new mother and child.

"How is Alecia?" Korpos asked as soon as I emerged.

"Very well," I replied.

"And the baby?"

"A boy," I grinned.

Korpos danced with joy at the news, hugging Demetri and slapping him on the back. "A boy? Oh wonderful news! Thank the gods, thank Artemis," he cried, turning and holding out his arms to embrace me. "Deepest gratitude to you."

I held my hands up to stop his approach. "I should wash, but you are most welcome. He is very handsome."

"Of course, of course, allow me to fetch you a clean chiton, I know my wife would not mind."

"Thank you," I said with a nod. Korpos rushed into the next room, still thanking any god he could think to name.

"Everything went well?" Demetri asked.

"Yes," I replied as Korpos returned, handing Demetri the clean material when he held his hand out for it.

"Korpos, you may come and meet your son now," the midwife said from the doorway of Alecia's room.

"Wonderful, wonderful!" he cried, clapping his hands and bustling inside.

"We should take our leave," I said, touching Demetri lightly on the arm.

He nodded and followed me back down the stairs. "Korpos and I made sure the baths would be ready whenever you finished with his wife. Would you like to go there now and get cleaned up?" he asked, stepping in the direction of the bathing area.

"I would, thank you," I replied.

17

The bathing area was a small square room with two baths set close together and a clay basin nearby. I dipped my finger in the closest one, pleased to find it almost hot.

"How is it?" Demetri asked.

"Perfect. I do not like a cold bath. When I was very young I would spend candlemarks on end in the hot springs, especially in the winter."

"Hot springs?" he repeated, thinking a moment before continuing. "Ah, of course, you said you were from the Army of Trachis. Were you born there?"

"I was."

"I don't know much about Trachis itself, but the hot springs are well spoken of – many a trader would praise them when they came to town from the south. I've always wanted to see them for myself."

"I have not found myself in Trachis or at the hot springs for many winters but they were always beautiful and very warm. Maybe one day I could take you to see them," I offered, surprising myself.

"I'd like that," Demetri grinned. He found a length of cloth slung over the rim of the clay basin and dipped it into the water it held. "Come, I'll clean your hands for you before you get in."

I stepped closer and waited. The intensity of the last few candlemarks was starting to dissipate – exhaustion taking its place – and I closed my eyes as Demetri worked to clean the blood from my palms and forearms.

"Do you still have family in Trachis?" he asked.

"You said you had experience with women birthing children," I said at the same time. I opened my eyes, finding his. Demetri looked away, replacing the cloth on the edge of the basin. He did not reply so I answered his question. "I still have family there but we do not speak."

He nodded, but it was more to himself than to me. He cast a glance at the door and took a deep breath. "I-I do have experience with mothers birthing children. I assisted Spyros' wife on a number of occasions. At times I have been allowed to spend time with the women of Spyros' household, to do the things they do." He paused again and I remained silent, letting him arrange his thoughts and tell me what he wanted to in his own time. He looked to the door again, a muscle in his jaw twitching. He drew in a deep breath, letting it all the way out again before he looked back to me. "One … one of the things I was allowed do was wash his wife's hair. Would you let me wash yours now?"

I watched him a long moment. I did not think that was what he intended to say when he started but the look on his face told me he was not ready to tell me yet. I did not take offense – he owed me no explanations. I would not push him to tell me what he was not ready to.

"It has been a long time since anyone has done that for me, so yes, I would like that," I smiled. Demetri turned his back as I removed my clothing and stepped into the bath, not returning his gaze to me until I was settled beneath the water, the flowers on top hiding my body beneath. He took my braid and undid it, fanning my hair out so it covered my shoulders and lay on top of the water around me. I had forgotten how good it felt to have someone else run their hands through my hair.

Demetri scooped the strands between his hands, fingers skimming over the protrusions beneath. I flinched and he stilled behind me. He slowly transferred all of my hair to one hand, pushing me gently to sit forward. I drew a breath, holding it as he ran his fingers across my exposed skin.

He caressed me; up and over the smoothness that rose from my back. "There's no break in the skin where your wings came out yesterday. Were these here … before?"

I gripped the side of the bath, releasing the breath I held. "Yes."

"For how long?"

"I noticed them almost a winter after my mothers were killed."

"Oh. Did you ever tell those who cared for you after your mothers' deaths about them?"

"No. You … you are the only person who has ever seen them. You are the only one who has ever touched them."

"Oh," he said again. "You're the only one I've ever shown my coins to." I had not forgotten there was one coin he had chosen not to share with me, but I did not bring it up.

Demetri returned his attentions to my hair, pouring warm water over my head before drawing his fingers through the easily-tangled strands. My fingers relaxed against the marble but it was a long moment before my heart returned to a normal speed.

The ease with which we had shared previously hidden secrets surprised me and I did not know why it felt so easy to talk to him. I felt a connection with Demetri. I wanted him to stay with me but I also knew *my* new life was war and death and he did not deserve to be in the midst of that. I had wrongs to avenge and he deserved to go to Athens and make a living in a field of his choice. He deserved to settle in one place, not live the nomadic life I was so used to. Even so ...

"Do you want to join me in here?" I asked.

He came to stand alongside the bath. "I ... er ... no. I can bathe in the morning before we leave," he replied.

I frowned as disappointment settled in my stomach. I should be glad of his answer, glad not to make more of what was – or was not – between us. "We should return to our room then. We have a long day of travel tomorrow," I said.

Demetri nodded in return, turning his back again when I stepped out of the bath and swapped my bloodied tunic for the chiton Korpos had given me.

"Would you like the bed tonight?" I asked as we walked the short distance to our room. "I am used to sleeping on the ground so it does not bother me, but I apologize you did not get the choice earlier."

"You don't want to sleep together ... i-in the same bed I mean," he asked, closing the door behind us.

"I ... we ... do you?" I asked, not sure I should.

He rubbed his chin, a slight grin on his lips. "Maybe I should be worried about sleeping close to *you* – you kicked out in your sleep a bit last night – I'm surprised I don't have bruises on my shins."

"You slept beside me? I ... I did not realize." I had not registered the closeness even in my sleep. I had never shared a bed with anyone, not even those gifted to me. I had spent a lot of time sharing tents or space beneath trees with the soldiers of course, but never a bed – I believed it too intimate, shared only by those betrothed or intended for one another. "I am sorry, it was unintentional," I murmured.

"It's fine, you didn't hurt me. Were you dreaming of what happened yesterday on the Plain?"

My mother's words from my dream floated back to me, *the decision shall not be yours.* I headed for the torch on the wall. "No," I replied. "If you do not mind, my shoulder would appreciate a soft surface."

Demetri crossed to the bed, crawling under the covers, his voice guiding me back when I extinguished the light. "May I ask where you're going on your journey? You follow the north path, yet you didn't bring warm clothing to protect yourself from the snow and wintry weather. I would deem you foolish, as you've enjoyed calling me on occasion, but I've seen you when angered, and I'm not sure it's wise to make fun of you." I heard the smile in his voice, and my own broke out, not that he could see it.

"You have a sense of humor, I did not know that."

"Sometimes," he agreed.

"Well, if you must know, I had intended to purchase a thick himation as I drew nearer my destination. Lucky for me, Andronikos had some to spare when we stopped there," I replied. I crawled under the soft animal skin, settling my hand on my arm and briefly wondering which way Demetri was facing. I did not have to wait long to find out – his breath tickled my cheek when he spoke again.

"Can I ask you something?"

"You may," I replied.

"Why didn't you ever tell anyone about the bumps on your back?"

"By the time I found them there was no one left to ask."

"Who cared for you after your mothers were killed?"

"My grandparents; Mother Alexis' parents, but it was strained between us. They banished my Papou Leandros – Mumma Skylar's father – and I did not confide in them about anything once that happened. I have never forgiven them for Papou's departure."

"That must've been lonely for someone so young."

"I did not let loneliness enter my thoughts. I focused on becoming a soldier instead," I told him. "Tomorrow we will enter the Pindos Mountain Ranges, the day after that we should reach the path that takes you to the Tymphaioi."

Demetri was quiet a long moment. "Our parting will weigh heavily on me. Not only do I consider you my first friend, but if you hadn't been at the lake, I wouldn't have had the opportunity to become more than just an orphaned slave."

I blinked in the darkness, his words cutting at me with their sincerity and the way they mirrored my own thoughts mere days before. "I am pleased you will have the chance," I murmured.

We lay beside each other in silence and I closed my eyes, glad for the warmth and softness of the bed beneath me.

*

Demetri berated himself for his cowardice. He knew he should have crossed the bathing room and pulled the lock down into place. He should have told Ava what he kept from her. But he was scared. Afraid she would not understand. Afraid it would be too much. Too soon. They barely knew each other, no matter what he had seen her do, no matter how he could accept that part of her. She may not be able to do the same for him. He could not blame her. He liked her and he didn't want to push her away. He needed to know if … maybe there was a chance …

*

Demetri's hand found my face, his long fingers caressing my cheek. "Back on the Plain … before the Persians … when I kissed you, I think you know that I wanted to do more than that …" he started.

I swallowed loudly. "I do."

"There was the start of something between us – I'm not wrong about that, am I?"

I covered his hand with my own. "Our futures are known only to the Moirai. You have your journey and I have mine, I do not know where my path will take me."

"That doesn't answer my question."

I drew in a breath, blowing it all the way out again before I replied. "You are not wrong."

"So if I was to abandon my plan to find the Tymphaioi and accompany you … would that be something you might like?"

"I …" I had no idea how to answer him. I was so used to being alone, to never questioning my choice to keep people at arms' length. But Demetri … something drew me to him even as I tried to keep my distance. "Maybe," I finally replied. "We … we should sleep, we have a long journey ahead."

I heard Demetri blow out a quick breath as he withdrew his hand. "Goodnight, Ava."

"Goodnight, Demetri." He turned over and, before long, his breathing changed.

I listened to the gentle sounds of him beside me, our conversation replaying in my mind. Demetri did not realize what he was offering to do. My path took me not only to Papou, but back to the Persians. We would take our revenge. How would he react if Papou or I used the amulet against them? He would know what to expect of course, but what if we chose to use it against them while they slept or before they attacked us? Both were possibilities and I did not know if I wanted him along to witness that.

Papou was an accomplished soldier like I was, but if Demetri was with us, our focus would be on his safety and that could put us all in danger. I was used to being responsible for others, but they were my fellow soldiers, we had trained together and knew how to spot a weakness in an opponent. Demetri had none of that knowledge and it was not something I could easily teach him, not something I *wanted* to teach him.

I squeezed my eyes shut. I should have told him the Tymphaioi were south of Athens rather than in the mountains to the north. If I had, he might already have reached the city and would never have known what I was capable of. *Philo might also still be alive*, the unbidden thought sprung into my head. I swallowed loudly. Many things would have been different. We would not have been together long enough for me to feel the pull of our connection. I rolled onto my back, closing my eyes and wishing for Hypnos to take me into his fold, but it was a long time before my wish was granted.

18

The following morning we packed up our few belongings and set off. Demetri did not try to continue our conversation from the night before and I welcomed the silence. I clasped my hand around the pouched amulet that once again hung from my neck and thought how, by the time Eos lit the sky the following day, I would have seen my Papou for the first time in ten winters. The thought stirred excitement and apprehension; I hoped I would recognize him and that he would not be angry with me for seeking him out. All those winters ago, he had said he would find *me*, and yet here I was, searching for him, perhaps before he was ready. But I had questions that needed answering – the sudden appearance of the amulet, and my wings, overruling his timeframe.

We travelled along the northern path towards the Pindos Mountain range, entering the first rocky outcrops as the light rain that had been falling turned to sleet, dropping the temperature abruptly. As we continued into the mountains, dustings of snow greeted us on the boulders and trees we passed. Further off in the distance, the impressive height of Mount Smolikos' peak was hidden beneath a dense mist, snow evident all the way down its side.

We ate two small meals as we walked and Demetri kept pace with me better than I had expected. He had found a fallen stick from a beech tree early on and used it to help traverse the stony paths as we continued higher and higher through the mountains.

Darkness had long since surrounded us and we were travelling side by side by dim torchlight through the continuing snow, when the snap of a nearby branch caught my ear. I held my hand up and Demetri stopped as I unsheathed my sword. The bouncing up and down of a torch made its way between the trees to our left and I positioned myself between the approaching light and Demetri.

A tall man dressed in black pants beneath a thick himation and snug leather boots in the same dark coloring, parted the trees. I recognized his clothing as that of the highwaymen who were stationed at frequent intervals throughout Greece. Travelers and traders had to pay their way and I had expected to come across at least one or two as I travelled through the ranges.

"Evening," I said, keeping my sword at my thigh.

"You seek passage north into Macedonia?" he asked, pushing back the hood of his himation.

"We do."

"Ten drachma." I nodded and took the coins from my pouch.

"I shall pay my own way," Demetri said, putting one hand on my arm as he reached beneath his chiton with the other. I only nodded in reply, returning half the coins to my pouch and handing over what I owed.

Two more lights approached from the overgrown path to the right. "The path is well used this evening," the highwayman mused as he took Demetri's coins and waited for the new travelers to reach us.

I knew the reputations of the highwaymen to be ruthless and deadly; they were quick to run anyone through who tried to cheat them or refused to pay, but still I kept my sword in my hand. If we ran into trouble, my immediate concern would be getting Demetri out of the way, then help the highwayman if he needed.

The owners of the lights were soon upon us and I was elated to see four herders. Their clothes were simple – chitons and thick himatia – and each man held a long wooden stick. They had no flock with them but I suspected they normally used the sticks to keep them in line or maybe used them as Demetri had to hasten their journey through the mountains.

As they paid the highwayman, I searched each of the shaggily bearded faces, looking for a familiar feature or a spark of recognition within. I saw nothing that told me one of them was Papou. Disappointment flared in my chest and they shifted uncomfortably under my gaze.

"It appears you are all headed north," the highwayman said, interrupting my intense scrutiny. "The snow is expected to become heavier tonight, you should take shelter in the caves just up ahead," he advised.

"Thank you," I replied, turning to the herders. "May we travel with you?" Even though Papou was not with them here, he might be nearby; maybe he had passed through earlier and was waiting for the rest of them to reach him at the caves.

The herders looked to each other, then down to my leg. I followed their gaze, realizing I still held my sword. I quickly returned it to my scabbard and gave them what I hoped was a reassuring smile. "I am sorry if I startled you." The nearest herder gave me a nod.

"Safe travels to you all," the highway man said, returning to the nearby trees.

"And to you," I called after him. The herders turned and set out along the north path ahead of us, I took the torch from Demetri and caught up to the herder who had nodded at me. "Have you travelled far?" I asked.

"Not far."

"You do not travel with your flock, are they already in the valley?"

"They are."

"Can I ask you about one of your herdsman? I see he is not with you tonight bu–"

"Your friend appears in need of rest," the herder interrupted, nodding in Demetri's direction. His feet shuffled across the ground and his head drooped, his chin almost touching his chest.

I crossed to him, sliding an arm around his waist and taking his weight. The herder moved off to join his fellow travelers, leaving me to help an exhausted Demetri.

Some time later the herders left the path, waiting for us to join them before entering the cave. I settled Demetri by the opening and helped the men gather wood. The herdsman who appeared to be in charge set about preparing a fire. The tinder soon caught and we divided up the food we all carried, eating within the fire's warm glow.

* * *

Demetri and the other men slept, their backs against one wall of the cave, as the senior herder, named Casaereo, and I spoke quietly by the fire.

"You have travelled far?" he asked me.

"Yes, from the south. My friend is unfamiliar with such a pace," I replied.

"You wear a soldier's uniform, and yet he does not."

"He is not a soldier." Casaereo considered my attire, but said nothing further. "I heard some time ago that a man called Leandros lived with you here in the mountains, is that true?" I asked.

"Leandros? Why do you seek him?"

"I knew him a long time ago. I believe he has answers I need."

"Did you know him from Trachis or Sardis?"

"Sardis? I did not know he was there. Are you sure of that?"

"When he first joined us, he spoke of his time in the east. He lost his lover there, after the rest of his family was taken from him."

His lover? Casaereo could only mean Nasrin, the woman my grandfather had lived with in Trachis before his banishment. Nasrin had gone with him when he left, and I had never heard of her again. This news would explain why. I sent up a silent prayer to her, once again cursing the Persians for taking the life of someone I had known and loved.

"How long has he been with you?" I asked.

"Eight or nine winters I suppose," Casaereo shrugged. "Each winter when we returned to the valley, he took his leave. But he was always on the path, awaiting our return when it was time to make our way into the mountains again. This past winter is the only time he has not met us."

"Which path did he take when he left you last winter?"

"The north one to Mount Smolikos."

"Mount Smolikos? That puts him within the boundaries of the Tymphaioi and Molossian warriors."

"Yes," Casaereo acknowledged. "Though there are few of them in the mountains at this time."

"Was his destination the mountain itself?"

Casaereo paused, watching the flames before finally answering. "I cannot be certain, but I believe so. Leandros believed there was something he had to find there. When he first came to us, he had suffered a great loss – his family. He wished to live the simple and mainly solitary life we have. He was quick to learn our ways and was a good herdsman who treated his flock with a firm but gentle hand. Over time, he appeared to come to peace with his fate. But the past few winters have seen that peace fade."

"How so?" I asked, pushing aside my own loss that threatened to rise in my chest.

"His body was still strong, but his mind weakened. He spent many candlemarks muttering and cursing and speaking of things we did not believe to exist, except in his mind."

"What did he say?"

"He spoke of an amulet, something very powerful he needed to destroy. We often heard him saying that he should not have wasted so many winters before going to search for it. He came to believe that the vertical cave in Mount Smolikos held this amulet and he intended to travel there to retrieve it."

"Did he say where he might go if he found it?"

"No, he was only upset that he was too late."

"And no one accompanied him?"

"No. He did not wish it."

"You were not concerned he would die on such a journey? His body is not that of a young man," I frowned, trying to keep my voice quiet even as my anger rose.

"We believed he would only travel to the base of the mountain – that

86

once he saw its great height, he would not attempt to climb it. It is my belief he has returned to his homeland for the final time, to make peace with the past and to live out his days in familiar surroundings."

Casaereo may have believed that, but I did not. "But if he *did* try to get to the vertical cave, how high would he have to climb – a third of the way? Half? Could he enter at the base of the mountain? Are there tunnels that meet the vertical cave there?"

The herder drew a breath before replying. "No. He would have to climb to the peak; that is the only way inside the mountain."

"Is there a path, or would he have to climb the rock face?"

"There is a narrow path which winds its way up the southern side of Mount Smolikos and back down the northern side but ... if you intend to follow him I would not advise you take the path in this weather."

"I appreciate your concern, but I must find him, it is very important. Maybe he was still looking for the amulet when the snow started to fall and is waiting at the top until the winter has passed before he returns," I mused.

"Perhaps," Casaereo conceded. "I see you are determined, akin to him in many ways. Is there nothing I can say to persuade you to wait until the winter has passed before you search for him?"

"No," I replied, lowering my eyes to the fire and wondering if Casaereo suspected that Leandros was more than just someone I once knew.

"It does not appear that your friend would be able to accompany you the entire way."

My eyes settled on Demetri's sleeping form and I shook my head. "No. His journey takes him to the west."

"West? It is not wise to travel alone on those paths. Can you not ask him to join you?"

I shook my head. "I would not ask it of him." In the morning I would convince Demetri to turn back; to go to Athens and be safe. "I will face Mount Smolikos alone. How long will it take to reach the peak?"

Casaereo considered his response a long moment before replying. "That is a difficult question to answer. On a clear spring day it takes *us* almost ten candlemarks, but with the snow that has fallen and being that you are unfamiliar with the path, it could take much longer. You should not begin your assent in the dark and if the snow is particularly heavy, you should wait until it lightens. There is little shelter once you begin your climb."

"I am grateful for the information. I will heed your warnings and hope to see you in a week, with Leandros, if you are still in the area," I said, reaching out my arm to him.

"We shall be here," he replied, taking my arm in a surprisingly firm grip. "And may the gods watch over you on such a journey."

"Thank you."

Casaereo found a place between two of his fellow herders and stretched out on the ground, pulling his himation over his body. I chose a space of my own and lay with my head on my arm, thinking about the next few days. If I started early and travelled all the candlemarks of the day, and overnight, I could be at the base of Mount Smolikos in two mornings' time. I could use that day to make my preparations and rest, ready to start my climb as soon as Eos lit the horizon the following morning, providing the gods favored me with clear weather. I could travel upwards all day and only the final part of my journey would be in the dark. I expected the path to narrow as I reached the peak, but I had torches to help me find the entrance to the mountain. After that, it would just be a matter of finding Papou inside.

As the fire cast flickering shadows across the walls of the cave, I thought about what Papou had spoken of before he left Casaereo. He wanted to find the amulet and then destroy it. But why? Why would he not want to use it against the Persians? Was his mind so deteriorated that he actually *wanted* to use it against the Persians but was confused, believing he had to destroy it instead? At least I knew he had not succeeded in that plan, but where was he? *Would I come across his lifeless body as I searched for him inside the mountain or along its path?* I shivered and drove the thought from my mind. Casaereo had said his body had still been strong. I would find him; I was certain of that truth.

19

I woke as the first rays of light colored the sky, Demetri and the herders still asleep when I quietly gathered my belongings and made my way out of the cave. By the time I had fallen asleep, I had convinced myself that leaving while Demetri slept would be for the best. Without me there, he would be able to make the right choice for himself and his future path – whether that be south and to Athens, or north-west towards the Tymphaioi. Of course if he chose the north-west path, the two of us would still be travelling in the same direction for at least a day. My advantage lay in that I could travel faster than him, and he had no idea where I was going so there was little chance he would think to search for my tracks ahead of him. I just had to hope Casaereo would not tell him of my destination.

"You were planning to leave without saying goodbye?" Demetri's voice startled me from my thoughts and I turned. He stood by the cave's entrance, his bag slung over his shoulder and sword belted around his waist.

"My journey does not end here like I thought. I have further to travel and I need to be on my way," I replied.

"Then I'll join you," he said.

I shook my head. "You should go south, to Athens where you belong, do not seek out the Tymphaioi, no good would come of it and they will not give you the answers you want about their armor."

"I don't want to find the Tymphaioi anymore. I want to join you."

"No."

Demetri approached in three quick strides and gripped my upper arms tightly, an angry set across his features. "You treat me like I need protecting, like I'm inferior to you but I'm not. I don't need your protection, but perhaps you need mine. You intend to climb the second highest mountain in all of Greece, alone, and for what? To search for an old man who might not even be there."

"You heard what I said last night?"

"Yes."

I broke his grip. "This is not your destiny, Demetri, it is mine."

"You can't know what my destiny is. You said it yourself – only the Moirai know our future, and I believe mine to be with you. I believe that's why we met at the lake."

"And what help would you be to me? You can barely hold a sword against boys with spears. You would be killed in an instant if you met a real soldier. I can travel for days on end and you can barely walk an entire day without needing a full night's rest. I will use the amulet again. I will kill and fight until I have avenged the death of my mothers and I will kill every Persian I find without hesitation. You will see nothing but death if you accompany me." The pain of my words flashed across his face, but I ignored it, knowing it was the only way to make him leave.

"It's not for you to decide what is for me. I'm free to make my own choices. It's true that I'm not used to such travelling, but it doesn't mean I can't. As for my skills with a sword, that's something I can learn. You can teach me."

"No," I said again. "I do not want you with me."

"I don't believe that," he said, approaching once more.

I stepped back, the solid trunk of a tree stopping me from going any further. "Do not doubt that I would leave you tied to a tree to prevent you following me," I warned him.

"I don't believe that either," he said, continuing to near.

"I did not help you at the lake just so I could be responsible for your death, Demetri." He reached out and placed a hand on my waist. "Do. Not," I growled, covering his hand with my own and throwing it off. He raised it and pressed his thumb into my injured shoulder. I drew in a sharp breath as the pain radiated through my body. I frowned and tried to break his grip, but he held firm.

"To travel alone with this wound would be foolish. I won't let you. I won't be responsible for your death either. I will accompany you to Mount Smolikos and wherever you travel after that," he said. Utter defiance was a side I had not seen from him since he had faced the boys at the lake, and though I tried to censor the feelings, my insides flared at its return, at his strength.

"You seem sure that being with me is what you want."

"I am," he replied, his breath tickling my face. He relieved the pressure at my shoulder but did not step back, leaning forward instead so his body ran the length of mine. He put his hand back on my waist. "My place is by your side, I'm sure of that."

My breath was suddenly hard to catch. He felt so right against me, in my life. I was quickly losing my resolve to deny him of joining me and I wondered why it did not bother me to want him to. To want this person in my bed as well as on my journey to find Papou.

"The journey up Mount Smolikos will not be easy. You heard what was said about it last night," I said.

"I did, and I believe that if I'm with you, you won't take undue risks and start in bad weather." Demetri leaned forward, pressing his lips to mine. He was warm against the cool morning air, but his touch did not linger, and when he pulled back I could still feel his mouth on mine. Wanted it on mine with an almost desperation. "Let me come with you," he whispered.

I raised my hand to place it on his chest, but he caught it, raising it to his lips instead. "You can come with me as far as Mount Smolikos. If you decide you want to continue on, I will let you. If not, I will accept that decision too. But if you do not come with me, you must promise to go south to Athens."

Demetri kissed my knuckles before entwining our fingers. "I accept your terms, but I have no intention of leaving."

I shook my head and gave him a tight grin. "I know and that is what scares me."

"Wh—" he started. I silenced him with a kiss of my own.

"Come on, we have a long journey ahead," I said when we parted.

I led him onto the small path, heading deeper into the Pindos ranges and towards Mount Smolikos. I could not think about what I felt for Demetri right now. I could not think about what would happen after we found Papou. What he might see me do. For now we were together and that was enough. He was everything I had not realized I still wanted – connection with another human. It scared the Tartarus out of me but I knew it was the truth.

*   *   *

We travelled all day through the snowy peaks of smaller mountains, the continual white numbing our toes as we walked. As Helios' light faded, we reached a second path – the path I knew headed west towards Mount Tymphae and the warriors Demetri had told me he no longer sought. I had paused, asking if he was sure he still wanted to accompany me. His answer had been a grin and a tug on my arm as he continued along the track we had been following. We travelled the entire night, the darkness settling around us with such completeness that it was difficult to see much outside the range of our torches.

Our pace was slower than if I had been alone and it took us until the following evening to reach the base of Mount Smolikos. We took shelter beneath a cluster of fir trees, crawling beneath their large green branches and huddling together for warmth.

*   *   *

When Eos drew us from our sleep early the next morning, we got our first look at the mountain towering above; thick conifer trees lined a narrow path littered with large boulders and rocks pushing up through the snow on an immediate incline. I understood why Casaereo had advised me not to start my climb in the dark. The path disappeared between the conifers only a few feet from us, but when I searched for it higher, I could again make out the winding line to the top between sparse, snow-laden trees.

I watched Demetri carefully as he too sized up the mountain track, fully expecting him to change his mind, regardless of his earlier insistence to join me. Instead, he smiled, picked up his bag and headed off up the path without a word. I gathered my own bag and caught up to him and, as we made our slow climb upwards, a silent final agreement was formed – we would help each other to the top and wherever our journey took us beyond that.

The falling snow, which had been our constant companion the day before, had disappeared, the sun streaming down onto us between the clouds. We spent the rest of the daylight negotiating the rocks, errant branches, slippery snow, and each other as we made our way to the top.

By the time we reached the peak, I was as exhausted as Demetri looked, our legs covered with scrapes and bruises from tripping and slipping in the snow and landing heavily against the rocks beneath. I had expected to find an obvious opening in the mountain when we reached the peak, but only flat rock greeted us. I searched along the path towards the north side of the mountain, but there was nothing there either and in the fading light I did not want to fall over the edge and find the quick death Casaereo had warned me about.

"We will have to take shelter here tonight," I told Demetri, pointing to the solitary fir tree that had found a way to grow on the narrow ledge. He only nodded in reply and, just as we had the night before, we climbed beneath the large branches, our backs resting against the mountain as we huddled together to rest our weary bodies and wait for morning.

20

I shivered and woke on the cold ground of an unfamiliar room. Two windows sat in the wall to my left, but no light penetrated them. Mumma Skylar loomed large above me, her face bright and mouth set in an angry line.

"Why do you huddle at the peak of Mount Smolikos? The Tymphaioi are to the south-west, you know this," she said.

I pushed myself into a sitting position, noting that I wore my full soldier uniform; greaves, cuirass, helmet. The himation I had bought from Andronikos was gone, and my aspis lay beside me, intact, as did my sword.

Mumma paced back and forth. There was something different about her. I had seen her angry before, worried even, but her movements and mannerisms did not seem to be her own. Seeing her unnerved me and I did not feel I should tell her of my true plans.

"I must have taken a wrong path," I replied.

She stopped pacing, her eyes flashing red as they pinned me in place. "Do not lie to me. You can follow a path as well as you can fight. Is it this boy who sees you stray from finding the warriors?" she asked, pointing. I followed her finger. Demetri lay beside me, his quiet snores lifting his shoulders as he slept, unaware of our new location. "You assured me he would not interfere and yet here you are, far from your intended destination."

I stood, positioning my body between the two of them. "He is no threat, it was not his choice to come here."

"You believe you have a future with this person," she said, a statement, not a question.

"I … I have not allowed such thoughts since you and Mother were taken from me."

"But you want to keep him safe from dangers. From the Tymphaioi."

"And what if I do? It is not your concern what I do with him. I will avenge you and Mother, but I will do it in my own time."

Mumma neared with frightening speed and I shrank back, the intensity of her angry stare startling me. "You do not have *time*. You need to abandon whatever foolish idea you have for being at Mount Smolikos and return to the Plain. Use the amulet and destroy the rest of the Persians who are coming. Embrace your fate as well as your past and know that with the amulet you shall achieve more than you have ever dreamed, more than I ever could."

"Tell me about the amulet, when did you use it? What happened?"

She turned suddenly, as if hearing something beyond the walls of the room and when she addressed me again she was distracted. "Leave the mountain. Leave the boy also; you shall have no need for him soon. Use the amulet against him if you must or just use it to leave this place," she ordered, disappearing from the room.

A chill ran through me and I knew she was gone. "I refuse to use it on Demetri. I will not hurt him," I called into the emptiness.

*

"Ava, wake up," Demetri's voice broke through into my slumber. "You were having a nightmare," he added when I opened my eyes.

I noted the soft light of morning filtering through the branches of the fir tree, relieved to find we were still at Mount Smolikos. "Sorry," I said, realizing I was lying across his legs. "We should find the entrance to the mountain." I drew my stiff limbs up, stretching them out beside us. My injured shoulder protested, but I ignored it, preparing to crawl out of our sheltered position when Demetri laid a hand on my arm.

"Wait. Do you want to talk about it?" he asked.

"No," I replied, giving him a quick smile. "I am fine. It was nothing." He released me, following close behind when I left. "There must be a break in the rocks here somewhere, maybe it opens like a door," I said, studying the stones.

Demetri put his hand against the mountain and felt along like I did. "Are you sure there's actually an entrance here?" he asked.

"Casaereo said there was," I replied. We continued to search and finally, near the edge of the ridge, I felt a small change in the rock face. I followed the gap with my finger; it extended all the way to the ground and a foot higher than my head. "Here," I told Demetri.

He joined me, sliding his fingers into the gap. We pulled on the stone and I sucked in a breath at the pain that lanced through my shoulder. The large section of rock opened outwards, revealing the darkness within. We were so close to finding Papou now.

Demetri retrieved our bags and handed me a torch, striking two pieces of flint together. The spark caught on the material and I sheltered it with my body as it flared to life.

"Ready?" he asked. I nodded, holding the torch out in front as we entered the mountain.

As we cleared the doorway, thick white strands blocked our path. I paused and held the torch up, trying to make out what they might be. Beside me, Demetri started to flail about wildly – he had walked directly into them.

"Get it off, get if off, oh gods get it *off*!" he yelled, swatting at his face and head. I stifled a laugh at his exaggerated movements; I had realized the threads were spider webs and I was glad it had not been me to walk into such a large one.

"Hold steady," I told him. He stopped thrashing and let me help pull the sticky lengths from his hair and back. I briefly wondered how long it would have taken the spider to build such an intricate design, but did not voice the thought.

"You are not fond of spider webs?" I grinned.

He shivered. "I don't mind the snares themesleves, the designs can be fascinating, but I fear the spiders who call them home."

"Me too," I nodded. I held the torch up again, noting other large webs strung between the wall beside us and the roof, which was only another ten cubits or so higher. "Come on," I said, making my way around the broken web.

"The old man we're looking for – Leandros – he's your grandfather isn't he? The one who was banished after your mothers died?"

"Yes," I replied, offering nothing more and glad when Demetri did not press me for details.

The space we stood in was round for the most part and, towards the middle, it was dark where the light from my torch and the stone door did not reach it. "Papou?" I called, heading in that direction. My voice echoed around the chamber, but no reply came back.

I continued forward and within a few steps, the light from the doorway diminished almost completely. The torch took over and soon revealed a spiraling staircase of stone barely three feet wide leading down into the middle of the mountain.

"It feels like there's something crawling around on my back, would you look for me?" Demetri asked, taking off his himation and swatting at his shoulders as he followed me.

I shone the light across his back. "I do not see anything," I told him, returning my attention to the staircase as I crouched down and held the torch above the second step. "Look at this."

"Who crafted those?"

"No-one. It is said the water that used to run through all the mountains here carved them out."

"Oh. Ouch! Something just bit me," Demetri cried, slapping the back of his arm. He took the torch and crouched down, holding it close to a small black thing twitching on the ground.

"Are you alright?" I asked.

"Yes," he replied. "It fared worse than me by the look of it."

"I am sorry, I did not see it before."

"Don't worry, I'm just glad it's no longer on me," he said, shivering as he stood. "Are we going down the steps you found?"

"Yes, they must lead to the vertical cave," I nodded, taking the torch back. I stepped carefully onto the first stone, finding it solid beneath my feet, and led the way, the torchlight bouncing across the walls with each descending pace.

The deeper we went, the narrower the passageway became and when the sleeves of my himation started to catch on the walls, I turned my body sideways to get through, telling Demetri to do the same. I continued to call for Papou, but it was only my voice that returned and after a while, I stopped, deciding to wait until we reached the bottom of the steps before calling for him again.

The torchlight dimmed and flickered, but provided enough light to see at least two or three steps in front until finally a light breeze swept across my cheeks and the torch came to life again. The brightness revealed the bottom of the narrow staircase and when I stepped out into another large open area, I found it was almost twice the size of the one at the top of the mountain.

"Papou?" I called. Again there was no answer.

"How far do you think we've travelled down?" Demetri asked.

"It is hard to tell. The stairs wound around, and they were steep, so I expect it would be a fair way."

"Are you sure there's no secret door out at this point?"

"I do not believe so," I replied.

"Then can we rest for just a little while?" I turned, finding Demetri leaning against the wall, his face pinched with pain and a light sheen of sweat across his forehead.

"What is wrong?" I asked, immediately crossing to him.

"My arm hurts … and … my chest."

"Sit down," I directed, wedging the torch into a niche in the wall above his head. I helped him to the ground and took one of our water skins, holding it to his lips. "Show me your arm."

Demetri turned the underside of his right upper arm to me. I had no trouble finding the bite. "It is badly swollen. How long has it been hurting?"

"Not long, we were over halfway down the steps, but it's getting worse." He suddenly paled and turned his head away, noisily emptying his stomach. He shivered and wiped his mouth with the back of his hand, laying back against the stone wall.

A trickle of sweat rolled down his cheek and I placed my hand across his forehead. "You might have a fever. Do you need to take off your chlamys?"

He shook his head, shivering again. "I feel like I'm sitting naked in the snow. Where is my himation?" I retrieved it from the bottom of the staircase and took it back to him. "Let me rest for just a few moments then we'll continue," he said, pulling it around his shoulders.

"I will go myself; we cannot be far from the cave now."

"No. I said I'd be with you," he insisted, pushing himself shakily to his feet. I supported his elbow as he stood, but he had barely straightened up before he cried out.

"What is it?" I asked, wrapping my arm around his waist. He crumpled to the ground again, clutching his calf.

"My leg, I can't move it."

I crouched beside him, kneading the lower half of his leg until the muscles relaxed beneath my hands. He gasped as the pain left him and I noticed the light sheen on his forehead was now dripping down his face. Dark marks beneath Demetri's eyes gave him a deathly hue and I shook my head against the image, taking the hot flesh of his hand.

"Demetri ... I do not know how to cure a spider bite."

His body trembled despite the heat. "Nor do I," he said, closing his eyes.

I took a deep breath as my thoughts raced. There had to be something I could do for him, I just had to think my way through it. I was familiar with herbs and medicines; I had applied plenty in the past, but never to a wound like Demetri had. It was not open; I could not simply apply the herbs and lay a cloth over the top, waiting while they did their work.

"I should clean the bite," I finally told him. "Maybe that will help with the swelling and take the poison from the area."

"No, I feel a little better. We must find your grandfather," Demetri maintained, trying to sit up.

"No," I said gently, putting my hand against his shoulder. "Let me clean it and then we will see how you feel." He nodded and slumped back against the wall.

I removed my himation and chlamys, soaking part of the latter with water from our waterskin and gently wiping the bitten area. Demetri continued to shiver, his teeth chattering loudly with each shudder but when I lay my hand across his forehead again, he was still hot to touch.

I drew my himation over his legs. "I once heard a healer say that if bitten by a snake you should keep still so the venom does not spread too quickly. We should do the same now. I will find the vertical cave and see if my grandfather is there while you wait here."

"I wouldn't be able to offer you much help at the moment anyway," he agreed.

"Lift your arm above your heart – if that can slow down blood loss from a sword wound maybe it can slow spider poison down too."

"Or direct it straight to my heart," he said with a weak smile.

"Do not say that," I murmured, wishing his words did not mirror my thoughts. With effort, Demetri lifted his arm and tucked his hand behind his head. I adjusted our himatia and chlamydes so they covered most of his body, then gathered small rocks, tinder and wood from nearby. I lit the tinder and pushed it between the wood, placing the rocks in a circle around them.

"You need to keep warm and still," I told him. He nodded as I took a second torch from my bag and lay it within reach of his hand, and the fire. "Just in case you need to keep more spiders away," I added with a faint grin.

"Thank you and … I'm sorry."

"Do not apologize for getting bitten," I said, putting a hand on his knee. "It will not do us any good. Besides, if it is anyone's fault, it is mine, for I did not see it when you asked me to look."

I squeezed his knee and took the torch, crossing to the opposite side of the mountain. When I looked back, Demetri's eyes were closed. I sent up a silent prayer to Asclepius before slipping through the small opening in search of the vertical cave.

I stopped abruptly as I exited the small tunnel; I was standing on the edge of the cave. There were more cobwebs, but they covered the top of the drop rather than the doorway I had come through. I crouched down, waving my torch across the abyss, burning the strands away and keeping an eye out for any spiders that might crawl up. Thankfully none emerged.

The cave itself was not quite as wide as my arm from fingertip to shoulder when I reached out. I held the torch in as far as I dared, but even then I could not make out the bottom. "Papou?" I called into the darkness. There was no answer. "Papou." Still no reply.

I could see why Papou had thought this place might hold the amulet – the rock that formed the vertical drop was almost the same color as the jet in the amulet, although the pieces near my hand were more green than black.

I dropped a small rock into the cave; it was a long time before it reached the bottom. I shivered. If Papou was in there, the rock should not have made any noise when it came to rest at the base. Besides, the thick webs told me that no one had been there recently. I had rope in my bag if I wanted to descend the cave for a closer look, but there was nothing to attach it to outside, and I did not relish the idea of making my way through more cobwebs below.

I did not believe Papou had been there, there was nothing to suggest that *anyone* had been inside the mountain in a long time. I frowned. Then where was he? If he had not travelled to Mount Smolikos, where had he gone? Was his strange behavior with the herders just a ruse? Had he really gone back to his homeland as Casaereo suggested – had he gone back to Trachis?

I shook my head and got to my feet, retreating through the small tunnel and back to Demetri. He was where I had left him, face still pale and sweat still raised on his forehead. There was a large amount of vomit on the ground beside him and I hoped I had not made him sicker by putting water on the bite.

I put my torch back in the niche of the wall and knelt beside him, placing my hand on his shoulder. "Demetri?"

He opened his eyes. "Did you find him?" he asked, looking past me to the tunnel.

"No," I replied. "We need to leave and get you to a healer. Can you stand?"

"I think so, but I'm so cold … and so tired."

"I know." I pulled my chlamys around my shoulders and held my arm out for Demetri to take.

He stood unsteadily and I helped him with his chlamys and himation, careful that the thicker cloak did not drag over the bite on his arm. I added my own to his shoulders and secured it before extinguishing the fire I had made. I stowed the second torch in my bag, retrieving the one wedged in the stone beside Demetri's head and slipping an arm around his waist.

"Ready?" I asked. He nodded, putting one arm around my shoulder and his other against the wall as we shuffled towards the stone staircase.

21

Our journey back up the stone steps was slow and painful. I was tucked into Demetri's side as far as I could go, but even so, the confined space made our climb difficult and his stumbling steps ensured my injured shoulder was squashed often against the unyielding wall around us.

By the time we reached the top, beads of sweat were dripping down Demetri's cheek and joined the ones on my forehead. Tremors continued to shake his body and he struggled to take the few steps across the flat surface before I set him down on the ground. I passed him the water and made him drink, but he barely managed one mouthful before it came back up.

He tried to raise his arm to wipe his mouth but could not get it above his stomach, his hand flopping uselessly back into his lap. I took the end of my chlamys, drying it for him. His breathing was shallow and the dark rings below his eyes had deepened.

I put my hand over his. "There is something I must find. I will not be long."

"Don't leave me," he pleaded, his hand gripping mine desperately.

"Open your eyes," I ordered gently. Demetri cracked them slightly and I nodded to him. "You will be able to see me the entire time," I promised. He nodded in reply and I stood, casting the light of the torch near the stone steps.

"Where are you?" I murmured.

Finally, my light picked up the small black body on the ground. When we had left Alecia and Korpos in Tricca, they had given us gifts of food, hairpins and a small earthenware pyxis as thanks for helping them with their son's birth. Alecia had several pyxides she kept her powders and jewelry in and she insisted I take one with me. At the time I had no need of such an item, but had accepted it graciously so as not to offend her. I was glad now I had.

I took the container from my bag, emptying the dregs of powder, and approached the spider. It had obviously still been alive after Demetri hit it and had tried to get to safety, but with only five good legs, it had not gotten very far. It now lay with its good legs drawn up by its body, and its broken ones jutting out at strange angles.

For the most part, including its legs, it was black all over, but along its back and over the end of its bulbous body, was a thin red line. I nudged it with my foot, the movement rolling it onto its back. Its stomach also had one red section, a strange shape, not quite rectangular, and yet not quite a diamond either, as if someone had dropped red clay from above and the shape was just how it had fallen.

I nudged at it again. Still it did not move. I placed the pyxis on its side and used the lid to scoop the spider inside. I secured it with the piece of twine Alecia had provided for that exact purpose, and wrapped it in the fabric of a spare chiton she had also insisted I take. When I was satisfied the spider was trapped securely inside the layers, I slipped it all back into my bag and returned to Demetri's side.

"We have to go."

"Wait," he said, reaching beneath the himatia and chlamys. "I want to show you something."

"Can it wait? You need more help than I can provide you with here, we need to leave."

"Please," he insisted. Knowing I could not simply haul him to his feet due to my injured shoulder, I blew out a long breath and nodded.

From beneath the folds of his clothing Demetri retrieved his pouch of coins, tipping them into his lap as he had the first day we met. He chose one and stared at it for a long moment before passing it to me. "I want to tell you about this coin," he said.

It was not one he had shown me before – it was the one he had held back. On the obverse was the image of a horse looking behind itself. On the reverse, a sandal below a strange creature with six legs. I frowned, not familiar with it. "What is this?" I asked, holding the coin up.

"A cicada. They can be heard singing to each other in the summertime."

"Oh. I have heard them when I have been on watch but never knew what they were called. What is the significance of this one above the sandal?"

He held out his hand and I gave the coin back. "To understand, you must look at the other side first." He turned it so the image of the horse faced me. "As with the dual heads and tails coins, I only made one of these. It was the last coin I made before I left Larissa and when it was done I destroyed the mold so another could never be cast." He shivered and I helped him pull the himatia closer to his body before settling myself beside him, our backs against the wall of the mountain.

"The coin tells a story. The horse represents Larissa, a place I both love and despise in equal measure, which is why its body faces one way and its head another." He turned it over, tracing the outline of the creature with his finger. "The cicada represents a long-held wish. Young cicadas don't live among other cicadas. The females deposit their eggs into the bark of a tree and when the eggs hatch they fall to the ground, growing under leaves and debris and feeding on root juice until they're considered adults. Then they make a tunnel and crawl to the surface, shedding their old skin and emerging strong and ready to sing in the world around them."

I frowned. "I do not understand. Is it your slave status you want to shed?"

Demetri shook his head and with effort crawled forward, shedding the himatia and chlamys as he knelt to face me. With shaking hands, he slid the fibula from his chiton, letting it fall to his waist. His chest was bandaged tightly from one side to the other, two hands' width wide, the mounds beneath contoured like the breasts of a woman, only smaller.

"Wait … You are … a woman?"

He hesitated and slowly shook his head. "Not exactly," he murmured. He unwound the bandage, his eyes downcast as he worked. "The night … the night Spyros found me with the silver … whipping me wasn't the only thing he had to do to me in front of Phaeops' father." I drew in a sharp breath as Demetri peeled the last layer back, exposing himself to me.

"Gods. Demetri," I whispered, a shiver sliding down my back. Where his right breast should have been, there was only a flap of skin crudely sewn together where a nipple should have been. The suture line ran from the breastbone almost back to his underarm. The left side was not as severely scarred – a neat line running beneath his breast, the nipple untouched and perfectly aligned in the center. That side was flatter than I was sure it used to be; shaped like a man's rather than a woman's, but without the trauma of its mate.

"What did he do to you?" I asked, hot flames of anger heating my veins at the mutilation before me. "*Why* did he do it to you?"

Demetri kept his eyes from me as he replied. "Phaeops and his friends have known what I … am for winters. They stumbled across the truth and that's when they forced me to make extra coin for them. They threatened to tell everyone if I didn't."

"Did they … did they touch you? Rape you?" I asked through gritted teeth.

"No. They couldn't ... they ... I ..." He drew in a deep breath and pushed himself shakily to his feet. I followed him, reaching out to steady him, my hand at his elbow. Demetri let his chiton fall all the way to the ground. My eyes followed it down, at first not understanding what I saw – what it meant.

"You are ..."

"Part woman, part man." A tear dropped to the ground between us. "An abomination."

"No. No," I insisted, balling one hand into a fist. "You are *not* an abomination." I slowly slid my other hand up to trail my fingers over the scars on his chest. Her chest. I circled him, my fingers sliding over smooth skin; chest, arm, shoulder. My breath caught again at the red, crisscross welts standing out angrily against the flesh of his back running from top to bottom.

"Demetri," I whispered again, tracing each pattern in turn. "How many of these are from that night?"

"Only the top ones."

"The others are from when you worked in the fields?"

"Yes." I returned to stand in front of him. Her. "Tell me what Spyros did."

Demetri swallowed loudly and closed his eyes. "Phaeops' father didn't know about ... me until that night. I was quite ... developed from a very young age so Spyros has always known what I am – it was why he bought me in the first place – to protect me from the other men who were at the sale that day. They had ... other plans for how I could be used, for how I could make money for them." My fist tightened but I stayed quiet. "When I started with the Celators, Spyros suggested I wrap my chest with cloth to make it less obvious that I had breasts, but when I was found with the silver and Spyros tried to whip me with my chiton on, Phaeops insisted I be stripped bare. With one look at my nakedness, Phaeops' father decided it was not merely enough for me to be whipped. He said I was ugly, an abomination against the gods, a liar. Spyros had no choice ..."

"There *was* a choice," I growled, a shiver slipping down my back. "There is *always* a choice. He should have stood up to those men, those ... bullies."

"In a way he did," Demetri said, opening his eyes. "He should've cut off both my breasts, that's what they wanted. Instead, he only cut off one and when I collapsed he turned the sword on them and told them if they didn't get out, he'd cut them to pieces too. They couldn't leave fast enough – they weren't fighters. They were noblemen who couldn't defend themselves, not against Spyros who was a huge man. He was gentle but he could look fierce, and standing there holding that sword, he was formidable.

"As soon as they were gone he took me home, tending my open, bleeding wound and telling me how sorry he was for what he'd done. His wife helped him and it was she who ... who shaped my left breast so it somewhat matched my right." Demetri laid a hand over his missing right breast. I released the fist and covered his fingers with my own.

"I am so sorry. But I promise you – you are not ugly or an abomination. You were not when you had breasts and you are not now that you do not. You are beautiful." I took a step closer, keeping my hand over his as I placed my other on his cheek. "You *are* beautiful," I repeated. I kissed him. Her.

"Thank you," he murmured. "You are kind to say so."

"I do not say it out of kindness. I say it because it is true. Do not believe what he said, what he told you – that was the lie. You are beautiful no matter the form your body takes." Demetri shivered and I reached for the discarded bandage and chiton beside us.

*

"This mortal keeps you from our bed again. Why?" Aphrodite asked, wrapping her arms around Ares' waist and pressing her lips to his shoulder.

"Tell me what you see," the god of war said.

Aphrodite focused on the two young people in the mountain. "Honesty. Trust. The blooming of a friendship, perhaps something more. He wears his scars on the outside, she on the inside. He shares his with her tentatively, yet bravely."

"And she shares hers with him."

"What happened to him? The scars on his back appear to be slave lashings, though the ones on the front ..."

Ares nodded. "He was a slave. He is ... was also born with both male and female sexual organs. He is a distraction," Ares grumbled, folding his arms across his chest.

"Or perhaps it is fortuitous they have met ... you have taken everyone from her – her mothers, her grandparents, she is alone, just as Skylar was for the most part. And yet, look how much stronger Skylar was, how much more determined she was to prove herself and be who you wanted because of what – who – she had to lose. He knows what Ava is capable of and still he remains. Just as Alexis did with Skylar. He could be useful. You could use their feelings for one another to advantage, just as you have before." Aphrodite placed her body between her lover and the mortals and looped her hands around the nape of his neck. "Come back to bed and allow us to share in our own pleasures. Whatever happens between the two of them this night is of no concern to us, is it?"

Ares' hands found her hips and he drew her closer. "Perhaps not and we can go ... soon, for you have always been able to distract me with talk of our coupling. You know I cannot refuse such offers."

"And I expect you never shall," Aphrodite grinned.

"I cannot imagine it," he replied, returning her grin. "But allow us to stay just a little longer."

22

With care I re-wrapped Demetri's chest, pinned his chiton in place and settled the chlamys and himatia at his shoulders before helping him back to the ground. The coin he had shown me, the story, it was not just any story, it was his story. It was her story.

"What does the sandal on your coin represent?" I asked.

"The sandal is for Jason and the huge adversity he faced in his quest to retrieve the Golden Fleece from Colchis with the Argonauts. He wasn't expected to succeed – but die in the attempt … which is the expectation of the fate that awaits a runaway slave," he said, confirming what I thought. Individually, the pictures seemed to make no sense, but combined with the history of the person who had crafted it, it made perfect sense.

I ached for Demetri's wish and for the cruelty he had suffered at the hands of those in Larissa, not because he had been disobedient and they had the authority to punish him, but because he had had the misfortune of being strong enough to survive being left to die on the path outside of Larissa and put within their unkind reach.

I could not catch a full breath, my chest clenching as a physical hurt pierced me deep in my stomach. I reached out a trembling hand and placed it on Demetri's. Previous to meeting him … her, I corrected myself, when stories of injustices were told to me, I felt only anger and wanted to exact revenge on those responsible. But for Demetri it was a deep sadness and a strong want to be able to take away his pain that I felt now.

"I wish your fate had not been to face such things," I told him.

He reached over and wiped my cheek. I had not even realized the tear had escaped. "Do not waste tears. My story isn't unique, most slaves wish for freedom, but few have the courage or opportunity to seek it."

"But you wanted to live like the cicada does; alone in a world without others your own age. Without boys who beat you and pursued you for telling the truth about them."

He smiled weakly and shook his head. "You misunderstand. My wish was that I emerged from my life in Larissa strong and ready to live the life I wanted in the world I discovered outside it. Yes, I've suffered at the hands of others and yes, I despise those who wronged me, but ... if we don't have challenges, how do we know what we're truly capable of? If Jason hadn't accepted his uncle's challenge, and gone on an impossible journey, he wouldn't have become the hero we know him as today."

I did not know how to respond. The man ... the woman who sat before me shared similarities with my own past; suffering tragedy that she did not wish for and could not have prevented. But where I used my mothers' deaths as a way to bring about revenge and destruction against those who had taken them from me, this surprising person used the adversities to spur them on to greater things. I did not know whether to hate Demetri or be in awe of him.

"I suppose we would not," I mumbled.

Mumma's necklace pressed against my skin, warm and hard as I drew in deep breaths to alleviate the sting in my chest. I did admire Demetri's actions, for wanting to become something other than what the tragedy had made him, but I knew that I could never feel the same. I was a soldier, a warrior, trained to kill those who carried out crimes against innocents, and just as I could not let the Persians go unpunished for what they had done to me, if the chance arose, I would not hesitate to kill Phaeops and his family for what they had done to Demetri. It was who I was.

I shivered and blew out a breath as a sudden, clear thought occurred to me: Demetri had held back that coin for a reason – he had thought he would be able to share it with me at another time in the future. "You think you are going to die," I frowned, watching him carefully. He nodded. I got to my feet, anger gripping me as I paced before him. "I will not let that happen."

He laid his head against the stone wall. "It mightn't be for you to decide," he replied, echoing my mother's words and causing me to pause in my steps.

My frown deepened. He was giving up; he ... he was not going to fight the poison in his system. "You have to fight," I demanded.

He gave me a weak smile. "I'm not ... one of your ... soldiers," he breathed. "You can't command me... I'm just a boy ... or a girl. I'm just a slave."

"No you are not. You are someone I ... someone I care for and I will *not* let you leave me without a fight." He closed his eyes, the smile still on his lips. "The night you came to tell me Philo died you said I had saved you and lost him; you believed I had traded his life for yours. If that really is the case then I will not lose you as well. Not here. Not now," I promised. Demetri remained silent, his eyes still shut.

Maybe I should use the amulet on him, maybe it would heal him. I reached for the leather around my neck, but something stopped me. Mumma had wanted me to use it against him when she came to me in my dream, what if it actually killed him? It had not saved Philo when I used it on him.

I left it where it was. No matter what I had to do or where I had to go, I would not let Demetri die. I crossed to him in two long strides, wrapping my arm around his waist and ignoring the protests from him, and my shoulder, as I hauled him to his feet.

"You are not going to die in this place, Demetri. I will get you help and you will soon be well again. I promise."

We cleared the stone doorway we had entered earlier and stepped out into the sunlight.

"Ah!" Demetri cried. He grabbed his head, staggering around the small ledge and pulling me with him. As we stumbled towards the edge, I jammed my heel against a rock protruding out of the snow.

I pulled Demetri back with everything I had and we crashed into the hard rock of the mountain. Sharp pain shot through my shoulder as Demetri landed heavily against me, his hands still covering his eyes against the harsh light.

I pushed him off my throbbing arm, struggling to free the hood of his chlamys from the two himatia he wore. I pulled it over his head and face as far as it would go, his body (or should it be *her* body?) immediately calming. I fell back against the mountain, sucking in several large breaths as my heart pounded loudly in my ears.

"I'm sorry," he panted beside me.

"What happened?" I asked, turning my head to his shrouded face.

"The sun. It's so bright out here."

"We have to get you to a healer."

"We can't start our descent now; the sun is more than halfway across the sky. We should make camp inside the mountain and start in the morning," Demetri said, taking two staggering steps back towards the entrance before crashing against the wall again.

"No. We need to leave. Now. And you are in no position to argue with me." I wrapped my arm around his waist again. "You need a healer sooner rather than later and I intend to get you to one."

"You might be right," he conceded. "But I'll just be a burden and danger to you in my current state. I should stay here. You should go."

"Do not be absurd, I will not leave you here alone where there is the potential for further harm. We will go together. Keep your chlamys over your face. I will guide you."

I did not know exactly where I was going to find a healer, but I had until we reached the bottom of the mountain to work that out.

*   *   *

Our progress was slow, Demetri managing to trip on or run into every rock or branch I warned him to avoid. Several times we fell to the ground, and often he landed painfully on top of me. I wanted to forgive his clumsiness but my frustration grew with each passing candlemark.

We walked side by side until nightfall and for the past candlemark Demetri had been quiet. My shoulder ached and streaming blood from cuts on my shins had long since dried, yet we were barely a third of the way down. I found a large tree, pinning Demetri against it with my body as I took out a torch and lit it. When I wrapped my arm around his waist again, his head lolled to the side, face paler than before. He had either lost consciousness or was asleep. I chose to believe it was the latter, but either way he became easier to handle and even though he was heavier, and I was basically carrying him, I was able to wend our way around the rocks and branches as required and continued down the path at a faster pace.

Without my himation I should have been cold, but Demetri's heated body kept me warm, and lulled me towards sleep. I fought against Hypnos, determined to get as far as possible before morning found us again. It was a battle I won, but when Eos lit the horizon the following morning, I could not go on. My legs trembled beneath Demetri's weight and refused to carry us any further. I had become immune to the aching of my shoulder, but as I sat Demetri against the mountain face, it made itself apparent and I sucked in a sharp breath. The sooner I found a healer for Demetri, the sooner they could look at my own wound. We just had to get there.

"Are we at the healer's?" Demetri croaked.

"No, but we will rest for a while," I replied. I sat down hard on the ground and pulled my chlamys around me. I would only need a few minutes rest, a half-a-candlemark at most, not that I could gauge such a short passing of time, but I would get us on our feet again soon.

As I lingered on the edge of sleep, my mind circled with thoughts of the man ... the woman beside me. I wanted a future for us after we left Mount Smolikos. I was fairly confident he ... she wanted it too. He had intimated as much before he showed me who he really was. If nothing else, I knew I did not want Demetri to die and I resolved to do whatever it took to get help for him. I just hoped he could avoid Hades' call until then.

"I want to thank you, Demetri," I mumbled.

"For what?"

"Coming to find me after Philo died."

"I couldn't just let you leave." I wanted to ask him why, but Hypnos claimed me. The question would keep.

*

"This is the one you believe you have waited for?" the man dressed all in black asked.

"Yes. As I explained, her recovery after her first use of the amulet was almost immediate," the god of war replied.

"Who is the boy?"

"No one important," Ares replied, waving off his question.

"He irritates you," the man grinned, scratching at his head – his golden crown the only break in his otherwise dark ensemble. "Why?"

"There is something she is not telling me about why they came here. I am certain it is his influence."

"You have spoken to her?"

"I have appeared to her, though not as myself."

"Ah, of course – as her mothers. You have encouraged her to use the amulet again?"

"Yes, but she has not."

"What are you going to do about that?"

"Ensure she has a reason to," Ares shrugged.

"How?"

"You shall see, Uncle. You shall see," Ares grinned, disappearing in a flash of bright light.

*

"Ava." I woke to Demetri's weak voice and insistent shaking.

The sun was high in the sky and – thankfully – there was no sign of snow. Demetri's face was still shielded by his chlamys and as I pushed myself to my knees, I saw a large pile of vomit on the ground beside him. My anger flared. I should not have fallen asleep. I should not have rested. I should have kept watch over him. I cared for Demetri, I wanted him … her … to be in my future, and yet I had slept when he needed me.

I took a corner of the chlamys and lifted it away. I barely caught a glimpse of the pale skin and deep purple marks beneath his eyes before he cried out, pulling it from my hands to cover his skin once again.

"Sorry," I said. "Come on, we have to go." He nodded his reply. I took Demetri's arm, laying it over my shoulders and pulling him up by his middle as he pushed weakly off the mountain face.

We continued our slow, stumbling descent – Demetri sleeping through most of the journey, waking only briefly to be sick or when pain gripped his legs. With the setting of the sun came a light dusting of snow. We were still only halfway down the mountain.

Demetri woke, turning his head and retching noisily onto a small shrub. "You can't … keep this pace," he panted, untangling himself from my arm and sitting down heavily. "Leave me here and continue your journey to find your grandfather."

"No," I replied, cradling my injured shoulder which was stiff and sore.

"You must."

"It is not up for discussion, Demetri. We will continue as soon as you are able." But even as I spoke, the snow started to fall heavier around us and a sharp wind blew up. It would be foolish for us to continue in the weather that was closing in. We would have to take shelter beneath the trees I could see further down the path.

"Take your himation, you're going to need it. I can take shelter beneath those trees just down the path and wait for you there." He pointed to the grouping I had seen. I shivered against a sudden breeze and opened my mouth to protest. "Don't argue with me, you know I'm right. You'll be able to travel faster down the mountain without me," he insisted. I drew in a breath and nodded, taking the himation and re-fastening it around my shoulders.

I would not leave him, but he did not need to know that. If the weather was kind, I would pick him up while he slept and continue our journey down the mountain. My shoulder painfully reminded me that it would not be that simple. It needed rest and new herbs and would not cooperate without at least one of those.

Demetri held out his arm and I pulled him to his feet, picking my bag up again. I kept hold of his hand as he headed for the cluster of small trees growing against the mountain face. We were only a few feet from them when I saw the crack.

"Demetri, stop!" I yelled, trying to drag him back. It was too late. Demetri put his foot into the crevice and the entire ground gave way under us.

I fell through the dark, groping for Demetri, for something solid, for anything to stop my fall. There was nothing except air around me.

23

Hades and Ares stood above the two, still figures inside Mount Smolikos. "Must you always be so dramatic?" Hades sighed. "Would another minor wound to the boy not have been easier?"

Ares shrugged. "Probably, but from this depth, my Chosen One shall have to use the amulet if she wants to get out."

"Are you certain they are not dead?" Hades asked, nudging the boy with his foot.

"I thought you of all immortals would know if they were – you are the God of the Dead, are you not? Do you not feel the souls entering your kingdom?" Ares sniped.

"I do, I just wondered if *you* knew the answer. They fell a great distance, mortal bodies do not often survive such treatment, as you well know."

"I am not a fool – I did not allow them to smash against the unforgiving ground. Well, not too hard anyway."

"Hard enough to stun, but not kill?" Hades asked, rolling the boy onto his side.

"Exactly." Ares replied.

"Well, as exciting as this has all been, Persephone awaits me in my palace and it is not long until she returns to her mother."

"I shall come to you once Ava proves she can do what we need. Father's throne shall not be his for long," Ares nodded.

"I cannot wait to see the look on my brother's face when we unseat him," Hades grinned, offering Ares his arm.

The god of war took it in a firm grip. "Our time comes, Uncle." Hades nodded and disappeared, leaving his nephew to wait for Ava to wake up.

24

I was flat on my back when I woke again. My body was numb, cold snow coating my face. I inhaled deeply and flexed my fingers and toes. They were stiff, but they obeyed and I had few aches and pains, though how *that* was possible I had no idea.

"Demetri?" No answer. I opened my eyes to complete darkness. "Demetri?" I called again, louder this time, my voice bouncing off unseen walls. Still he did not reply.

I blindly felt the ground beside me. Rocks, stones, water. A lot of very cold water. *Where are you?* I rolled onto my side and this time my shoulder and legs objected to the movements. I ignored them and found my bag nearby, briefly wondering how the precious contents I had stored there had survived the fall. I took a torch and flint from the top, deciding to wait until I could see before reaching inside too much further. The pyxis could have smashed and I did not relish the idea of handling the spider in my bare hands. I shivered with the thought and concentrated on getting light.

I wedged the wooden handle between my thighs and struck the flint together. It took several attempts for my shaking hands to create a spark big enough to catch on the head, but eventually a dull glow lit the area. I started pulling out the contents of my bag. I ate two loose dates and set aside a length of rope. The chiton which held the spider was bundled up just as I had left it and when I cautiously felt for the pyxis, I was relieved to find it still held its shape beneath the layers. I put it aside as well and drew out my last item – a tunic. I unrolled the material, releasing the white shell with its orange inside. It had been a gift from Mumma Skylar for my birthing day, the last I had had with my mothers. Mumma had missed the actual day, having been with King Cleomenes in Sparta, but brought back the unique item to make up for it. I had cherished it when she gave it to me and when they were taken from me less than a moon later, I treasured it even more, ensuring it was always among my few possessions wherever I went.

The fragile spine on one end had broken, the fragment still wrapped in a fold of the material. I closed my eyes, holding it reverently as tears formed behind my lids. "I am sorry," I whispered. Without Philo, the murex shell was the only physical reminder I had of my mothers other than the leather bracelet I wore. I pressed my lips to the cool whiteness, swallowing the lump in my throat.

A long moment later I opened my eyes and re-wrapped the shell in my tunic. I replaced everything and with the torch light stronger now, I held it out and shone it around the area, finding the black mass I was looking for.

"Demetri!" I cried, scrambling over to where he lay. "Demetri, wake up!" I urged, shaking his shoulder. He did not move. I dropped the torch, the head sizzled when it hit the water, but it did not go out. I rolled him onto his back. "Please Demetri, please wake up," I whispered.

I could not lose him. I had failed Philo, I could not fail Demetri too. I raised my eyes and spoke into the darkness, hot tears pouring down my cheeks. "Hades, do not take him from me, I beg of you. I need him. Mumma, if you can hear me, please, speak on my behalf. I ... I want Demetri in my future. Please, help me. Help him ... her." I squeezed Demetri's himation between my hands, shivering as snow continued to fall from above, settling on my head and shoulders.

"Do not leave me, Demetri. Please. Fight to stay in this world with me. I care about you in a way I have for no one before. I should have told you. I am sorry I did not stop you from coming with me to this place. I should have tied you to that tree at the base of the mountain, or woken the herders to keep you from following me. Please, fight. There is something between us, you know that. I do not know if I love you but maybe ... maybe one day I could feel that way. I want the chance to find out." I laid my head on his chest and sobbed into the soft material above his cold body.

*   *   *

It was not until sometime later when my cries subsided, that I realized two very important things. One; I could feel the gentle rise and fall of Demetri's chest and two; I could hear his heart beating beneath my ear.

I wiped my eyes with the back of my hand and placed my palm on Demetri's stomach. It rose and fell with each shallow breath he took. I closed my eyes and sent up a prayer of thanks to Asclepius, Hades and

Mumma. The torch spluttered beside me and I rescued it from the water, its head immediately brightening. I blew out a deep breath. He was alive. The gods had heard my prayers, and granted them. Now I just had to figure out how to get us out of wherever we were.

I stood gingerly, almost collapsing again when a shooting pain gripped my right knee. I rubbed at it as I limped around. "I do not believe it," I murmured, my torch lighting up a formation of stone steps. They were the ones Demetri and I had come down after he had been bitten by the spider. I raised the torch higher. The bottom two steps were visible, but the rest were covered by rocks.

I found the notch in the stone wall for the torch where Demetri had sat and tried to free the ones at the bottom. They would not move – wedged in solidly – and I had to presume they went all the way back up to the top.

I stood with my hands on my hips, looking from the concealed steps to the cave around me. The whole area was about a third of the size it had been, filled now by clumps of large stones, small shrubs and a steady stream of water.

I took the torch and spun around, twisting my knee again in the process and sucking in a loud breath as I waited for the pain to subside. I followed the flowing water back to the small tunnel I had taken to the vertical cave. The tunnel itself was blocked by boulders, but the water had found a way between them and poured into the larger area I stood in.

I returned to Demetri and put my hand on his stomach again. He was still breathing in the same shallow way that reminded me of Philo's breathing on the Plain. I refused to let the memory engulf me and stood abruptly, propping the torch against a large boulder and dragging Demetri by the arms to a pile of rocks. The water was lower there, three rocks sitting out of it. I got him on top of them and even though his head flopped forward onto his chest, the rest of him remained stable against the wall.

I took the second torch from his bag and stowed it in mine, looping it over my shoulder and approaching the side of the mountain. I held the torch higher, searching for a way out. There looked to be a break in the wall several feet up, but I would have to climb up to be sure. The rocks on the ground beside me were round and too unstable to stack up to use as steps, but I noticed ridges and niches in the wall itself. I put my fingers in a few of them and found they were deep enough for me to get a decent grip.

Again I lifted the torch, mapping out a path upwards, niche by niche, ridge by ridge. There seemed to be a negotiable track and if I could make it to the top I could find out how far we had fallen. After that, I would need to find a way to get Demetri out if he did not wake up.

I checked on him again and set small rocks in a circle on one of the large boulders, propping the torch inside and pleased to find it provided enough light for me to also find my way up the wall.

I raised my right arm, nestling my fingers in the first niche. I pulled myself up, placing my left foot on the first ridge. It was a solid base but I braced myself, knowing what would happen when I lifted my left arm to the second niche. Drawing a breath, I reached up, pain immediately lancing through my shoulder as I pulled upwards and placed my foot on the second ridge. I exhaled loudly and continued up, trying to block out the pain by focusing solely on my task. As I placed my fingers onto another small ridge, something scuttled over my finger. I quickly drew my hand away, but the movement was enough to put me off balance and my feet slipped from their holds. I dropped the short distance to the ground, freezing water splashing up my legs and agony shooting into my twisted knee as I landed.

"Ow, ow, ow," I yelled, grabbing at my leg. "By the gods that hurts," I groaned. I leant against the side of the mountain again as I waited for the pain and the beating of my heart to lessen. "Damn spiders," I muttered.

As my breathing returned to normal, a dull light started to illuminate the cave, my chest warming at the same rate as the brightness. With a frown I took the amulet from beneath my cuirass, its heat immediately spreading through my fingers and up my arm. The shooting pains in my knee and shoulder dulled to a low throb. *Can I control when or how the amulet's power appears?* I wondered. The thought had barely occurred to me when the amulet dulled again. My frown deepened but I returned it to my tunic.

I took another breath and hauled myself back up the rock face. Without the discomfort in my shoulder, I was able to quickly climb the twenty or so 'steps' to the break I had noticed in the rocks, and I did so without meeting any more small creatures. I dragged myself up over the edge, breathing hard as I lay on the snowy ground. After a few moments I pushed myself to my feet and drew the torch and flint from my bag.

As far up as I could see, the side of the mountain had fallen in on itself and rocks and a few trees lay strewn around. I turned in a circle, taking in the density and types that still stood nearby. There was a cluster of conifers, similar to the ones we had slept beneath the night before we started our climb. I made my way over to them and realized that the path was not as steep as it had been before the ground collapsed beneath us. That could only mean one thing; we were at the bottom of the mountain, and those *were* the trees we had slept beneath that first night.

"Thank the gods," I murmured.

The first of Eos' rays painted the sky and I knew I had to find a way to get Demetri out of the mountain. There was no way I could carry him up the way I had just come, but if I did not find a solution quickly, the water filling the mountain would drown him. Spurred on by that thought alone, an idea started to form.

I shed my bag, taking the rope from it and working quickly to secure it around the nearest fir tree. I dropped it back through the hole and crossed to the conifers. The branches hung low, heavy with the weight of the snow they held and several had snapped from the trunk. I knelt down on my good knee and pulled one of the larger branches free of the others. The green foliage was soft and thick, the wood unbending and strong – it would be perfect to construct a litter, I just needed something to secure it with.

I lowered myself backwards over the edge of the hole into the mountain, stepping my way down the wall and back to Demetri and his bag. I had seen a rope coiled in there when I took the torch and I was glad he had thought to bring it.

The stream coming through the rocks at the far side of the cave was now gushing, and the water level had risen much quicker than I had expected. It reached my thighs as I splashed across to Demetri, my breath hard to catch in the cold. I grabbed his bag and scaled the wall again, the amulet's earlier relief starting to wear off as I pulled myself up the hanging rope. A few pebbles fell from above, shaken loose from the edge with the movement of the rope, but they were tiny and did not hurt me.

I shed my himation and laid the rope from Demetri's bag on the ground, gathering branches and shaking the snow from them as I lay each in place, putting smaller ones on top before tying them all together. I intended to pull Demetri along behind me and, with the mountainous areas we would have to traverse, the litter would need to be reasonably thick to protect his fragile body so I added two layers of soft bark from the nearby juniper trees as well, carefully checking the bark for spiders or webs – the last thing I needed was for Demetri to get bitten again, or me.

When I was done and every part was tied in place, I had about five cubits of rope left to pull it by, which would be more than enough. I tested its weight, pleased to find that it slid easily over the snow. With Demetri on top it would, of course, be much heavier, but it would do nicely. I pulled my rope back up out of the mountain, alarmed to find the end of it wet. I peered down, noting that the torch no longer shone beside Demetri, the water lapping at his waist. I quickly tied the ends of the ropes together and lowered the litter into the mountain, following it down as soon as it rippled the surface below.

I waded across to Demetri, towing the litter behind me. I pinned it against the wall with my hip as I awkwardly pulled Demetri into the water, turning him over and sliding the litter beneath him as I did so. The water level was rising quickly around us and by the time I got Demetri beneath the hole in the mountain, I was treading water. I found a boulder to stand on and hoisted myself up, using the niches in the wall to return to the surface. I stood at the edge and gripped the rope tightly in both hands, taking a moment to brace my right foot ahead of the left.

I counted silently then pulled with everything I had. Intense pain tore through my shoulder, reverberating through my entire arm. I dropped the rope, falling backwards as I grabbed at my flesh. When I took my hand away it was stained red, as was the cloth, the blood seeping through and trickling down my arm. I waited for the comforting, familiar warmth of the amulet to make itself known beneath my cuirass, but it remained dark and colorless. I frowned, but took a deep breath, refusing to abandon my task. Amulet or not, I had to get Demetri out of the icy water. My shoulder would heal.

I stood and returned to the rope, taking it between my palms and preparing myself. I pulled as hard as I could, trying to compensate with my right for the weakness on my left, but it was no use. The only movement came from the small stones at the edge of the hole. They fell into the mountain, no doubt showering Demetri and the water below.

As I dropped the rope and tried to come up with another solution, the edge where I stood started to tremble and shift, the small stones that had been falling gave way to larger ones and suddenly it collapsed altogether, dropping me back into the icy water below.

25

The cold robbed me of my breath when I hit the water. The shock of it, along with the inability to use my left arm properly, hindered my progress back to the surface and I struggled for long moments before I came up coughing tiny pebbles and water. I groped about for the litter, holding tight when I found it.

I drew in deep breaths and surveyed Demetri's face and head. There was no blood or bruises to suggest that any of the rocks had hit him on the way down. Even so, I put my hand on his stomach. The slow rise and fall was still there and I closed my eyes, thanking Asclepius again.

Numbness had taken over my body from the tips of my toes to just under my armpits, my chest expanding in exertion even as my teeth chattered. The rate the water was rising, there was a chance we would be spat out onto the path above within half a candlemark. I could just wait but with the temperature of the water, I quickly dismissed the option. I would not survive more than another few minutes in the cold; the parts of my body that were not already numb, burnt with the pain of their impending fate.

As if sensing my fear of what was to come, a warmth started at my chest. At first, I thought one of Helios' rays had heightened enough in the sky to stream down onto me, but then my shoulder blades started to itch and the curious bright orange glowed out from the amulet.

I shivered as Mother Alexis appeared in front of me, bobbing with the rising water at Demetri's head. She smoothed the hair from his forehead.

"You shall freeze to death if you stay here," she said, meeting my eyes. "Use the amulet to save yourself."

"Only if it saves Demetri too," I told her. "Mumma wanted me to use the amulet *against* him. But I will not risk his life ... her life just to have mine. It has to save us both."

Mother reached out, her fingers wisping across my cheek in a tender gesture. "My sweet girl. As you have grown I see your loyalty and kindness for those you care for has not diminished. You have my word that no harm shall come to Demetri if you use the amulet here." She smiled as she spoke and the pain and injustice of her loss hit me again with such fierceness that I found it hard to swallow around the lump in my throat. This was my *mother*. She had tended every scrape and cut, every fever and cough I had suffered with tenderness and care until the day she died. She would not lie to me.

I nodded as my shoulders prickled. I struggled and freed myself of my chlamys and cuirass, laying both on top of Demetri in case my wings emerged again. I drew the pouch from between my breasts, sliding the amulet out. It warmed my fingers and arm, but it was not nearly as hot as it had been on the Plain. "Can I fly us out of here with my wings?"

"Perhaps," Mother replied. "We shall have to wait and see."

I held the amulet out in front of me as the pain at my shoulder blades started. It was not as intense as the first time, similar to needles pricking at my flesh rather than the stabbing of swords. I turned to watch the long black poles lengthen and change into wings behind me as a bird cried out overhead.

A settling calm flooded my veins. I could do this. I *would* do this. I could save us from the freezing water, from the collapsing mountain. I would get Demetri the help he needed. He would survive, we both would. We would continue on and live our lives as the Moirai had intended – the distress of these past few days a mere memory; inconsequential happenings on my journey towards greatness.

I smiled at my mother as the amulet glowed brighter and changed color. The glowing orange gave way to yellow, the yellow to green and the green to blue, at first pale, then a much darker shade.

The power built. My blood filled with heat that snaked from arm to chest to stomach to leg. With one hand gripping tightly to the litter, and the other around the amulet, I kept my eyes on my mother. *Take us from the mountain*, I silently demanded of the amulet. Almost immediately a slither of blue burst from the amulet, hitting the water beside us. The dark liquid dropped, yet we did not sink with it, rising instead.

"Good girl," Mother said, smiling and tapping my cheek. She disappeared again, making me shudder.

The water swirled below us, just as Charybdis did when she created her whirlpool in the Strait of Messina. Solid, yet pliable it rose up, pushing Demetri and I towards the opening of the mountain. My head and shoulders topped the edge and I pushed the litter over the side, grabbing a small shrub and pulling myself out after it. I turned back to the mountain, expecting to find the water spilling out behind us, but it had withdrawn and when I looked down into the cave, I saw it was no longer a cylindrical stairway, but simply a wide mass of coldness half-filling the cavity.

The amulet's power continued to course through me and I stood, my big, black wings spread out behind me as I took in the snow-covered path and trees. I had done it. I had saved us. I *was* invincible. I could command fire. I could command water. I had power like the gods. The knowledge was undeniable.

I was ready to take Demetri to help. The amulet could do no more for him, it had got us out of the mountain, but the rest was up to me. I brought the gem to my lips in thanks. It was still glowing dully but I returned it to the pouch around my neck. I knew it would return to its solid black color until I needed it again. It was time we were on our way.

Fly I commanded. My wings flapped behind me but I did not leave the ground. *Well, it was worth a try,* I shrugged. I pulled Demetri from the edge of the mountain and set about separating the rope attached to the branches beneath him from the one on the tree. The ends had fused together and I could not see where to disentangle them from one another. I drew my sword, choosing a place just above where the two ropes met. Raising my weapon above my head – my shoulder not painful in the least when I did so – I started hacking the thick cord in front of me.

My movements were fast, frenzied almost, and I had very little control of my swings. Several times I missed the rope completely, my sword smashing into the ground or the rocks that stood nearby. But I did not care, I was alive. I had a gift, something that would only enhance my impressive fighting skills. With the amulet I would not be stopped. I would be able to do anything I desired. It was an intoxicating thought.

My actions continued until I was too exhausted to go on and the power that had engulfed me suddenly dissipated. My wings retracted beneath my skin and the pain in my shoulder returned with an intense fierceness. I stumbled to the ground with the force of it. My eyes fell to the rope. My sword had barely even chopped halfway through.

"How can that be?" I murmured. Setting aside my sword, I crawled to retrieve my himation, pulling it around my shoulders as I huddled close to Demetri's body, shivering violently as exhaustion overcame me.

As I fluttered on the edge of sleep, a shadowy figure appeared beside us, placing a hand on Demetri's head. He gasped. I tried to sit up again, but the large hand stilled me and I fell into a dreamless sleep.

*　　*　　*

When I woke, the sun was well past the highest point in the sky and my clothing was dry. Water had banked the side of the mountain and streamed past my head, thankfully forging a path beside rather than over me. I had no doubt it would still be icy and I had no wish to feel it again so soon.

I pushed myself to a sitting position, my shoulder continuing its dull ache and my legs stiff. The memory of the shadowy figure I had seen earlier returned and my brow furrowed. *Had there really been someone else with us or had I already entered Morpheus' realm and dreamt it?* Demetri's eyes were still closed, his face pale. I put my hand to his cheek, noting how cold it was. I closed my eyes, hesitantly reaching out to touch his stomach. I was rewarded with his shallow breaths and I blew out my own, opening my eyes again.

I tentatively got to my feet, re-sheathing my sword and hobbling back and forth to stimulate the blood flow. My knee was swollen and bruised and I had to hold it out straight as I turned. For all my wild slashing earlier, the two ropes were still joined and, while I could just untie mine from the fir tree and use it to pull Demetri along, there was a chance that they would separate at an inopportune time as we travelled. I was not prepared to take that chance.

I pulled Demetri down the path away from Mount Smolikos until both the cords were taut and up off the ground. I took a torch and some flint from my bag. When flames danced from the head, I held it beneath the fraying binding and burnt it the rest of the way through. The severed ends dropped to the ground and I let the cold snow extinguish the flames as I did the same with the torch.

I crossed to the large fir tree and collected my rope, coiling it and placing it in my bag before putting both our bags on Demetri's legs. The memory of my actions with the amulet flared in my mind. It was not like the first time I had used it. The amulet had not helped me to kill, but to survive. Maybe it was due to the hematite Demetri spoke of – he had said it was a protective element. But how did it know? Could it feel what I needed or was it just because I had addressed it silently? Again I had questions with no answers. Yet. I needed to find Papou, then maybe I would get them. *If* I found him. I did not know where I should even look now.

My eyes fell to Demetri's face and I pushed the thoughts aside. I had another important task to attend first. I brought to mind the large map Moeris kept in the tent back at the Pass of Coela. It showed every mountain, town, village and settlement in each direction from Trachis to deep into Macedonia. I knew that the closest two settlements to Mount Smolikos were Konitsa and Tymphae, both south-west, though not along the same path. Cold fingers slipped down my back as I acknowledged it; Konitsa was home to the bloodthirsty Molossians, a small tribe of warriors even more fierce than the Tymphaioi Demetri had wanted to find in Tymphae.

*

"You see how quickly she recovered again?" Ares asked, his tone full of excitement. "I can feel the strength of her power flowing through me. It shall not be long now. I shall have to test her once more to be absolutely certain, but we are so close."

"She appears to be the one," Aphrodite nodded.

"Finally," Ares murmured.

"She needs to heal though. Her shield arm shall be useless in the coming war if she does not take care of it soon," Aphrodite mused. "It does not appear she intends to use the amulet to do so."

"No, she is stubborn that way, just as her mother was," Ares grinned. "If she is determined to heal as a mortal then I shall allow it. But once she has recovered, I am going to appear to her. Her third test shall be under my instruction. For now, I shall send her towards fierceness for her healing to begin."

*

I shivered again. I had no choice; Konitsa or Tymphae was where I would find a healer and Demetri needed someone as soon as I could find them. I just had to hope that the cold weather would keep the Molossian war hounds close to home with the men, rather than roaming the mountains searching for unwitting prey.

The pouch holding Mumma's amulet dangled around my neck and I knew it would be unwise to enter either tribe's area with it there if I wanted to keep it. I took my bag and emptied the contents carefully onto the ground beside me. With the tip of my sword, I sliced through three stitches at the bottom, opening the hole and slipping the pouch inside. I drew the stitching together again and pushed one of Alecia's hairpins through each side of the material to keep it shut.

I returned everything and placed it back on the litter, taking my cuirass from Demetri's chest. I removed my himation and pulled the bonded material over my head, crying out as it dragged over the arrow wound. The material covering it was once again sodden with blood and I knew that when I got myself a new aspis, I would need my left arm to be strong and healthy to wield it. If I left it as it was, it would make me sick – it needed to be kept clean and dry. I took the cloth from the hole and threw it aside. I retrieved Demetri's spare chiton from his bag and cut three wide strips from it.

"Sorry," I murmured. Gritting my teeth, I raised my injured arm to hold the end of the first piece of material across the gaping hole. I wound it around my arm and back, tucking the end beneath the layers and pulling as tight as I could. I hoped it would stay in place until I reached a healer.

I returned what was left of Demetri's chiton to his bag and put my chlamys and himation back on. I wrapped the other two lengths of material around my hands and tucked the ends beneath the layers just as I had with my shoulder. I flexed my fingers, glad to find they did not hinder my movement too much. I did not know exactly how long my journey would be, but if I did not protect my palms from the rope, I would be unable to drag Demetri with me, or protect us against anyone who tried to harm us as we travelled.

I re-sheathed my sword and got to my feet on trembling legs. I turned so Demetri's head was facing the path leading down Mount Smolikos rather than up it and looped the cord over my right shoulder. With a deep breath, I took my first steps towards Konitsa and Tymphae, the litter sliding smoothly across the snow behind me.

26

I trekked through the pouring rain, head bent against the fierceness of the weather, eyes forced shut against its onslaught, unable to focus on the slick ground beneath my feet. I had left Mount Smolikos a day ... maybe two days ago, I could no longer remember. The constant rain and thunderstorms had followed me almost the entire distance. I hoped I was still headed in the direction of Konitsa or Tymphae. It should not be taking me so long to reach one of them.

Rivulets of water flowed in a steady stream down my forehead, in and around my eyes and off the tip of my nose and chin. Some snuck beneath my tunic to saturate the skin beneath, while others flowed down the outside of my mud-spattered himation, adding to the slickness of the ground I fought hard not to slip on.

Every step reverberated through my twisted knee and the arrow wound in my shoulder. In the dark of the last night I had tried to rest my right arm and use my injured left to pull the litter behind me. That had been a mistake and now my arm hung uselessly by my side, the stream of blood the experiment had caused long gone, along with the length of Demetri's chiton I had had there.

I could no longer feel the fingers on my right hand or, thankfully, the rawness of my palms scraping against the rope as I walked. That material had also been lost long ago and the open wounds drank in the water from the skies, cleaning themselves.

Demetri's continued silence tormented me, but I could not bring myself to stop and check on him. I did not know if I could start again if I stopped, but more than that, I was afraid he was dead and I did not want to face that truth. I prayed to Asclepius to keep watch and heal him if what I most feared had not yet happened.

As lightening lit the sky and fields around me, I looked up. *Was that...?* I blinked, uncertain if I had really just seen what I thought I had. Thunder rumbled loudly overhead and another sharp crack showed me the same scene: sheep, a herd of them, and just past them, several small lights in the windows of three houses side by side. I willed myself on.

The sheep started to bleat, stepping aside to make a path through their number for me to pass. As I entered the flock, the fierce sound of barking hounds reached my ears and I shuddered involuntarily, sending another wave of pain through my body. I tried to move closer to the sheep for protection, but they backed away, their cries loud and more frequent.

The hounds made their own way through the flock, barking and growling. I did not want to incite their anger any more than I already had so I stopped where I was, hoping they would appreciate my caution and not attack me, or Demetri. They continued to close in and the lightning showed them in all their ferocity. Their hair stood on end despite the pouring rain, droplets caught at the tips. Sharp teeth with spit (or maybe it was just rain water?) dripped from their lips as they snarled. They paced through the sheep with their large paws and sharp claws, watching me as I watched them from lowered eyes. I did not know what to say to calm them; I had never been so close to a hound, and never close enough to one I knew would rip my throat out if I made the wrong move.

In another flash of light, I saw them stop, their growls quieting as they focused on something behind me. I had no time to turn and see what it was before the cold blade of a knife pressed against my throat.

"What are you doing here?" a voice rumbled.

My legs would no longer hold me up and I collapsed painfully to my knees, dropping the rope and landing on my right side in the mud. Several pairs of feet surrounded me and loud, harsh voices yelled, but I could not make out anything they said until someone slid thick arms beneath my knees and around my back and scooped me up.

"We shall take them to Theron and Irina's, they can tend their wounds, then we can question them," he said to the others.

"Please, help my friend first," I rasped, my voice barely loud enough over the thunder and rain. The man who held me only grunted and with carefully placed steps, carried me out of the deluge and into a warm room. He deposited me on a rug in front of a large fire, Demetri placed next to me, both of us relieved of our himatia. I closed my eyes, starting to shiver again. Their footsteps faded away, the house quiet except for the crackling of the fire.

Soon enough a lighter set of steps approached. I opened my eyes again as a big man with broad shoulders and thick thighs looked Demetri over, catching my eye when he spoke.

"Your friend has no blood and no obvious wounds, yet he is not dead. Does he simply slumber?" he asked in a gravelly voice. I shook my head. "I did not think so – my men attempted to wake him, but he did not rouse. What happened?"

I cleared my throat to speak. "He was bitten by a spider, on his right arm."

He lifted Demetri's arm and inspected it. "What sort of spider?" He spoke with an accent that was vaguely familiar, but I could not place it.

"I do not know, but I brought it with me. It is in the pyxis in my bag. I believe it is dead." The man nodded and retrieved the items, shaking the spider out onto the floor. He pushed at it with his finger before taking a long, skinny instrument from the nearby table and holding its legs out from its body as he stared. He made a few noises in his throat and then checked Demetri again.

"Irina, is that bath ready yet?" he called suddenly, making me jump.

"It is," a woman replied, entering the room. She crossed to me and tried to free the fibulae that held my chlamys at my shoulder.

"I do not need a bath. I just need to stay near the fire to get warm," I said.

"You are soaked to the skin and shall catch a death of cold if you do not get warmed up soon. A bath is the quickest way to do that," she soothed, cupping my face gently in her hands and looking me over.

"You need those injuries attended to as well," the man added. "Irina shall take care of you while I attend your friend. When was he bitten?"

"A … a few days ago, I am not sure how many," I replied, frustrated I could not provide him with the exact information. "Please … do not remove his chiton, only his outer clothing. That is all you need to do to get to his wound." He considered me a long moment, his eyes sliding to Irina briefly, before he nodded.

"Has he been this way the entire time?" he asked.

"No, he started vomiting soon after he was bitten. He was also sweating profusely and got very tired."

"When you attempted to rouse him, you could not get a response?"

"No, we fell when I was trying to find him help."

"Fell? From what?"

"Mount Smolikos. Part of the side collapsed," I explained. "After that, he did not wake again."

"I see. Well, the spider is a black widow and he has had the venom inside him for a long time, not to mention any other injuries he may have sustained in the fall. I shall do what I can for him."

"Thank you," I replied.

"Come now, I shall assist you with your bath," Irina said, taking my arm and helping me to my feet. I let her peel my saturated chlamys from my body and guide me to a small room towards the back of the dwelling, realizing that she stood almost two feet taller than me.

"I appreciate your concern but I can bathe myself," I insisted.

"I have no doubt you are more than capable, but your travel appears to have been long and arduous and it is not a weakness to seek help at the end of such journeys."

"I ... I do not wish to seem ungrateful but my body is no–" Irina put a finger over my lips.

"As a healer I have seen much. You need not be afraid I would discuss anything with anyone. Theron too shall respect your request about your friend unless it becomes necessary in his treatment. We wish only to see you both well again."

I drew in a deep breath and studied her face. She seemed like she was telling the truth but after so many winters of hiding the nodes on my back, suddenly there would be two people who knew of my secret shame. It did not sit well with me, but right now I was too exhausted to put up any more of a fight. I gave her a nod and let her undress me.

With practiced efficiency, Irina took my cuirass and tunic from me, making sure the material of neither item touched my shoulder, or the many cuts and bruises she found across my cold, wet skin. She helped me into the clay bath that stood against the far wall, its design almost identical to the one in Tricca with deep sides and a length great enough for someone to sit inside with their legs stretched out. I settled into the warm water, finding the only comfortable position for my battered knee to be drawn half way to my chest and rested against the side.

I gasped when I immersed my right hand in the water and pain shot through it. I drew it from the bath again, frowning. The hand I had been unable to feel for so long as I walked was red raw, layers of skin torn away in jagged lines – and not just on the palm, my fingers were the same. The pink of the skin exposed was so bright and looked soft, but I was not about to touch it to confirm. I tried bending my fingers, but the movement sent another agonizing stab up my arm.

Irina took my wrist gently. "It served you well on your journey and I shall heal it too. When did you get this?" she added, pointing to my shoulder as she dipped a cloth into the water and drew it down my other arm.

"Many days ago," I replied.

"It appears it is from an arrowhead." I nodded weakly in reply. "Did you have it cauterized to stem the bleeding?"

"No, but herbs were applied to it within a few candlemarks."

"It appears you have reopened it ... several times perhaps. It is not healing well. What herbs did you use?"

"I do not know; they were prepared for me by someone else."

"A healer?" I shook my head. "You understand that after I clean it, I shall have to cauterize it?" A knot formed in my stomach as I looked down at the wound. A trickle of blood leaked out and I knew she was right. Even with everything that had happened the day on the Plain, I still should have had Andronikos or Agapios seal it for me – or done it myself when I stopped by the Peneus River. I knew better than to leave a wound open.

"I understand," I replied.

Irina took a large jug, pouring water down each of my arms, spending extra time around the wound as I shut my eyes against the stinging. My chest, stomach and legs received her gentle treatment, before she put a deliberate hand on my uninjured shoulder and pushed me forward. I resisted for the slightest moment before drawing a breath and exposing my back to her.

She did not draw in a breath or cry out, simply dipping the material back in the water and cleaning my back as she had the rest of me. When she was finished with the cloth, she set it aside and took the jug again, holding it high above me. I closed my eyes as water cascaded over my head and down my body, caressing me with its warmth. For the first time in days all my aches and pains melted away. I wondered if it was the faint scent of flowers the water gave off as it splashed around me that caused the change.

Irina touched my shoulder. "It is time to get dressed, then I shall take care of that shoulder and your hands." I opened my eyes and let her help me from the bath. She dried my body with care and covered me in a warm, dry tunic. "Come," she encouraged. She led me back to the main room and sat me by the fire, the room now devoid of anyone else.

"Where is my friend?"

"He is resting," Theron said, entering the main room again. "I have done what I can; the rest is up to him. You can join him when Irina is finished with you."

Irina sat me in a chair to wait while the two of them worked at a small table preparing the medicines for me. I lay my head against the back, staring into the crackling fire and letting it warm and lull me towards sleep while blocking out thought of what was coming.

All too soon, Irina returned to my side. She placed a length of iron among the flames and pulled a second chair close as Theron handed her a small bowl. "Yarrow shall help heal the cuts," she said, taking my hand. She spread the mixture over the damaged area and I sucked in a breath, my mind rudely drawn from its contented dozing. Irina was gentle, but no touch could be gentle enough against such ravaged skin. "When was the last time you ate?" she asked.

Had I eaten at Mount Smolikos? I definitely had not since. "I do not know," I replied, shaking my head.

"Then I shall fetch you some broth when I have finished here." I nodded, instantly famished at the mention of food.

When Irina was satisfied every part had been attended to, she bound my hand in soft linen, tying the ends together and effectively preventing me from forgetting I could not use it. She passed the bowl back to Theron, who stood silently beside us, and he handed her something in return.

"You shall need this," Irina said, holding up the object.

It was a thick, round piece of wood. I inhaled deeply, knowing what it was to be used for and immediately losing my appetite. I opened my jaw and Irina placed it between my teeth. I bit down, watching as she took the iron from the fire with thick cloth. The end glowed brilliant red, dulling as it cooled. Theron stood behind me, placing his large hands on my upper arms and pinning me in place. As Irina neared, the heat radiated from the end of the iron. I drew another breath and held it.

"Ready?" Irina asked. I nodded and closed my eyes. My body tensed, my senses on high alert. Theron's hands tightened and Irina drove the iron into my skin. I bit down hard on the wood, screaming around it. My body bucked against Theron's strong grip as the blinding pain shot through me. I fought hard not to pass out but it was too much. My body shut down.

27

I woke in an unfamiliar room, my shoulder barely aching. For a moment I could not remember where I was, or how I had gotten there. The course fibers of an animal skin scratched against my bare limbs when I moved and the memories returned. I swung my feet over the side of the bed, pleased to find that for the most part, my body did not hurt and my arms and legs obeyed my wishes to move.

With my covered hand, I struggled to pull away the material of my tunic to inspect my shoulder and when I did, I found it tightly bound, just as my hand was. It would have to wait. I wondered how long I had slept, the sun lit the horizon outside the small window of the room, but as I had no idea where in the house I was, I did not know if it was dawn or dusk light I saw.

My bag hung over a chair on the opposite side of the room and I hobbled towards my few possessions. My twisted knee was still painful, but the utter exhaustion I had felt had disappeared. I was eager to find out how Demetri was, but I needed to know the amulet was where I had left it. I pushed my hand to the bottom, my fingers finding the hairpin. I released it and drew the pouch out, checking the contents and relieved to find the amulet still inside. I returned it to its place and left my bag on the chair, noting my sword was not with the rest of my things.

I crossed to the doorway and entered the main room, stopped by a cold blade at my throat.

"Put that away. She is our guest," Irina scolded.

The weapon remained where it was. I looked into the face of the man who held the knife. He had deep blue eyes and grey, shaggy hair that reached his shoulders. His long, light colored beard was laced with strands the same color as his hair and he was taller than me by at least a foot-and-a-half. The forearm closest to me was wide and bare, except for the lone strand of leather crisscrossing upwards from his wrist to his shoulder to attach the battered leather and linen over his chest.

"Ava!" a voice I recognized cried.

I turned to see Demetri stand so suddenly that the chair he had been sitting on fell backwards.

"Demetri!" I smiled, pushing away the blade and rushing to him.

"Ava?" someone echoed.

I put my arms around Demetri's waist and pressed my head against his chest. Against her chest. He held me tightly for a moment before pulling away and taking my face in his hands, kissing me fervently. For a moment I was too surprised to return it, but as he pulled me closer, I closed my eyes and reveled in the sensations it drew. He was alive, he was here, with me. We had both survived and we would be together, wherever our journey took us, just as I had prayed we would.

Demetri broke our kiss and looked me over intently as I did the same. The color in his cheeks had returned and the deep purple marks under his eyes had all but disappeared. He looked completely well again.

"I was afraid you weren't going to wake up," he said.

"I thought the same about you." Rough hands pulled me from Demetri's embrace and spun me around. The man who had held the knife to my throat pulled the bottom of my tunic up, revealing my left thigh. He put his hand over the scar there. "What are you doing?" I yelled, slapping his hand away and taking a step back.

The man dropped his knife, his knees following – and finding – the floor beside his weapon. "Ava," he whispered. "By the gods."

"Leandros, what are you doing?" Theron asked, approaching the three of us.

My mouth dropped open at his words and I stared down at the man before me. "Papou?" I asked. He lifted his eyes to mine and we stared, unbelieving, at each other.

"I did not think I would ever see you again," he finally murmured.

"Who is this?" Theron asked.

Papou took a deep breath and gathered his dagger as he returned to his feet. "This is my granddaughter; Ava."

"You said you had no family left. So who is she really? Is she the reason you have stayed longer with us than usual?" another voice asked. I turned, finding a man towering Theron.

"Silence, Origenes," Theron said, holding his hand up. Origenes' face was a mass of scars that continued beneath his clothing and across his closely shaven head. His arms were twice as wide as Papou's and his legs resembled the trunks of trees. He folded his arms across his chest, staring viciously at me, but said nothing further.

"We seek Ava's grandfather for his blessing, we intend to wed," Demetri offered. My head spun in his direction as my eyebrows shot up. The words were unexpected, though it would explain the kiss.

Theron placed a hand on Papou's shoulder. "It appears there is much to discuss this evening. We shall leave the three of you to your words. Come, Origenes. I am certain you have hounds to feed and men to command," he said, turning to the giant behind him.

"You cannot trust these two … strangers in your home, the three of them could have planned to meet here."

"I see no evidence of that, Origenes," Theron replied. "So far the two young ones have been no trouble, and Leandros has never given us reason to doubt *his* loyalty."

"No good has ever come of his presence here," Origenes murmured, a flash of pain crossing his face, quickly replaced by a deep scowl. "Besides they are awake now, and recovered, that could change. They could slit mother's throat, or yours, and be far from here before we even know you are dead …"

"We are perfectly safe. Trust me," Irina interrupted, staring hard at Origenes. The deep lines sunk even further into Origenes' forehead as he matched her gaze.

"I shall see you out," Theron said in a voice that left no room for negotiation.

Origenes followed Theron to the door. "I shall be out here all night. No one leaves without my knowledge."

"We are grateful for your vigilance," Theron said. He opened the door, letting a cool gust of wind and a large, black war hound in, Origenes making his way out into the night.

"I too shall take my leave and return in a while," Theron added, nodding to Irina, then the three of us, before closing the door.

I tensed at the hound's bounding approach. He made a beeline for Demetri, licking at his hands and putting his large paws against Demetri's stomach as he tried to reach his face.

"Down boy, down," Demetri laughed; a sound I was not sure I had actually heard before. The hound obeyed, sitting by his feet as Irina took three chairs to the fire.

"I shall prepare something to eat for you."

"Thank you, Irina," Papou said, Demetri and I echoing his words.

Papou limped towards the fire, taking the chair closest to it. I watched him, thinking how much he had changed in ten winters. I sat beside him, unsure what to say now that we were finally together, as Demetri seated himself in the other empty chair.

"You have grown much," Papou said, staring intently at my face.

"And you are an old man now," I replied with a grin. Laughter burst from Papou's chest and the apprehension that had settled in my stomach lifted. He reached his arms out, clasping my face between his hands.

"My darling Ava, you have your Mumma's dry wit and Alexis' beauty." He kissed my cheek, the wispy hairs of his beard tickling my face. I smiled as I caught the slightest hint of beeswax on his hands.

"I was told you had gone to Mount Smolikos, but instead you are here ... where is here exactly?" I asked.

"Konitsa," he replied. I nodded, glad that even in my weakened state I had found one of the small settlements I had intended.

"You do not seem to be being held against your will. You are here intentionally?"

"I am."

"Casaereo said you were headed for Mount Smolikos, but we went there – it did not look like you had been there."

"You met Casaereo? Where?"

"At the Thessalian-Macedonian border."

"He was well?"

"He was," I nodded. "Did you go to the mountain?" I pressed.

"No, I have been here since I left them last winter."

"Why did you tell them otherwise?"

"I did not want them looking for me when I did not return to them as I always had. They are not young men anymore, they do not attempt such heights."

"Why? What is here in Konitsa that sees it so?" Papou did not answer immediately, his eyes darting between Demetri and me, settling on Demetri when he spoke again.

"So, you have travelled here to seek my blessing?" he asked, a wary smile lighting his face.

"Papou, why did you come to Konitsa?" I continued.

Demetri put his hand over mine and squeezed gently. "That is not exactly our true intent," he answered.

"No?" Papou asked, his eyes settling on mine again.

I exhaled loudly, but accepted the change of direction in conversation. For now at least. "We met at Lake Xynias half a moon ago," I told him.

"Your ... er ... reunion did not speak of such a recent meeting."

"Though our time together has been short so far, we've been through a lot," Demetri replied.

"Oh?" Papou asked.

I met Demetri's stare and offered explanation. "Victory over old foes."

"Loss," Demetri added.

"Collapsing mountains."

"New found abilities and the sharing of long-held secrets."

"I see. So, where were you both headed?"

Demetri waited for me to answer first. When I did not, he said, "I sought the Tymphaioi, though my direction had me travelling the wrong way. It was Ava who told me it was so."

"Why do you seek the Tymphaioi?"

"They wear certain armor that I want to learn about. It's made up of small iron squares and I believe it would be almost impossible to penetrate during a battle."

Papou considered his next words. "The armor you seek shall not be found with the Tymphaioi," he finally said. "Wait here." He stood and crossed to the door of the house, calling to someone and carrying on a quiet discussion when they arrived. He returned, carrying a covered object in his arms and laid it on the table, a tinkling, metallic sound filling the room. He pulled the material aside, revealing a solid chest piece with hundreds of small bronze plates held together with lengths of leather.

Demetri jumped from his chair, joining Papou at the table as I followed, my hand cold where he had removed his. "This is it. This is what I've been searching for." He reached out, running his fingers over the bronze. "May I?" he asked, pointing to the cuirass.

"Please," Papou nodded. Demetri picked it up and turned it over to reveal the same pattern at the back. Each piece of bronze was square in shape with a rounded bottom, roughly the length of Demetri's middle finger high by half that wide.

"Where did you get this? Did you spend time with the Tymphaioi?" he asked.

Papou shook his head. "No. This is from the tribe of the Dassaretae or Dexaroi, not the warriors you speak of."

"The Dassaretae? They are Illyrian-born, are they not?" I asked.

Papou shook his head. "No. There *is* a north Illyrian tribe named Dassaretii as well but the Dexaroi are a Greek tribe – the northern most sub-tribe of the Chaonians here in Epirus. The people of Konitsa and I have spent much time with them over the winters." He turned back to Demetri. "It is made from bronze, not iron as you suggested, and though iron would be far stronger, and heavier, I do not know how you would fashion the holes for the leather to be threaded through. When the casts for the bronze are made, the holes are created within that mold."

Demetri nodded, studying the armor before him. "It's even finer than I imagined it would be. Can you help me create one of these? I would like to have one when we take our leave."

"I am not certain the Molossians would wish for me to share such knowledge, but I shall ask," Papou said, covering the armor again. He opened the door and handed it to someone outside.

"I would appreciate that," Demetri nodded as the three of us returned to our chairs by the fire.

"And why have *you* travelled this far, my darling? Has something happened to your grandparents? Have you assumed the throne in their place and wish to rescind my banishment?"

I shook my head. "No. Agrias and Melina still walk in this world, though I have not seen them for many winters. I serve in the army and Agrias commands me from afar."

"You are of the royal line?" Demetri suddenly interrupted.

I waved him off. "In name only, I have no interest in taking over as queen when they pass on. Maybe if things had been different I might have considered it, but now …"

"Why didn't you tell me?"

I turned to him, my anger stirring. "What purpose would it have served? I have not lived the life of a princess; I have not been groomed for the position. I told you, it was better for us all to go our separate ways and never speak of such things. I am a warrior and I will never be anything else."

"I see you also have your Mumma's fire," Papou stated. I did not miss the sadness in his voice, but I would not let what he said to simply pass this time.

"And how would I know what traits I share with either of my mothers when you left without a fight? You left me there with no one to speak to me of them."

"I am certain Moeris would have if you had asked it of him. Or your grandparents, had you not fled from their home," he replied, though his tone was not unkind.

His words immediately cooled my heated blood. "How do you know that is what happened?"

He shrugged. "I may not have physically been there, but I did not completely abandon you, even if I believed it would be for the best."

"Ava," Demetri said, laying his hand over mine. "Perhaps it is best if I left the two of you to speak alone."

"No, please stay. I am sorry. Your words just caught me off guard," I said, threading my fingers through his. Now that we were reunited I did not want to lose sight of him, and he did not deserve the anger I had shown him. I drew a deep breath, blowing it out again before I spoke. "I have not seen myself as Princess of Trachis for a long time. I did not want the title and ran, as Papou said, to avoid it."

"You have a lot to discuss with your grandfather, you and I can talk afterwards. Damon and I will wait for you outside," he said, indicating the hound at his thigh.

"But Origen–"

Demetri leaned across and kissed me. "Don't worry, we'll be safe enough." I frowned but let him leave. Theron would soon return and ensure Origenes did not harm Demetri. I hoped.

28

When the door closed behind Demetri, I turned back to Papou. He stared at me for a long moment before he spoke. "I owe you an explanation. Several perhaps."

"I have many questions for you as well," I agreed. "My first is how you knew to look for the scar on my thigh."

He inhaled, blowing it out slowly before he replied. "I was there, that night in the mountains. Do you remember Nasrin?" I nodded. "After I was banished, she and I joined the fight against the Persians in Sardis."

"Casaereo told me she was killed there. I am sorry."

"She was," he confirmed.

"Sander and Kleitos never told me you were there with them."

"I asked them not to. You had suffered so much loss already, I did not want you to know of Nasrin."

"But if I had, I could have spoken to Agrias and Melina. Maybe they would have let you come back given you no longer had anyone else."

"I did not believe it was best for me to be near you. I had caused the deaths of so many I loved already. I did not want that to be your fate as well."

"What about what *I* wanted?"

"I could not allow that to influence my decision. I missed you so much, but after I lost Nasrin as well as your mothers, I thought it was best I stayed away."

I shook my head, unable to understand how he could have made such a decision. "So what were you doing in the Othrys Mountains that night then?"

"I had been with Casaereo and the herders for two winters and when Casaereo told me he had business to attend in the south at Tricca, I offered to accompany him. It was the only time I did so – given that you almost died because I was there." His eyes traced the contours of my face and I knew the memory of that night was replaying in his mind. "I had intended to sneak back to Trachis to check on you, and to find out if you had joined Moeris in the army, but I came across some of the soldiers at Othrys instead. I heard them talking and knew you and Lysistratos would be out hunting the following day. I remained nearby, I was going to approach you if the two of you got separated."

"But instead I stole away under the cover of darkness to look for *you*."

"Yes. But I have always wondered; how did you know I was there?"

"You did not keep as hidden as you thought, the scouts saw you on their way back to camp and when I questioned them about the appearance of the stranger, I knew it was you."

"You sought me alone, why?"

"Moeris would never have granted me permission to go if I had told him. And I did not want anyone else there. I thought you might leave again and it would be another four winters before I had the chance to see you again."

He dropped his eyes to the fire. "Instead it has been ten long winters."

"If you saw what happened, why did you not help me? We could have defeated the thieves together and saved the old woman."

He met my eyes again. "I should have, I know that. But I ... I wanted to see what you were capable of, how much your skills resembled Skylar's."

"You would have let me die just so you cou–"

"No, of course not. When I saw you fall, I made noise in the trees; to the thieves it would have sounded as though more soldiers approached. That is why they fled."

"I did not hear the sounds you speak of," I frowned. All I remembered was the blood pounding in my ears as my life drained from me. "When they left, why did you not show yourself? Why did you not take me back to camp?"

"I followed them for itinerary, sending them to Hades in quick succession. By the time I returned, the soldiers had found you and Moeris found me."

"Moeris?" I murmured.

Papou nodded. "He wanted to know the same as you. He accused me of being selfish and foolish for leaving you. He told me I should have never left you there to die, that it was only through Philo's loyalty and love that you were still alive."

"Philo kept me warm until they got there. I owed him more than what he got," I said, tears welling in my eyes for my recently lost companion.

"Where is Philo now, did you leave him south of the mountains when you came to find me?"

I drew in a shaky breath and shook my head. "His was the loss Demetri spoke of. He died on the Thessalian Plain."

"I am sorry," Papou said, taking my uninjured hand. "He was a good horse, a loyal friend. He would have done anything for you. Every soldier deserves such a steed."

I nodded and blinked back the tears. "I could not save him."

"I am certain you did everything you could, as was always your nature."

I shrugged. "I should have done more. He too was killed by Persian soldiers."

"What? The Persians have come to Greece?"

"You seem surprised, but it is not the first time." I took my hand from his, anger replacing my sadness. "I faced them in Marathon. We crushed their attack. The past winter has seen our army stationed north of Trachis in case they decide to come for us through their allies in Thrace and Macedonia."

"Is there talk of it?"

"It is only talk at the moment but I would not put it past them." Papou nodded and I returned our conversation to its previous path. "Moeris did not tell me he had spoken to you at Othrys. When I confessed why I had been out there, he sent men to look for you, but they found no trace."

"He did not send anyone. He came himself. I am not surprised he did not tell you we had met. It did not end well between the two of us. He had watched you grow in a way I was denied and was very fond of you. He was angry, afraid that you would die. He told me never to come looking for you, that unpleasant things would happen to you if I did."

"He threatened my life if you ever returned?" I frowned.

"No, no. He loves you; he would never harm you. But he believed you would put yourself in danger if you sought me out again. He did not want that any more than I did, he would not want it now I am certain. I returned to the herders and spent subsequent winter moons to the north, rather than the south. I convinced myself Moeris spoke true and that you were better off."

"I would have been better off with *you*."

"Ava ..."

"No! You should have taken me from Trachis when Melina and Agrias made you leave."

"My darling girl, I wanted to. You must believe me, but I was afraid for you. Afraid that just as I was not able to protect your mother and grandmother, I would not be able to protect you."

"So you ran away, as a coward does, leaving me to grow without a family, without anyone to love me. In a place I despised!" I cried, the hidden, devastated nine winter old child bubbling to the surface. I stood, pacing the area between the chairs and the fire.

He followed me to his feet but did not approach. "Please, I understand your anger, but I did not inten–"

"What did you think I needed protection from? What did *they* ever need your protection from?"

"It does not matter," he said, suddenly refusing to meet my eyes.

"Of course it matters. Do you think I would be standing here if it did not? You told me before you left that when it was time, you would find me and tell me everything." I saw the fear on his face. He knew of the amulet's power. He knew one day I would have it and what would happen when I did. Anger flooded my veins. "You should have told me. Mumma should have told me what her amulet could do."

"What ... what amulet do you speak of? What has happened?"

"What do you think?" I replied, scowling at him. "Do not pretend you do not know the weapon I speak of."

"No, this ... this cannot be," he muttered, slumping back onto the chair.

"It is," I said. "I will prove it to you." I moved with purpose to the small room I had woken in and ripped open my bag. As I took the pouch from its hiding place, a thump sounded from the main room. I dropped the amulet and ran back. Papou was no longer by the fire and the large wooden front door stood open, a cold breeze whipping through the room and enraging the fire in the hearth.

"No!" I yelled, balling my left hand into a fist as I rushed after him. I would not let him run from me or leave without me again. I stepped through the doorway, almost colliding with Demetri.

"What's wrong?" he asked. "Where is Leandros going?" I shook my head and tried to step around him. He grabbed my arm, but I shook him off.

"Go inside Demetri, I will return soon."

"If you're going somewhere then Damon and I will accompany you."

"I do not need an escort," I told him sharply as a shadow fell over us.

"Neither of you are going anywhere," Origenes rumbled. "Get back inside."

"Leandros and I have not finished our business."

"It is not a request," Origenes boomed, pinning both my arms to my side as he lifted me off my feet and placed me back in the warmth.

"Then do not let him leave. If he tries to, stop him, and bring him back here. Do you understand me?"

"You do not command me, Girl."

I crossed to the fire and the piece of iron Irina had used on my shoulder. I took it awkwardly from the hearth in my bandaged hand, holding it as though it were a sword as I faced Origenes again. "Maybe I should challenge you then," I said.

"What is your true purpose here?"

Demetri placed a warning hand on my arm. "We told you already, we seek her grandfather's blessing for our union. It was only the weather that caused us to get disorientated and end up here instead of Tricca where we thought he was."

"You expect me to believe such a story?" Origenes asked, sliding two swords from the table beside him – mine and Demetri's. "You speak words of innocence, yet your weapons and clothing suggest something else."

"I know how it looks but you *must* believe us, we would not be here if ..."

"Do not try to speak sense to him Demetri, you will not succeed. He is loyal to his tribe and would stop at nothing to keep them safe. I respect that loyalty." I squeezed the iron in my protected hand and advanced on Origenes. "But you will not keep me from what I seek," I warned the larger man.

"Tell me why you are here," he snarled.

"Return our weapons and maybe I will give you answers." I brought the iron up until we stood, facing off – swords to iron.

"I do not believe that the weapons belong to you, especially not to him," Origenes said, nodding in Demetri's direction. "He is no warrior and you are not an Amazon, and Amazons are the only women fighters in these lands." I pressed the iron in my hands to Demetri's sword as Origenes slowly returned mine to the table, getting a better grip on the one he held.

"You are right, *I* am just a metalworker," Demetri said. "The sword you hold is one I made. I can teach you to make it if it would help prove we seek nothing more than what we've told you."

"Why would I do that? So you have another weapon to use against us?"

"No, you could use it against your enemies ... enemies who are not us," Demetri hastened to correct himself.

"So now you admit you are our enemies?" Origenes said with a smirk. He was playing with Demetri, a tactic I had used myself on more than one occasion. Fluster and confuse until you had an easy opportunity to behead or run your opponent through with your sword.

I pushed Demetri sideways, stepping between the two of them and raising the iron higher. "We are no enemy of yours unless you make it so," I told him.

Origenes grinned and pushed his sword against my iron. "How proficient are you with a weapon, Girl?" he said.

I smiled and positioned my feet, the right slightly more forward than the left, holding the iron as tightly as I could in my bandaged hand. "Better than you," I replied.

Origenes rolled his shoulders and took his own stance, barely settling before he advanced. The sound of iron on iron filled the room. Each meeting of our weapons reverberated down into my hand, but I felt surprisingly little pain. Damon barked but did not approach as we fought and from the corner of my eye, I saw Demetri pulling the hound out of our way. I was not as capable as usual with the bandage on my hand and Origenes movements were less than fluid, his strength making up for it somewhat. I defended and attacked, holding my own against his onslaught as we rounded the room, knocking chairs and the table over in our wake.

"You are fortunate it was Leandros who found you and not me, I would have killed you before you reached the flock," Origenes said, blocking my attack.

"And how do you think he would have reacted once he knew who I was?"

"Who is to say he would have ever laid eyes on your body? He does not know everything we do here."

"Enough!" Theron's voice shouted behind us. "Lower your weapons, both of you."

29

I waited. Origenes waited. Both of us determined not to be the first to surrender.

"Now," Theron roared. Origenes slowly lowered the sword and I followed with the length of iron, my chest heaving with the exertion of the unexpected fight. "What is the meaning of this?" Theron asked.

"It is nothing," Origenes said.

"My grandfather left and we were not finished our conversation. Origenes would not let me go after him," I replied.

Theron nodded slowly and put a hand on my shoulder. "I shall find him. You shall finish your conversation. I give you my word." Theron and Papou had obviously known each other for many winters. I hoped he could convince Papou to stay and talk to me.

"Thank you," I nodded.

Theron took the sword from Origenes. "To which of you does this belong?" he asked, addressing Demetri and me.

"It's mine," Demetri answered before I had a chance to claim it.

Theron held it up, examining the guard with its carvings, just as I had. "It is very impressive. Where did you get it?"

"He *says* he made it," Origenes spat.

"I was asking the boy," Theron chided. "Is that true?"

"Yes," Demetri nodded.

Theron looked back to the sword. "It is made of iron, not bronze."

"Yes," Demetri repeated. "I suggested that I could show Origenes how to make a similar one, but I don't know if you have the materials I'd need."

"He cannot make such a weapon," Origenes snarled.

"What would you need?" Theron asked, ignoring Origenes' comment.

"Do you make your own swords or knives?" Demetri asked.

"No. Our main weapon is the Sarissa. You would call it the long spear," Theron replied.

"A good weapon for hunting animals in mountainous areas," I acknowledged with a nod.

"We often acquire knives," Origenes said. "They are quite useful when we need to flay our prey. These questions should be directed to me. I am the one who makes our weapons."

Demetri shivered, but met Origenes' eyes. "Very well. Are the tips of your spears made from iron?"

"Only when we have no bronze; iron is an ugly material."

"To some people, but it has many advantages," Demetri replied calmly. He pointed to his sword in Theron's hand. "To craft a sword similar to mine would take several days. I need specific items. If you can provide them, I'll prove to you how iron is better."

"What items?" Origenes rumbled.

"A furnace, bellows, a hammer, tongs, water, wood or charcoal if you already have it, but most importantly, some iron ore."

"We have all that," Origenes replied.

"You have iron ore?" I asked skeptically.

"Just because we do not *use* iron weapons, does not mean we do not have ore."

"Then it is decided," Theron said, taking the iron from me and propping it back at the hearth. "Demetri shall show us how he made such a fine weapon. There shall be time for further discussions while we learn."

"Not tonight," Irina's voice interrupted. "Demetri needs at least another night's rest to recover his strength and I am certain Ava would wish to join him … and she certainly needs more time."

"But …" Origenes started.

"They shall *not* be joining you tonight," Irina cut him off in a firm voice. "You have items to gather which may take several candlemarks. You may return in the morning."

"I shall be here at first light, then we shall find out how much truth lies in your words," Origenes said.

"We shall be here," I told him, squaring my shoulders and staring him down. He turned and ducked through the doorway, his footsteps loud as he crunched across a dirt path. Theron gave me a nod and followed the other man out, closing the door behind them.

Irina put a hand on my arm. "Come, eat. You and Demetri must have much to speak of as well."

"Would you remove the cloths from my shoulder and hand?" I asked.

"In the morning," she replied, guiding me to the upended furniture. I nodded as she and Demetri righted the disturbed table and chairs and she settled me into the nearest one.

She left the room, returning moments later with two steaming bowls of broth and fresh bread. My stomach rumbled its appreciation at the smell that filled the room and I thanked her.

"You are most welcome. Enjoy your meal, I shall see you in the morning."

"Until the morning," Demetri and I echoed.

Demetri pulled the bread in two, offering me half before starting his meal. The smell of the broth called to me seductively and I tucked in heartily, alternating between dipping the bread into the bowl to soak up the liquid, and just picking it up and drinking it as though it were wine in a goblet.

"What happened with Leandros, did he refuse to answer your questions about the amulet?" Demetri asked.

"I did not get to ask him any." The large hound, Damon, dropped to the floor beside us, his huge paw resting on Demetri's foot, his head on top of that. "He seems to be fond of you," I remarked, shuffling my chair back ever so slightly. The hound may have taken a liking to Demetri but I still remembered the way they had looked at me when we arrived – as though I was dangerous – or worse; food.

Demetri smiled and scratched him between the ears. "Yes, and I of him. You don't need to be afraid, he won't hurt you."

"You did not see him and the others the night we arrived."

Demetri smiled even wider. "He wasn't with them. He's considered the runt of the litter, a disappointing equivalent when compared to his brothers. He's no war hound."

"I see," I murmured, content to keep my distance. "How long have we been here?"

"What exactly happened at the mountain?" Demetri asked at the same time. We smiled at each other.

"You first," I said, finishing the last drop of broth.

"Theron says we arrived the night before last."

"So I have been asleep almost two days?" I asked with surprise. He nodded, absently scratching at Damon's head, which was resting now on his thigh.

"Yes. I was afraid you weren't going to wake at all, but Irina told me I had to be patient, you had a lot of healing to do."

"I was not as unwell as you."

"Maybe not but what happened? I remember the spider bite and returning to the peak of the mountain up those stone steps and wanting to rest under some trees. Then I was falling. Where did we land?"

"Deep within the mountain again," I replied. "It caved in on itself. Water filled the inside and I used it to float us out again." That was close enough to the truth. He did not need to know the exact details of how we got out.

"And then you walked all the way here?"

"I did. When did you wake?"

"Early yesterday afternoon."

"You seem quite healed."

He nodded. "I am. Theron said he used chamomile to relax my muscles and willow bark to reduce the pain from the bite so my body could fight the poison. Then he applied a mixture of salt and honey to the bite itself. When I woke I was famished, and a little weak, but the poison had left my body." He held his arm up; the bite itself had almost disappeared, the area marked with only a small, red dot. I went to touch it, momentarily forgetting about my bound hand. Demetri smiled and took me gently by the wrist. "Irina said you did a lot of damage to this."

I nodded and looked down, remembering the bright pink skin. "Rope burn," I confirmed. "Tell me though, did Theron leave your chiton on once he had tended to you? I asked him to do that."

"He did, thank you, I appreciate it."

"Well, I knew you did not have another chiton to change into," I grinned. "I cut it up to protect my hands and shoulder, for all the good it did in the end."

He returned the smile. "I owe you my life. Again. So perhaps we'll consider ourselves even. I'm so glad you came back to me."

"So am I," I replied, stifling a yawn.

Demetri stood and offered his hand. "You need more sleep, perhaps it would've been better to leave the fighting until you'd recovered a little more."

"Maybe," I agreed with a grin. I took his hand, letting him lead me to the room I had woken in not so long ago, and sending up another prayer of thanks to Mumma Skylar and Asclepius for his recovery.

When we reached the small bed, Demetri loosened his grip. I held tight and pulled him down onto it with me, our bodies stretched out as we faced each other.

"There isn't room for the both of us," he said. "I'll sleep on the floor."

"No. Please. I am not afraid to sleep close with you. I am not afraid or appalled by who you are or what you showed me. I meant what I said at the mountain – I think you are beautiful, regardless of what form your body takes. You are not an abomination, or a beast, which I heard the boys at the lake call you. I did not know at the time why they said it, but I do now. They were threatened by something they did not understand. But they too were wrong." I leaned forward and placed a tentative kiss on Demetri's lips. "Maybe we can talk some more about it all tomorrow?" He only nodded. "Then for tonight, please stay. I cannot let you go. I want you with me."

Demetri smiled shyly and put his head on his arm. "Well how can I refuse when you put it like that?"

"You cannot," I replied.

"Thank you for accepting me for who I am," he murmured.

"Thank you for trusting me enough to share yourself with me," I nodded.

30

Morning found me wrapped in Demetri's warm embrace, the course animal skins drawn around us providing an extra layer of heat. I could imagine no better place to wake and I knew he … she had given me something I had not realized I still yearned for – someone I wanted to share my life with. When I was very young I had thought I would find that person as I grew, just as my mothers had found one another. But after they were killed, I pushed those dreams aside, believing it safer and less painful to never care for another, in case they too were taken from me.

When I first joined the army, Lysistratos had told me everyone – even soldiers – needed the love and support of those both inside and outside the barracks. He had believed we would become firm friends, like we were when we were children. I had not thought I needed such friendship. I thought the bond I shared with my fellow soldiers would be closer than friendship. And it was, to a point. But Lysistratos had been right – it did not matter that I did not want it, or seek it, but he, and Eumelia, and I *had* become close again, like family.

But our friendship was not the same as the love he and Eumelia shared. It was not the same as what my mothers had had. Their love was different, special, to the point of exclusion of everyone else sometimes, how they seemed to only see each other, even in a crowded room. Theirs was a love that had endured many winters, never wavering in its intensity. Eumelia was my oldest friend and she and Lysistratos had found the same sort of love and I was happy for them, but I had stopped expecting that one day I would find it for myself.

But now there was Demetri. I recognized the kindred spirit inside him – someone who had kept so much of himself hidden, protected from the rest of the world – and I realized I wanted the chance to explore the possibility of sharing my life with someone else, of sharing it with him ... her? I was not sure what that even meant. Of how I should think of him ... her.

Demetri's arms tightened ever so slightly around me. "Good morning," he murmured. "This is a nice way to wake up and not painful in the least – you slept peacefully."

I rolled onto my back, unable to keep the smile from breaking out. "It is, and I did." I already knew he had feelings for me – his story about why we were there made that obvious – but I wanted to know how deep those feelings ran. "Can I ask you something?"

"Of course."

"The story you gave about us being here ..."

He grinned. "I wondered when you were going to ask me about that. I hope you're not angry."

"No, not angry. But why ... why make it so specific? Why infer there was ... so much between us?"

"I thought about a lot of things as I recovered. You mostly; I didn't know if you were going to wake up and I couldn't bear that thought. I wondered, if I said out loud how I felt, that perhaps it would bring you back to me ... just like you did."

"What do you mean?" I frowned.

"It's hard to explain, but it must've been after the mountain collapsed. I wasn't awake, I know that, but I heard your voice. I heard you ask Hades not to take me. I heard you say that there is something between us, that you might one day love me. That you wanted the chance to find out."

"Oh," I said, lowering my eyes.

"Didn't you mean it?" he asked after a moment's pause. My eyes shot back to his and I saw the hurt and fear written across his face. I rolled onto my side, my injured shoulder complaining only slightly as I reached up to trace his furrowed brow.

"I meant every word," I assured him. He exhaled, the grin returning to his face as he placed a hand at my hip.

"I'm glad to hear that, because I think I'm in love with you and I don't want to lose you."

My breath caught in my chest, joy flooding through me. I leaned forward and kissed him, his lips soft and warm against mine. "You make me feel things I have never felt before, Demetri," I whispered, placing my bandaged hand on his cheek, and wishing I could feel his skin.

"Is that bad?" he asked.

"No," I replied. "Just, surprising, and a little unsettling."

"You make me feel a certain way too."

"A good way?"

He increased the pressure on my waist and drew me closer. "Yes, in a very good way," he said, our lips meeting with renewed purpose. His tongue slipped inside my mouth, hand gliding down my thigh and lifting the hem of my tunic to caress the skin beneath.

A spark of heat ignited in my stomach and I lay my hand against his chest, his breath catching. I felt his excitement and my own body responded. I wanted him ... her? I needed her. Him. Them. I wanted to know not just her thoughts and words, but her body. His body. I wanted to feel him against me, skin against skin, with nothing to separate us.

I broke our kiss, sliding my hand from his chest to his chin, raising it ever so slightly so our eyes met. "Can I ask you something else?" He nodded. "Having both male and female ... parts ... which sex do you feel most like? On the Thessalian Plain, you asked me which choice of lover I preferred. I meant what I said – that I have no specific preference but I just ... wondered which part of *you* wanted me, desired me, felt something for me?" I stumbled, not sure how exactly to ask, or do it without causing offense.

He gave a small smile. "All of me fell in love with you. I don't really feel *more* like a boy or a girl. To keep me safe, Spyros raised me and introduced me as a boy but in the privacy of his home, I was often taught and allowed to worship and serve the household as a girl ... I suppose I don't think of myself as one or the other specifically, but a combination of both. Now though ... I suppose I should feel more like the man I resemble. Is that what you would want?"

"I do not know if it is my place to tell you how you should feel," I murmured.

"But if we were ... together ... how would you want to introduce me? As your male lover or your female lover?"

I hesitated, considering my answer. "Honestly, I do not know. I have never introduced anyone as my lover. I have never had a ... relationship with anyone for more than a night," I replied. "But if I was to introduce you ... well ... I do not know what is more true for you, and without breasts I suppose it would confuse people if I said you were a woman ... Not that you have to have breasts to feel like a woman I suppose, I mean I ... er ..." I trailed off, knowing I was making a complete mess of my answer.

Demetri laughed and drew me close again. "I think I know what you mean ... and at least you didn't say you didn't want us to be together."

"I think you already know that is what I want," I replied. "But what about you? How do *you* want people to think of you because I think that is more important than how I want them to?"

"I-I don't really know either. I guess ... for now, while we're here ... we should let Theron and everyone continue to think I'm male. I will be Demetri to them. But ... perhaps when you and I are alone ... perhaps you would think of me as a woman?"

I nodded slowly, taking in his ... her request. "Has your name always been Demetri?"

"Ever since Spyros bought me. I don't remember if I had one before that, at least not a proper one, there were plenty of derogatory ones."

"What would you like your name to be when it is just us? Do you have a feminine name you like?"

"Well, I have always liked the name ... Demi. If it doesn't feel too strange for you to call me that ... It means half of something."

"Demi," I repeated, trying it out. "It is perfect and it would be my privilege to do that."

"Thank you. Now, enough talk, it is time I showed you how I – all of me – feels about you."

"Oh you think so, do you?" I asked, heart soaring at his – her – words.

"I do."

Demetri – Demi – I silently corrected myself captured my lips, effectively silencing me. It would take some getting used to, this new boy-girl in my life. But I wanted it, welcomed it. I wanted all of her and all of him at once. His hand slid from my hip to my thigh. Or was it her hand? The growing desire was making it hard to think about anything other than what she was doing to me. Her lips trailed down my neck as her hand found its way beneath my tunic. Maybe if I thought of the top half of her body as female, and the lower half as male, that would work ...

I gasped as Demi took the skin of my neck between her teeth. I gripped her head, holding her against me as I pushed my body into his.

"Why are they not ready to leave?" Origenes' voice boomed from the other room, rudely drawing me from the pleasures of the hard body beneath my hands.

A quieter voice responded – Irina's perhaps – but I could not make out the words.

Demi's head shot up, a scowl on her flushed features. I put a hand on her cheek and drew her face back to mine. "Ignore him," I insisted, pushing into him to emphasize my point. She groaned but shook her head.

"I don't want him to come in here. I don't like other people seeing my body, but yours is definitely not for others to see, *Princess*," she replied. I was taken back at the unexpectedness of the word, but when her hand found my breast, I found I did not wish to berate her for the use. "You're mine," she said, squeezing my heated flesh. Her lips took mine again, my insides soaring at the claim she made on my body. At the claim she made on me.

I immediately missed the contact when Demi drew away, rolling off the bed and crossing to the door. Heat continued to surge through me and I mirrored the calming breaths Demi was taking as I pushed myself to my feet as well. His excitement was still evident and did nothing to calm my hammering heart, but I reached for my cuirass and awkwardly pulled it over my head. She was suddenly behind me, hands at my waist preventing me from doing the cuirass up.

"Not today," she murmured. "I've enjoyed seeing you in just a tunic. It flatters your … attributes." I turned within her hold and leaned close so our bodies touched once more. She closed her eyes, hands tightening.

"You said my body was only for you to see," I teased, failing to keep the grin from my face.

"It is, but the men here already see you as an enemy," she replied. "They don't need another reminder of that."

"You hope that is how they see me. Perhaps without my cuirass I would be seen as a conquest," I muttered, my smile disappearing. Her eyes flew open, her worry evident. I forgot she would not see things as I did. I drew my hand down her chest to soften my words. "For you I will leave it here today, but do not get used to it. I am a soldier and prefer to wear my weapons and armor."

She shook her head and slid her hands to the small of my back, drawing me even closer. "You are a woman first, and a soldier second and that is how Demetri *and* Demi prefers it." She leant down, kissing me briefly before drawing my cuirass back over my head and letting it to drop to the floor. I wanted to give into my desire and taste the sweetness of his body, of hers, regardless of Origenes' presence in the next room. I fisted the material at Demi's chest with my unbound hand and kissed her again. She groaned but stepped away, a pained look on her face.

"No," she said, but it was more plea than conviction. "I want you more than you can know, but we can't. Not yet."

I swallowed and nodded, taking control of myself. She was right – we would have time after she … he showed Origenes his metalwork skills. His name is Demetri, I reminded myself. When there were others around he needed to be Demetri. Besides, I needed to talk to Papou and learn what he knew about the amulet. I swallowed again, retrieving my cuirass from the ground and returning it to the back of the chair. It would be strange not to wear it, but it was only for a day, and I had been without it almost three now, another would not matter.

I handed Demetri one of the himatia from the end of the bed and we carried them into the main room of Theron and Irina's home, attempting to settle our breathing and look like we had just woken, rather than doing what we actually had been.

31

Origenes paced by the fire, hands balled into fists. Theron and Irina sat at the table with another man I did not recognize – not at first anyway.

"Papou," I murmured. The long beard was gone, his face more lined than I had expected, but overall his features were the same as the ones I remembered from ten winters ago. My dear grandfather whose departure I had mourned along with my mothers.

Irina indicated the seats opposite her and Demetri and I took them, Papou giving me only the briefest of nods before returning his eyes to his food. I allowed him his silence, thankful at least that he was still there.

"Eat quickly, then we go," Origenes grumbled.

"There is no hurry," Irina said, rounding the table.

"Humph," came Origenes' reply.

As she had promised last night, Irina took the cloth from my shoulder and Demetri drew a sharp breath. The wound was a purple-grey bruise, having closed significantly compared to the last time *I* had seen it. The skin around the hole was a healthy pink and it seemed I had avoided any further illness after reopening it so many times.

Irina undid the dressing on my hand as well, revealing the pink palm and fingers. They were still raw, but new skin was starting to grow over the damaged areas and it was more stiff than painful when I tried to close my hand into a fist. Irina checked me over carefully, taking her time, and I could not help wondering if she was doing it deliberately, just to annoy

Origenes who was huffing by the fire. I smiled at the thought.

"You are healing well," she sounded pleased, "we shall leave the cloths off for today, but your hand at least shall still need protecting should you intend to use it for swordplay or similar." I nodded as Origenes muttered beneath his breath. Everyone ignored him and Irina continued. "You may accompany Demetri today if you so wish."

"Thank you," I said, taking an apple, some figs and a wedge of cheese from the middle of the table. Irina returned to her chair as Demetri smiled, giving my arm a quick squeeze.

We finished our meal in relative silence and as soon as we were done, Origenes herded us outside. I noticed our swords still on the table by the door, but Theron shook his head as I reached out to take mine.

"Later," he promised.

I hesitated, but left it where it was, turning back to Papou. "Are you joining us?" I asked.

"Soon," he replied, briefly meeting my eyes. I watched him a moment longer before nodding and following Origenes.

As we cleared the doorway of Theron and Irina's home, Damon came bounding across the grass. Origenes rolled his eyes at the hound and I took a step closer to Demetri who greeted Damon warmly. I shook my head at the strange pairing. I would have preferred if the first non-human friend Demetri had made in Konitsa was not a vicious war hound, but I now understood that you could not always help who you were drawn to, or what form they came in.

Origenes led us to a dwelling with a straw roof sorely in need of repair on the edge of the settlement. Smoke billowed from the chimney, but we did not enter, continuing instead to the back. The area we found ourselves in contained no trees, no grass and no flowers. A light dusting of snow covered the ground, light brown dirt visible beneath the bare patches.

A group of men stood along the perimeter; faces hard, set, in watchful concentration, arms folded across their chests or holding tightly to spears should they suddenly need them. I did not miss the huge hounds that stood beside them, held back with thick leather wrapped around their masters' hands.

As we approached, a chorus of rumbling from the animals filled the air and my breath caught at our close proximity to the beasts. Damon bumped past my thigh, emitting a deep growl of his own as he placed himself between me and the other hounds. I looked at Demetri, who gave me a tight smile. Origenes impatiently beckoned us to join him in the middle of the cleared area.

It was a long time since I had been in the metalwork shop at Ophelos' house in Trachis – our weapons brought to the barracks for us rather than us visiting the shop – but it looked like the Molossians used much of the same equipment. A square, clay construction stood waist high in the middle of the space with two animal skins connected by short lengths of clay. Just like the ones in Trachis were, they were made of goat skins, the same as our water skins. Nearby, three wooden half-barrels sat, the first filled with charcoal, the second sand, and the last with water. Large stones were scattered beside them and a flat rock, at about the same height as the clay structure, stood beside those with a pair of tongs and a hammer resting against it.

"Did I get everything you wanted?" Origenes grunted, indicating the gathered materials. Demetri stepped forward, inspecting each item in the semi-circle. Damon matched him step for step, his eyes flicking between me, Demetri and the other hounds. Demetri picked up several pieces of coal, the tips of his fingers instantly blackening. He returned them to the pile, ignored the sand and water, and moved across to the flat rock. He tested its stability by trying to rock it from side to side. It remained in place. He nodded and picked up the tongs, testing how wide they would open. When he was satisfied with those, he picked up the hammer, gripping it in his palm and bringing it down deafeningly on the top of the rock. He nodded again.

Papou joined two warriors on the opposite side of the clearing, his head bent to theirs as he spoke. They nodded, their eyes finding mine, but they were not hostile as they stared. I drew my eyes back to Demetri as he approached the clay furnace and held his hands above the top; the heat of the fire inside shimmering the air between them and the structure.

"Well?" Origenes pressed, joining him.

"I don't need the sand," Demetri replied.

"How do you intend to make your cast?"

"Iron doesn't need a cast. But the fire needs to be hotter."

"I lit it well before first light, it should be sufficient," Origenes countered.

"The bronze you use is a soft metal and turns to liquid at a much lower temperature. Iron needs far more heat; all the ore and impurities burn away and we're left with a solid mass of iron called a bloom, and *that* is what I'll make the sword from."

"So how do we increase the heat?" Origenes asked.

"The charcoal needs to fill the entire furnace," Demetri replied. Origenes nodded and helped Demetri drag the barrel of charcoal to the fire, tossing in piece after piece until Demetri signaled it was enough.

*   *   *

After my fourth attempt to talk with Papou failed, I gave up. The Molossians watched our every move and interrupted us with apparently urgent, and yet rather useless, information for my grandfather whenever I tried to speak to him. I retreated to a tree on the edge of the clearing, kicking at the fine dust beneath it. I had my suspicions that Papou had planned the interruptions, maybe to protect the position he had formed since arriving and to cement the belief that we were not there to conspire against the Molossians. But more than that, I wondered if he did not know how to speak to me of what he knew of the amulet and my mother.

Either way, his behavior angered me and I wished my hand was not so damaged so I could rid myself of the frustration by attacking an unsuspecting tree, or better yet, sparring with a large opponent. The Molossians were not swordsmen – I could see they preferred their spears – but I had no doubt that Origenes would enjoy another scrap, whether Theron allowed it or not.

* * *

As the candlemarks passed, Demetri poked around in the fire, sending sparks and flames high into the air as he directed Origenes – who was crouched beside him – when to pull the animal skins up and down. Origenes appeared to have formed a grudging respect for Demetri, no longer shouting demands when he wanted something, but rather asking what or how he could assist. The turnaround in the fierce warrior's behavior was almost comical, but I knew that I too had been easily charmed by the young metalworker in a short amount of time.

Damon had long since stopped trailing Demetri everywhere and ambled over to where I sat beneath the trees. After his unexpected show of protection when we arrived in the clearing, I found myself slightly less wary of him and held my hand out in a gesture of goodwill. He sniffed at my fingers briefly before flopping to the ground, his head pinning my thigh in place. I shook my head, but smiled, wondering how Damon could possibly be so different to the rest of his brothers, and why, with their influence so close, he had not grown in size and temperament as they had. I settled a tentative hand on the soft fur of his back and raised my eyes to the furnace. Demetri was explaining its construction and the benefits of the animal skins to Theron and some of the other warriors who had huddled closer, warming their hands as they listened.

"When working with iron, bellows are always used. By pumping air inside the furnace, it increases the temperature much faster than what the fire can achieve alone."

"May I?" Papou asked, approaching and indicating the bellows.

"Of course," Demetri nodded.

Papou knelt on the ground and pushed the skins down, one at a time, his eyes focused on the top of the furnace. He increased his pace, flames shooting up into the air. The other warriors cheered and a smile split his face, revealing the face of the younger man I had once spent every morning with at the Melas River.

"You've done this before," Demetri said with a grin.

"Many times," Papou admitted, getting to his feet again and slapping Demetri on the shoulder, his voice low enough that I did not hear his words when he spoke again.

*

I dozed beneath the tree; a combination of the pale sun, Damon's warmth at my legs and the himation around my shoulders. I was pulled from my impromptu slumber by a sudden shudder and a deep growl from Damon. The fur on his back lifted as he tried to stand but I held him in place, turning my head to find Mumma Skylar sitting beside me against the tree trunk. Damon settled once again on my thigh, his eyes still on Mumma as I stroked his thick coat.

"I am pleased to see you have recovered," she said. I was not concerned that the men would see or hear her, they were paying no attention to me, and Demetri had not seen her on the Plain when she had stood directly in front of him. Still, I kept my reply quiet.

"As am I."

"I see you have found allies to help you in your fight against the Persians. They are fierce. You have made a wise choice."

"They are not allies."

"Then why ...?" she trailed off. I followed her gaze to the furnace. "Leandros ... Father," she corrected, but the way she spoke his name unnerved me. "This is why you travelled north against my wishes – to find him." Her eyes returned to me, anger rolling off her.

There was no point denying it any longer. "Yes. I sought him for answers about the amulet."

"If you had questions, why did you not ask me? I would have given you the answers."

"You should have told me when I was a child," I said, my voice rising as I spoke.

"You speak true, I should have, *we* should have," she admitted. "But do not imagine your grandfather has your best interests at heart. He shall attempt to turn you from the path I have set you on."

"Why would he do that? You are his daughter. He loved you, he still loves you."

"Do not pursue him for answers, leave this place and I shall tell you everything you want to know."

"No. I am not leaving until *he* has told me everything."

159

"Do not disobey me. Leave him here to die an old man's death and return to the south where you shall have everything you ever dreamed of," she warned, bright red momentarily replacing the familiar blue in her eyes.

"I am not going anywhere," I told her, drawing out each word. She opened her mouth to speak, but instead disappeared.

32

"Ava?" Demetri's voice made me jump. "Are you alright?" he asked, his hand warm on my thigh.

I met his eyes as Damon stretched behind him. "What? I … yes. Why do you ask?"

"You were calling out. Were you dreaming again?"

"I … I must have been," I replied, looking back to where Mumma had sat. "How is the furnace coming along?" I added, shaking my head.

He offered me his hand. "It's ready for the ore." I let him pull me to my feet. "What did you dream of? You look troubled," he said, his hand cupping my cheek.

"Do not be concerned," I assured him, smiling and placing a kiss on his lips. He nodded and took my hand again, leading me to the furnace.

Mumma's words and her appearance in general concerned me. I needed to talk to Papou as soon as possible and if he would not make the time, then I would force him to listen regardless of who was nearby.

The men moved aside when Demetri and I joined them, Demetri crossing to the ore and picking each piece up, testing its weight. "This one," he announced, returning to my side. "When the iron is taken from the ore, we'll be left with a piece roughly two thirds of the size."

"Shall it still look like a rock?" one of the warriors asked.

"Mostly, yes, just shinier," Demetri nodded.

"I did not know swords were rock shaped," the same man said.

Demetri smiled as the others laughed. "I'll explain how we get the shape

161

once we have the iron bloom."

Papou stood opposite me, watching Demetri dig through the charcoal, flames licking at his hands as they escaped. I tried to catch his eye, but he was careful not to look in my direction. I stepped out of the knit of men and made my way to him.

"We need to talk," I murmured.

"Not now," he replied, never taking his eyes from Demetri.

"Then when?" I questioned, my voice a little louder.

He met my eyes. "Over dinner. Now quiet, I need to hear what he does next."

"Oh please, you know how to do this just as well as Demetri does," I hissed. "Whenever you came back from battle you and Mumma would spend candlemarks repairing your swords and shields in Ophelos' workshop."

"I have given you my answer," he frowned, casting his eyes about the group. "Please."

"Fine. But be warned, I will not wait any longer." He looked me over, that sad look on his face again. I wondered what he was remembering. He nodded curtly and excused himself, waving Theron over and striking up a conversation when they met at the edge of the clearing.

I huffed out a breath, glad that we had at least settled on a time to talk. I took my place between the men, trying to concentrate on what Demetri was doing in the hope it would drive the unease of my mother's visit and the impatience of my talk with Papou from my mind. Demetri made a large hole in the center of the charcoal, placing the piece of ore he had chosen inside. He dragged the coals back over it, filling the furnace to the top again with more charcoal.

"Why do you burn charcoal, why not just put the ore straight into the fire?" Origenes asked.

"As the ore burns away, the iron is left to mix with the smoke of the charcoal. The combination of the two produces a much stronger product than iron alone. The charcoal also makes the iron easier to shape, and sharpen, which I'm sure you understand is important for a sword," he replied.

Origenes nodded and Demetri smiled at me. I took his hands, looking them over. They were warm and red where the flames had found them, black where the charcoal had smudged them. "You should be wearing something to protect these," I scolded.

He closed his hands around mine and drew them to his lips. "When I remove the bloom, I'll use the tongs, I promise." He placed his hands on my hips, turning me to face the furnace and drawing my back to his chest as he pulled his himation around my own. With the sun starting to make its descent across the sky, the temperature around us had dropped and I was grateful for the extra layer. I was also surprised at how content I was at the feel of a pair of arms around me.

"How many candlemarks until we can remove the bloom?" Origenes asked.

"Not until morning," Demetri replied.

"Then you shall have plenty of time to return to the house and eat and sleep," Irina said, entering the clearing.

"We could leave for a while, as long as someone is willing to stay behind and pump the bellows," Demetri said.

"I shall do it," Origenes volunteered.

An animated conversation taking place between Papou and Theron caught my attention. "I will be back in a moment," I said, squeezing the arm around my waist. Demetri nodded and released me.

"What is wrong?" I asked as I approached the two men.

"Nothing that concerns you," Papou said.

"Theron?" I asked, ignoring my grandfather.

"I dispatched men this morning to hunt for food. They are not back yet."

"And that worries you?"

"No, well yes. They generally return before lunch unless they find a pack of animals. If that is so, they do not return until the sun has passed the highest point in the sky, but they always send word. I have heard nothing from them this day."

"So you need someone to look for them? Papou and I shall go, we are both skilled trackers if you show us the path they took," I said.

"You shall not join me," Papou insisted.

"Why?" I asked, rounding on him.

"Turn such ideas from your mind Ava, you still need rest. Leandros shall go alone," Theron added.

"Bu—"

"Irina would have my innards for dinner if I allowed it."

"Yes, I would," Irina agreed, passing us on her way back to the house.

"Wait here with us until we know more," Theron said, laying a hand on my shoulder.

"It seems you will go to any length to avoid our discussion. But you *will* tell me what I want to know before long," I growled, spinning on my heel and stomping back to the furnace. I would return to Irina and Theron's with Demetri as expected, but Papou would not get far before I followed. I would track him down and he would tell me everything he kept from me.

"What is it?" Demetri asked, opening his himation once again for me.

"Nothing important," I replied, sliding in against his body. I watched Papou take Theron's arm and shake it. He cast a glance in my direction and I stared unflinching at him until he turned on his heel, much as I had done, and left the clearing.

"So why do you favor iron?" Origenes asked.

"Over bronze?" Demetri replied. Origenes nodded. "Well, when you make a bronze sword, you cast it rather than forge it as you do an iron one and there are many times within that casting process where the outcome is unfavorable. For example, the liquid could have air bubbles or pieces of charcoal in it if you aren't vigilant enough. Or sometimes the entire thing falls to pieces when you open the mold. The blade can crack when you're hardening the edge, and if that happens, you can't do anything about it; you have to melt the bronze down and start all over again. Also you have to wait up to a moon before you can test the weapon. If it doesn't work then, again, you have to start all over again. It's a very time-consuming process. When you compare that to iron, even though the furnace is set up differently and you don't work with a liquid, you start and finish with the same solid item – iron."

"I know of some of the problems you speak, the bubbles and charcoal, but I have never made anything larger than arrowheads. To melt them down and begin again has never been a bother to me. Although having to begin a sword again would be rather frustrating after so much work," Origenes acknowledged.

"You certainly need a lot of patience and skill." Demetri agreed.

"And are these common, the ... what did you call the type of sword you have?"

"Xiphos. No. Spears are still the main weapon of choice for most armies, just as they are for you," Demetri said. "The Spartans do carry swords sometimes, but they're much shorter, only a little larger than daggers. The swords I create are almost twenty-eight inches long and weigh just over four pounds. I've heard some far-off lands use single edged swords, but I believe our double-edged ones are better as they can thrust and cut," he said, demonstrating with his hand. "With a single-edged blade you can only cut, and even then it's similar to a chopping motion. With our swords, you have the advantage of being able to use it from whichever side of your body it's needed, and it can be used in just one hand."

Origenes nodded as Demetri removed his himation from around me, taking my hand instead. "If you would excuse us, we have food and ... sleep to attend. I'll return in a candlemark or two and relieve you of bellows duty," he said, addressing Origenes with the last of his speech.

"I shall be here," Origenes nodded.

"The bath is ready for you," Irina said to Demetri. "And I shall leave your food on the fire for when you are done."

"Thank you," Demetri replied with a nod.

Hand in hand, Demetri and I returned to the bathing room of Theron and Irina's house, Damon trotting along beside us. "You are not hungry?" I asked.

"Famished, but I thought maybe we could bathe and finish what we started this morning before we eat." He stepped closer, breath hot when he pulled me close and kissed me.

The thought of a hot bath ... and everything else he wanted to do was more than appealing, but I did not want to lose Papou's trail if Demetri – Demi – I corrected and I spent candlemarks reveling in one another, which it seemed like she was suggesting.

I broke our kiss and took a step back. "Irina bathed me when I arrived, so maybe I could bathe you instead, like you did me back in Tricca. In the vein of continuing what we were earlier, I would like to show you how *I* see you – a body. A woman. A man. Hidden, scarred but not broken. Someone I care a lot about."

"I would like that," Demi smiled. "Damon ... stay," she added, the hound obeying the request and standing guard in the doorway.

I crossed to the door, closing it most of the way as Demi removed her clothing. I returned to stand in front of her, helping to unwrap the bandage across his chest and setting it aside. *Her* chest, I reminded myself. She kept her eyes from me, that shy look back on her face as I offered her my hand and led her to the bath.

She stepped over the edge into the flower-covered water, their scent wafting up to greet me as Demi submerged herself. On a table beside the bath was a long, curved tool I knew to be a strigil. I had never used one but knew that wealthy men and women used them to remove dirt and oils from their skin when they bathed. An amphora of oil stood beside the strigil but I left them both where they were for the moment, taking a cloth instead and gently wiping the back of Demi's neck. She sat forward so I could reach her back and I was careful as I ran it across the raised scars. I continued down each arm from shoulder to fingertip before dipping the cloth back in the water and squeezing it out.

I stepped along the side of bath until I could see Demi's face. "Your chest?" I asked. She closed her eyes a moment before nodding.

"Do you want me to stand up or ... or do you want to join me in here?" she murmured.

"Whatever you feel most comfortable with," I replied.

"You can come in," she whispered.

I placed the cloth on the side of the bath. "Alright." Her eyes never left mine as I took the fibula from my tunic. I stepped into the bath and knelt in front of Demi; her legs outstretched either side of me.

I took the cloth again and drew it across her collarbones before moving lower. The flat skin and the wounds were mostly healed but there were remnants of herbs recently applied so I was gentle as I removed them. I reached for the oil, coating my fingers and spreading it over her chest in gentle circles before taking the strigil. It was as long as my arm from wrist to elbow, smooth and made of wood in a dark color with a slight curve at each end. I drew it down each of her arms, letting her get used to the feel of it across her skin before I met her eyes again. I held it up and she nodded in reply. I drew the strigil lightly over her skin, removing the oil and the last of the herbs, careful to avoid her nipple on the one side, and the scars on both.

"All done," I murmured. "Do you still need herbs on your chest?"

"Thank you. I do, but they're in the other room."

I nodded in reply and stepped out of the bath. "We can get them before …" I left the rest unsaid as Demi's eyes traced every inch of my naked flesh. My skin prickled in response. She pushed herself to her feet, the water cascading off the ends of her fingers to drop back into the bath below before stepping over the rim to join me.

"I think the herbs can wait," she murmured, roughly pulling her chiton on and offering my tunic to me.

Taking my hand, Demi led me past Damon, through the main room and into the bedroom. I barely had time to register the existence of our swords on the table before Demi's hands were at my waist, lips meeting mine hungrily. She slid her hands down to my thighs and in one smooth motion lifted me up. I wrapped my legs around her waist (his waist?) and fisting my hand in her hair as I felt him rise beneath me. She took us to the bed, body covering mine, warm and hard and I shivered as I fumbled with her chiton, desperately trying to free it.

"Well this *is* romantic," a voice pierced the quiet around us.

33

Demi – Demetri I reminded myself – jumped from the bed. I followed, grabbing the closest sword – which happened to be his – and positioning myself between him and the newcomer. Damon rushed into the room, hackles raised and teeth bared as a deep rumble emanated from his throat.

The stranger wore dark boots and pants and a black and red sleeveless leather vest that exposed the impressive array of muscles along his arms and across his chest. He was taller than me, though not by much and the dark hair that reached his shoulders was perfectly groomed. His face was flawless, as though crafted by the gods themselves. His dark eyes flashed red, captivating me momentarily when I looked into them.

Damon's growl turned to a deafening bark, resembling the vicious war hound he was supposed to be. "Sit," the stranger roared. Damon obeyed for a moment then ran, whimpering into the main room. The man laughed. "You know with Philo's sad demise, perhaps a new pet is required. What if I made him a proper war hound, only stronger, more vicious?"

"Who are you?" I asked, ignoring his offer. He made no reply, flicking his hand in a dismissive motion instead. The sword I held flew across the room and into his waiting palm.

He held it up and looked it over, spinning it expertly around his wrist. "This is very nice." He drew it back beside his head like it was a spear before sending it sailing across the room where it lodged, blade first, in the stone wall behind us.

He did not resemble someone I had heard referred to as a 'magic bearer' and I did not know any man who possessed the strength he had just showed us; except Heracles, and he had been dead a very long time.

His gaze settled on mine. "Finally, we meet face to face."

"Apologies, but you have me at a disadvantage, you would be …?"

He laughed, the sound filling the entire room. "I am a little insulted. Do you not recognize Ares, God of War, when you see him?"

"God of War?" Demetri repeated.

"What do you want?" I asked, folding my arms across my chest.

"You and the amulet," he replied.

"What amulet?" I asked.

He wagged his finger at me. "Do not do that. We both know you possess a powerful amulet made from jet and hematite. It has been passed down from mother to daughter through generations of Skylar's family, one after the other, until it reached you." He pointed at me as he said the last words and took a step closer. I stayed where I was, raising my chin slightly.

"What makes you think I still have it?"

"Oh I doubt you would go anywhere without it after what you did to those Persians on the Thessalian Plain. But I notice you no longer wear it around your neck. Why ever not?"

"It clashed with the leather on my cuirass."

Ares threw his head back and laughed again, shaking his finger at me for a second time. "You certainly have Skylar's humor."

"What do you know about Mumma?"

"Oh I know plenty about both of your mothers, and I know they very much want to see you use that amulet again, to take your revenge on the Persians, just as I would."

"What interests you so much about the amulet?"

"It is sacred to me, it was made for *me*," Ares replied, starting to pace. "Your mothers never told you of your history, of your ancestors. If they had, the knowledge that you can wield the amulet would not have shocked you; you would have been prepared for the changes that happened when you did."

I frowned, recalling what I knew of my family line. "Papou Agrias came from Macedonia, he is of the royal Argead line. His nephew is Alexander, King of Macedonia, just as Agrias' brother – Amyntas – was before him. Agrias is now king of the Malian tribe at Trachis, his queen, Melina, a Malian woman he took as wife. None of them have ever grown wings and defeated their enemy with a gem like I did."

"But you have known for some time that Skylar did," Ares countered. "And Agrias and Melina are not your only grandparents."

"You speak of the power coming from Mumma Skylar's lineage, but we are not linked by blood. I was born of Mother Alexis' body so Papou

Leandros and I are not true ancestors in the manner you speak."

"And yet you have harnessed the power of the amulet," Ares shrugged, halting his pacing to face me. "What do you know of Skylar's mother, your grandmother Zita?"

"Nothing. I never met her and Mumma and Papou never spoke of her."

"Have you ever heard of the Keres?" I shook my head. Ares looked past me to Demetri. "What about you?"

"No," Demetri replied and I was glad his voice was strong.

Ares nodded. "Shall I tell you a story?"

"We had no plans for stories before we went to bed tonight," I said. I was somewhat curious about what he would say, yet eager to be rid of him so I could go after Papou as I had planned. I had even more questions for him now. Everything else between Demetri and me would have to wait.

"No I do not imagine you did, but you are going to get one anyway. Stay," he grinned. I opened my mouth to speak, but no words came out and my arms and legs refused to move when I expected them to.

From the corner of my eye, I saw Demetri edge towards the table. "Uh-uh," Ares chided, shaking his head. Demetri halted in his movement but I was not sure if it was his choice, or the god's. I frowned and, as I had no choice, waited in silence for Ares to go on.

"The first Keres – the five daughters of Nyx, Goddess of the Night – were given their purpose by their sister, Eris, Goddess of Discord. Unseen by mortals, they flew above the battlefields, forbidden to attack or cause death to those below. They drew strength when a warrior was felled, swooping down to feed upon their blood, before carrying the carcass off to Hades in the Underworld."

"They sound lovely," I smirked, pleased my voice at least had returned.

Ares smiled and continued. "I had long called Eris friend and after many winters of asking, she allowed me charge of them. She made me promise I would allow them to continue their duties and I had no hesitation in allowing it. In turn I requested assistance from the Moirai, convincing them to keep me informed of any mortal men destined for a violent death."

"Why?"

"I assigned each Ker one of the named mortals, instructing them to follow them from the day of their birth until the day of their predicted death. When they fed on their charge, the strength they gained was more than any other.

"They were magnificent to watch and I often wished I could send them into battle for me. They were akin to the Persians when given a task – insatiable for the fight – desiring the carnage and bloodshed that would follow their attack. Unfortunately, they began to want the same and instead of waiting for their assigned mortal to die, they began to incite fights in marketplaces and homes. Strangers, friends, brothers, sisters, mothers, it did not matter who it was. They joined the fray, killing all in their path, leaving the bodies where they fell.

"As you can imagine, I was not pleased they had disobeyed me, nor was Hades who had to collect the bodies himself and take them into his realm. I saw no choice but to banish them from the lands. I told them never to return."

"I am presuming they did," I said.

Ares nodded. "Many winters later, they came to Olympos, begging me to allow them to re-join me above the battlefields and swearing they would only feed from those I assigned them when their time was done. They had been living with the Valkyrie clan to the north and asked me to go there with them – the Valkyrie were going to create a powerful amulet – something that befitted my title as the God of War. All I had to do was provide a drop of my immortal blood."

"Valkyries?" I muttered. "I thought their existence was only a legend."

"All legends begin in truth," Ares replied. "With my blood and a particular Ker's merged within the amulet, we would be forever linked and that bloodline would always carry my mark." He knelt down, burning a three-sided shape into the ground with his finger.

"Every Ker in the line since that day has had this symbol on their left shoulder. The Valkyrie told us that one day a great warrior would be born to the family. She would not be as the others before her were; she would be extremely powerful, a force not to be taken lightly. Someone to be reckoned with. She would be able to control all four of the amulet's elements – fire, water, air and earth. When I learned of Skylar's existence, I believed she was the one, given she was half-mortal. Her mother was one of my Ker and Leandros her mortal mate. But I was mistaken." Ares waved his hand above the shape and it disappeared.

He returned to his feet. "Each time a female child in the line was born I tested her, not immediately, but when I believed her ready, when she displayed certain … traits. Of course, while I waited for your mother and you to be ready I had to endure nineteen *mortal* winters, and that is quite a stretch longer than usual.

"I have aided scores of Ker children to control the amulet, to help them bend it to their will. They in turn agree to allow me to guide them and protect them, lending my assistance when they want it. But no one has ever been able to conjure more than one element … no one that is, until you."

"You're misinformed, she has only used it once," Demetri said, his teeth gritted.

Ares looked him over and a smile crossed his face. "Only once you *know* of."

Demetri snatched up my sword and raised it in Ares' direction. "I said you're wrong, she only used it once on the Plain," he insisted.

I felt my limbs release from Ares' hold as the god watched on, amused. "I will deal with this," I told Demetri, disarming him before he could defend himself, and pushing him towards the bed. He stumbled and fell to his knees.

Ares was at my side in an instant. He slid my sword from my hand, returning it to the table, his mouth close to my ear as he spoke. "I saw what using the amulet unleashed inside you; the power, the want."

"What's he talking about?" Demetri asked.

"You did not speak of that to him, you knew he would not understand," Ares murmured. I wanted to respond, but my voice failed me again. "When I spoke of the Keres' passion for carnage, you knew exactly what I meant, did you not?"

His fingers caressed my cheek and I was drawn to the seduction in his voice. My skin tingled at the feelings he spoke of; how I had desired to leave Greece and take my revenge directly to the source of my hatred. "The power that coursed through you … the bloodlust, the desire … It made you feel alive, thirsty for more."

"I felt indestructible," I agreed, my voice barely above a whisper.

Ares circled me, threading an arm around my waist and holding me firmly against his chest as he whispered into my ear. "Can you imagine feeling that way *all* the time? I can help you release that power, help you harness it so it obeys your every wish and command." I closed my eyes, surrendering to his words as Demetri's voice called to me distantly. "I could make you the most powerful force this side of Olympos. You would be unstoppable. Feared. Revered. Loved."

Demetri called to me again.

"Where is the amulet?" Ares asked, his hands tightening around my waist.

"My bag," I replied as desire pulsed through me.

"Get it," he whispered.

I opened my eyes – my bag was already in his outstretched hand and I took it from him, freeing the amulet from the pouch and holding it up. It swung back and forth and I swore I could feel its power, waiting there for me to command it.

Demetri's voice was even more distant when he spoke my name again.

Ares took the leather from my hands, settling the amulet between my breasts. His fingers skittered along my collarbone and a deep craving flared within me. "You do not need this boy. You have me now," he crooned. "Just say the word and I get rid of him." He circled me again, his face barely inches from mine, his perfect pink lips close enough to touch. I wanted to touch them. I reached out, running my finger along his bottom lip.

Ares smiled. "Show me your mark and I shall prove to you that you are the one," he whispered.

"Ava!" Demetri's voice was louder, but I could not tear my eyes from the god of war's mouth.

Ares leaned forward and kissed my neck, his hands sliding beneath the himation at my shoulders. Suddenly I was wrenched from the warmth and seduction I had been drawn into. Demetri held me tight against his chest with one arm. My sword was in his other and he swung it wildly in front of us. I could feel him shaking.

"Leave her!" he yelled. We had only taken half a step before Ares was there, Demetri's hands separated from my body.

I turned as Demetri hit the wall behind us, sinking to the floor, stunned. "Demetri!" I cried.

The hold Ares had had on me was well and truly broken. I took a step towards Demetri. Ares yanked me back by the hair, roughly discarding my himation and searching my left shoulder for the mark he had spoken of. The skin was bare. He checked my right shoulder. Still he found nothing. I grabbed at the hand that held me, struggling as he wrenched the top of my tunic down, exposing the tops of my breasts.

"I said leave her," Demetri roared, rushing at Ares and hitting him at full stride. He bounced off the god and fell to the floor, dazed. Ares barely moved, but the motion was enough that he released me and I crumpled to the ground.

Ares rolled his shoulders and adjusted his vest as he stared me down, his face no longer friendly or seductive. "You *are* the one. I know it, as do you. This is not finished, your time is coming," he said, his voice deadly serious. He looked down at Demetri. "You had better not get in my way again." With that he vanished and I shivered, rushing to Demetri's side. To my Demi.

"Are you hurt?"

"No," she replied, pushing herself off the ground. I put my hand under her arm, but she shook it off.

"I don't need your help."

"Demi ..."

"He could've made you do anything he wanted. He could've killed me and you wouldn't have cared. You told me you'd never used the amulet before the Plain. You let him kiss you," she shouted.

"Is that why you are upset? Because he *kissed* me?" Demi crossed her arms as the urge to laugh at her behavior bubbled up from my stomach. I managed to control it, blowing out a long breath instead. "Demi, I would not *willingly* let the god of war kiss me. He had some sort of ... hold over me. I cannot explain it but when he spoke, it felt like we were the only people here. But the next time he appears, I will not be so captivated by him. I was unprepared. It will not happen again."

"And your lie about the amulet?"

"I did not lie to you. The second time I used it was at Mount Smolikos, after the mountain collapsed. It helped us get out again. I used it to help you."

"Maybe you hoped you'd kill me like you did those Persians, that way you wouldn't have to concern yourself with me."

"Do not be foolish," I snapped. "It was after I realized how I felt about you that I used it. I was not going to let you die there. I did what I had to."

She clenched and unclenched her jaw but said nothing more. I crossed to her, reaching out to smooth the frown lines above her eyebrows. "There is only one person I want kissing me Demi, and it is not Ares."

"So you say."

I growled deep in my throat and ripped the fibula from her chiton, exposing her chest. I slid my hands inside, cupping what was left of her breasts as I kissed her hard. My tongue found its way into her mouth as hers battled mine in return.

"Do not doubt me. *You* are the one I want, not him," I panted when we parted.

"Theron!" the desperate yell cut through the silence around us and we both jumped.

34

Demetri gathered our himatia from the bathing room as I grabbed my sword and we ran from the house. Papou stood where I had met the sheep flock several nights before, hands on his knees, puffing mightily. Theron, Origenes and several other warriors appeared; spears at the ready, eyes darting around to find the source of the danger.

"What is it?" Theron asked.

"Persians," Papou panted.

"Here? That makes no sense," Theron replied. "They have never ventured this far east."

"You," Origenes growled, raising his spear as he turned to me and Demetri. "I knew we should not trust you. You were the diversion, sent to distract us with your talk of sword making, while your army had time to surround us."

"No, I swear, they're not our allies," Demetri said, holding his hands up.

"I shall kill you," Origenes shouted, bursting forward. Papou stepped into his path, knocking the spear from Origenes' hand and laying him out cold with a sharp blow to the temple.

Papou addressed Theron. "They are not under Ava's command."

"But they *are* here because of me," I added, sheathing my sword. Ares said my time was coming, and it seemed that the God of War was an impatient man.

"Why? Were you fleeing from them when you arrived?" Theron asked.

"No. But I can stop them."

"You cannot," Papou said, meeting my eyes. "You must not."

"It is the only way to save these people. I will not let them to lose their lives for me."

"It is too dangerous."

"It is the only way," I insisted, taking the amulet from my tunic. It glowed orange and warmed my fingers. Its power filled me. I welcomed it. "I know what it does. I can destroy them all."

"I shall not allow it."

I advanced on Papou. "You refused to talk to me when there was time; you refused to acknowledge what you obviously know to be true. Now there is an advancing enemy, *our* enemy and I can kill them all without losing anyone else. I will use the amulet like my mothers want me to and I will win. If you do not want to stay and see what I have become, who I *truly* am, then go. Take the Molossians with you for their spears are not needed in this fight."

"Give me the amulet," Papou ordered, holding his palm out.

I gripped the gem tighter. "No."

"I cannot allow you to do this. You should have been free of its curse."

The heat from the amulet roared through my arms and chest. "I have no further use for you, old man."

Papou's face transformed into a grimace and he roared as he charged, sword held high above his head. I took out my own, meeting him solidly, the sound of iron against iron filling the air.

"I beg of you. That amulet is evil and shall take everything you hold dear from you, my darling."

"You are merely jealous that it makes me a better soldier than you ever were," I snarled, pushing upwards against his sword as he pushed down on mine. He was stronger than I had expected, but with the amulet's power coursing through me I held my own against his attack.

We rounded the clearing – sword to sword, iron to iron – until finally I took his feet out from under him and he crashed to the ground. I stood above him, my chest heaving, sword poised to run him through.

"Ava, no!" Demetri cried.

"They are here," someone screamed.

"Not today, old man," I murmured, spinning my sword in my hand and slamming the pommel against his temple, just as he had done to Origenes.

I straightened and faced the gathered army; three hundred Persian soldiers in white cuirasses and yellow head coverings less than two hundred feet away. Beside me, Demetri took Papou's arms and dragged him towards the houses. Theron did the same with Origenes, shouting orders to the Molossian warriors who fled towards the clearing with sudden purpose.

"Cowards," I muttered. They were clearly not the vicious warriors I had heard tales of, but scared mountain men who, when faced with a greater number than their own, chose to flee instead of defending their homes and people.

Demetri neared and when our eyes met, he flinched ever so slightly. I recognized his stance as one of confusion. He wanted to escape the destruction he knew I could inflict, yet his love for me held him in place.

I focused once again on the soldiers and took the amulet from my neck. The orange was brighter and hotter now. I drank in its power like a dying man would water. A light breeze lifted my hair, calling to me to conjure the air element Ares had spoken of. My shoulder blades itched and I stood straighter, dropping my himation to the ground as I waited for my magnificent black wings to emerge.

I shivered as Ares appeared beside me. "Your grandfather does not appear pleased that you have the amulet," he said.

"He is not my foremost concern."

Ares laughed and put his hands on my shoulders, his thumbs caressing the small nodes high on my back. "What do you think of my army? After your display on the Plain with only thirty men, I thought you could do with a challenge."

"How many did Mumma face when you tested her?" I asked, ignoring his question.

Ares circled me and I met his eyes. "More," he replied with a grin.

"Make it as it was that day. Show me what she faced."

He laughed again. "You truly are everything I have waited for." He turned towards the army, holding out his hand, his palm facing the sky. The soldiers before us shimmered, their clothing and armor transforming into a mass of black leather and colored plumes standing tall on their helmets. They stood so close together it was almost impossible to tell where one man ended and the next began.

"How many?"

"One thousand soldiers. My soldiers, not Persians."

"They hold no weapons, it does not seem a fair fight with what I have."

Ares shrugged. "You wanted it just as it was that day." He motioned to the silent group and one soldier emerged, the long blade of his sword held against Irina's throat. "It was Alexis held in such a manner back then, but this shall do. Prove who you are. What you can do."

I refocused on the entirety of the army, glancing only briefly at Irina. Her face was pale, eyes large, but somehow I knew I could dispense of the army without hurting her. I raised the amulet until it was level with my chest, warmth filling me from head to foot as, with very little pain, my wings extended behind me, the sheer fabric of my tunic no match for their powerful ends. The cry of a bird rang out around me. I smiled. It cried for me, for who I was and what I could do.

The breeze became stronger. I gripped the amulet tightly, urging the wind to come. The jet turned from orange to a cloudy grey, then silver, as though a fire's worth of smoke was trapped inside the gemstone.

"Ava ..." Demetri breathed. "Please don't do this. There are too many of them,"

"Quiet," I commanded. "Ares will not let them kill me. If I die then the Keres' line, my line, ends. There is no one to pass the amulet on to."

"And what about Irina?"

"She will not be harmed."

"You are placing a lot of faith in the God of War. He's not known for *saving* mortals."

"He will not let me meet Hades in the Underworld. Now, get back."

"No."

"Now, Demetri." Still he did not move. I took a sideways step and turned the amulet on him.

"What are you ...?" I swept Demetri up with a gust of wind, setting him down again several paces from where he had been. His mouth gaped open but he did not approach me.

I turned back to the army; they had started to advance. The amulet glowed even brighter. The wind heightened and my hair whipped across my face. Suddenly the sky darkened. At first I could not see what was causing it, but slowly they came into focus. Birds; thousands of big, black vultures raced across the sky towards Konitsa. The flapping of their wings overhead was deafening as they circled the sky above the army, as if waiting for my command. I took a step forward, aiming the amulet directly at the soldiers.

"Archers!" Ares shouted. Bows appeared in the soldiers' hands and they immediately raised them in response. "It is up to you now," Ares said, stepping aside.

I nodded and focused the amulet on Irina and the man who held her. "Free her," I murmured.

An almost invisible grey streak flew from between my fingers, and lodged itself in the soldier's shoulder, sending him sprawling backwards. With the impact, he released Irina. She scrambled away and I turned to the army. Their arrows were trained on me, but I did not give them the chance to fire. The wind buffeted me where I stood, gaining in speed and power. A bright speck of silver sat on the outside of the amulet, begging to be released.

"Now," I whispered. It bolted away from my hand, encircling the army and trapping them inside the wall of howling wind. The bows were ripped from their hands, sent spinning upwards into the wind chamber, as one by one the soldiers rose from the ground to join their weapons in my swirling creation.

The birds screeched in reply, soaring out of reach of the wind tunnel. They ducked and weaved as one, a great dark mass, before turning their beaks towards me, their red eyes locked with mine. Within moments their shadowy outlines became clearer, their bodies no longer resembling birds, but women. I grinned again, knowing they were my ancestors, my kin. They were part of me. They were the Keres. My wings flapped behind me and I inched forward. The Keres looked to me. I knew what they wanted, I could feel their desire. I wanted it too. I nodded.

They dove down through the trees and into the tumbling mess of bodies and weapons. They pecked and clawed whatever they could find. The soldiers cried out, arms flailing about their heads as they tried to protect themselves. Their screams were quickly drowned out by the animals. The Keres worked together, some holding the men high off the ground with their clawed feet, as others attacked any unguarded flesh they could find. They ripped off clothing and armor, sinking their teeth deep into the exposed skin. They fed mid-air, reveling in the taste of the blood. I was drawn to join them, could almost taste the blood in my mouth and feel the flesh as it came apart in their hands.

I laughed, triumph filling me, as I watched the flock scratch and maim with their sharp talons, pecking the eyes from the soldiers with their long beaks. The bloodshed and carnage the vultures created fueled the desire raging within me. I was proud of them, proud of their obedience to my will. I hoped Ares would send more soldiers to replace the ones so easily killed, but I could not find my voice to ask him.

Demetri's hand suddenly covered mine on the amulet. He was trying to take it from me. I rounded on him as a familiar adrenaline coursed through my body, more powerful than I had ever felt it before. Demetri's face was a mask of terror, but when our eyes met, something flickered in his and changed. Suddenly it was not lust for blood that welled within me, but lust for Demetri. For Demi. For him. For her. For what *she* made me feel and for how *he* would make me feel it. Desire surged between us through the amulet. The woman and the man inside the body before me felt what I did; heat, control, unrestrained desire. Lust. Demi smiled and gripped tighter. Triumph and fiery desire crossed her features and I recognized the hunger; she would have me with a passion and need deeper than anything she had ever known. In return, I wanted to devour her. Own him. Be one with him. Heat crackled in the air, exciting me, calling to me as a rush of wind swept us off the ground. I released the amulet and it hung in the air beside us, never wavering in the intensity it had created.

Suddenly I knew who Demetri was – a woman from head to waist, a man from waist to toes. That was how she made sense to me. Two halves of a whole. She or he depending on what part of her touched me or where I touched him. Demi seized me by the waist and pulled me against her hard body. She kissed me fiercely, hungrily. I fisted my hands in her hair, drawing her closer still. She drove her tongue deep into my mouth and my own fought for supremacy in hers. Her body burnt my fingers, which only served to fuel my desperation.

I ripped the chiton from her body, throwing it aside. It disappeared immediately in an updraft of the maelstrom that raged around us. She swept my hair from my shoulders, finding the hollow of my collarbone with her teeth. I dug my fingers into the scars on her back from the slave-boy lashings as she freed me from the confines of my clothing. Her eyes journeyed over my skin from top to bottom, pausing mid-way back up. She traced the dark shape on my ribs with her fingertips before cupping each of my breasts in her hands.

I drew her eyes back to mine, pressing my lower body into his and capturing her lips as her hands enthralled me. Skin against skin our bodies met. The power around us intensified. Her hands possessed me, moving ever lower, her lips trailed down my throat to my breast, my body writhing beneath the heated ministrations. With her lips and hands she brought me ever closer to the point of my desire, in turn caressing and possessing my most intimate areas, inflaming me with the longing she delivered.

I could feel him hard against my thigh and I longed to feel him inside me. I put my hand on her cheek. She looked up, breaking the sweet contact at my breast. The black of her eyes burned red and I glided my finger over her chest, teasing the remaining nipple into a hard point. Demi gasped, her back arching into the contact. I flattened my hand where her breast should have been, never stopping the pressure at her nipple.

She closed her eyes, her fingers quickening against me, his hardness pressing forward to join them.

"Gods … I want you. Please," she whispered.

"Yes," I replied. She opened her eyes, sliding her hands around to grip my backside. I gasped at the need I saw reflected on her face and I put one hand on her shoulder, easing onto him.

A guttural groan escaped her as he pushed into me, filling me and heating me from the inside. Her hands held me firmly as we moved together, soaring higher within the vortex, higher than the birds I had conjured with my amulet until finally our desire reached its peak and we found sweet release.

35

An enormous clang like a hammer crashing against an anvil shattered our intimate entanglement. Demetri and I were flung apart with incredible force. I remained caught in the updraft of the wind for several moments before the air stilled and I drifted back to the ground, the amulet landing beside me. I returned it to my neck, the intense beating of my heart drowning out all other sounds.

I wondered if I had dreamt the birds, the army, what had happened between Demetri – Demi – and me. There was no sign of her, or of Ares' army that had stood before me and been decimated by the Keres. The only reminder the soldiers had been there were the fine tendrils of grey smoke drifting across the darkening sky. The warmth and power from the amulet lingered and I knew it had been real; I had not been unknowingly drawn into Morpheus' realm.

My tunic lay in a heap beside me and I settled the material around my body as I got to my feet. I shivered, struck by how silent the path was. "It appears your lover has left you," a quiet voice said beside me. "Perhaps he was not as fond of you as you believed."

"Maybe," I agreed, rolling my shoulders.

"He is nothing but a weak mortal. He is not worthy of one of such standing."

"She has strength you can only dream of but there are few who are worthy of my body," I replied.

Ares laughed and placed his hands on my waist. "No mortal shall ever have you again. You belong to me, to the gods now."

I brushed his hands from my waist and faced him. "I do not belong to anyone, if you want any part of me you will have to earn it, just like anyone else."

He laughed again, taking my chin in his hand. "I have waited so very long for you. You *shall* belong to me, I feel it."

Swiping his hand away, I picked up my himation from the ground. "We will see."

A shiver ran the length of my spine as Ares disappeared and my eyes found Papou's crumpled form. The addictive, calm heat the amulet had filled me with vanished and, with a faintly sick feeling, I ran to my grandfather.

I knelt beside him as I shook his shoulder. "Papou?"

He groaned and relief flooded through me. His eyes cracked open, finding my face. "What did you do?" he asked.

I dropped my eyes to my hands. "I am sorry, Papou, I never meant to hurt you."

He grimaced and pushed himself upright. "I know." His eyes darted around. "The army? The amulet, did you use it?" I nodded, keeping my eyes from his. "By the gods," he whispered. "And you destroyed them all?"

"Everyone Ares put in my path."

"Skylar and Alexis never wanted this. They believed they had broken the cycle," he muttered.

"You are wrong, Papou. They *did* want this for me. They came to me – both of them – in my dreams. It was Mumma who delivered the amulet to me before I set out to find you."

"It was not them, can you not see that? Ares knew the one weakness you had and he used it against you. You must not use it again, do you hear me? Not ever."

At his words, I knew the truth; the odd stance Mumma had when she visited me in my dreams, the flashing of her eyes, the reason I had been reluctant to tell her of my plans to find Papou – it had never been she or Mother Alexis in Morpheus' realm – it had always been Ares.

"Today was not the first time I made the amulet bend to my will," I admitted.

Papou grabbed my chin, forcing me to look at him. "How many times?"

"Tell me what you know of the amulet," I countered, pulling my face from his grip.

"How many times have you been able to call on its power?" he asked again, fear evident across his features.

"Three."

He closed his eyes and drew in a deep breath. "What element did you destroy that army with today?"

181

"Wind," I replied, too ashamed to mention the Keres and the part they had played in the destruction.

"Has it always been wind?" he asked, opening his eyes and holding his hand out to me. I shook my head. "What else?"

I got to my feet, pulling him with me. "Fire and water."

He shook his head back and forth, sliding his sword into its sheath. "It cannot happen. Not to her," he muttered.

I placed my hand on his arm. "Papou, please, tell me what you all kept from me when I was a child. Ares told me the origins of the amulet, but you and Mumma and I ... we do not share blood so how come I can control the amulet's power?"

"What else did Ares speak of?"

"He said he had been waiting for me and that he would help me harness the power of the amulet and control the elements."

"He continues to believe," Papou whispered, his eyes searching the area again. "Where is Demetri?"

"I do not know. We were ... together and then I found myself on the ground and he and the Persians were nowhere in sight."

"How close was he to you when you used the amulet?"

Heat crept up my neck and I could not look at him as I answered. "Close."

"Did he touch you? Did he touch the amulet?" Papou pressed.

"What does it matter?" I asked keeping my eyes focused on the trees far to the east.

"I need no specifics, but your avoidance tells me the two of you were together in an intimate sense. That would explain his sudden absence."

"How can you be sure?" I asked, returning my eyes to his.

"Do you love him?" Papou asked instead. I shuddered as a flare of heat rippled through my veins and the calm feeling returned, my wings throbbing beneath my skin.

I shook my head. "The love of a mortal is not for me. I wanted him for nothing more than pleasure, for a diversion and entertainment along my journey, but he could not withstand the pleasures he received in return."

Papou stared at me again for a long moment. "The words you speak are not your own, and I have heard similar ones spoken before. You *do* love that boy. I shall find a way for you to remember that, for both of you to remember."

I dismissed his words with a wave of my hand. "I should not have sought you. I should have let Ares guide me from the start. I should have got my answers from him. *He* is my future; *he* shall help me destroy my enemies ..."

Papou advanced, squeezing my arms furiously between his hands. "Do not *ever* speak such words. There is much I must tell you, much you must understand about the amulet, about our family and what it would mean if you used it again. So much I should have told you before it came to this. Ares is controlling you even now; he shall destroy who you are and all the goodness inside you if you allow him to."

I wrenched myself from his grip, anger heating my blood even further. My wings pulsated beneath my skin and I set my feet, waiting for them. They broke free, lengthening behind me, flapping slightly when I commanded it of them. Papou took a step back, eyes wide, hand resting on the pommel of his sword.

"Why should I care about the past now when I am so clear about my future? I must use the amulet to destroy the Persians."

Papou shook his head. "No." He drew his sword, raising it high above his head. I was so surprised by the gesture I did not even reach for my weapon in defense as he brought his down on the closest of my wings. A crack echoed off the buildings behind us like Papou had struck iron against stone. His sword bounced off, the motion sending him stumbling backwards as it did me. The sting of his blow registered in a dark area of my mind and I dimly noted the spots of blood that fell to the ground beside me.

"By the gods," Papou murmured. My wings retracted into my skin, a dull throb accompanying the action and discharging the seductively warm liquid coursing through my blood. I shook my head and picked up my himation, drawing it around my shoulders and pulling it close against the sudden chill.

"Why?" I managed. "Why would you do that?"

"Forgive me," Papou said, remaining where he was, sword still in hand. "I thought it was the only way to break you from his hold. To rid you of your wings. But ... but Ares already has a greater hold on you than I imagined. I fear I shall not be able to tell you everything before he finds a way for you to use the amulet again." I said nothing. "You must promise me you shall not use the amulet again, I beg it of you. You must fight him."

I did not know if I *wanted* to fight Ares. His words filled me with such a sense of truth. It felt wrong to question them. But part of me also knew that what I felt and the words I had spoken to Papou were not what I really believed. I loved Papou, and Demi, and did not want to hurt either of them. I could not.

"Gather your belongings and wait for me here," Papou directed.

"What about the Molossians?"

"They shall not return until morning. After you and I spoke last night I told Theron and Irina you possessed the amulet. I was concerned you may use it while we were here. We agreed if you did, they would take their people into the mountains and wait for morning before returning. I could not be certain how the amulet would affect you and I did not want them to die if you were unable to control your impulse to kill."

"Irina ... I ... she was being held by one of the soldiers but I ... the wind pushed her out of harm's way. I think."

"If you did not see her die with the soldiers then she shall be safe. She shall be with Theron."

"How can you be sure?"

"I just am."

"You speak like Theron and Irina knew of the amulet's existence already."

"They did, though they have never seen what it is capable of."

"How?"

"I have known them both for many winters, they knew Zita."

The familiar lilt in Theron and Irina's words ... "You are all from the same area," I ventured.

"From the Thracian tribe of the Bessoi, yes," Papou nodded.

Oh," I murmured, unsure how else to reply. I knew nothing of Papou's history. When I was a child, the stories I heard from he or my mothers of their pasts started when they all met in Trachis. Back then, I had never thought to question where any of them had been before that and by the time I was old enough to wonder about it, they were all gone.

"Where do you think Demetri shall go now you are separated? He said he sought information on the armor of the Tymphaioi; with what little I showed him, would he return to his home with that knowledge?"

"He would not go home," I replied with a shake of my head. "Athens is where he intended to go once he had it so if I were to guess, I would say there."

"Athens it is then," Papou nodded. "Gather some food from Irina's kitchen, we shall head south and find Demetri's trail." I hesitated, afraid that if I went inside, Papou would not be there when I returned. As if sensing my worry, Papou took my hand. "I shall not leave again without you. Ever. You have my word." I nodded and climbed the steps of Theron and Irina's home, casting a glance back to Papou, who gave me a tight smile.

I went directly to the bedroom, my eyes automatically finding the bed. *I heard you ask Hades not to take me ... I heard you say ... that you might one day love me ... I think I'm in love with you and I don't want to lose you.* Demetri's – Demi's – words speared through me. Her bag was gone, as was her sword – which I had last seen sticking out of the far wall. What if I never saw her again? Grief gripped me at the thought, much as it had when I found her cold, motionless body in the mountain. I groped for the wall to steady myself, a knot forming in my throat, my breath refusing to come.

I knew now that I loved Demi not just because she was the first person I had shared my secrets with, but because she had made me *want* to share my life with someone else, someone outside of the soldiers, outside the only life I had known for so many winters. I wanted her more than I had thought it possible to want someone. There would not be anyone else for me. In my heart I knew it was the truth and not even Ares' seductive voice in my head could drown out that certainty. If what had happened between us when I used the amulet this last time had made her run then I would find her and try and repair it. I needed to tell her how I felt. I needed to tell her I loved her. I swallowed. I had not told anyone I loved them in ten winters. Not since … my mothers. I had to tell Demi I would never use the amulet again if she asked it of me.

Papou had told Casaereo he wanted to find and destroy the amulet … was that the only truth he shared with him when he spoke of it? "I will destroy the amulet like Papou wanted to. He will never have to fear me using it again," I told the empty room as I gathered my bag.

"No!" another, much louder, voice filled the room, sending a shudder through my body. "The amulet is your destiny. I am. Nothing and no one shall stand in your way. You shall fight and kill. You can take your revenge on anyone, or any nation who has ever wronged you. You can avenge your mothers. You can be unstoppable and you shall enjoy every second of it."

I expected to find Ares behind me when I turned, but there was no one else in the room. "I will not," I insisted to the emptiness. "My destiny is my own to make." I closed my eyes as my body shook again. I knew Ares was gone.

As much as I wanted revenge on the Persians, I wanted Demi too. Somehow I knew I could not have both. There would be dire consequences whichever choice I made. I could not, would not, make any decision until I knew what Papou and my mothers had kept from me for so long.

"What are you not telling me Ares?" I asked the empty room. This time he did not answer.

36

"I thought you said she was the one. Why is she resisting what you offer her?" Hades asked, pacing across the polished marble floor of Ares' palace.

"She is not the first in her line to do so," Aphrodite mused, her eyes finding her lover's as she brushed her hair.

"Not helpful," Ares snapped. "She shall come around."

"When? None of her actions have been as those before her, even if you knew that would be so," Hades continued. "We have spoken already of how fast her recovery was, but she should not have such a will to deny you. How is it so when she has had no one to warn her against you all these winters?"

"She shall do what I want. I just need to convince her what I want is what she wants. Removing the boy was the first step. It shall be easier now," Ares replied.

"It had better be."

"Perhaps your line is dissolving rather than evolving as you believed with her grandmother," Aphrodite shrugged. "Zita called forth the water element, but Skylar reverted to the fire."

"And Ava has used both, plus the wind element," Ares growled, disappearing.

37

Papou and I made our way south from Konitsa, travelling until well after the sun had dropped behind the mountains and shrouded everything beyond the glow of our torch in darkness. I waited quietly, impatiently, for Papou's explanation and when the moon was at its highest point, he started to speak.

"I know you have many questions. I once had to travel a similar journey to this with your Mumma, but that makes it no easier. Before I can explain about Demetri's departure, I must tell you where this all began. Where it began for me." He looked to me and I nodded for him to go on. He nodded in return, his eyes focusing again on the path ahead of us. "You said Ares told you where the amulet came from ... what did he say exactly?"

"That the amulet was made for him by the Keres, who had been with a clan of Valkyrie since he banished them. They said they would obey his wishes again and that the Valkyrie could make something very powerful, if he agreed to provide them with a drop of his blood. He did, and with his blood and one of the Ker's combined, the amulet became sacred to him and that particular line," I replied.

"He spoke the truth on that at least," Papou acknowledged. "Your grandmother, Zita, was a Ker. I did not know that at first, but once we were in Konitsa, she spoke of what that meant in detail. Did Ares tell you what the Keres did?"

"Yes. They were assigned to mortals destined to die a violent death, and when they fell, the Keres swooped down and fed on their blood before carrying them off to Hades in the Underworld."

Papou nodded, his face grim when he spoke again. "I was born in Thrace, to the Bessoi tribe. Our people were the protectors of the Satrae – priests and priestesses who lived on the highest mountain of the area – interpreting the words of the gods, just as the Delphic Oracle does in Greece.

"As first-born I was immediately named a warrior and when the time came, I took my place as defender of the tribe. Zita was assigned to me. She followed me for many winters without me ever knowing. As I grew, and she came to know my thoughts and my ways, she fell in love with me. One day she appeared to me – something that was highly forbidden – and as soon as I laid eyes on her, I fell in love with her too.

"I was in many battles and at the end of each of them Zita would come to me, tending to the wounds I had received and offering advice on how to avoid such injuries next time. At first I did not understand how she could have seen me fight, and I would tell her I did not want her so close to such danger." He smiled as he remembered. "She always laughed and said I did not need to worry. Eventually I learned it was because she was high above the battles, not in the mountains or on the plains where I fought. One day I was badly wounded and as I lay on the ground, I knew it was my time to meet Hades, but Zita would not allow it. She swooped down and took me far from the battlefield. She defied her duty, her family, her ancestors' vow to Ares, and she healed me, telling me she could not live without me."

"Is that when you went to Konitsa?"

"Yes. We remained there for a number of moons, until she found she was with child. She feared her family would feel the baby so we left and it was then she told me of her line; her *curse* she called it. She never wanted that life for our child and we agreed never to tell her of it. We travelled south through Thessaly and Boeotia, moving on every half-moon or so until we reached the Peloponnese.

"By the time we arrived in the south, the constant travel became too much for Zita and we stopped in a small village near Sparta. We were there for just over a moon, until the night she birthed your Mumma. That night everything changed. Do you remember the mark your Mumma had on her left shoulder?" I nodded, bending down to scratch the three-sided shape into the ground with a small stone. "Zita had one too, just the same," Papou said. I wanted to tell Papou about the shapes on my ribs, but I held my tongue.

"Through her mark, Zita could feel the Keres, she knew they were coming for us. She could not tell if they knew about the baby, but she was certain if they found Skylar there with the mark, they would take her back and raise her as one of them. Zita was supposed to kill me, but ..." he paused. "But instead they killed her," he finished. I reached out and took his hand, holding it tightly. "I took Skylar, having promised Zita that we would continue to move from town to town, to never stay in one place for too long. She had told me it was the only way we would stay safe. Zita hoped that with Skylar being half-mortal, and without influence from her family, she may be free of the curse.

"I had barely reached the olive grove near the house when the Keres arrived. They flew down from the sky, long flames trailing them. They were huge with faces and bodies of women, wings akin to that of birds. They dragged Zita and the owner of the house outside, setting fire to it. Zita's wings erupted from her shoulders and she pounced on that poor man, ripping apart his flesh with her claws and her mouth until she had taken him apart piece by piece.

"I believed – just for a moment – they would forgive her for leaving, but they did not. They turned on her, biting and tearing at her body as she screamed. I could stand it no longer and I did not want our daughter to bear witness to such bestiality, so I fled into the trees and far away from the small house."

"Papou," I whispered.

He squeezed my hand. "I kept Skylar safe just as Zita wanted. I travelled from town to town, village to village, working at whatever trade they needed most; Fisherman, Baker, Craftsman, Celator. But I never drew a sword again. Not until Skylar was twelve winters old." He drew in a deep breath, exhaling it all the way before continuing. "We were in a small town called Anticyra, near Delphi. We had plans to move on within the day, but as we packed our few belongings, a mercenary and his men attacked. There was no time to get everyone to safety and besides, my warrior's heart still beat inside me. I could not leave a defenseless town full of farmers to the hands of plunderers and rapists. I had no choice but to stay and fight. Skylar too felt a similar calling.

"She was remarkable, showing no fear in the face of the battle. She took my sword from my scabbard, cutting down two of the men before I had a chance to stop her. I armed myself with spears and we defended the town almost single-handedly. I was afraid for her, for what it might mean, but I put away my fears, choosing to believe that she had inherited *my* fighting skills, not her mother's Ker instincts. I knew it was the amulet that perpetuated the strength of the Ker, and neither of us possessed it.

"After that, Skylar was determined for us to rid the countryside of mercenaries and thieves, to go to the aid of defenseless farmers who did not know how to protect themselves from such attacks. She insisted I teach her all I knew about defense and attack, having realized I was not new to battles. I admitted that I had once been a great warrior. I agreed to her request not only because I knew it would mean we would always be on the move, but because I believed she was headstrong enough to attempt it on her own and she would have been killed if I did not aid her.

"For seven winters we travelled the lands offering help where it was needed, fighting tyrants, armies, slavers and thieves. News of us reached many ears and we aided, among others, the Spartan king against an Athenian tyrant and the people of Stratos against the Epirotes. Skylar joined me among the ranks of every army until one day, as we travelled to Agrias' palace at Trachis, she was badly injured.

"We were there almost a moon before Skylar was strong enough to even hold a sword and I led Agrias' men in drills and mock battles, seeing her as often as I could. When she recovered, I learned that she had fallen in love with your mother – the Princess of Trachis – who was promised to another. Soon after Skylar and Alexis spoke of their feelings for one another, Illyrian and Epirote forces arrived and we were dispatched to defend Trachis for the king."

"I remember that story," I said, the memory from so long ago resurfacing. "When the army arrived, Mother was captured by … someone, I do not remember his name."

"Melanthios," Papou supplied.

I nodded. "He stole her away from the palace, hiding out at the hot springs. But Mumma found them, killed Melanthios and saved Mother. Mother said Mumma was her hero as she always saved her when she needed it."

Papou nodded, dropping his eyes to the stony path beneath our feet. "They loved each other very much. I was so happy when Skylar found someone who made her as happy as Zita, and then Nasrin, made me. When the Illyrian threat was quelled, I left, travelling to Konitsa where Nasrin was. Unfortunately, the Keres found Skylar six moons later, while I was still away, and you grew inside Alexis." Papou took his hand from mine. "We shall rest here tonight," he said.

"But Demetri …"

"We can travel faster than he can, we have time to rest." He put his bag on the ground, finding small sticks and tinder for a fire. I blew out a deep breath but shed my own bag, placing rocks in a circle and laying larger branches from nearby trees inside them.

When the leaves and twigs had caught, Papou continued. "Zita's mother, Dianthe, was the first to make herself known. She told Skylar who – or rather what – her mother was. She told her of her family history, omitting of course their part in Zita's death, and painting me as a villain for keeping the 'truth' from her."

"I understand how she felt," I murmured, poking at the fire with a spare stick.

Papou did not respond but it was a long moment before he spoke again and I did not meet his eyes. "Ares gifted the amulet to Skylar, telling her it would increase her abilities and provide her with many more. He promised to help her use it for good – playing on her wish to protect Alexis and their unborn child, as well as those who could not protect themselves, just as she had since she was twelve winters old. She believed everything he and Dianthe told her – and would not believe what I said."

"She sent word to you in Konitsa?"

"No, by the time they spoke to her, I had already returned to Trachis. But she was so angry with me for what I had kept from her that she would not speak to me. It remained that way until after she used the amulet for the first time. At first, she could not call forth its power, not until Ares provided the incentive for her to do so. He sent an army to attack the city and capture Alexis, threatening to do her harm. Only then was Skylar able to harness the fire element and defeat them to save her."

"Until I used the amulet myself, I did not believe the story Moeris and some of the other soldiers told of Mumma vanquishing an entire army with fire."

Papou nodded, but the gesture was more to himself than to me. "It was a … surprising, terrifying day for many."

"I can only imagine," I murmured, my thoughts turning to Demetri and the day on the Plain. "Do you think Ares and Dianthe knew about Mumma before she was in Trachis? Or that they knew you had gone, and so went to her? Maybe they saw you as a threat," I eventually asked.

"I doubt they saw me as a threat, and I do not have an answer for you – I have always wondered how long they had known of her by the time they made themselves known," Papou replied. "Perhaps it was just luck and they saw her mark one day, or perhaps they felt her power when she reached nineteen winters."

"But she only ever used *one* of the elements – that day with the army?"

"Yes. I was so grateful she was not who Ares believed she was. Until you were born, the question hung between us all of whether the title would fall to you or not. We did not believe it had but now … now you have …"

"I have been able to use three of the elements," I finished.

Papou nodded. "Yes. But just as when Ares gave his explanation to Skylar, he has left out many truths when speaking to you about what it would mean if you really are the Chosen One, able to command all four of the amulet's elements."

"What do you mean? What would happen if I used the last element?"

Papou's eyes met mine briefly before settling on the fire before us again. "If you are indeed Ares' Chosen One and you command the power of the last element, you shall be lost to me. To Demetri, and to yourself. Ares is not going to aid you or protect you. He is going to use you for his own purpose. He would have complete control over you. You would do his bidding. He could call on you whenever he wanted and you would not be able to resist or deny him," he replied in a grave voice.

I frowned. "I do not understand, how could the title of the Chosen One fall to me anyway? Mumma and I do not share blood, we are mother and daughter in name only."

He exhaled slowly. "You do share blood. You are of Skylar's body just as much as Alexis'."

38

I frowned and shook my head. "I do not understand, how can that be?"

"Before the Keres arrived, your mothers discussed having a child. It was to grow inside Alexis, and when they journeyed to the Heraion of Perachora near Corinth, they learnt that part of them both could be used in the creation. Do you remember Thaddeus?" I nodded. "He and Alexis were very close and he agreed to help your mothers. When the three of them came back from Hera's temple, you had been created inside Alexis with parts from all of them."

"So Thaddeus is … was … my father?" I asked.

"Yes."

"He … he died that night in the palace. He tried to save them," I murmured.

"Yes," Papou confirmed.

I swallowed loudly. As a small child, I had loved Thaddeus and his wife Hesper as though they were uncle and aunt and they had always treated me as kin. They were kind, yet firm in their discipline; Lysistratos and me often joining their own four children in rough games in their apartment or in the courtyard of the palace, even after Tritonos died. The five of us – Lysistratos, me, Nikomachos, Pamphilos and Eumelia – were always together … until the night that changed everything. I had mourned for Thaddeus, along with my mothers, in the days and moons that followed, never realizing I lost all three of my parents that night.

The same day Papou was banished from Trachis, Hesper took her own life at the cliffs near the west gate, unable to bear the thought of living without Thaddeus. Those of us left had tried to be there for each other in our grief, but it was the start of our separation from one another – at least until Lysistratos and me had reconnected at the barracks, Eumelia and me soon after that.

Tears slid down my cheeks as the pain I always worked so hard to keep down settled around my heart. Papou moved to my side, wrapping an arm around my waist and holding me as I cried.

"Forgive me, my darling," he finally said, kissing the top of my head. "I kept this from you for so long. I should have told you so you could mourn for him properly, just as you mourned for your mothers."

"I farewelled him in my heart just as I did them," I replied, as my tears slowed. "I was just a child, I could not have understood. Besides, I was not the only one left to grow without parents, my … half-siblings Nikomachos, Pamphilos and Eumelia were left behind too."

"As Tritonos would have had his life not been cut short," Papou nodded.

"I … I never knew how much family I still had there after you left. I thought I was alone." I paused, closing my eyes as I sent silent words to all of them. "Maybe that is why Nikomachos and Pamphilos did not stay in Trachis," I mused.

"Perhaps," Papou agreed. "Shall I go on?" he added after a long moment.

"Yes," I replied, opening my eyes again.

"When it became apparent that Skylar was not his Chosen One, Ares told her that her daughter – that you – would be far more powerful than she; that the Ker bloodline was strong in your veins. You were the one he had been waiting for, he could feel it. He told us that when you were old enough, he would return."

I wiped away the last of my tears, my brow furrowing again as I straightened. "Why did none of you speak of it as I grew? Why did you not warn me? Did you not believe what he had said to be true?"

"We believed he was mistaken – you had no mark – nothing that indicated you had any Ker blood in you. I cannot tell you how relieved we all were when we saw that bare patch of skin on your shoulder the night you were born."

"But I do have a mark. It is not on my shoulder as you all thought it would be, but with everything I have so recently learnt from Ares and you, I have no doubt it is the mark of the Keres."

"Show me," Papou said, fear crossing his face once again. I stood, removing my himation, chlamys and cuirass and pulling my tunic up, revealing the dark mark on my ribs that Demi had traced in the wind tunnel.

Instead of a single, three-sided shape, it was like two, one opposite the other with the bottom line of both removed in the middle.

Papou joined me by the fire, staring intently at it. "By the gods," he whispered. "That must be the completed mark Ares spoke of after you were born. But it was not there that night ..."

"Ares was in Trachis when I was born?"

"He made Alexis birth you three moons early," Papou murmured distractedly. "We all checked you so thoroughly. How did we not see it?"

I frowned but did not press him for further details on Ares' presence – there would be time for that story later. "It was not always this shape; it started as a small, dark dot that I thought nothing of for the longest time. But when the knobs started to grow hideously from my back, I saw that it had changed too. As the winters passed it spread out, becoming an obvious shape, not just a drop of dark color against my skin."

"What knobs?" Papou asked.

I re-settled my tunic and pulled my himation and chlamys around me again, leaving my cuirass off for the moment. "The ones on my back – where my wings sprouted from when I used the amulet. They started to grow soon after you left Trachis. I did not tell anyone about them and I had no one to explain what they meant or why they had suddenly appeared – if they should even be there. If you had been there, I am sure I would have asked you or shown you, but you were gone and I could hardly send a messenger to look for you with such questions. They were a source of shame and secrecy for me ... until I met Demetri. He was the first person to ever lay eyes on them."

"I ... I am sorry," Papou whispered, settling his gaze on the flames again.

"Did Mumma ever speak of hers to you?" I asked.

"No. I do not know if she had them ... before."

"Then she was fortunate," I said quietly.

We were silent a long while, each lost in our own thoughts until I spoke again. "Papou, when I used the amulet, I did not become a Ker; I did not grow claws as you said Zita had, just wings. Did Mumma change when she used it?"

"The only truly obvious difference was the wings, just as it was for you," he replied.

"Why did she not use her wings the night she was killed? Could she not have saved herself and Mother by drawing on some sort of … I do not know what to call it … Ker powers with them?"

"She no longer had them."

"Did they disappear when she was unable to use the amulet again?"

"No," he replied. "I cut them off."

"What?" I said, jumping as the fire crackled loudly beside me.

Papou poked at the embers. "When Skylar used the amulet to save Alexis, she changed before my eyes. It was not just the wings. I saw the power of the amulet overtake her. She was different, scary, powerful, and even more intent on destroying the ones who had attempted to hurt her wife than I had ever seen. Once Alexis was safe and Skylar had killed the soldiers Ares had conjured, I saw an entirely different kind of power run through both Skylar and Alexis."

I dropped my eyes to the fire as I whispered, "Lust."

"Yes," he confirmed. "A wall of fire sprung up around them, hiding them from my view, and that of Trachis' army. They partook of each other's body in the most intimate of ways and when they were revealed to us again, Alexis was repulsed at what had happened between them. She begged Ares to take her far away from Skylar. She did not intend to ever return."

"Why?" I asked.

"You must understand that the power of the amulet for someone who is not of the Ker line is a very different thing. If they come into contact with you while you are using it, they are subjected to those same feelings of desire and power. But once the amulet's influence is taken away, they are left with only an intense desire to be far from where you are." I did not know what to say. "Was today the first time you and Demetri had been together in that manner?"

"Yes," I replied, my voice barely above a whisper.

"Then I believe his feelings would be further intensified. To be bound together under the amulet's influence with someone you truly care for is so much more powerful than if it had been with someone you cared nothing for at all. Demetri shall be confused; he shall have forgotten what you truly mean to him, much as I suspect you had when you first spoke with me … afterwards." I could only nod in answer. "When I finally found Alexis and took her to Skylar, she was not herself; she was so angry at what they had done inside the fire. It was not their first time together, but it did not diminish the revulsion she felt. She spoke of how Ares had made her see the truth; that Skylar was nothing more than a ruthless killer and would stop at nothing to get what she wanted, using people for her own pleasure, regardless of their wants or desires.

"Ares told Alexis that being with Skylar would only put her, and the life of her unborn child, in danger. He told her that she should cut all ties with

Skylar before it was too late and the ones she truly loved were taken from her. I attempted to make them remember the truth of who they were, to remind them that they had always been stronger together, but Ares' hold was strong."

I closed my eyes, wondering if Ares had already found Demetri and poisoned him against me. "So, when I had said all I could, I did the only thing I could think of to break the spell he had them under: I cut off Skylar's wings."

"Did it release them?"

"Yes."

"Is that why you tried to cut mine earlier?"

"Yes, but yours are far stronger than Skylar's ever were."

"Oh." I pushed a charred log further into the flames as I thought about what he had told me. "Do you think Ares has spoken to Demetri already?"

"If he has not by now, it shall not be long. The amulet could not have influenced Demetri or sent him away unless he cared deeply for you and you for him. But just as Skylar had me to find Alexis, so you have me to help you find Demetri, and when we do, we shall ensure that all is as it should be."

"I hope it can be so," I whispered. We sat in silence for a long time, watching the fire's flames lick the wood we had placed in its reach. Papou had not been able to cut my wings off as he had my mother's. Was it because they had been there, beneath my skin, for so long? Even if he had been able to, would they have just grown back? Would cutting them off have guaranteed an end to Ares' influence over Demetri?

"Do *you* think I am Ares' Chosen One?" I finally asked.

"It would appear so," Papou murmured.

"The night they died, I remember Mumma's words to the Persian who stabbed Mother Alexis. She said, 'she is not of the line. How many times must we speak of this? She has no mark. There is *no* connection with her.' I realize now they were talking about me, and yet somehow the Persian knew the truth about who I really was, about what I would become."

"Yes," Papou said. "Because he was no Persian."

"What do you mean, who was he?" I frowned.

"Ares," Papou growled. "There were no Persian soldiers at the palace that night. The God of War cloaked his own warriors in Persian colors to give you an enemy you could name. He wanted it so whenever you saw Persians on our shores after that time, you would remember your parents and want to exact your revenge. He intended for you to grow with a hatred for the yellow caps, for he knew that when the time came, he would be able to manipulate you easily."

"If you knew all this, why did you not come back for me, to teach me what I should do to resist him or to find a way to stop it?" I asked, my blood heating.

"As I said earlier, I did not believe there was any need. Skylar and I spoke at length after you were born and without the Ker mark we did not believe you would be able to use the amulet even if she allowed you to test it when you were older ... not that she would have allowed you to test it, had she lived."

"Why did you or Mumma not destroy the amulet when you knew what it could do? Why allow it to exist at all?"

"It is not as simple as that, if the amulet is cracked or broken in any way, the power inside shall be released and Ares, or someone else, would be able to harness it to get what he wants."

"What *does* Ares want to do when his Chosen One proves she can use the amulet?"

"He intends to challenge Zeus as ruler of the gods. Alone, he would be outnumbered, even if he found allies in some of his brothers or sisters. But with the amulet ... well you have seen what it can do. If Ares was to win, our world would be changed forever. We would never live in peace, there would be no beauty left anywhere – just perpetual war, death and destruction. Our world would be destroyed."

"We cannot let that happen," I said quietly. In that moment I knew with certainty that I did not care if I was Ares' Chosen One. I did not want to follow the path he had set me on. I would not be manipulated by him any longer and I would not help him get what he wanted. I would be strong, as Mumma Skylar had been. I would do what I had to and stop Ares from getting his wish. I would find a way to negate the amulet's power forever. And I would break Demetri from Ares' hold.

"Wait ... has Moeris always known what happened to my mothers, like you have? That it was not a Persian soldier, but Ares who killed them?"

"Yes," Papou nodded.

"Why did he not tell me?" I murmured "After all this time ..."

"I asked him not to. Made him swear he would not. I held no fear you could hold yourself against Persian soldiers when you were faced with them, or sought them out, but I knew you would attempt to find Ares, to challenge him and I did not want to lose you to him."

"And yet you almost did because you did not tell me of my past, my family." I shook my head, unable to think about what my life might have been had I sought out Ares for my revenge instead of the Persians. "The night you left, you told me that when it was time, you would find me and tell me everything, but if I had not found you, would you have returned?" I asked instead.

"I do not know," Papou replied, his face grim. "At the time I did not mean the words, I only wished to comfort you. But the more winters that passed, the more I believed I had made a mistake, that I had failed you. I wish to believe that come the end of this winter I would have left Theron and Irina and returned to Trachis, but I cannot be certain."

"Sometimes facing those from our past can be too hard," I muttered.

"Indeed," he agreed.

We sat, staring at one another over the flames of the fire for a long time, but no more words were exchanged. Eventually I nodded to him, settling down and pulling my himation tighter around me. "Goodnight, Papou. I am glad you are here with me."

"Me too. Goodnight, my darling," he replied.

39

"With all I have told you, do you still wish to find Demetri?" Papou asked as we continued our journey south the following day.

"Yes. Even if he chooses not to stay with me, I want him released from Ares. I owe him that much."

"Then we shall not stop again until we find him," Papou nodded "The further he gets from you, the stronger Ares' grip shall be. If you are up to it, we can be at the Thessalian border in two mornings' time and he should not be far ahead of us."

"My wounds have healed well enough not to slow me down, but are *you* still able to keep such a pace?"

"My winters of travel have served me well, I shall not slow you down," he replied with a tight smile. I nodded and we hastened our pace.

*   *   *

Just as Papou had promised, we arrived at the Thessalian-Macedonian border two mornings later, the same highwayman guarding it as before. "It is good to see you again, your trip north was fruitful?" he asked, offering his arm.

"Yes, thank you," I replied, taking it firmly.

"Your friend came through late in the night, I offered him a safe place to rest, but he wished to continue."

"Yes, we sent him on ahead to deliver a message," Papou replied before

I had the chance to formulate a convincing story.

"He travelled with a large hound, I have never seen one so big, though I have heard stories of their existence," the highwayman continued.

"A hound?" I frowned – it must be Damon.

"He must have found him wandering in the mountains," Papou supplied again. "Come, we should be on our way."

"Take care if you intend to take the path along the mountains south of Gomphoi, I have heard of strange happenings in that area," he warned.

I had a feeling I knew what he was talking about but asked anyway. "What sort of happenings?"

"Traders who have travelled north on that path since you were here have reported a mound which they believe to be dead Persian soldiers. The flesh and bone have been burnt away, leaving only ash beneath the singed uniforms. The heat required would be immense, yet there appears to be no evidence of fire around them."

"Perhaps their burning took place elsewhere and the uniforms disposed of there to protect those who carried it out," Papou suggested.

The highwayman shrugged. "Perhaps, though the men say the ash is in such a fragile state that when they attempted to touch it, they could not, it was taken away on the wind before their very eyes."

"We shall stay further east on the Plain," I assured him. The screams of agony which had filled the Plain that day returned with uncomfortable ease. I still considered the Persians my enemies, even if they did not kill my mothers as I had always believed, but I did not want to think about the immeasurable pain they would have felt in the last few moments as they burned. "Has there been Persian retaliation since?" I asked, trying to drown out the sounds in my head.

"No, but I believe it shall not take long once they hear of it," the highwayman replied.

"Then we should be on our way," I murmured.

"Safe travels," the highwayman said. I nodded my reply and Papou and I continued on, my grandfather saying nothing about what we had heard. I suspected he already knew the truth.

*   *   *

During the dark of the next night, we reached the edge of the Pindos Mountain Range and entered the northern point of the Thessalian Plain. We kept to the middle of the Plain, away from the mountains to the west, just as the highwayman had suggested. I was relieved we would not travel the path Demetri and I had taken; I did not want Papou to see what I had done. *I* did not want the reminder of the carnage the amulet had enabled me to create. I just wanted to find Demi and free her from Ares' hold. But when the sun lit the horizon the following morning, we still had not met up with her.

Papou and I walked in silence, a light breeze lifting my hair. But it was not the breeze that made me suddenly shiver. I turned, drawing my sword from its sheath and finding Ares before me.

"It is impressive how you know when I am near. I have never known another mortal who can feel my presence as you can," he grinned.

"How fortunate for me," I deadpanned.

"Ares," Papou spat, his sword firmly in his grasp.

"It has been a long time, old man," Ares acknowledged.

"One thousand winters would not be long enough," Papou growled.

"What do you want, Ares?" I asked. "I know the truth now, about the amulet and my family. I will never use it again. I will never let you control me."

"Perhaps," he shrugged, turning and addressing Papou with his next words. "I had not thought to kill you all these winters. I had believed you too weak to return and tell Ava what you knew, and we can all agree that is true. But I had not considered *her* attempt to find you."

"There is much you do not consider," Papou taunted.

"True, but I do believe in correcting my mistakes."

Ares raised his hand and a perfect, solid sphere of purple appeared in his palm.

"No!" I yelled, putting myself in front of Papou. "You will not kill him because he told me the truth."

"Oh I do not intend to kill him ... not yet at least, but he shall help me get what I want."

"I shall never help you," Papou disagreed.

"Quiet now, old man," Ares sneered. The sphere shot out of Ares' hand, swerved around me, and swept Papou up inside. Papou beat his fists against the side and I could see him yelling, but no sound penetrated the circle around him.

"Now, where were we?" Ares asked, turning to me again.

"I was telling you to go to Tartarus," I replied, drawing my eyes from Papou and resting them on Ares as I held my sword higher.

The God of War laughed. "I do so enjoy our banter. But you are not strong enough to resist me for much longer. I can feel your defenses weakening." His words wrapped around me as warm as the himation I wore. "There is part of you that *wants* to join me. Life would be easy again, you would have renewed purpose. Fight, kill, and be rewarded. Just as it was before you began this silly journey to find your grandfather. Before you met that ... boy."

I knew I must fight him, but his words were like a caress. The amulet warmed my chest and flowed down into my stomach.

"I can feel the amulet's power, can you?" he asked softly, his lips at my ear.

"Yes," I whispered. He traced the leather at my neck, drawing the amulet from my tunic. The soft orange glow grew brighter in his fingers and a smile crept over his face.

"There have been times since I gave you this that I have not been able to sense its presence. I wondered if it was because you did not wish to use it, but then you did, and both of you have grown stronger in my veins. You *want* to join with me."

"No," I claimed, but I was not convinced of the answer myself.

"Yes," he whispered, taking my hand and closing it around the gem. "Allow me to show you how close we are to getting what we both desire."

"If I use it again you will control me," I countered as my shoulder blades prickled.

"Only if you use the final earth element," Ares corrected. "You are free to conjure any of the other three elements you wish. You can use them as many times as you desire without agreeing to join me … unless you want to of course, you need only give yourself to what I offer and it shall be done. I can show you."

"No," I said, shaking his control over me. I took a step back, releasing the amulet.

He frowned. "You cannot deny me, I am much stronger. I am your destiny."

"*I* control my destiny and I do not choose you."

The calm control enveloped me again as he neared. "You *want* to be with me. I can give you purpose. You would be powerful, feared, worshipped. You would command great armies and be immortal. Your power shall match mine and we shall rule together, forever."

With his words, the sword in my hand rose of its own accord. I could see my future, see everything he promised. I wanted to know if I could really use the fire, water and wind again – if they would manifest themselves in the same way as before. I had to know if they would bend to my will as Ares bent me to his.

Ares stepped back and smiled. I could feel him inside me, rushing through my veins, filling me with his power, calling me to use mine. To prove that everything he had spoken of was true. I sheathed my sword and shed my cloaks and cuirass, the tunic I wore still carrying the holes my wings had made when they broke free back in Konitsa. As if the very thought of them was enough, they painlessly extended, spreading out behind me and catching the gentle breeze.

I took my sword again, spinning it around my hand until the blade faced the ground. I gripped the hilt tightly between my palms and smiled at Ares as I plunged it deep into my thigh. There was no pain but I could feel the cold iron deep in my flesh. I drew the sword out again, dropping to my knees as blood poured from the wound.

Ares joined me on the ground. "Heal yourself," he commanded. "Hold the amulet over your leg, just as you did with Philo."

"It did not help Philo," I countered.

"He may have had a little help in his final candlemarks," Ares grinned. I felt no sadness or fury as his words sunk in. In battles many good soldiers, many faithful steeds, died. I knew that, it was simple truth and I would spend no more time mourning his loss. I would not have need of a horse once I joined Ares anyway. I had wings; I would fly wherever I wanted to go. "Hurry, before you lose too much blood," Ares ordered.

I took the amulet from my neck, the deep orange of the jet radiating heat and intense light. I held it up, my gaze finding Papou's as he stood, trapped in the bubble, eyes wide with fear. For a moment, Ares' hold on me broke and pain ripped through me. I could deny Ares what he wanted. I could let the life drain from me and he would never be able to use me, or the amulet, to get what he wanted.

As if sensing the change, Ares grabbed my chin, forcing me to look at him as he wrapped his other hand around mine. "Do it," he urged.

The calm assurance immediately returned, the pain in my leg disappearing. Ares released me and I dropped my eyes to the gash. I held the amulet over the wound and whispered, "Heal me." The amulet glowed brighter, the orange inside intensifying until a single bolt of light flew from it to my leg. The blood immediately ceased flowing out of the opening and within moments, the cut had disappeared altogether. There was no scar, not even a mark where I had driven the sword through my skin.

I looked up, meeting Ares' triumphant smile. The amulet cooled in my hand, its effects vanishing as I returned it to my neck. My wings retracted beneath my skin and I reached for my chlamys and himation.

"You are magnificent," Ares said with pride.

"I will serve you well," I replied with a grin.

"That you shall," he agreed, "that you shall."

He turned and released Papou from the bubble. "No … no…" Papou cried, falling to the ground.

"I win, old man," Ares laughed, helping me to my feet.

"You have shown me what I am capable of, now I will show you just how powerful *I* am. Take me to Demetri, he is a loose end and will only stand in our way when we try to carry out our plans, I must eliminate him," I said.

"Allow me," Ares offered.

"No. I want to do it."

Ares smiled again. "As you wish, I shall take you to him."

"Bring the old man too," I added. "I will get rid of them both." With one hand on his chest, I leaned in. "There is much to be done in our plans, but I hope you will leave time for pleasure too."

He grinned. "Pleasure and power are mine to offer and I shall ensure your needs are met as often as you require, with whoever you require." Ares reached down and picked Papou up by his cuirass, holding his hand out to me. "Come, I shall take you to the boy."

I took his offered hand, my arms and legs growing heavy, like invisible hands were pulling them towards the ground. My feet suddenly left the stony path. The Thessalian Plain was gone. Complete and utter darkness surrounded us. Warm air rushed past my bared skin and in and around my eyes, making them water. I squeezed them shut, my head and stomach both rolling with the haste of our journey. I remained awake as long as I could, my limbs frozen in place; arms at my sides, legs unbent and rigid as they trailed my upper body through the dark. My stomach threatened to return the last food I had eaten until finally I succumbed to Hypnos' realm.

40

I jerked awake when my feet hit something solid and I found myself standing in a small room.
Thankfully my stomach and head had stopped spinning and my limbs had returned to their usual pliable selves.

"That was quite a journey," I murmured.

"Indeed," Ares replied. Papou stood the other side of Ares and the fierce barking of a hound filled the room. "Hush," Ares roared.

The beast quieted immediately and I saw it was Damon. He stood protectively in front of Demetri; fur raised down his back, teeth bared, ready to attack.

"How did yo–?" Demetri started, shrinking back against the wall.

"I am a god, how do you imagine?" Ares shrugged.

"You told me you would keep me safe. Why did you bring her here?"

"Because I asked him to," I replied, taking a step forward. "We have unfinished business."

"Get away from me," Demetri shouted.

"Ava, please, you must fight him, you must not allow Ares to win," Papou pleaded.

"Your words are useless, old man, I am his now and I will not be swayed from my path," I replied.

Ares laughed and pushed Papou into a nearby chair. I turned to the God of War, putting my hand on his chest again and slipping it beneath his leather vest to caress the exposed hairs.

"Leave me with them and prepare something for me to use the final element on."

He brought his hands to my waist. "Why not use it on these two mortals? It would be a fitting way to bring about their end. They die as you are reborn, ready to carry out my deeds, and your own desires."

"It is tempting, but they are no challenge. An old man and a runaway slave boy are not worthy of such power. I have defeated whole armies with the amulet. I want more. We will take our power to Olympos and defeat Zeus and those loyal to him. We will kill them and rule as we were destined to; together, unstoppable and magnificent. Greater than Zeus and Hera before us, greater than the Titans before them, we will bring about chaos and destruction like this world has never known and we will rejoice as time after time, blood is shed in our names."

"Ava, no," Papou cried.

A triumphant grin spread across Ares' face and he tightened his grip on my waist. "I always knew you were the one, that you would be everything I had waited for. You shall have your wish just as soon as you are done here."

He kissed me on the cheek as I said, "Go now and prepare everything. When I am done I will call for you and we will start our reign."

He grinned and disappeared. Cold fingers slid down my spine and I knew he was gone. I turned to Papou. "Are you hurt?"

He hesitated a moment before shaking his head. "You are not ..."

"Under his influence? No," I replied. "Ares obviously spoke the truth when he said that would not happen until I used the fourth element or I truly wanted to join him, but he thinks I will bend to his will if he speaks certain words. Instead, I spoke the words *he* wanted to hear."

Papou smiled as he stood and crossed the room, taking me tight in his arms. "You are so much stronger than I had ever hoped," he said, his voice catching.

I returned his embrace. "It will take a lot more than that to convince me I should do what he wants."

"When you stabbed yourself I thou–"

"I know and I am sorry for frightening you," I cut over him. We parted and I turned to Demetri who still stared warily at me, crouched against the wall. I took a step towards him and Damon emitted a deep growl. I held up my hands. "Hush, Boy, I will not hurt either of you."

Damon stayed in position but did not leap as I approached. I kept my eyes from his and offered my fist instead. He stood a few moments longer before whimpering and licking at my hand, relaxing his stance and letting me pat his head and back as he leant into me.

"Good boy," I crooned, keeping my voice quiet. "Now sit." He obeyed and I gave him another pat before taking a step towards Demetri.

"Get away from me. You used me for your own pleasure. You wish for nothing but power. You used me. I hate you!" he screamed.

Papou advanced, his hand raised, but I grabbed his arm. "No! You know his words are not his own." Papou nodded and lowered his arm as I addressed Demetri again. "You felt the amulet's power, Demetri; you know that I could not stop what happened, that I did not wish to end it any more than you did."

"This was not my fault. Ares said you would say it was my fault."

"That is not what I said," I interrupted, trying to keep my voice calm, despite my anger. "It is no one's fault what happened between us. It is not the way I would have chosen for it to happen, no matter how much I wanted it. Somewhere deep inside I know you know that."

"You let him control you and you would do the same to me if I let you, but I won't, I–"

"Listen, I had an entire speech prepared for what I would say to you when I found you, but we do not have time. I need you to be quiet and listen. I am not under Ares' control. If I was, you would already be dead. Both of you would be. Do you remember what you said to me when Ares first appeared to us in Konitsa?" Demetri did not reply. "You said that Ares could have killed you and I would not have cared. That was true. But take a good look at me Demetri: I am not lying to you. I would not be here if I did not care about you. If I did not *love* you. I may not have been searching for love or for the whisper of what I thought was no longer for me, but it found me. *You* found me and I do not want to lose you."

"You spoke words you knew Ares wanted to hear, how do I know you're not telling me what you think I want to hear?" he countered. "He said you didn't really care about me, that you just pretended to when you knew that was how I felt. You wanted my body for your own pleasure – so you could say you'd been with … someone like me."

"Since we met, has there *ever* been a time when I made you think I was just pretending to care about you or what you have been through? Have I *ever* given you a reason to think that I would play with your emotions just so I could take you to bed or give you reason to doubt how I felt about you?"

"Ares said he came to Konitsa that night to save me, to stop you from getting what you wanted."

"He did not try to *save* you when the Persians arrived in Konitsa and I used the amulet against them. Can you not see that he has been filling your head with lies so you leave and he can claim me for himself?" I drew in a deep breath and took a step towards him. Demetri drew back so I went no further. "Before I used the amulet in Konitsa, you told me Ares was not known for saving mortals. You were sure of that, why do you now believe everything he says? He never wanted to save you, but *I* do. I will not let him win, but I need your help."

"I can't help; I'm nothing but a runaway slave, just like you said."

My anger flared, my hands balling into fists. This was not my Demetri, this was not my Demi. I faced Papou again. "Papou, what you will hear me say will be confusing but in time we will explain it." He frowned, clearly wondering what I was talking about but he nodded in reply. I faced Demetri again. "The boy I know would never see himself as just a slave. The woman I know wanted something more for her life," I said, advancing.

I drove my hand beneath Demetri's chiton and pulled the coin pouch from his waist. I opened it quickly, spilling the coins on the ground. I found the story coin and held it close to his face. "*This* is the Demetri I know. The strong, courageous person who dreamed of more than what life had offered so far. The boy who created the most beautiful coins I have ever seen. The girl who captured my heart with no more than simple truths and a gentle nature." I grasped his face between my hands, our eyes locked.

"I will not let you die or have you live the rest of your life hating me for the lies Ares told you. I will not let you leave my life when you have become so important to me. You are mine, Demetri. Demi is mine. And I am yours. Ares cannot win if we face him together. I love you. Hear me when I tell you this." I kissed him hard, holding firm even as he resisted, arms flailing against me.

When I finally let go, his eyes rolled up into his head and he slipped from my hands, collapsing to the ground. I dropped to my knees as Damon bounded over, whimpering and licking at Demetri's face as if he thought that would wake him. I cradled Demetri's head in my hands as his eyes fluttered open again.

"Ava," he murmured. He pulled himself to a sitting position and rubbed the back of her head. "Ugh, my head. Why didn't you catch me?" he grinned.

A laugh burst from my chest and I lay my hand on his cheek, kissing him again. When we broke apart I studied his face. His eyes were clear, the wary look gone, replaced by his familiar grin. He threaded his hands in my hair, touching his forehead to mine.

"I'm sorry about what I said, I didn't mean it," he whispered. "Somehow, I knew, but I couldn't stop myself. Thank you for what you said, to your grandfather too. I love you too. I don't want to be without you. Ever." He kissed me fiercely, releasing my hair and pulling me by the hips onto his lap. I returned his affections just as ardently and my breath soon grew short as my hands travelled across his body.

Papou cleared his throat behind us. "I am pleased that you have returned to yourself, Demetri … er … Demi … What do you prefer? Never mind, we shall talk about the rest of that later. For now, there is much to discuss about Ares.""

"Indeed," I grumbled, breaking our kiss.

"Demetri is fine for now," he added.

"Done," Papou nodded.

Reluctantly I disentangled myself from Demetri's embrace and got to my feet, a flush creeping up my neck as I faced Papou. Demetri scratched Damon between the ears, the large hound bumping his head against his thigh.

"I gather you have a plan," Papou asked as he sat back in the chair.

"I do," I replied. "You said that we cannot break the amulet without releasing its power, but what if we were able to separate it?"

"I do not see how it would be possible, the two pieces are too closely entwined, if either section is brok—"

"That is where we need Demetri's help," I interrupted, turning to him. "Do you remember the night Philo died, when you first saw the amulet?" He nodded. "You told me you thought the amulet was made of jet and hematite; that separately they should be harmless, and it was only when they were together that it was a dangerously powerful weapon."

"I did," he confirmed, his brows knitted together.

"Is it possible to soften the hematite and release the jet from within its grip, without compromising either of them?"

He drew in a breath as he considered it. "Maybe."

"Papou is there *anything* that Zita or anyone else told you that would have you believe we should not try it?"

Papou shook his head. "No. But destroying the amulet was never something Zita and I talked about."

"So … if we release the power trying to destroy the amulet, Ares wins. But if we do nothing, he will find a way to make me use that fourth element and still win," I said.

Papou nodded. "It appears we have to attempt to separate it," he conceded.

"I agree," Demetri added.

"Good. We have to work quickly, before Ares discovers that the two of you are still alive. Will we need a furnace like in Konitsa, Demetri?"

"Yes. Luckily for us, we're in Kierion; they have a large metal workshop here," Demetri replied with a nod. "I'd planned on staying here for a while, to try and make the armor Leandros showed me."

"Do you know the man who runs the workshop?" Papou asked.

"I do. I met him once when he visited Larissa. His name is Kratos. He'll have everything we need but what do we do with the separated pieces? How are we going to defeat Ares?"

"I do not know yet, but maybe separating them will be enough," I replied.

Papou crossed to the door. "Come," he said. We followed him out, Damon trotting along happily beside us.

"How did you come to have Damon?" I asked.

"I don't know," Demetri replied. "But when I woke up after … after the whirlwind, he was there with me. I was grateful for his company, I felt as though he was the only friend I had."

I drew in a breath and nodded. "I am glad you had him."

Demetri took my hand. "I'm pleased I have *you* again," he smiled.

41

Kratos' workshop was impressive and much like the one at Trachis as opposed to the basic setup in Konitsa. The workspace consisted of two rooms, I was not sure what the second room held, but the first was dim and hot, with a raging furnace, open on one side and its glow providing most of the light for the area. The bellows connected to the side of the furnace were made from smooth, dark animal skins relieved of the fur. Tools hung neatly from the wall above a large table, with barrels of water, charcoal and ore occupying one corner and an anvil stood in the middle of the room, large enough for four men to use at the same time.

I shed my himation and chlamys and lay them over the back of the chair on top of Demetri and Papou's — the two of them beside the table against the far wall, discussing the various tools above it.

"The furnace is already almost at the temperature we need for softening the hematite. We'll hold the amulet above the coals with these tongs," Demetri said, choosing a long-handled pair with thin tips. "The amulet's power doesn't extend to the leather that keeps it around Ava's neck, does it?"

"No, I believe it is just in the jet and hematite," Papou replied.

"I agree," I added, stepping over Damon, who had made himself comfortable on the floor near the door, to join them. "If the leather held any power, I am sure it would have changed like the amulet did before I commanded it, and I felt nothing."

"Good, then I'll remove the leather so it doesn't catch fire in the

212

furnace."

I nodded, taking the amulet from my neck and handing it to him. He selected another tool from the wall – it looked to be a smaller version of the tongs – and cut through the leather, drawing the severed end through the loop of hematite at the top of the amulet and dropping it to the bench.

"What can I do?" I asked.

"Are you happy to hold the amulet in the flames while I pump the bellows?"

"Of course," I replied.

Demetri handed me the tongs and led me to the furnace. I clasped the jet firmly, but carefully, between the two ends of the tongs, leaving the hematite exposed as I waited for Demetri to take his position by the bellows. He gave me a nod and I placed the amulet deep inside the furnace above the coals. He pulled up and down on the animal skins, sending long flames, swirling smoke and bright sparks over the amulet.

After only a few minutes I saw the hematite start to weaken and I drew it out of the flames. Demetri joined me, taking the tongs from me, his eyebrows pulled together in thought. "It looks like I misjudged the temperature of the furnace. It should've taken half a candlemark at least to soften this much."

We re-joined Papou at the table, Demetri setting the amulet on top. "Are you ready?" he asked, looking first to me, then Papou.

I swallowed. This was the moment that would determine whether beauty and love would ever exist again in our world, or if we were destined to live forever with nothing more than death, destruction, and perpetual war. It would determine if Ares would win, or if *we* would.

"Wait," I said, putting my hand on Demetri's arm. "If this does not work I want you to remember that I love you. I know that being here, with me, with us, is not where you expected to be when you left Larissa, but I am really glad that you came into my life. You are more than *I* expected to find when I left the soldiers. I never expected to find someone I wanted to spend time with … my life with."

"You think we're going to die," Demetri murmured.

"Maybe," I replied. "But if we do not, I cannot guarantee that I will ever really be myself again. I might hurt you – both of you," I added, meeting Papou's eyes. "My choices will not be my own, but I need you to both remember that I would never deliberately harm you if I had the choice. I will fight as fiercely as I can, but I am not convinced that I can win if the full power of the amulet is released."

Papou stepped to my side, laying his hand on my shoulder. "We all understand the risk that separating the parts of the amulet has, but it is the only way." He pressed his lips against my forehead. I nodded and gripped the hand at my shoulder, squeezing it tightly. "You deserve a moment of privacy, but the hematite is beginning to re-harden, so a moment is all you have," he whispered. I nodded and he busied himself at the far table. I wrapped my arms around Demetri's waist and drew him … her close.

"I love you," he breathed.

"And I you," I replied.

He kissed me. I could not bear the thought that I would ever hurt him but I knew the power of the amulet – the way the heat coursed through my veins and drove me to say things I did not mean and do things I would never have imagined possible. If only I could fight the feelings enough to get Demetri and Papou away from Kierion, then maybe they could live out their days far from my destructive force. If only I had the power inside to guarantee such a wish.

Demetri and I parted and I turned to the amulet on the bench. "It should be me who separates it," I said.

Demetri hesitated, but eventually nodded. "You'll need these," he said, choosing a pair of thick leather gloves from a hook above the table. I pulled them on, finding the insides soft and warm, molding to my fingers as soon as I got them into position.

"Stand back," I warned. Demetri and Papou took several steps away from me.

I drew in a deep breath blowing it all the way out before I bent over the small gem. With my thumb and forefinger, I held each end of the amulet, carefully manipulating the hematite at the bottom of the amulet with my other hand. Silently the hematite released the jet from its grip and when the gap at the side was big enough, I pulled the jet from the center, grasping it in my palm and sending up a silent prayer of thanks to whichever god or goddess wanted to claim it.

Tentatively Demetri and Papou stepped closer, smiling at me as our eyes met. "W–"

"No! You must not separate them," a loud voice shattered the silence within the workshop. I jumped, almost dropping the piece of jet I held.

I turned, finding a barrel-chested man leaning against the anvil in the middle of the room. He wore a dark leather apron over an orange chiton draped across the left side of his body, leaving his impressively muscled right shoulder and arm exposed. On his head, he wore an oval cap and dark tufts of curly black hair escaped from the sides and back. His beard was thick, but neat, reaching only to the base of his chin and I noticed that his left leg – which was visible around the edge of the anvil – was lame and twisted, causing the lean of his body.

Damon looked utterly unimpressed by the arrival of the newcomer. He looked directly at him, but merely yawned and resettled his head on his paw, snoring quietly once again. It was not Kratos, the owner of the workshop, I had met him earlier. The man that stood before us appeared not so much a man as a ...

"Hephaestus?" Demetri breathed, eyes wide and brows high on his forehead.

I looked back to the man – the great god Hephaestus – as he nodded. I opened my mouth again but a shooting pain drove deep into my back and I dropped to my knees. My wings were trying to emerge, the pressure as they pushed upward far greater than I had known it before. I dropped the jet on the table, fumbling to remove the gloves and my cuirass, throwing them aside as Demetri and Papou crowded around me. We had failed.

"What is it?" Demetri asked. I could not reply, pain clouding my vision as disappointment settled in my stomach. I squeezed my eyes shut, waiting for the familiar ripping sensations to start but something was wrong. My wings could not break the skin. They fought beneath my flesh, stabbing me in anger at my body's refusal to let them escape.

"Ares," I panted, scanning the room with a sudden shiver. Demetri and Papou followed my gaze with alarm, but he was nowhere to be seen.

"I shall deal with Ares, but you must all stay here until I return," Hephaestus said, disappearing.

I raised my eyes to the jet on the bench. I expected it to be glowing, but it was not. It was still the same solid black it had been when I separated it from the hematite. I felt almost ... hollow at its appearance. "My wings cannot break free. They *want* to react to the amulet, but cannot," I panted. "I do not feel any of the usual confidence it fills me with either."

"So Ares can't turn you against us, we've beaten him," Demetri insisted.

"I do not believe that," Papou said. "There must be more we do not know; Hephaestus would not be here otherwise." As Papou spoke, Hephaestus reappeared. His leather apron and chiton sat askew across his massive chest, his cap slightly off-center.

Demetri helped me to my feet, the pain at my back subsiding with each passing moment. Hephaestus adjusted his clothing and limped across to the table, reaching for the separated amulet. I blocked his path, taking the hematite and jet before he touched them.

"Why have you come? Why did you say we should not separate the amulet?" I asked.

Hephaestus paused in his approach. "Please, I mean you no harm. I am only here to help release you from Ares' grip. I had hoped to arrive before you chose to take this path, but my plan took longer than I anticipated."

"How did you even know what we intended to do with the amulet?" I asked.

"I have seen everything you have been through for some time now and if you allow me, I can help you."

"What do you know of the amulet?" Papou asked.

"Why do you want to help us against Ares?" Demetri asked at the same time.

Hephaestus sighed, backing up until his thighs touched the anvil. He rested against it as he addressed Papou. "I have known of the amulet's existence for longer than I care to remember. I learned of it from my former wife, who took great pleasure in divulging not only its power and intended use, but all the ways it was protected against being destroyed."

"So breaking it is not the only way the power can be released?" I asked as the pain in my back disappeared entirely, along with the hollow feeling.

"No," Hephaestus replied, shaking his head. "As you have witnessed, the hematite and jet can be separated with no apparent, immediate disaster, but should they stay unconnected for more than a few candlemarks, they shall release the power, just as they would if either of them had been broken."

"I cannot reconnect them. If I do, Ares will find a way to make me use them. He will get what he wants," I said.

"He can attempt to, but I believe I have found a way to harness the power of the elements to work *against* him rather than for him."

"How?" Papou asked.

"As long as the jet and hematite are set within one weapon, the power can run through them. If they are touching each other, as they were in the necklace, they shall obey Ares, but if they are not, then the power belongs to the wielder of the weapon." Hephaestus addressed me specifically. "You are more than capable with a sword, and Demetri is, as you have observed, one of the most talented metalworkers ever to be blessed with such a gift. I suggest we fashion *your* weapon to include the jet and hematite so you can do battle with Ares and defeat him once and for all."

"How?" I asked, skeptical of his plan.

"The jet can be set in the pommel on the end of your sword and covered to hide its existence," he replied.

"Silver would be the quickest to melt and would blend in with the rest of the pommel. We can use my coins," Demetri suggested.

I turned to him and shook my head. "Absolutely not, they are precious to you."

"As you are to me," he replied, turning back to Hephaestus. "What about the hematite?"

Hephaestus hesitated. "Demetri, you must understand, if you include something of your own in the weapon you shall be linked forever with Ava and with the power of the sword. Is that what you want?"

"Yes," Demetri immediately replied.

"Dem–" I started. It was one thing to say he … she loved me, but another to be forever bound to me.

"You don't want us to be together?"

"It is not that, but do you not want to take a mom–"

"I don't need to," he assured me.

"A contribution from Demetri shall make the power of the sword even stronger," Hephaestus said, catching my eye.

Demetri shook his head. "I'm no one of great importance. I'm just an orphan who was fortunate enough to be found before I died of exposure. I have no power to add to the sword, but I'll give Ava anything she needs to help her defeat Ares and to keep her in this world with me for as long as the Moirai allow."

"Even orphans have parents," Hephaestus corrected.

Demetri took my hand, his eyes boring into mine. "I don't need to consider this decision, I've known almost since we met that I wanted to be with you and I haven't changed my mind, even with everything that's happened."

I had no chance to reply, not that I could have even if I wanted to, before he kissed me. His words touched me deep inside, wrapping around my heart and claiming it. Papou cleared his throat and Demetri broke our kiss.

"Thank you," I whispered.

"The thanks has always been mine," he replied.

"What about the hematite?" Papou asked, returning our conversation to its former path.

"The hematite can be smelted down and placed within the guard. Ava shall be able to harness the power as it travels from the jet in the pommel, through the hematite in the guard and into the blade," Hephaestus replied.

"Why should we take your word that this is going to work against Ares, and not *for* him? How do we know he has not asked you to pretend to help us, while you actually aid him?" Papou continued.

"I have no love for Ares, only a deep desire to punish and take my revenge," Hephaestus replied. "You mortals enjoy hearing stories of the struggles of your gods and heroes, so I suspect you have heard of mine."

I picked up my cuirass from the floor, laying it over my cloak on the chair. "Long ago, your wife, Aphrodite, had an affair with your brother, Ares and brought great shame and ridicule to you," I offered.

"Yes. And the knowledge of their continual and unapologetic betrayal lingers deep beneath my breast, causing me the deepest of pain, such as I have only experienced once before."

"But you must have had other lovers, could your pain not be diminished by them?" Demetri asked.

"Could yours?" Papou asked quietly. From the corner of my eye I saw Demetri's mouth open and close silently. Finally, he shook his head and dropped his eyes to the ground.

"I have had many lovers, but never while I called Aphrodite my wife," Hephaestus said. "The women I sought out never belonged to another god or man. I have waited many of your winters to seek my revenge on my brother and when I saw the two of *you* had met, I knew that finally my time had come. You have my word; I shall not turn against you, I am loyal to you."

I met Hephaestus' eyes and saw the truth in them. "Then let us get started," I nodded.

42

"You shall be safe here in the workshop, but Ares is waiting for you to emerge. When I ... spoke with him before, I told him this was nothing more than a house and that the two of you were enjoying some time alone," Hephaestus said, nodding at Demetri and me.

"Ares would not have taken you at your word," Papou countered. "He would not expect either of us to still be alive."

Hephaestus took the individual parts of my sword which Demetri had deconstructed in preparation for the jet and hematite to be added as he replied. "No, he did not. But he cannot enter unless I allow him to."

"He can wait," I said, checking the bubbling mixture of Demetri's silver coins in the small skyphos above the flames. "Once we have the jet and hematite within the sword, he can do anything he wants, but we will be ready."

"Indeed," Demetri agreed, pulling the melted pieces of hematite from the flames in front of him.

"The jet," Hephaestus requested, raising his hand. Papou held it out but did not release it to Hephaestus. The god just shrugged and measured it against the side of his finger – it reached the length of his first knuckle and half the width on his smallest finger. He compared that to the length of the pommel, nodding once before pushing his measuring finger straight through the top of the pommel.

My mouth dropped open at his strength – I should not have been so surprised by the feat – he *was* God of the Forge after all. A cylindrical length of iron dropped to the ground, bouncing against the base of the anvil with a metallic ring as his finger cleared the bottom. He inspected his work, nodding once and holding the altered pommel out to Demetri.

"Now it shall hold the jet," he announced.

"Well, that certainly quickens the process," Demetri grinned.

"And now for the hematite," Hephaestus murmured. "When it is done you can re-fit the hilt and by then, the silver shall be ready to be poured around the jet."

"And then the sword will be ready to use?" I asked.

"Yes," Hephaestus replied. He widened the gap which fitted the guard over the tang below the hilt. "Pour the melted hematite into here, Demetri. When it cools, the guard shall be attached securely to the tang on the blade."

Hephaestus slid the guard into place over the tang and Demetri poured the molten iron into the hollow. It hardened almost instantly and even I knew it was not possible for it to cool so quickly; Hephaestus had to have influenced that process too.

With the hematite set, Demetri took it to the nearest barrel, immersing the blade, guard and tang in the water. It bubbled and steamed for a few seconds before he pulled it out again. Obviously satisfied with what he saw, Demetri returned to the anvil, handing it to Papou. Papou re-secured the hilt to the tang, wrapping the leather from the amulet around it – just as Demetri's sword had on its handle – before Hephaestus placed the pommel at the very end of the tang.

"How does the silver fare?" Papou asked.

I checked the small vessel again; it was pure liquid. "It is ready," I replied, taking it from the furnace.

"Place some in here first," he said. "That way the jet shall not be sitting directly against the tang, I do not want to take the chance the jet breaks when you strike your first blow with the sword, no matter what Hephaestus says about who it will obey."

I nodded and poured a small amount in the hole as Papou set the jet carefully inside. He nodded to me again and I emptied the rest of the silver in, enveloping the gem in the steaming liquid, stopping only when it was level with the top of the pommel. The silver hardened instantly.

"There is one more thing we need to add," Hephaestus said, holding his hand out for the sword. Papou passed it to him and Hephaestus dragged his finger down its middle with an ear-splitting screech. The noise sent a deep shudder through me, the iron peeling away like it was the consistency of fleshy bread when taken straight from the fire, rather than the hard metal I knew it to be.

"What are you doing?" Demetri cried, covering his ears.

"How far are the two of you prepared to go to stand against Ares?"

Hephaestus asked, meeting first Demetri's, then my eyes.

"As far as needed," I replied without hesitation.

"I would do anything," Demetri agreed.

Hephaestus nodded. "And you are prepared to be bound together forever in order to achieve this?"

"You have already asked this of them, why do you ask once more?" Papou frowned.

"I must be certain," Hephaestus shrugged.

"I'm prepared to be linked with Ava for the rest of my days in this world, and the next," Demetri said, taking my hand.

"As am I," I agreed with a smile.

"Very well," Hephaestus nodded, grabbing our entwined hands and holding them above the sword. He slashed a long line down our forearms, holding tight to us both as we writhed with the sudden pain.

"What are you doing?" Papou and I cried at the same time. Hephaestus did not reply.

My blood mixed with Demetri's as it slid onto the waiting iron of my sword. It sizzled and popped before disappearing into the vein Hephaestus had carved in the length of the blade. When the last of it had disappeared, Hephaestus released us.

"It is done. The sword is ready to be used against Ares," he said.

"What is it with you gods? You seem to derive a perverse pleasure in seeing our mortal blood spilled," I yelled, pressing the cloth Papou handed to me against my arm.

Hephaestus grinned. "It is not pleasure from seeing your blood spilled that I seek ... and you have no need of the material, your wound is already healed." I frowned, but realized my arm no longer hurt. I pulled the cloth away, finding the long gash gone.

"You could've just told us you needed our blood," Demetri muttered.

"I could have, but this was faster," Hephaestus shrugged. "Now, are you ready to stand against Ares?"

"I am ready," I nodded, taking my sword from his outstretched hand and spinning it around my own. It felt like it always had – same weight, same balance – even the addition of the leather to the hilt felt as if it had always been there. I was ready to fight for those I loved and for every innocent mortal who, at this very moment, had no idea of the danger their world was in. "Do not let Ares enter the workshop, we will go out and meet him."

"As you wish," Hephaestus replied. "I shall keep my distance, but should you require aid, you need only call."

I slid my sword into its sheath and put my cuirass and chlamys back on, leaving my himation; it would be far too bulky to fight in and I would need every advantage I could get in the coming battle with Ares. Damon stood and stretched, yawning loudly and shaking the last of the sleep from his body as he waited by the door.

"It is time to finish this," I murmured. Papou and Demetri nodded in agreement and we filed out into the bright sunlight. I had barely taken three steps, when Ares appeared.

"You betrayed me! You allowed these two worthless mortals to live and now you seek shelter with a god so lame, that even *your* powers outweigh his," he yelled, advancing. "What did you do to the amulet?"

"What needed to be done," I replied, folding my arms across my chest.

"You had me believing every word you spoke; that you had aligned yourself with me, that you welcomed what I was offering and that you would forsake your mortal self and be mine."

"You saw what you wanted to see, not the truth. It seems that even the great God of War is not infallible," I smirked. Ares roared and I thought he would charge me, but instead he disappeared. My smirk vanished and I pulled out my sword, spinning around as I tried to predict where he would reappear.

I did not have to wait long: Demetri yelped as Ares grabbed him by the hair and lifted him off his feet. His other hand held Demetri's sword at Papou's throat. "I do not know what you did to the amulet or how you believe you have altered the destiny I know you are fated for, but I *always* get what I want, and you shall be mine. We shall finish this once and for all just where you suggested – at Olympos." He disappeared again, taking Demetri, Papou and Damon with him.

"Ares! Bring them back, *now*," I demanded, my voice echoing around the empty streets of Kierion. "Hephaestus!" The named god appeared. "Take me to Olympos," I ordered.

"Of course. I should have known Ares would not fight you in the mortal realm. He has always enjoyed a show, and what better place to have his moment than in the home of the gods?" He held his hand out. "Aphrodite and Hades shall no doubt attempt to aid him. I can deal with them, but only you have the power to stop Ares. Only *you* can alter the destiny he has carved for you and save us all."

"If I fail and become what Ares wants … if I become his *true* Chosen One, promise me you will keep Papou and Demetri safe for as long as they live."

"The weapon you hold is extremely powerful; one made with the blood of gods and with eternal love. Have faith in yourself and in your love and you shall be victorious," he replied instead.

I hesitated a moment before nodding, hoping I had not put my trust in the wrong god – and that eternal love was what was fated for Demetri and I. Gripping my modified sword tightly in one hand, I took Hephaestus' offered one with my other. I took a deep breath and prepared myself for the heavy, rolling sensation I knew would accompany our journey.

43

I shivered as I woke to a cold, dark ground, my sword still gripped tightly between my fingers, but Hephaestus no longer beside me. I murmured a quiet word of thanks to him and pushed myself to my feet, taking in the room as I started my search for Ares. It was a cavernous area, its walls and ceiling colored in the purest white I had ever laid eyes on. Two large thrones sat empty at one end of the room, and it was eerily quiet. The ceiling far above sloped gradually upwards towards the middle until it reached its peak. Light streamed in from the rounded windows and Doric columns stood in the walls between them around the perimeter of the room. More columns stood in the middle of the room, the floor between tiled in a bright blue.

I could not help crossing to one of the windows and peering out at the white clouds. The tip of Mount Olympos was far below, just visible where the cloud was thinnest away to my left. I turned from the window, noting there were no solid doors, just archways leading off into other rooms. I made my way through one and into a second room. There was no one inside it either and it was similar in design to the first, although there were no blue tiles. Statues of Zeus and Hera in various poses lined one wall and I ran past them on my way to the next room, skidding to a stop when I cleared the doorway – Papou and Demetri were bound together, back to back, against one of the columns, their mouths covered with cloth, their eyes closed. Damon kept watch beside them, whimpering and pawing at the ground. The hound looked up, his whimpers turning to a sharp bark. I held my hand up and he quieted as I took a pace towards the three of them.

"So glad you could join us," Ares' voice echoed around the room.

Damon growled deep in his throat and came to stand beside me, the fur of his coat tickling my bare legs. I scanned the room, finding Ares lounging against a column. He pushed himself from the marble as I tightened my hold on my sword.

"Where is the amulet?" Ares asked.

"Safe from you," I replied, twirling my weapon around my hand.

"Come now, you are one of only a few mortals to be brought to this place. A mark of respect would be to tell me what I want to know."

"Not in this life or the next," I said.

Ares laced his hands behind his back and started to pace. "You know, you and I taking Olympos from Zeus and Hera would have been magnificent. Do you wish to hear of what I had planned for us? Perhaps I can convince you to change your mind about aiding me."

"Speak of it if you want, but I will not change my mind," I shrugged, taking a step towards Demetri and Papou.

"We shall see," he murmured, smiling again as he continued. "Well, being that I do not care as much for palaces or architecture as my father, I planned to have you divide Olympos down the center … of course with your immense power that would also have split the mountain and much of the mortal world below, but that only added strength to my plan." He paused and looked up at me. I froze, trying to look interested in his story. "With the earth opened up, the Underworld would have been exposed and in the ensuing battle Zeus, Hera and those loyal to them would have been on one side and you and me on the other. There would be no way to fight but across the abyss and if someone should fall, well, Hades would be there to catch them and either heal them or finish them for us. Not to mention our Keres, they would have enjoyed swooping down and dragging their share of the immortals into the dark depths of Tartarus."

"What about Zeus' thunderbolts, or that purple sphere you used on Papou, could you not have just thrown those at each other and be done with it?" I asked.

"Of course, and with each hit, more and more of the palace would have crumbled away until there was nothing left, but it lacked the … finesse I wanted for the encounter between me and my father," Ares replied.

"That battle will never happen. You cannot have the amulet's power. Or me."

"So, you are still refusing to join me of your own free will?" Ares asked, the hint of a smile playing on his lips.

"Always," I replied.

"So be it," he nodded. He raised his hand, a purple flash of light exploding from his palm. I ducked as it hit the wall behind me, sending chunks of marble raining down. I covered my head and scrambled towards Demetri and Papou.

Ares fired again, demolishing the wall of windows behind them. Falling debris from a column glanced my shoulder, knocking me to the ground. Damon placed his body over mine, his growls deepening. I rolled out from under him, jumping to my feet as Ares raised his hand a third time.

"No!" I cried. I slashed out with my sword, but the bolt hit Damon in the side. I backed up as his huge body got even bigger, the underside of his belly soon above my head. His newly-formed, identical three heads turned in my direction; saliva dripping from their lips as they bared their teeth. Each huge mouth opened, releasing a tremendous bark, the sound echoing deafeningly around the white-walled room. Ares laughed as I backed into the wall behind me. Damon padded towards me.

"Damon," Demetri shouted. The hound paused, turning its heads in the direction of the new voice. I raced around the distracted beast, my eyes darting between Ares and the littered floor under my feet as I took shelter behind an intact pillar. The God of War allowed my escape from the hound but watched me carefully – no doubt wondering if I was going to bring the amulet out to defend myself.

Damon padded towards Demetri. Slowly. Calculating. Demetri stood defenseless, his arms still bound behind his back, but I saw that Papou was also awake, the two of them talking quietly.

"It appears you shall have to decide who to save – yourself or your lover."

I tore my eyes from Papou and Demetri and faced Ares, gripping the sword in my hand tighter and ensuring my body was ready for anything.

"There is no choice. Both of us will leave here alive," I told him.

Ares laughed again and flicked his hand sideways, just as he had in Konitsa. This time my sword remained where it was and his smile faltered ever so slightly. He brought his hand up and tried to take it again. Again nothing happened.

An ear-piercing screech filled the air and I turned, startled to find twenty or thirty Keres flying in through one of the newly created doorways. Their clawed hands held long swords, and they dipped and dived at me, their faces filled with hate and fury rather than the triumph and unity we had shared in Konitsa.

I slashed at the creatures, their sharp claws sliding past my defenses and tearing at my skin. I took a number of them down in response, striking off wings and arms as they swarmed. I fell to my knees under their weight, continuing to swing wildly, their squeals of pain reverberating inside my head and threatening to stop me. I squeezed my eyes shut and kept on fighting, determined not to let our kinship sway the decision I had made to see them as my enemies.

Finally the beasts closed in so much that I could not bring my sword up or around to inflict any damage. *Maybe the Keres would be the ones to end my life, not Ares.* I had barely finished the thought when the snarling started. Damon's sharp teeth ripped chunks of flesh from the Keres' bodies as he dove into the crowd. One of his three mouths grabbed my chlamys and lifted me to my feet. I sliced the heads from the two nearest Ker before pulling myself onto his back and pressing my heels into the hound as I had so many times with Philo. He took off towards Ares and I kept my body low behind his heads, hoping Ares had not seen me mount him. Damon slid to a halt several feet from the God of War and I slipped from his back, catching sight of the surprised and slightly apprehensive look on Ares' face as he unsheathed his sword and faced the beast.

Papou and Demetri stood, alive and safely hidden, behind the only column still standing in the room. Demetri caught my eye and gave me a nod and a tight smile – I returned both. I could defeat Ares. The two people standing behind that column were *mine* and I loved them with everything I had. Ares would never control any part of me that took me from them, I would not allow it. Not ever.

The sword in my hand seemed to warm in tune with my thoughts and I squeezed it tightly between my hands. Damon stepped towards Ares and I crouched low at his side, matching my footsteps with his larger ones, still hoping I was as hidden from Ares' view as he currently was from mine. Damon suddenly stopped, the hair on his body bristling as a deep growl emanated from his chest.

"Ava," Ares called. I could hear the smile.

"All I need is a distraction, boy. Can you do that for me?" I whispered, resting my hand on Damon's leg. One of his large heads turned and nodded. His eyes refocused on Ares as his knees bent ever so slightly in a position I recognized. I stepped away from Damon and Ares came into view.

His smile widened. "Enough games. It is time to finish this so we can rule Olympos together. Forever."

"That is not going to happen," I told him, bringing my sword up into a defensive position and planting my feet solidly. Ares shrugged, raising his own sword and taking a step towards me.

Damon set himself momentarily, then sprung towards Ares, bringing one of his three mouths down onto Ares' outstretched arm and pinning him to the ground with a large paw.

Ares yelled and dropped his sword, slamming his free hand against the leg that held him. Damon flew from the god's body, sailing through the air before hitting the floor and skidding into the other room with barely more than a whimper.

"Damon!" Demetri cried.

Ares got to his feet and surveyed the damage to his arm. I took advantage of his distraction, rushing at him with my sword held like it was a spear. I was within arm's reach when Ares looked up, but he could do nothing as I drove my weapon into his stomach. I lodged it as deep as the guard.

He grinned, hands finding the hilt. "Silly girl. A sword cannot hurt me."

"A normal sword, no," I agreed. His smile faltered as he grabbed at the object stuck firm in his flesh. His face paled and his breath hitched in his throat.

He looked down in astonishment. "What have you done?" he whispered.

"What I had to," I replied.

Ares dropped to his knees, hands still wrapped around mine on the handle. "Do not believe this is over between us," he panted.

"The power of the amulet is broken. You will never control me."

"I shall come with armies, with assassins. I shall bring the full force of the Persian army down onto your head; the brothers, the sons, the fathers of all those you murdered, I shall fill them with the desire to conquer every city between Trachis and Athens and I shall not stop until you are dead or at my side, you can be certain of that."

"You can come, but I will be waiting, *you* can be sure of that," I told him.

Ares drew the sword from his body, a metallic screech accompanying the action. He opened his mouth to speak again but a light as bright as a thousand suns poured from the wound. I put a hand up to shield my eyes from the glare, as pure agony ripped through my shoulder blades. I dropped to the ground, my sword still in my hand as it slipped from Ares' stomach. I could not catch my breath. My wings broke free, tearing through my skin, tunic and leather cuirass with such force that I could not move. The fierceness and pain of their emergence was worse than I had ever experienced. The long flames of heat that had once excited and empowered me, burned me from the inside as agony rushed through my blood.

I gripped my sword with aching fingers and trembling arms. The ground shook beneath me and I squeezed my eyes shut, concentrating on only the leather between my palms as distraction from the torment raging inside. Heat, pain, numbness, it was too much. I was sure I was going to burst into flames at any moment. Part of me welcomed it. I could not bear the torture. I was dimly aware of shouting voices as the fire inside consumed me. Something blew across the back of my head. I surrendered to the darkness willingly.

44

"She wakes," Papou's voice flowed through my mind.

No pain. No heat flooding my veins, only a faint, hollow feeling inside. I opened my eyes, finding two cautious faces and one joyful one above me. I sat up, noting that no one offered to help.

"What happened?" I asked, trying to read their faces.

"You defeated Ares," Hephaestus grinned – he looked so excited I thought he might start dancing.

"We cannot be certain of that," Papou replied, frowning. I looked around the room, I could see why. We were still at Olympos, the white-walled room in a state of devastation; walls blown away, window arches barely holding together as pieces of marble dropped towards the world below. Strong, magnificent columns that had once held up the ceiling now nothing more than shattered lumps and fine dust. But it was the deep crevice that split one room from the next that made me understand Papou's fear.

"Did I ...?" I did not need to finish the question – Papou's face gave me the answer.

"I have told you, if she was under Ares' influence at all, she would have killed you as soon as she woke," Hephaestus said, addressing Papou before turning to me. "Do not be concerned with that, yes you did it, and yes it appears that you harnessed the power of the earth element, but the amulet's original intentions did not flow through you, you were not under Ares' command then, just as you are not now."

"You are *not* under his influence, are you?" Papou asked.

"No," I assured him. "But how could I harness the power and not be in his grip?" I frowned.

"The addition of my blood to the sword tempered the effect of Ares'," Hephaestus answered. "When you ran him through and opened up the ground, you sent him straight to the cage I made for him, just as I hoped you would be able to."

My frown deepened. "I do not understand, when did you add *your* blood to the sword?"

"It seems I'm not just a ... a half-man, half-woman orphan like I thought," Demetri replied. "I'm half-god too. Hephaestus is my father."

"What?" I asked, my mouth gaping at him. Demetri dropped his eyes to his hands and nodded. I looked between him and Hephaestus. "Is that how you knew what we intended to do with the amulet?" I asked.

Hephaestus nodded. "Yes. When I saw my child had met you, I was filled with joy. I could finally have my revenge on Ares. But more than that, with your immediate and total acceptance of him ... her I hoped she could finally have what I had never been able to provide – a family who loved him. Someone who loved him for who he was without insisting he ... she ... pretend otherwise. Of course, there was no guarantee that the two of you would fall in love, or that you would be able to resist Ares' charms. I am just grateful that you are as strong as you are or the outcome may have been very different today." He put a hand on my shoulder, but I could only nod, trying to process his words. *Demetri – Demi – was half-god? Who was his mother? Maybe he was a full god. Maybe that was how he was able to recover from the spider bite even after so many days. Was it Hephaestus' dark shadow I had seen at Mount Smolikos ensuring Demetri lived so we could carry out his plan against Ares?*

Hephaestus' acknowledgement of my quick acceptance of Demetri – Demi – my love for her, did he influence me in that? I did not think so. The only other gods to have that kind of power were Aphrodite or Eros and I knew neither of them would have helped Hephaestus. I had not stopped before to consider why it did not matter to me, when I realized I was in love with Demetri, if she was female or male, but maybe because I had not known him one way or the other for very long I was not shocked or surprised, or been unable to reconcile that with the image I was then shown. Maybe the sex of the person we fall in love with is not important. I had fallen for Demi for who she was inside, not because of the body Demetri found himself in.

And my wings ... they had broken free when I stabbed Ares, but the pain was now gone, replaced by a faint emptiness, and the large extensions did not overshadow me. What had happened to them? What did it mean? Was it really over?

Damon's cold nose snuffled against my hand and I looked down at the hound. His body had returned to its former self, with no outward sign of his change or wounds from his clash with Ares except a light dusting of white marble powder.

"Thanks for the help," I murmured. I cleared my throat and scratched the top of his head. He nuzzled me again before dropping to the floor, placing his head on his paws in his familiar way.

I undid my chlamys and let it fall, reaching a tentative hand to my shoulder to undo my cuirass. Demetri helped me take it over my head and I held it up. There were two jagged holes at the back where my wings had pushed through and I wondered, briefly, if there was any way to patch them without making them more obvious.

"It might be time for a new cuirass," Papou said, stepping closer and running his fingers over the leather. He offered me his hand and pulled me to my feet, taking me in a fierce hug and crushing his lips to the top of my head. I wrapped my arms around his waist, squeezing him in return.

"You're bleeding," Demetri suddenly said, his hands scrambling to pull my tunic from my shoulders.

"Wait," I ordered, unwrapping my arms from Papou. Demetri paused and I took a deep breath, sliding my trembling fingers beneath the material. I gasped as I touched the smooth, flat skin at my shoulder blades. No lumpy flesh. No shameful bumps. Nothing. I drew my hand away again – there was no blood. It must only be on my tunic. I knew with a sudden certainty that I was free of Ares' curse and the amulet's power. My wings were gone. They would not return. We *had* defeated the God of War.

I turned to Hephaestus. "You said Ares was in a cage, but why did you not let the sword's power kill him?"

"I could not. Zeus knew of my involvement with you and I would have been banished, we gods are forbidden from killing each other and I would not wish to incur our father's wrath."

"But if Ares had managed to challenge Zeus, he would have killed as many gods as he had to, and I suspect his true plan was not to take them alive to the Underworld, but to kill them, Zeus in particular."

"You may speak the truth, but I am not my brother, and whilst I have enjoyed finally taking my revenge, I would never have had you kill him. He shall be trapped for eternity in the metal cage I forged and that is a far worse punishment for him. Knowing what could have been, and what shall never be. Ares shall never have any hold over you. He shall never be able to make you bend to his will again, not unless you desire it."

I shook my head. "No thank you. I am satisfied with what, and who, I have here."

"I believe it is time we took our leave of Olympos," Papou said, looking around the broken palace.

"Of course. I shall return you to Kierion to collect your belongings.

Where do you wish to go after that? Perhaps Athens where Demetri has longed to be for so long?" Hephaestus proposed.

"Maybe Trachis?" I suggested. Papou and Demetri looked at me with surprise. I met Papou's gaze as I explained. "Agrias and Melina deserve to know the curse is broken and maybe I can persuade them to lift your banishment."

"You do not have to do that for me, I would be happy wherever you are, if you would allow me to accompany you," he replied.

"I want you with me, and maybe it is time I accepted and acknowledged who I am too. In Trachis. To the people of Trachis." I took Demetri's hand. "Would you stay if I asked it of you?"

"Nothing would make me happier," he replied, smiling as he added, "maybe I'll really ask your grandparents for their blessing of our union. They seem accepting of unique pairings in Trachis."

"Wh-what?" I stuttered.

Demetri and Papou laughed and Demetri swept me up into his arms, kissing me. "Let's return to Kierion, then ... home?" he asked when we parted. He returned me to my feet, arms still encircling my waist and eyebrows lifted beneath his hair. I swept the long strands off his face – her face – as I smiled.

"Home," I confirmed.

45

I placed my sword into the sheath at my thigh and tied the leather strings of my cuirass at my shoulders and ribs. I pinned my chlamys at my shoulder, hiding the jagged holes in the leather and linen and looped my bag across my body as Demetri and Papou gathered their own belongings. We woke Kratos and made our goodbyes, leaving him with coin and the thick himations from Andronikos as payment for the use of his workshop. We would not have need of the heavier cloaks once we returned south; our winters far milder than those of the north regions we had been travelling in.

The town of Kierion was situated on a small hill above the Apidanus River, a fortified wall protecting it from enemies. No soldiers stood along its length and the gates remained open, allowing us immediate access into part of the Thessalian Plain known as the Plain of Pharsalia below.

Papou turned his face upwards to catch the sun's rays and inhaled deeply. "Ah, smell the flowers on the breeze and feel the warmth it brings. Spring shall soon be upon us and the Plain here shall be filled with the stalks of wild crocus and narcissus flowers." I grinned as I looked at him – recalling how he had taught me of the flowers and plants that populated the area around Trachis when I was a child.

As we followed the gentle downward slope and joined the Apidanus River, a voice hailed me on the wind. I turned, Lysistratos' familiar figure leading another from the gates. I raised my hand in greeting, realizing that the man with him was Moeris – and he did not look pleased.

"By the gods, it is her," Lysistratos yelled, throwing aside his shield and the broken parts I recognized as my own. He ran, grabbing me up in a crushing hug when he arrived. "I was so worried. Moeris is too but he pretends it is only anger that drives him to find you," he murmured.

"I have missed you as well," I said, gripping him tightly. "I truly call you brother now."

He released me, a frown furrowing his brow. "What?"

I gave him a tight smile. "Later, I must see Eumelia first, there is much to discuss, much for her to learn."

"Where have you been?" Moeris demanded finally reaching us, his feet sending up angry puffs of dust. "When I met with Agrias he said he had not spoken to you. Lysistratos and I have spent almost a moon searching for you and when we found your broken shield and discarded greaves at Lake Xynias, we did not know what to think."

"I am sorry, Moeris, I did not mean to worry you," I replied, resting my hand on his arm. His heart beat furiously beneath the skin, but his face softened and finally he wrapped his arms around me.

"How could I have faced the king and queen if you had been harmed? I should have insisted on joining you on your journey."

"It was one I had to make on my own. Besides, I am well, and I have been reunited with someone I have not seen for many winters."

I felt Moeris' body stiffen as he released me slowly, his eyes finding first Demetri, then Papou. "Leandros," he rumbled, the two men staring each other down. "Who is the boy?"

Demetri offered his arm without hesitation. "I am Demetri."

Moeris ignored it, his eyes finding mine again. "What reason did you have to find your grandfather after all these winters? Why did you not speak of your wishes to me?"

"There is a lot we need to discuss, but for now, just know that without Papou, you and I would not be standing here together today. I sought him for answers, for vengeance, but I received much more than I expected. It is good we are together again. All of us." Demetri lowered his arm and I took his other hand, holding Moeris' gaze. "We must not repeat the mistakes of the past, it will not do any of us good."

Moeris eventually nodded, turning to Papou. "It has been many winters and we did not part as friends," he acknowledged.

"You speak true, and I have regretted it ever since, but I hope we shall be able to repair that past and call one another friend once again." Papou held out his arm. Moeris gripped it tightly, drawing Papou into a hug, the two of them slapping one another on the back.

"As do I, for I have missed you. Do you intend to return to Trachis?" Moeris asked as they parted.

"Yes, though I am not certain Agrias and Melina shall be as pleased to see me again."

"Melina still holds grief and anger beneath her chest, but perhaps with the passing of so much time things shall be ... different," Moeris shrugged.

"I expected as much, but I hope it is so," Papou said with a solemn nod.

Lysistratos held his hand out to Demetri and they shook. "I am Lysistratos. You travel with very little, do you call Kierion home?"

"No. Once it was Larissa. Now it shall be Trachis," Demetri replied, his cheeks coloring slightly as he caught my eye. I smiled and squeezed the hand of his I held.

"Our city shall be more fortunate for it," Lysistratos continued. "Do you have a trade?"

"Um ... yes. I worked as a Celator and in the metalwork hut," Demetri replied, resting his hand on the hilt of his sword. Lysistratos' gaze fell to the item and he grinned.

"You have an intricate design on the guard of your sword, may I see it?" Demetri nodded, drawing the weapon from its sheath. I took my hand from his and Papou joined them in quiet conversation.

Moeris stepped to my side and we watched Papou and Lysistratos as they admired Demetri's handiwork. "I did not realize you sought such affections, if I had, I would have encouraged you to leave long ago," he noted.

"I did not know of it myself, it was not something I intended to find when I left the Pass of Coela," I replied.

"That is often the way of it," he nodded. "I am pleased for you anyway. There is much joy to be had when you find one you wish to walk this world with," he added, laying his arm over my shoulders.

"Thank you," I replied, wrapping my arm around his waist.

A flash of light lit the Plain and Hephaestus appeared before us. Moeris and Lysistratos jumped, drawing their swords and holding them in the god's direction. I reached out a hand to both men. "Do not be alarmed, Hephaestus comes as friend, not enemy."

"Hephaestus," Moeris murmured, immediately lowering his weapon and his eyes. "Forgive me, magnificent God of the Forge, I meant no disrespect."

"Do not fear me, Mortal. These are friends?" Hephaestus asked, turning to me.

"Yes. We serve together in the Army of Trachis."

Lysistratos returned his weapon to its place, turning to me with a wry smile. "It seems there is much you have to tell us of your adventures these past weeks."

"There is," I replied, returning his grin, knowing Lysistratos loved a good story.

"You are ready to return to Trachis then? I can take all of you, if that is your wish," Hephaestus suggested, holding out his hand.

"I think we will walk," I replied.

"How else would we travel if not by foot or horse?" Lysistratos asked.

"The immortals travel in a unique manner, but now is not the time to experience it again," Papou answered. "There is much to discuss before we arrive in Trachis, friendships to be repaired and new ones to be formed. The days we spend together are required to see it so."

"As you wish," Hephaestus acknowledged with a nod.

"Perhaps you would travel with us a way and share the story of my birth and how you came to know my mother?" Demetri asked.

"Of course, my child."

"Child?" Lysistratos queried, his mouth dropping open.

"We will share the story as we journey home," I promised him with a smile.

"The next time you insist on leaving, I am not letting you go without me," Lysistratos laughed.

"I cannot imagine I will ever have such an eventful journey but you know I would wish for nothing less than to have you at my side."

We followed the Apidanus River south through the Plain towards the Othrys Mountains and the region of Thermopylae beyond. Hephaestus started his story and I slipped my fingers between Demetri's. Maybe I could finally find peace with the past. I had always thought it would come with the deaths of Persian enemies at the end of my sword, but now it seemed it would be with the strength of family – new and old.

I would never forget my mothers or the injustice of what had been done to them, and to me. But now I knew the truth of why it had happened, and by who. No longer would I let misguided hatred for Persian soldiers drive my actions. I would always defend Trachis from enemies, whether they be mortal or immortal, but I would do it with truth – and love – to guide me.

ACKNOWLEDGMENTS

Firstly, thank you for coming back after Dark Thermopylae, I know it was hard for some of you to do so, but I really appreciate it and hope this book, and Ava, has captured your hearts and imagination just like Skylar and Alexis did. There is still some of them within her, which I hope shines through, but she is definitely her own person.

To bring in a character like Demetri/Demi felt right for their relationship to Ava, but I was afraid I would not do justice to the struggles and triumphs those in the LGBTQI community face as they search for their truest selves. I hope I have not offended you – Ava's stumbles are my own in some ways in how she can understand who Demetri is (in a way that is not confusing to the reader). I hope I have treated you all and what you feel/are going through/have been through with respect. My own journey as a lesbian woman has been easy compared to what so many of you go through and I know how lucky I am. You are all beautiful, no matter the form your body takes. You are loved. You matter. Not only do my characters truly believe that, but so do I. Find those who will nurture you and care for you. Find your tribe and be who you feel you truly are inside. I would be honored to find myself in your tribe if the opportunity ever arose, so if you want to reach out and contact me, I will be here.

A HUGE thank you to DR and Ashley who I asked to read this book before it was released because I was … scared that I hadn't done the people in it justice – Demetri/Demi especially. Thank you for your suggestions and feedback and for setting my mind at ease just a little, I don't think it'll be the last time I ask you to help me out (and I hope you'll say yes again)!

To my editor, Kristie, thank you for reading this book AGAIN – I know I made a major change that I didn't tell you about, letting you experience it as a reader rather than an editor knowing what's coming. That first version you saw years ago is still essentially here, even though I have returned to some of the things you weren't crazy about (like conjunctions). But now I have a reason for it – speech changes and we're moving on with the times! Thank you again for being here to steer me when I stray too far from the mark, you know I appreciate it.

To my wife, Renee, and daughter, Ava, thank you for loving me, supporting me, putting up with me and being my family, my greatest loves (see, I put both of you before the dog and cats and my characters) and my sounding boards. I'm so grateful to have you both with me on this journey – my writing one, and my life. I love you guys.

ABOUT THE AUTHOR

Belinda Harrison was born and raised in a country town in North East Victoria, Australia. She spent some time experiencing 'big city life' in Melbourne and Sydney in her twenties where she held jobs in a packaging company, an online gaming firm, various temp positions and a hair loss treatment center before the lure of the country recalled her.

She joined her family's business in the world of retail plumbing and appliance sales – which is when she started writing the Thermopylae Bound Series – before deciding to leave the familiar and join another well respected local firm in the Real Estate sector where she worked in Commercial Property Management.

Belinda then decided it was time for another change and moved across the road to the local newspaper where she looks after Circulation, writing after hours and around family commitments (and book club).

She currently lives in 'the best part of Victoria' with her wife Renee, daughter Ava, Charlie the dog, and cats Caesar and Max.

You can find Belinda on the following social media platforms: Instagram (belindagharrison), Twitter (beharrison78) or Facebook (Belinda Harrison Author) or join her mailing list at www.belindaharrison.com for bonus short stories. And don't forget to leave a review of this book, or any of the previous ones in the series on Amazon or Goodreads to help spread the word.

The final book of the Thermopylae Bound Series *End of War in Thermopylae* will be released in 2020.